G R JORDAN'S

Unravel Your Destiny

The Treasure of Captain Estes

The Treasure of Captain Estes

First published by Carpetless Publishing in 2023

Copyright © G R Jordan, 2023

This novel is entirely a work of fiction. The names, characters and incidents portrayed in it are the work of the author's imagination. Any resemblance to actual persons, living or dead, events or localities is entirely coincidental.

G R Jordan asserts the moral right to be identified as the author of this work.

G R Jordan has no responsibility for the persistence or accuracy of URLs for external or third-party Internet Websites referred to in this publication and does not guarantee that any content on such Websites is, or will remain, accurate or appropriate.

G R Jordan

First Edition

ISBN: 978-1-914073-99-1

Cover art by J Caleb Clarke

Jcalebdesign.com

Interior art by Sean Counley

www.seancounley.com

G R Jordan

"The cave you fear to enter holds the treasure you seek."

Joseph Campbell

<u>Acknowledgement</u>

To Louise for play testing and support, thank you for all your help.

And to all my kickstarting backers, I may have built this tome, but you brought it to life. Thank you all.

TABLE OF CONTENTS

How to Play

This is an adventure where YOU are the story! YOU will make the choices that decide your future and YOU will pay the consequences. In order to do this don't read this book through like a normal book. Instead, when you reach the end of paragraph 1, choose one of the options presented and go to that section. Continue to read from there until you are given another choice to make.

Your character (and later, your vessel!) undergoes various changes, collecting items, losing items, and will have notable incidents happen to them that affect gameplay later. This is tracked in various ways. One of the most important ways to track these is the codeword list. During gameplay you may be asked to tick or untick codewords. Do this on the codeword list sheet in the appendix at App 01. You may print out or copy any of the appendix sheets as many times as you want for personal use when playing the gamebook.

The other sections of the appendix apply at various times during the game, and you will be directed to the appropriate appendix section when required. There is a large section explaining how to voyage around the New Southampton seas which takes you through this when you get your vessel. But you start on your own with so very little so further explanations are saved until the appropriate part in the gamebook.

The game uses dice in some of the decisions. Usually this is a D100. This can be performed on an app for your computer or phone or by using 2xD10 where one is the "tens" and one the "single numbers".

So, gird yourself and get ready to jump into the fray. YOU may win, YOU may lose, but whatever may YOU have a lot of fun doing so! Turn the page for "The Treasure of Captain Estes".

The Treasure of Captain Estes

For years, You, Mary Hastings, lived a charmed life as the daughter of a plantation owner far out towards the Americas. Life was good and the sun shone as your father sent goods back to England and the other colonies. You wanted for nothing and watched as others toiled for your father in the fields of the island around New Southampton. You would see large wooden cargo vessels with their sails unfurled, coming to the island, and on occasion saw the busy docks where goods were sold and transported onto the vessels. There were troops from England at the garrison and a vibrant market with fruit and goods.

But there was a darker side to your home of New Southampton Island, for on the opposite side of the island far from New Southampton was the illegal port of Strangar, a haven for pirates and criminals who had managed to fend off the attentions of the garrison as long as you'd known. The seas around New Southampton were a running battle between pirates and the cargo ships as well as Spanish forces who came for territory and anything else they could gather on the way. Your father warned you that beyond plantation life was a world where everyone grabbed what they could from anyone else in whatever way possible.

You had heard tales of murder and bloodshed, executions, and revenge but your father had kept you well hidden from it, a promise made to your late mother. But one night it came to the plantation in the form of Captain Estes. The Spanish Captain was well rumoured as a grabber of gold and treasure and he attacked your father's plantation, in search of the Cross of Cadiz, a golden relic your father had bought many years before after it had been stolen some one hundred years before from the cathedral in Cadiz.

You watched as Estes first killed your stepmother outside and then ran a sword through your father in his study. You fled down the stairs and hid in a tiny hole built into the wall of the kitchen pantry. Dressed in a long white gown and in bare feet, you cried from shock and sorrow before looking down at the cross hanging around your neck, a gift from your birth mother not long before she died. It took you back to when she had passed and her last words on her death bed.

"The family must go on. I have no son, only you, my daughter and you must take over from your father one day. Swear on the cross to me, swear it my child."

You were but a child and you swore as asked, but now those words stir something in your heart. You will rise and restore the fortunes of your family, even as they crumble around you. You may be a mere girl, blonde and slender in frame, a perfect wife in waiting as your father put it, but now you have to become something stronger, and maybe darker. You clutch the cross around your neck and swear again to your mother to ensure the family goes on.

Where shall you go? What can bring back the wealth and name of your family? "Estes!" You say the words through gritted teeth. He has the Cross of Cadiz, the heirloom of your family. He is taking your wealth from around you. You swore to your mother so you will see Estes dead and his wealth in your hands, along with the Cross of Cadiz.

You wipe the sweat from your hands, push your blonde hair from your eyes. As much as your heart is stirred, you realise you are an eighteen-year-old girl, hiding from a large Spanish force, and you wonder what your first move should be. Time to decide at *1*.

G R Jordan

The Treasure of Captain Estes

1

You peek out from your hide and can see some Spanish soldiers in the kitchen. You know that you could run back up the stairs and see if Estes is still there to confront him, but some time has passed. Or you could confront the Spanish soldiers for, if you can get to the kitchen door, you might be able to escape into the plantation fields. Or you could try and head to your father's small armoury and find weapons with which to fight.

Do you

Run up the stairs in search of Estes – **437**

Confront the Spanish soldiers – **898**

Go to your father's armoury – **1084**

2

You raise your hands and turn away slowly before suddenly rushing at the door and barging into the barn. In the dim light, you see several bound men and two others both of whom are holding pistols. Pistols that have now fired at you. You feel the balls hit you from the barrels and you are thrown back off your feet. You manage to stumble out of the door, pushing the pirate from outside to one side in a desperate effort. You run into the street. If you have already lost a body part go to **370**.

Otherwise, you need a Doctor, and fast! If you don't find one within 4 entries, you must go to **370**. Return now to **1112 and remain clear of the barn.**

<u>3</u>

You fire your cannons towards the shore, but no one shows. You see huts go on fire and the land becomes devastated around the settlement. After letting the dust settle, you spy the land and see the utter devastation you have caused. But there is no one there. They must have fled. You take the small boat ashore with some crew but all you find is the wreck of a village. If they had anything of value, it's gone.

You've made sure this place is no longer worth visiting. You may no longer return to the south of the island for it's just a wasteland. So, what's next?

Do you

Tell the crew to sail to the north of the island – **468**

Route for the centre of the island – **746**

Decide to set sail - **consult the voyage chart**

<u>4</u>

You send for your offering, and it is brought before Tom who touches it carefully, examining it. He smiles and a child takes your offering away.

How many Doubloons did you offer?

Up to 1,000 – **566**

More than 1,000 up to 5,000 – **771**

More than 5,000 up to 10,000 – **1321**

More than 10,000 – **964**

5

Do you have the codeword **Trap**, if so – *92*. If not, read on.

As you walk along the path, eyes blurred from the endless jungle, you swoon a little and feel your right foot begin to fall in front of you. You are suddenly pitched into a deep trap, and you scrabble with your hands which slows your fall. However, you hit your head before you land. When you wake you see that the trap is deep, but you can climb up the roots. However, you have no idea how long you've been here.

Roll a D100 (or 2xD10)

00-35 You have only been out for a few minutes

36-79 You have been out for a day. Mark off 1 day from your voyage chart.

80-99 What a hit to the head. You've lost two days. Mark off 2 days from your voyage chart.

You climb up with difficulty out of the pit, disorientated about how you entered. **Tick codeword Trap.** There are two ways you can go but you don't know which one you came in by. Do you

Go this way – *116*

Or try this way – *38*

6

You get hit by lots of darts dart and fall to the floor. When you wake up you are in the same room and have managed to drag yourself back to where you started on this floor. You don't realise now, but will when back at the ship, that three days has passed since you collapsed. **Add 3 days to your voyage chart. Go to *396***

7

There is no sound from outside the room and it all looks safe to continue. What will you examine now?

The desk – *1305*

Brass Sextant – *1446*

The picture of the woman – *640*

The drawers – *255*

The charts – *348*

<u>8</u>

Reduce your Waters Strength Chart by 1. The current is too strong and sweeping you north. Your foot scrapes the bottom briefly and you think you may be able to drop a pole and take a rest. Do you

Float North – *1253*

Drop a pole – **Make a note of this section and go to *694***

<u>9</u>

You pull up the pages of parchment and sit down on the wooden chairs to read. It takes some time to read through and the crew with you get frustrated, but you find the tale fascinating. These are the words of Estes, his account of trying to work out this place. You read over the important bits and try to commit them to memory.

"I hid my money in five places; The Waters of Myra, The Drops of Daniel, The Bulls of the Plain; The Wall of Fire, and The Winds of the World. Each treasure chest was left beyond these strange phenomena. To simply reach them is a trial without knowing the path and I lost many good crewmates working out the path. But I took each trial and I have suffered for it. They may say I die in battle in the future but in honesty, I am already dying for something is wrong inside."

"The strangest thing about this place is how it disappears at sunset. And how that sunset is shorter than we would think. Maybe an hour shorter. I would have been caught out by it except I was forewarned and yet I still left crew behind one occasion. When I returned, they were not here which makes me wonder what dangers walk this place at night."

"The poles are important, but I will not say which and note all my secrets lest I lose these writings. But save to say, never strike off the paths for there is no coming back from what lurks in the jungle."

There is a lot of manifest notes and tales of his crew which frankly are rather dull. **Tick the codeword Notes.**

What now?

Look at the crude map – *1160*

Just get on with things and leave the hut and

Strike out for the path – *1039*

Look at the poles – *703*

<u>10</u>

You approach the main tables and the seller smiles at you and begins to show you his wares. You return the smile and watch the two guards who seem to have deemed you a fit person to be at the stall. When the seller turns his back, you carefully sneak an emerald into your back pocket. The seller then presses hard for you to buy something, but you laugh graciously and say not today and walk away from the table. **Tick the codeword Emerald** in your inventory. You seem to have got away with it, so what next.

Do you

Try the provisions stall – *1368*

Look at the whiskey and ale stalls – *155*

Or return to the street – *496*

<u>11</u>

You seem to go through your doubloons quickly with a number of pirates stepping forward and when you get back to the vessel you see that your new crew is there. **Increase your crew size by 1 as long as**

the vessel has room. If not, you have wasted money on a new crew that cannot come with you.

Among the crew is a former first mate of the dreaded pirate Santiago. He tells you that Estes used a cursed compass to find the island that he left his loot on, and that a cursed compass went down with the Marie Santiago last he heard.

What now?

Go to see Blind Tom – *681*

Visit the provisions isle – *334*

Go back to the Wild Isle – *879*

Explore the dark isle – *397*

Approach the pirate king – *1348*

Decide you have had enough of Hells Deep and set sail - **Consult the voyage chart and set sail**

12

Reduce your time by 1.

If your time is in the following gaps (57-53 or 42-38), then go to *1037*.

As you stand at the door, you can hear nothing at all from inside. All is silent and the only sounds you hear are the odd flap of a flag from the rather dour wind.

Do you

Hide where you are – *103*

Route South – *1435*

Creep East – *174* (More options over the page)

The Treasure of Captain Estes

Go North – *42*

Sneak West – *1393*

Open the door and enter the building – *382*

13

The gypsy looks at you with pity and invites you to sit down. She calls for a flagon of ale and watches you sup it slowly.

"Not used to it, are you," she says. "I used to be a low down runt too, scavenging the streets and hoping for the day when I could be something again. And now, I do alright, I manage to get by on my own terms. Let's see if we can get you started. Wait outside and I'll be out with something for you."

She seems genuine enough but why outside. What is it she is going to do?

Do you

Get up and wait outside – *685*

Or say no thanks and instead if you haven't already

Approach the bar – *669*

Walk over to the single pirate – *838*

Go over to watch the pirate playing the mouth organ – *1421*

Or leave – *1112*

14

5 Skull 0 Scales 0 Coins

The pirates all begin to laugh heartily and then the one you bet with takes out a pistol and shoots you at point blank range. They find you in the early morning dumped at the roadside. You did know it was a risky game. Maybe don't play it next time at *1*

15

The pirates soon turn back to their ale while the bar maid simply gives you a cursory glance. You are here for a reason, so you had better get their attention.

Do you

Ask if any of the pirates have a crew and a vessel – *1408*

Or leave them and explore the rest of the tavern

Talk to the gypsy woman – *711*

Walk over to the single pirate – *838*

Go over to watch the pirate playing the mouth organ – *1421*

Or leave – *1112*

16

You are taken through some wooden corridors and then up a flight of steps into a room with a fire burning in a hearth and a chaise longue in front of it. A woman with long, dirty blonde hair rises from the furniture to turn and face you. She is dressed in a fine black long-coat with breeches and she grabs a large floppy hat to place upon her head.

Have already given your name, Mary Hastings – *650*

If not

She sweeps in front of you gazing intently at you. You find it hard to tell if she is disgusted or pleased with your appearance.

Are you

Dressed in a long-coat – *267*

Wearing a night gown, even if it's cut to look like a slave – *215*

The Treasure of Captain Estes

<u>17</u>

You arrive at the small nuggets of islands known as Hell's Deep, where the pirates hide out. It is a place you have heard of but not one you thought you would ever see. Here lies extreme danger because if you are not thought of as a pirate you will be thrown out at best, killed at worst. There are also disputes amongst pirates and you will need to watch your back.

As you approach the islands, a small barge is sent out to meet you and you see a bald man on board with a large sword and a woven band over his long-coat. The barge comes alongside, and he asks permission to come aboard. You grant it and he bows before you before producing a large scroll.

"Welcome fellow scourge of the seas, you are at the kingdom of the free, lorded over by Captain Ariel, Bloodletter of the High Seas. He bids you welcome but demands tribute from you unless you can show your worth."

Your first officer says that the man is looking for status or an amount of treasure will be demanded for entrance to the pirate kingdom. You wonder if this a matter best left to your officer, but you also think you may have goods on board that would qualify you to gain entrance.

Do you

Have the codeword **Password** – *21*

Leave it to your officer – *1241*

Decide you have an item you can offer to prove your worth – *229*

Offer doubloons – *1297*

Decide the price is too high and leave Hells Deep – **Consult the voyage chart and set sail**

18

You return to your ship, sodden, but clutching your findings. Take a look at each item (**Check your code words**) you have in the list in order from top to bottom.

Wall Frame – *1326*

Crate Scroll – *31*

Desk Scroll – *1138*

19

Black Robert gives a sudden sniff and then looks at you with wild eyes. "We are a galleon, and I am the most identifiable pirate in this part of the world. We will go at night, and you will go alone. If they caught me ashore, they would hang me straight away."

So, that's that. Looks like your choice is made for you. Go to *307* to sneak in during the night.

20

You wander along the path, unsure where you are and reach a junction. Which way now?

Left – *1359*

Right – *612*

Turn back – *575*

21

"Ah, one of our own," says the bald man. "The king is delighted that you join us."

The man turns and signals to vessels that are gathered around the entrance to the islands, and you sail into the small group. Go to *473* to continue your adventure.

22

Add a modifier of 30 when asked in the next section. Go to **207**

23

You are back at the temple and the steps down to the hall beneath the ground are still blocked. There's nothing here to see or do now. You check the sun and realise you can go north - **202** or south - **1329** along a jungle path. Choose now.

24

"While we are here in Malin's Town, I have a contact who could help us get some money. Or maybe even some information. Let me go to town."

You wait while Simon disappears, and he comes back a few hours later with a gentleman in tow. In your Captain's quarters, over rum, he tells you how Estes has buried his treasure on an island that is hard to locate. He can offer no help in finding it but he knows that the island has several trials to be overcome in order to reach the treasure. He can obtain information about one of these trials if you are prepared to commit a *dark run* for him. This is contraband goods. There are three drop-off points; The Bird's Paradise, The Abandoned Island, and Hell's Deep. If you do this and then return to Malin's town he will have the information. He looks nervous as he asks if you will accept.

Do you

Accept – **263**

Reject the offer – **1247**

25

Reduce the Hot Strip by 2. If this places you on a Fire spot add 20 to this section's number and go there for the walls have moved. There are walls of fire to the north, west, and east, so you route south from your current location. Go to **251**

<u>26</u>

You wander along the path, feeling woozy, but reach a junction. Which way now?

Left – *612*

Right – *1453*

Turn back – *526*

<u>27</u>

Reduce the Hot Strip by 1. If this places you on a Fire spot add 20 to this section's number and go there for the walls have moved. You can see fire to the north and to the west.

Do you

Go South – *1123*

Go East – *744*

<u>28</u>

You walk over to the fire and gently shake the man asleep there awake. He gives his head a shake and then looks you up and down. You ask him if he can help you by telling you about the local seas. He gives a smile and invites you to sit down. You purchase him an ale and he tells you about his journeys around the New Southampton seas. Among his tales are those of a Kraken horn that keeps the dreaded Kraken away when it attacks in the far east seas. When you ask where to find one he says the Abandoned Island but warns it will not be easy to obtain.

"You need to find the temple. But be warned, it is guarded by something horrible."

You ask what but he refuses to say anymore except that you should be wary of coming to the temple by the north beach. You ask if he was there once, and you see him go pale. He stands up and excuses himself before quickly leaving the tavern.

You think about talking to the merchants, but they seem to be leaving. The barmaid is showing no interest in speaking to you, so you decide to go back to the crossroads to plan your next move. **You cannot return to the Malin's Town Alehouse. Go to *802***

29

You raise a hand and yell for music. The rest becomes a blur as everyone seems to be in a good mood and ready to celebrate. When you wake up, you find it's 3 days later and there's food missing but the crew are in a buoyant mood.

Increase your crew morale by 3 levels. Reduce your provisions by 1 due to excess food eaten at the party. However, you have wasted 3 days on the party and recovery which must be added to your voyage.

Now continue the voyage at **654**

30

Reduce the Hot Strip by 1. If this places you on a Fire spot add 20 to this section's number and go there for the walls have moved. There are walls of fire to the west and east. You can route south or north from your current location.

Do you

Go North – ***772***

Go South – ***648***

31

You open the crate scroll and it is blurred, some of the writing having been affected by the water. What you can make out seems to be referring to some sort of weapon. It mentions a green, prickly algae, and it's defensive properties, but what it refers to is washed over and unreadable.

Is this useful? If you have more items return to *18.* If not, the island still looks unappealing and barren, and your first officer agrees it is not worth exploring. The wreck is now fully underwater and shifting, making it too dangerous to go back to. I guess you're out of luck here.

Set sail for a new destination by consulting the voyage chart.

<u>32</u>

You gulp as through your eye piece you see a Spanish war galleon, armed to the teeth with cannon, one of the most feared sights on the seas.

Is your vessel speed *Very Slow* – *852*

Otherwise, your first officer tells you to flee as no good will come from an encounter with this beast of a vessel. You agree and you strike a course away from it, taking a day to be assured you are clear of them and can return to your course.

You return to your voyage but must **add 1 day extra to it** for this diversion.

Continue the voyage at *654*

<u>33</u>

Reduce your time by 3. You feel the wall and your hands fix on what you touched before. It feels like a small picture frame.

You can take the frame if you wish but must put it down your breeches or inside your shirt as you need your hands free to feel around. If you take it, note the code word Wall Frame and note where you place the frame.

You now stand with your back to the wall where you found the frame. On your left is more wooden wall while right and ahead is clear water.

The Treasure of Captain Estes

Do you

Step forward – **44**

Turn right and walk forward – **663**

<u>34</u>

You turn to walk back towards the start of this cliff path but as you walk a sudden wind blows you and you feel a gust. Then a vicious blast of cold air lifts you clean off your feet, taking you to the air and off the path and down to the rocks at the bottom of the cliffs. You are dashed instantly.

Well, you cannot say you weren't warned! No turning back. *And once you start do not turn back, for you cannot and live. These are cursed cliffs, enter at your peril.'* Remember that bit.

You can reset to the start of this puzzle at *1366* if you want or start all over again at *1*. That was a long haul, and you did so well, just not well enough.

<u>35</u>

Reduce your time by 5. Anything you were holding in your breeches is gone. Untick that item. You reach forward and feel clear water ahead but on your left you feel a large barrel blocking your path. On your right you can feel hatch handles but not the same feel as those you grabbed on the outside of the hatch to the forecastle. There's also clear water behind you.

Do you

About turn and step forward – **1344**

Walk forward – **715**

Open the hatch to your right and step through – **1209**

36

"Mary, it is Mary. Terrible business about your father but you're alive and that's good news. Come with me, I'm Robert Grimshaw, and we need to have a chat. After all I think you'll be wanting your lands back and the head of a certain Captain Estes."

You know the name Grimshaw, one of your father's associates he only spoke of rarely, but he trusted him. You hold out a hand and the man shakes it before he calls over some men who whisk you away from New Southampton and off to your destiny. Go to *1417*

37

You race across to the far side of the room, hearing darts fly, but make it successfully. There's a rope below you, leading down to another floor. Behind you are the remains of darts on the floor but you don't know if it's a trap that will spring again.

Do you

Climb down the rope now below you – *303*

Run back across the room – *1388*

38

You wander along the path and reach a junction with three paths off it. Which way now?

Left – *1050*

Middle – *26*

Right – *73*

Turn back – *5*

39

You turn asking for everything your vessel has, and the crew respond. Everyone is working hard but the cargo vessel is wise to your move and sails away from you. No matter what you do you don't seem to close the gap and after a day you know you need to call the pursuit off. You return to your voyage but must **add 2 days extra to it** for this diversion.

Continue the voyage at **654**

40

You wait for the tune to finish and endure the monkey jumping from watcher to watcher and the music plays on. As the tune comes to a halt, you realise that the pirate you were talking to is gone. Shaking your head, you walk away before realising that something is missing from your person. **Check your codewords. The second ticked item is gone. If you have only 1 ticked item, that is gone. If you have no items ticked (just what have you been doing?), then you realise it was just a light tickle and carry on.**

Leave the music and

Approach the bar – **669**

Talk to the gypsy woman – **711**

Walk over to the single pirate – **838**

Or exit the tavern – **1112**

41

Reduce your time by 1. You step forward and feel open water ahead and to your right. However, on your left is a large barrel blocking your progress.

Do you

About turn and step forward – **237**

Turn right and walk forward – **1381**

Reduce your time by 1.

If your time is in the following gaps (52-48) and you are not hidden, then go to *1037*. If you are hidden, you see a guard on his patrol and must remain hidden until he clears the area. Reduce your time by 6. Now continue at the plain text below

If your time is in the following gaps (22-18) and you are not hidden, then go to *1128*. If you are hidden, you see a guard on the enclosing wall patrolling and must remain hidden until he clears the area. Reduce your time by 6.

If neither of these apply, continue at the plain text below

The dark interior of the inner fort is barely lit by the occasional brand, and you can see a large building before you with a bolted barn type door. It has a guard on a smaller door, but he clearly cannot see you in the shadows. It appears that this will be a hard building to get inside but you can try.

There is a gate out of the enclosed centre of the fort in the wall, and it is open. To the south are more buildings. To the east is a path and what looks like a small hut. To the west is a large building with no guards outside.

Do you

Hide where you are – *915*

Route East – *174*

Creep West – *785*

Sneak north – *103*

Approach the building before you to break in – *1023*

43

Reduce your Waters Strength Chart by 1. Ignore this if you have just jumped in. The current is terribly strong and you are swept north. There is nothing you can do except float to *346*

44

Reduce your time by 1. You step forward and there is still clear water before you. On your right you feel a cage while there is a wooden wall on your right.

Do you

About turn and step forward – *157*

Walk forward – *281*

45

You descend the stone steps down to the quayside and note that you are being watched closely. As you pass by the docked vessels, you try to make conversation with those on guard but they simply tell you to beat it. You feel like you are unwanted and that if you don't get a move on out of here, you may get moved on in a more unpleasant fashion. But you still need a vessel. Or do you require something else? A tall pirate with a drawn cutlass approaches you and demands to know your business on the docks.

Do you tell him

You wish to obtain a vessel and crew – *1012*

Tell him you need a doctor – *1093*

Say that you are just looking – *329*

Claim you are lost and leave quickly – *699*

46

No, it's in the right cup, so you lose your stake. Hope you didn't bet too much. Want another try? If so whose game

Look to join the one-legged pirate's game – *1181*

Engage in the stumpy pirate's game – *1316*

Play in the female pirate's game – *618*

If not go to *64*

47

You try to get close to the tables to sneak away with a jewel, but the guards are watching you closely as you make a grab for a large emerald. A hand grasps your shoulder and you are carried out to the street where you are tossed into the dust and dirt of the walkway.

Do you have the codeword **Prominent** – *942*

Otherwise pick yourself up and **tick the codeword Prominent** in your list. Now return to the street at *496* and please stay away from the market.

48

You wander along the path, feeling breathless, and reach a junction. Which way now?

Left – *1218*

Right – *797*

Turn back – *399*

49

You cannot stop yourself, but you manage to take the pole and swing it sideways, jamming it into the rock. The wind howls and you stay flat as you crawl your way back to the entrance. The wind does not abate until you are back at the junction. You breathe a sigh of relief, but you are faced with the same choice minus your pole.

Remove the circle around your chosen pole and untick the codeword. You may choose another pole to use if you have one. If so, circle that codeword and continue.

What will you do now?

Walk and enter

Barcelona – *431*

Seville – *530*

God knows – *1229*

Or crawl and enter

Barcelona – *1254*

Seville – *342*

God knows – *815*

Or do you beat a hasty retreat – *34*

50

1 Skull 2 Scales 2 Coins

That's a win. The pirate opposite grunts and looks annoyed but you gain your prize. **Tick the codeword of your prize, keeping your stake item**, and return to *1060*

<u>51</u>

This is an expanded explanation of voyaging (or a repeat if you are struggling) and how to use the various charts and timers at the rear of the book. Any of the charts may be photocopied for use by players as you may need a few of them!

Okay, let's start your first voyage.

There's a chart of the seas around New Southampton in the appendix at *App 02*. Print a copy of this out as you will be using it a lot.

There is also a Voyage Log (*found at App 03*) where details of your vessel are entered, and changes are recorded. Fill this in now, if you have not already done so. The initial details are given when you met your first mate.

Now, fill in a trip planner (*Found at App 07*) stating where you are departing from and where you are going to. To calculate the normal trip time, find both the departure point and the destination on the Passage Time Chart (*Found at App 05*). It does not matter which is on which side of the table but find the box where the row and column cross.

In the box are 5 figures, which are the number of days a vessel will take according to its speed. The first figure is for a very slow vessel and the last for a very fast vessel. The numbers are as follows for the various speeds.

Very slow / Slow / Moderate / Fast / Very Fast

Enter the result in the planned days section of your trip planner. What happens on the trip will decide the actual days taken.

Next decide if you are on half rations. You must be on half rations for the whole trip or not at all. If you do not have enough rations for the whole trip, you must go on half rations.

Your provisions are in the cargo hold and are eaten at a rate dependant on the size of crew. Each cargo hold section of provisions is equal to 5 days food for a medium crew. A large crew will eat one section of provisions in 3 days, while a small crew will make them last 10 days. If you go onto half rations you must mark on the time chart when you do this. You cannot do this for more than 30 days or the crew will mutiny. Keeping rations at a sensible level is important. And yes, you must work it out. Sometimes you need to go and get provisions at a port out of your way.

The easiest way to denote provisions in your hold is to use the letter P in the section and then place a number (3, 5, 10) indicating the days of eating for the crew and a letter (S, M, L) to indicate the crew size. These will need to be adjusted if your crew size changes.

Provisions can also be destroyed in the narrative, as they are in the hold. Yes, it's annoying but beware.

At the end of your trip and arrival at your destination, intended or otherwise, you should remove the rations used and strike off the days taken, both planned and extra. If you are told the trip is cut short, you will be told how many days to take off your planned time.

Once you know your planned time you need to know which section to go to start your voyage. Go to the Passage Start Point Chart at *App 06* . Find the Departure point and Destination on different sides of the chart and then the box where the column and row meet. In the box are four dice roll results. Roll a D100 (2xD10) and then go to the resulting section to start your voyage. You will be instructed when you must repeat this process to start another voyage.

Having completed this section as part of a voyage plan, now go to the resultant section. Maybe bookmark this section or take a note of the number in case you need to revisit for your future voyages.

VERY IMPORTANT: At some point, hopefully, you will have discovered enough information and collected the required codewords to locate Estes' treasure. If you think this is the case, don't keep sailing around but instead look at the Passage Start Point chart and go to the explanations at the bottom of the page, specifically section 5. You cannot complete the adventure if you don't go here at some point in your game!!!!!!!!

Remember to update your Voyage Time and Voyage Log on arrival at your destination!

52

You sail close to the Brigantine under a white flag and are welcomed on board by Captain Jeboe. He needs nothing from you but is prepared to sell you provisions at 15 doubloons per provision and he can spare up to 10.

Add provisions to your hold as you see fit up, to 10 provisions at a cost of 15 doubloons each.

After trading, Captain Jeboe bids you a farewell and you sail on. Continue the voyage at **654**

53

As you walk back you see the pit of snakes but note that many seem to be escaping and coming your direction. Fortunately, most seem to be still in the pit but the few that are out come slithering towards you band then bear such fangs that you start to run back to your vessel. As you look behind the snakes come for you and as you push the small boat back out and row to your vessel, you feel such a sense of foreboding that you resolve to never come back here. **You may not return to the dark isle for the rest of your adventure.** So, what next?

Go to see Blind Tom – **681**

Visit the provisions isle – **334**

Enjoy yourself at the wild isle – **879**

Approach the pirate king – **1348**

Decide you have had enough of Hells Deep and set sail - **Consult the voyage chart and set sail.**

54

Reduce your time by 1.

If your time is in the following gaps (27-23 or 17-13), you see a guard on his patrol and must remain hidden until he clears the area. Reduce your time by 6. Now continue at the plain text below

If your time is in the following gaps (52-48 or 12-08), you see a guard on the enclosing wall patrolling and must remain hidden until he clears the area. Reduce your time by 6.

If neither of these apply, continue at the plain text below

You keep to the shadows, but no one comes. What will you do now?

Do you

Hide where you are – *1393*

Route South – *1197*

Creep East – *103*

Go North – *785*

Approach the building before you to break in – *989*

55

You show your item to the man who examines it and smiles before asking you to tell the story of the item. You fix your audience with a tale of high adventure, heavily embellished and they are impressed with you. The man with the wooden crutches tells you to sit with him and you spend a few hours listening to his tales of the sea. You pick up some possible pieces of information.

"The guards at Hell's deep won't take a bribe but they can be passed with a wink." **Tick codeword Password.**

"The bird's at the Paradise need a whistle to scare them otherwise they'll be all over you."

"They say some type of people live near the Marie Saratoga but didn't see them when I saw the wreck."

After an afternoon's carousing you leave and wonder what your next move should be. You return to the crossroads to plan your next place to visit – *802*

<u>56</u>

You get hit by lots of darts and fall to the floor. When you wake up you are in the same room and have managed to drag yourself back to where you started on this floor. You don't realise now, but will when back at the ship, that three days has passed since you collapsed. **Add 3 days to your voyage chart. Go to *843***

<u>57</u>

You dive back down after taking a large breath. The vessel is large and you wonder where to look at. You checked out the port side of the vessel last time, where this time?

Do you swim to the

Stern of the vessel – *1422*

Bow of the vessel – *94*

Starboard side – *1212*

Keel – *1413*

Or instead

Clamber on board - *603*

Return to your vessel – *894*

<u>58</u>

The man seems a little affronted, but he calmly steps away leaving you with decisions to make.

Do you

Approach the jewellery stall – *1158*

Go to the provisions stalls – *1368*

Or return to the street – *496*

<u>59</u>

You step forward towards the gap and your crewmates stand back to watch your efforts. You get ready to run the gap between the rock formations and try to time it so there are no bulls running toward you but in truth it's hopeless trying to find a clear run. You'll have to avoid the bulls as you go.

You take a run towards the middle of the gap and watch carefully to see what bulls come towards you. Go to *641*

<u>60</u>

The Malin's town alehouse is a sleepy affair with a few quiet merchants drinking in the corner. A rather buxom woman is tending behind the bar, and you can hear the sounds of a kitchen coming from the rear of the building. The whole building has a somewhat homely feel, and you notice that the warm fire has a rather stalwart figure napping beside it.

Do you

Approach the barmaid – *354*

Talk to the merchants – *598*

Wake the napping figure – *28*

Leave the tavern and return to the crossroads – *802*

61

You return to the base of the mountain and take a moment to gather yourself once at the foot. There are two paths away from the mountain, one a canopy covered path to the north, the other a more open topped path to the west, although it is still surrounded by the dense jungle.

Do you

Head north – **435**

Take the path west – **477**

Return up the mountain – **1177**

62

The pirate places a coin into the central cup of three and turns them all upside down. His hands then become a blur as the cups are moved around at pace before being reset in a line.

"Now call," says the pirate, indicating you should choose the left cup, the middle cup or the right cup.

Do you choose

Left – **377**

Middle – **787**

Right – **104**

63

"Are you Jalibert?" you ask.

"Who wants to know?" asks the man, angrily.

"Albert sent me. He said you can heal my wound."

"Come quickly," says the man and takes you to a vessel behind him. In the dark depths of the hold, you are tended to by a woman and allowed to sleep and rest. **Untick the codeword Shoulder Wound**.

You are in the hold for at least two days and then Jalibert comes to you in a flap.

"Captain Fareham is looking for you, and he is close. You need to go." You are taken to a wagon and hidden under some straw. The cart begins a journey of many hours before coming to a halt. After the rickety journey, you ache but are given a long-coat, breeches, and boots to wear, as well as a hat.

"Before you is Strangar. You'll be safe from Fareham here but beware it is no place for a lady."

With that, Jalibert simply leaves you. You know **you cannot go back to New Southampton**, so seek your fortune out in the pirate haven of Strangar. Go to *671*

<u>64</u>

You have left the games of chance so what next?

Make for the small houses – *1304*

Explore the tavern – *363*

Go to see the fights – *84*

Decide this is not a place you want to explore and return to your vessel - *314*

<u>65</u>

Go to *1361*

66

You cry to the crew to let the vessel run as fast as she can as you race for the Brigantine. But you are up against a trained crew who use the weather and the sea magnificently. After a day they are gone from sight. You return to your voyage but must **add 2 days extra to it** for this diversion.

Continue the voyage at *654*

67

The sailor looks delighted with the **Promissory Note (Untick the codeword)** and he tells you to wait here while he goes to get his crew for introductions. You stand waiting for twenty minutes before you hear a cry from out on the water. Turning around you see the sailor on a small rowing boat, the note being waved about in the air. As he does a flurry with his hand as a way of a bow, he overbalances and falls into the water.

From behind you, you hear someone say, "I see Captain Courageous has robbed another poor sod of their money. Total con man, and a drunkard."

You slump your shoulders having wasted the money but there's nothing for it but to look again. Go to *117* and choose another option.

68

You step onto the pillar with a sigh of relief. There are pillars to your right, directly behind, diagonally to your front right and diagonally to your rear left. You can see a small item on the pillar diagonally to your front right.

Do you step

To your right – *985*

Diagonally backward left – *531*

Diagonally forward right – *238*

Backwards – *448*

69

You grab hold of one of the treasure caskets as it strikes your foot. Desperately you haul it with you to the vessel and feel the arms of your crew haul you aboard. Soaking you gasp for breath and look around to see who else has been rescued. Not all of the crew from the small boat are standing there and some of the treasure caskets are missing. You realise you have lost 80% of the treasure that was in the small boat. **Adjust this amount now on the Island Time Chart.** There is a silence among the crew but there is little else you can do. Go to **725**

70

You wander along the path, wondering if you'll get out of here, and reach a junction. Which way now?

Left – **399**

Right – **1218**

Turn back – **797**

71

The vessel is brought to a halt, and you spend 2 days clearing the rats from the ship. You may not have got them all, but they are back at sensible levels, only seen in an occasional dark corner.

You have taken 2 days to clean up and you must add them to your voyage time. However, your crew are happier so raise your crew morale by 2 levels.

Continue the voyage at **654**

72

Oh dear. The guard does slide but forwards and right into you knocking you to the ground where you are seized by his fellow soldiers following behind him. Your hands are bound, and you are taken back to the garrison and to a livid Captain Fareham.

The Captain knows the value to him of your father's lands although they have been ransacked and he forces you to become part of his plan and you are married in private. Fareham now owns your father's lands and keeps you locked up for the next year. When you don't respond to his advances and wishes to be a passive wife, he has you taken away in the night and disposed of. Your last thoughts are that your family remains unavenged. Try again at *1* and remember enemies are everywhere, even those people who help.

73

You wander along the path, dreaming about being back on the sea, and reach a junction. Which way now?

Left – *48*

Right – *664*

Turn back – *1414*

74

The following morning Timmers marches into the cells along with the fort commander. In fairness the man is a piece of work. He is soft soaping the commander, talking about an impetuous scamp of a cabin girl.

Do you have the codeword Caught – *221*

If not read on,

When he gets a chance, Timmers tells you to stay quiet and you are led out to your vessel and then taken on board. You see a lot of items removed from your cargo hold, but soon you are sailing away from the fort. Timmers the diplomat has come through, you are free.

Remove half of your treasure from your stores. If you had no treasure, reduce your provisions down to half of their current level. Reduce your crew morale by 2 levels. You're alive but not by much. You have also lost 1 day, reduce your time chart by 1.

Now consult the voyage chart and set sail for your next destination.

75

Reduce the Hot Strip by 2. If this places you on a Fire spot add 20 to this section's number and go there for the walls have moved. There are walls of fire to the north, west, and east, so you route south from your current location. Go to *1173*

76

You wander along the path, palms becoming sweaty from the heat, and reach a junction. Which way now?

Left – *1008*

Right – *581*

Turn back – *1071*

77

Reduce your time by 2. If your time is in the following gaps (52-47 or 22-17) then go to *1377*. If not continue below

The papers in the hut are copious and have large scrawls of ink across them. It seems that someone had a bit of temper filling some of this in and you see ripped parchment everywhere. But everything on the page is numbers and you understand they are shipping notes, certainly no use to you.

Do you

Wait in hiding – *926*

If you haven't already

Look at the scrolls on top the barrel – *1332*

Move to the north quarter – *1176*

Move to the south quarter – *519*

78

Together you race onto the wall, but the cry has gone up and you see many guards ahead. From behind you hear feet approaching up the stone steps. There appears to be no escape.

"If we charge them, they can only defend themselves one at a time because the wall is so narrow here." You look ahead and Diggory is right, the wall is narrow. But it is also not that high here. You could jump over it to below. You look around. Is the tide in? Are you close to the bay, even? You know the water laps high against the wall when the tide is in, from your visits to New Southampton. But parts of the garrison are untouched by water. Just where are you. You can't tell.

Do you

Charge the guards with Diggory – *91*

Tell Diggory to jump the wall with you – *1221*

79

You have been here before and got the treasure. There's no way you are climbing those hilly paths again. Turn around and re-join the jungle path at *171*

<u>80</u>

Reduce your Waters Strength Chart by 1. The current is pushing you north. However, you think you can reach an eddy that seems to allow a way south but to get there will be incredibly hard work. There is an easier eddy to reach which may allow you to head east. Do you

Swim South – *338*

Float North – *1083*

Swim East – *1027*

<u>81</u>

Reduce your Island Time Chart by 1

You trek along the path, and everything seems to be a mass of green. There's a fork in the path, and you wonder which way to go. You can take either fork, or you could always head out into the jungle off the path.

Do you go

Left – *854*

Right – *245*

Strike out into the Jungle – *1347*

Turn around back the way you came – *1129*

<u>82</u>

You grab the rope and begin to descend but you see so many birds begin to swoop towards you. You blow your bird whistle which sends the feathered throng scattering and lets you descend to the base of the formation where you can decide your next action. Go to *1439*

83

You are back at the trap you fell into. You carefully walk past it and on to the end of the path. Go to **38**

84

You walk over to the various makeshift fighting rings that occupy a part of the island. There are many sweaty pirates sparring off against each other and you see plenty of broken teeth and copious rum being drunk. You certainly don't fancy your chances in any of these fights, but you think that some of these pirates could boost your crew. Alternatively, you could just walk away having seen some pugilistic entertainment.

Do you

Want to attract some crew – **121**

Decide to explore another part of the island

Make for the small houses – **1304**

Explore the tavern – **363**

Approach the gambling groups – **1424**

Or decide this is not a place you want to explore and return to your vessel - **314**

85

You feel around the crates and find one which is open. Searching inside you feel what appears to be a leather bound scroll. (If you have found this before the crates are merely empty) **Take it if you wish and tick the code word Crate Scroll if you do. Also, do you put it in your breeches, shirt or teeth to hold it as you need your hands free? Record your choice now in your notes.**

Reduce your time by 3 for the search. You now have your back to the crates. Ahead and left is clear water, but you feel a wooden wall on your right side.

The Treasure of Captain Estes

Do you

Walk forward – *541*

Turn left and walk forward – *588*

86

The pirates give a hearty laugh and shout at you to stand still while they take their reward. You are grabbed by them and without any hesitation they remove the body part you proffered for playing the game. You are then thrown back out onto the street, holding your wound, and almost screaming in pain. You need a doctor and fast, as you can see you are bleeding out. Start a count from now. You can turn to five more entries before your wound overcomes you and you will pass out onto death.

Return now to *262* **after which your entry count will begin**. Wait for nothing and find that Doctor. If you don't find the Doctor after 5 entries go to *370*.

87

This hasn't gone well and getting out of a fight now will be tricky. Let's hope you still have some manoeuvrability and speed.

Is your manoeuvrability

Good, Great or Reasonable – *682*

Poor or Lacking – *1086*

88

Do you have the codeword **Bird Whistle** - *82* If not, read on.

You grab the rope and begin to descend but you see so many birds begin to swoop towards you. More than that they attack you and you soon fall off the rope and down to the hard rocky ground below. You land heavily and the crew take you back to the vessel where you spend 2 days recovering. **Add 2 days to your voyage chart**. Once you feel like standing again, you return to the base of the formation and ponder your next move.

Do you

Enter the rock formation via the wooden door – *303*

Try and climb the rope outside the formation again – *362*

Leave the Bird's Paradise – **consult your voyage chart**

<u>89</u>

Do you have the codeword **Monkey**. If so – *836*. If not, continue below

You arrive at a clearing in the jungle where stands a covered statue of a monkey. Around the monkey's neck is a gold chain, maybe some 4 yards long. Before the statue are 3 different pedestals, each rising in height, side by side. You can reach the chain from the bottom pedestal. An older child could manage it from the middle one, while a toddler could manage it from the top one, if the child could ever get up there. Do you

Try and reach the gold chain from the

Lowest pedestal – *743*

Middle pedestal – *1450*

Highest pedestal – *390*

Or retreat back down the path – *1066*

<u>90</u>

Reduce your time by 1.

You step into the darkness and then feel around. There's nothing in front of you, nothing to the side and obviously nothing behind. On your left side you can feel a wooden wall.

Do you

Step forward – *416*

Turn left and step forward – *1339*

About turn and step forward – *343*

<u>91</u>

You get behind Diggory and together you charge at the oncoming guards. Diggory was right, the gap is narrow and sure enough you all collide and fall over. But you fall sideways off the wall and land on your head on the stone below. You black out instantly and die shortly after. It was a bit of a risk but you can try again at *1*

<u>92</u>

You are back at the trap you fell into. You carefully walk past it and on to the end of the path. Go to *116*

<u>93</u>

"Good money, eh?" says the man with the long scar.

"There are no grasses here," says the barmaid coming out from the serving area. "And we don't give information to strangers." She produces a loaded musket and tells you to leave. You walk out, disappointed and don't notice the man following you until he jumps you from behind. He knocks you to the ground and rummages in your pockets. **Untick the codeword of the smallest item in your codeword list.**

You pick yourself up and walk back to the crossroads annoyed at your foolishness. **You cannot return to "The Dog's Knackers" in the future. Go to** the crossroads at *802*

94

Diving down to the starboard side you see a horrible sight. Along the wooden side of the vessel is a skeleton with algae growing off its dull bones. The head is missing but otherwise the skeleton looks intact. It is held in place by a long spear thrust through its missing gut and snagging on the bottom rib. You feel a chill in the warm water and realise it's not the environment.

You may grab the spear if you wish, pulling it from the wood. If so, tick the code word Spear.

You're out of breath and so surface again. Having caught your breath, what next.

Do you swim to the

Stern of the vessel – *1422*

Starboard side – *1212*

Keel – *1413*

Or instead

Clamber on board -*603*

Return to your vessel – *894*

<u>95</u>

The crew have a weary look about them as they stare at the storm you are going into. There's a humid feel to the air, even more than the normal and you can see the storm clouds rising.

How bad is the storm?

Roll 1xD100 (2xD10) and go to the result below

00-20 – **Wild**

21-65 – **Strong**

66-00 – **Mild**

Check the result in the below table along with your vessel's storm handling ability and go to the appropriate section.

Storm Handling	Weather	Section
Good	Wild	*420*
Moderate	Wild	*957*
Poor	Wild	*220*
Good, Moderate	Strong	*175*
Poor	Strong	*842*
Good	Mild	*1464*
Moderate, Poor	Mild	*643*

<u>96</u>

You're a wanted person and you've drawn too much attention to yourself. The guards yell at others out in the street and you are soon surrounded. With such a force you are trapped and are taken away to the garrison and thrown into prison.

Captain Fareham of the garrison visits you and tells you that he intends to marry you, and he does so in quiet, keeping you locked up in the jail. Fareham now owns your father's lands and keeps you in your cell for the next year. When you don't respond to his advances and wishes to be a passive wife, he has you taken away in the night and disposed of. Your last thoughts are that your family remains unavenged. Try again at *1* and next time try and be more discreet.

97

You swoop low suddenly, before pitching forward. You can hear voices but in truth you cannot make them out. Are they saying something in concern, or simply shouting at you? Soon your eyes fog over, and everything turns to black. You have lost too much blood and have died. You never got that shoulder wound seen to. Try again at *1*

98

You see a white bull running directly at you and it doesn't look like it will move to avoid you. You are in the middle channel. What will you do?

Go right – *783*

Stay in the middle – *1047*

Go left – *298*

99

You push the pole down in the water in an attempt to jam it into the depths but it fails to stick on anything. Wore, it slips from your grasp in the crazy current, and you lose the pole. **Untick the codeword Red Pole**. Now return to your previously noted section.

100

The gypsy takes one look at you and turns away, ignoring you completely. You hear a number of pirates laugh and you feel very conspicuous. You try one more time to initiate contact but the gypsy woman simply stands and leaves. I guess she didn't like the look of you.

What now? If you haven't already,

Approach the bar – *669*

Walk over to the single pirate – *838*

Go over to watch the pirate playing the mouth organ – *1421*

Or leave – *1112*

Vessels Engage In The New Southampton Waters

101

3 Skull 0 Scales 2 Coins

You lose. (If you lost a body part go to *86*) **Untick the stake item from your codewords**, and return to *1060*

102

"You need to learn how to mould a man to your will," says Diggory, and he strides up to the second officer and grabs a hand, pinning it to one of the masts with a knife. "We have a position for second officer. If someone doesn't volunteer quickly, I will make it a vacant position."

A hand is raised at the back of the crew and a man steps forward. He takes the knife out of his crewmate's hand and cleans it, handing it back to Diggory.

"Sorry, Diggory, matter seems settled."

The crew take a step back and Diggory smiles at you as they disperse. You see how the crew look at you though and you wonder if you have made the right move here. You can tell over the coming days as although they obey your commands quickly, they seem to watch you closely. **Reduce your crew morale by 1 level.** Now continue at *654*

103

Reduce your time by 1.

If your time is in the following gaps (57-53 or 42-38) and you are not hidden, then go to *1037*. If you are hidden, you see a guard on his patrol and must remain hidden until he clears the area. Reduce your time by 6. Now continue at the plain text below

You can see before you the shadow of a large building with a single person wooden door and iron grills across the windows which also have shutters behind them. There appears to be no one on guard.

To the south, west and north, you can see buildings similar to what is before you while to the east there is a small building, although the dark makes it hard to see.

Do you

Hide where you are – *1281*

Route South – *1435*

Creep East – *174*

Go North – *42*

Sneak West – *1393*

Approach the building before you to break in – *1240*

104

Roll 1D100 (2xD10) to find where the coin actually is. Did you roll?

00-33 – *777*

34-67 – *573*

68-99 – *911*

105

You wander along the path, and almost stumble before you reach a junction. Which way now?

Left – *1414*

Right – *48*

Turn back – *664*

106

Go to **875**

107

Reduce your time by 1. You walk forward and find a wooden wall straight ahead. However, on your left and right is clear water.

Do you

Turn left and walk forward – **343**

About turn and step forward – **1339**

Turn right and walk forward – **416**

108

You step close to the shrine, and you can hear a howl begin like nothing from this earth. It says the word "penance" in a tone that indicates threat and death. You shiver at the sound and watch as writing starts to scroll across the chest in blood. However, it appears to be in Spanish and you cannot understand what it say. "Blast it," you cry, "I need English!"

The writing suddenly changes to English and you tremble at the words you see.

A penance is paid, or I shall have your head.

You can feel a presence close by and are unsure how to proceed. Will you really have to pay a cost to "Estes"?

Do you

Place something on the shrine from your inventory – **584**

Step away from the shrine – **479**

109

"Hey hey," says a pirate, "looks like someone looking for work. You can cosy on up to me, gorgeous."

"Hey boys, simmer down," says the bar maid, "she's one of mine. Into the back room, girl, told you before not to be late."

The men at the bar are staring at you, awaiting your response. You feel uncomfortable but you don't know the bar maid either. There's a knot in your stomach but you'd better do something.

Do you

Run – *273*

Sit down with the pirates – *751*

Take the bar maid's offer and go into the rear room – *1028*

110

You can't believe yourself, maybe you can just read the wind, but you grab hold of a crewman and haul him by the neck to the edge of the vessel and sling him out into the water beside the sloop. Before he lands in the water, he is grabbed by a throng of spirits, spectres which are wispy and white, but which also devour the man before your eyes.

Behind you, Martha is on her knees holding her hands up to the sloop before you, worshipping it. You join her and feel something in your soul grab you. Darkness fills you and you are carried away, speaking words in a language you never knew.

You sacrifice so many crew but a little while later you are standing on the deck again and the wind is blowing steadily with all storm clouds gone and the sea only showing a slight roll. But inside you feel powerful but horrible, like a tainted soul. You have a new master now.

Lower your crew morale by 3 levels. Lower your crew by 2 levels. Tick the codeword Darkness. What have you done?

Now continue your voyage at *654*

111

As you approach the doors one of the large men in overcoats blocks your path and demands what your business is within the guild. He is friendly enough, if firm, and certainly much larger than you.

Do you

Tell him you wish to join the guild – *726*

Say you are here on the business of your captain – *439*

Pretend to be lost and requiring help – *122*

Offer a bribe to gain access – *1310*

112

You scream as loud as you can and some men on horseback arrive. They are the New Southampton garrison and cut down the Spanish soldiers before further Spaniards arrive. In the melee, you disappear into the crop fields, able to hide out of sight. Go to *647*

113

You step onto the cliff edge pleased with yourself and then a suddenly chill runs through you as a maniacal laugh erupts from nowhere. The cliff ledge begins to crumble, and you desperately try to hang onto something as all around you tumbles to the sea below. You must have done something wrong, erred in some part of the puzzle. You see your crewmates' horrified faces as you finally slip off the ragged edge you are holding onto and descend to your end in the crashing waters below.

So near to Estes' treasure but with something missing. Where did you go wrong? You can try again at *1* or you can always reset to the start of this puzzle if you like at *830* (remember to untick the following codewords: Aisle, Pew, Rosary, Transept if ticked). This time make sure you know your path across before you try.

The Treasure of Captain Estes

<u>114</u>

You pick yourself up off the stone floor and look around you. Across from you is another cell with a prisoner. He is wearing a sailor's uniform and looks like an officer. The man is tall and lanky and is staring at you.

"Someone said Fareham had picked himself up a little wife. Did you not behave, Mary?"

You glower at the man but are also aware that at the moment you have no friends. The bars of your cell are solid and there is only one little window above, beyond your reach.

"Who are you?" you ask.

"First officer, Diggory Hurst, ma'am. I am here for daring to usurp Captain Johnstone, the most incompetent and dangerous captain in the British fleet. If I had not, we would all be dead. As it is, the crew have escaped although we lost the ship. Currently, they are in the bay in a small sloop they have acquired. Tomorrow I am tried for mutiny, and I need to rendezvous with them, or I will shortly be dead."

You stare at the man unsure if he's telling the truth.

"If you would be so kind as to help me, I think we may both escape this incarceration. I will need that cross around your neck. I need to signal the crew and unfortunately my mirror was taken from me when they saw my last signal. The matter is also urgent as the light is currently in our favour and I can signal for maybe the next hour or so. So please trust me, Mary Hastings."

How does he know your name? The man is maybe in his thirties and has a battered face. Is he a criminal? Can he be trusted? The cross is of deep sentimental value.

Do you

Ask how he knows you – *759*

Throw him the cross – *1018*

Refuse to help him and await your fate – *884*

115

You turn and run straight into Captain Fareham, an officer at the garrison who has been at your mansion many times. In his late thirties, you know he has had eyes on you as a potential wife and could be a route to safety.

"Mary, thank God you are alive. I saw your father and thought they had got to you as well. Come now, quickly and I'll get you to the garrison. You'll be safe with me."

He takes your hand and runs quickly up the stairs and then down the second set at the far end of the mansion. Soon he has you on a horse riding with an escort to the garrison. At least you are safe for the moment but what plans the captain has for you remain to be seen.

Go to *1031*

116

You wander along the path, getting flashbacks to your parents, and reach a junction. Which way now?

Left – *1071*

Right – *5*

Turn back – *581*

117

The docks are awash with sailors and gentlemen, slaves and servants, working hard in the hot sun. Many vessels are being off loaded, others stocked for voyage, and a few seem to have little life about them. You need a vessel and a crew, so this may be the place to get one.

You look around and see three opportunities to explore. Nearest is a man in a full blown long-coat and a tri-cornered hat telling tales of the sea to a small, gathered crowd. People are laughing with him and seem in awe of his tales. Beyond him is a small hut, with a sign on the door stating that commissions are taken for voyages. And further on is a rickety pier with a large man sitting, whittling on a stick, with a sign saying the vessel is for hire.

Do you

Approach the storyteller – *410*

Go to the hut – *753*

Walk to the rickety pier and the large man – *140*

118

You find the pull of the main current tough to overcome to get to the eddy, but you do it eventually. **Reduce your Waters Strength Chart by 1.** You swim through to the eddy. Go to *285*

119

You grab the handles of the chest and your hands burn. You scream in pain and stumble almost into a wall of fire, but you stagger here and there momentarily lost in your pain. When you recover, you are not sure where you are.

Reduce the Hot strip by 2 and go to *1420*

120

If this is at least the second item you have examined then roll 1xD100 (2xD10,) and consult the table below

2nd item	3rd item	4th item
00-39 – *959*	00-59 – *959*	00-89 – *959*
40-99 – read on	60-99 – read on	90-99 – read on

Well, guess what, they are chairs, some with rather delightful rose patterns on them. And if you want to, you can sit on them. Seriously, they are chairs and you've wasted time looking at them.

Do you

Examine the desks – *1239*

Check out the cabinets – *1405*

Peruse the charts on the wall – *371*

Or leave the room and return back to tunnel – *558*

121

How much are you prepared to offer to join your crew? Who knows if it costs more here to get crew or not? Decide how much you want to put aside for the new crew:

300 doubloons – *1017*

500 doubloons – *1261*

1000 doubloons – *710*

If you can't afford this, return to *84* and choose again.

122

"Excuse me but I'm lost," you say and watch the door man approach. He grabs you by the collar and tosses you to one side.

"Well, this isn't where you were looking for."

You scurry off as the man looks quite large.

You cannot return to the Mariner's Guild in daylight, during this visit to Malin's Town, as you are now identified as a loser.

Do you

Come back at night in an attempt to gain access when the building is closed – *742*

See to the needs of your vessel and crew – *903*

Try to earn some money by signing up to a cargo run – *1335*

Visit the taverns for information – *802*

If you have had enough of Malin's town, then **consult the voyage chart and set sail**.

123

You see a brown bull running directly at you and a white bull to your right. You are in the middle channel. What will you do?

Go right – *392*

Stay in the middle – *466*

Go left – *547*

124

You walk to the merchant district of the small town and see the impressive Marnier's Guild building complete with a small wooden frigate, about one quarter size, outside. The building shows little in terms of wear and tear and has two large wooden doors at the front. Above them, is the small round emblem of a ship's wheel, that denotes the guild. You can see two large men in smart overcoats standing at either side of the doors, and wonder if you will be able to get in. As the main guild in the area of New Southampton, they keep track on all vessels and may have details of where Estes went before his demise. Whether they will tell you about that is another matter.

Do you

Approach the doors – *111*

Come back at night in an attempt to gain access when the building is closed – *742*

Decide that this may not be the place for you and instead

See to the needs of your vessel and crew – *903*

Try to earn some money by signing up to a cargo run – *1335*

Visit the taverns for information – *802*

If you have had enough of Malin's town, then **consult the voyage chart and set sail**.

125

Reduce your Island Time Chart by 1

You trek along the path, weary and grumpy. You find a multi-fork in the path, and you wonder which way to go. You can take one of the paths, or you could always head out into the jungle off the path.

Do you go

Left – *151*

Right – *429*

Straight ahead – *407*

Strike out into the Jungle – *1077*

Turn around back the way you came – *1223*

<u>126</u>

You sail into a small opening that has three exits from it. The rocks are spaced here, and you can turn easily. There are exits from the channel to the northeast, northwest, and southwest. All are wide channels so where next?

Do you

Sail northeast– *1349*

Route northwest – *244*

Go southwest – *452*

<u>127</u>

You step forward to the raging heat aware that you will not last that long inside the Walls of Fire. You think about your possessions and wonder do you have anything with you that will help. But there's nothing. This is truly a risky challenge.

You wander round the outside of the flames until you see a solitary entrance. You know the casket is somewhere in the middle of the flames but not where.

Check the Walls of Fire diagram (*App 10*) as you will enter the challenge from the southwest corner. All descriptions will reference to the cardinal points. The heat is so intense it is hard to look up and you must shield your eyes, so you are judging where the walls are by the base of them. The walls are 5 movements deep in both directions and you will move in the north, south, east and west directions.

Also check the Walls of Fire Hot Strip (*App 11*) which is a countdown from 25 to zero. At zero you will be overcome by the heat and be forever trapped inside the walls. Follow the section marked on the Strip when this happens. Also tick off the Strip when instructed. If the text asks if you are on a fire spot this is indicated on the timer (*App 11*) by an FS alongside the time remaining.

You step forward into the challenge and find that your path is blocked to the north and the west. You can step back out but what is the point and so take a move to the east, arms up against the heat. **Reduce the Hot Strip by 1. Go to *1065***

128

You open the chest and see a piece of parchment inside. The voice hisses," I curse you, child," and then the feeling of eeriness and loathing vanishes. You look at the parchment which shows a bearing from a location known as the smiling face. **Tick the codeword Bearing B**

You wonder if this bearing will help you. For now you are at the top of the rock formation and need to descend, so take the rope and climb down to the level below. Go to ***470***

129

He eyes you suspiciously as you walk back to the street. You make no move and when you are back in the middle of the street, he gives you some advice.

"Tavern over the road if you want a good time. Doctor at the docks to clean you up. If you're short of coins, you can catch the game at the entrance to Strangar. Just don't wander up to anywhere unannounced. We don't like it."

With that he returns to his "sleep" at the barn door. Return to ***1112*** and choose somewhere else to go.

130

You are fortunate as you are beside cover and hide straight away. Go to ***1190***

131

You ignore the strange feeling and reach for the gold. As you do so, the chest falls away as does a section of the wall. They swing back and down, creating an opening to the outside of the rock formation. The floor you stand on tilts up, forcing you to fall forward and out of the rock formation and down to the hard surface below.

You are knocked unconscious and the next thing you know you are on your vessel, attended to by your first officer. You've lost a day from the fall but will you go back to the formation as you are still moored beside it. **Add a day to the voyage chart.**

Do you

Return to the rock formation – *1439*

Decide this is a bad idea and leave the Bird's Paradise – **consult your voyage chart**

132

Your crew stare in horror as you give the order to round many of them up. Your first officer looks at you but then a large tentacle is seen approaching the vessel and they give a nod of approval. Crewmates scream as you select them for sacrifice and order your first officer to throw them from the vessel. The day seems to darken as you order more overboard in what seems to be an endless horror. Your feel like your soul has been gripped by something else.

But the plan works. After two hours of sacrificing, the kraken returns to the depths, apparently sated. But your crew look at you with a horror that pierces you.

Reduce your crew morale by 4 levels. Reduce your crew by 1 level. You have been tainted with the horror you have just committed. Tick the codeword Darkness if you have not already.

Now continue your voyage at *654*

<u>133</u>

Reduce your time by 2. If your time is in the following gaps (55-53, 35-33, 24-23 or 04-02) then go to *810*. If not continue below

You wait in the shadows seeing no one move.

Do you

Wait in hiding – *519*

If you haven't already

Investigate a slum – *847*

Take a look at the latrines – *386*

Move to the west quarter – *493*

Move to the east quarter – *678*

Leave the fort for your vessel – *535*

<u>134</u>

You see a white flag go up in surrender from the opposite captain and you soon board the vessel. In the hold you find the following: **Roll 1xD100 (2xD10)**

00-25 – **40 provisions and 400 doubloons worth of cargo (6 spaces)**

26-50 – **An empty hold**

50-75 – **A hold full of captured Spanish priests. You may take them, but they take up 4 spaces. (Tick the code word Spanish priests. They add a level to your crew when calculating rations.**

77-99 – **You find treasure taking up 14 spaces and worth 300 doubloons a space. You may fill up what your cargo can hold.**

You must now decide what to do with the captain of the other vessel. You could leave him adrift with his crew, or you could scupper the vessel and its crew. You find the idea of taking the crew and vessel along with you cumbersome and unpractical. You look at your own crew wondering what they would expect of you and compare that to your own morals.

Do you

Leave the vessel and captain adrift – *696*

Scupper the vessel with the crew and captain on board – *1124*

<u>135</u>

"I am no wench, sir, but a sailor!"

The alehouse erupts into laughter at your statement, and you hear the words "Feisty little beggar from somewhere nearby." Clearly they are not impressed and the portly man reaches for you again.

Do you

Shove him hard – *946*

Pull your knife on the man – *1298*

Saddle up to the man to gain information – *1038*

<u>136</u>

For all that the wreck gives an aura of foreboding, the water is crystal clear, and the day is sunny. You dive from your vessel to a large cheer from the crew and swim down until you are at the port side of the vessel. The name Marie Saratoga is painted on the side, and you see large scratches across the side of the vessel. The marks are deep and gorged in some fashion, like a massive claw had torn into the wood.

You would gulp at the sight, but you are underwater and that might not be useful. Instead, you swim back to the surface to grab a few breaths. As you tread water, you wonder what could have caused that. Maybe you should investigate further. Or maybe that would be foolish. You could always just clamber on board and examine the wreck from the inside.

Do you

Dive back down to investigate – *57*

Clamber on board *-603*

Return to your vessel *–894*

<u>137</u>

The mud path is dense, and you dare not step off it into the thick green plants that lie beyond, fearing that they will close up behind you, trapping you in an endless humid jungle. You hear nothing, no bird life, no animals or insects and everything feels eerie. Sweat rolls down your face as the path now forks before you, left and right. Which way do you go?

Left – *639*

Right *–70*

Turn back – *612*

<u>138</u>

You take the knife and run at the first soldier. You are like a wild thing, enraged by your father's death, and you slit the man's throat from behind. The second soldier turns and drives a knife into your shoulder causing you to yell. But the fire is burning within you and with your other hand you drive the knife into his throat.

Stumbling for the door, you realise your white gown is bloodstained **(tick the codeword Shoulder Wound)** and you clasp a hand over your wound. Making for the fields, you hide out until the morning.

Your wound is sore, and you worry about an infection setting into it. You have managed to stop the blood flow and it has clotted but you are not in great shape.

The Treasure of Captain Estes

By dawn the house is burnt to the ground, but the New Southampton garrison soldiers are in charge, having chased away the Spanish forces. You can see Captain Fareham, an officer at the garrison who has been at your mansion many times. In his late thirties, you know he has had eyes on you as a potential wife and could be a route to safety. He's taking charge and you know he will look after you if you go to him now. From there you could plan your next steps. But he is a powerful figure and may seek to simply take whatever's left of your father's lands for himself by taking you for his wife. You know you'll get little say in the matter now your father is gone. It's a risk but one that may pay off in the short term, given your wound which will certainly get the best of treatment that New Southampton can offer.

Your other options are riskier. You could head into New Southampton, but you have no money on you and without your father, you will have little say in what other people do. On the other hand, making for Strangar, the illegal port may bring you opportunities to go after Estes but at what cost and danger. Remember you have a wound which needs attention.

Do you

Go to Captain Fareham and ask for his help – *1315*

Walk into New Southampton – *1114*

Head for Strangar – *671*

139

You see a brown bull running directly at you and it doesn't look like it will move to avoid you. You are in the middle channel. What will you do?

Go right – *783*

Stay in the middle – *466*

Go left – *1047*

140

The man continues to whittle on his stick as you approach and seems to completely ignore you. You look beyond him but can see no one around. Do you know this man? Have you been sent to him?

Have you the codeword **Jalibert** – *63*

Otherwise, do you

Offer him a **Bottle of Whiskey** – *813*

Threaten him with a weapon for information – *675*

Ask about getting a crew and a vessel – *730*

141

You peer into the main shop from the dressing room until you see Madame Le Vert is alone and you sneak up behind her. Using your weapon, you threaten her by putting it in her back so she cannot see you. She then lies on the floor while you take one of the men's long-coats, a pair of breeches, a hat and some boots for a disguise before exiting out of the dressing room window. **Note you are now in a long-coat disguise.**

On dropping down to the alleyway, you quickly make your way back to the main street where you mingle with the crowds. Go to *1166*

142

You step onto the pillar, and you stumble for a hair raising moment but regain your balance. There are pillars to your right and in front and behind.

Do you step

Forwards – *170*

Backwards – *1409*

To your right – *166*

143

Reduce the Hot Strip by 2. If this places you on a Fire spot add 20 to this section's number and go there for the walls have moved.

If you have codeword Fire Chest, there are walls of fire to the north, south, and east. You can route west from your current location. Go West at *831*. Otherwise read on.

There is a treasure chest at your feet, but it is between the three walls of fire and could be extremely hot. You could wait for it to cool down as you shield it, or you could simply grab it. There are walls of fire to the north, south, and east. You can route west from your current location.

Do you

Go West – *831*

Shield the treasure and wait for a few moments to let it cool – *895*

Grab the chest – *309*

144

You sail into a small opening that has four exits from it. The rocks are spaced here, and you can turn easily. There are exits from the channel to the north, south, southeast, and southwest. All are wide channels except to the southeast which is narrow and will require a vessel with good manoeuvrability. Where now?

Do you

Sail north– *1270*

Route southeast (only vessels with good manoeuvrability) – *1030*

Go southwest – *159*

Sail south – *1448*

145

Is your vessel manoeuvrability

Great or Good – **400**

Reasonable – **965**

Poor or Lacking -**999**

146

You remember the small noiseless horn that you found, and you place it to your lips. You blow with all your might but there's no sound from it. However, it silences the song of the mermaids, and you see your male crew begin to come round from their trance like states, pulling themselves back from the water.

You order your crew to route away from the mermaids who pursue initially. But you blow the horn and keep the mermaid song at bay. By the afternoon, the mermaids have given up pursuit and you are able to all relax after a narrow escape.

Raise your crew morale by 1 level. Now continue your voyage at **654**

147

Reduce your time by 2. If your time is in the following gaps (40-35 or 10-05) then go to *1322*. If not continue below

You sneak up on the wagon and peer inside. There is nothing obvious, but you can see a pile of straw which you could search under. Otherwise, the cart is empty.

Do you

Look under the straw – **577**

(further options over the page)

Or

Wait in hiding – *433*

Investigate the flagpole – *602*

Move to the North quarter – *1176*

Move to the South quarter – *519*

148

You watch the guard pass by from your hiding place, keeping a track on them, but unable to move freely while they are about. It takes them a while to clear the area as they look here and there. **Remove 6 time.** Finally they are clear but you have had to abort your previous action. Return to *926* and choose again but ignore the time adjustment at that entry this time round.

149

You wait in your vessel as Diggory goes into Malin's Town to find your contact and give him the good news. He returns alone and has in his hands a piece of parchment. It has details on how to complete the "Waters of Myra" whatever that is. **Tick the codeword Myra.** Now decide if you should stay in Malin's Town or depart.

Do you

See to the needs of your vessel and crew – *903*

Try to earn some money by signing up to a cargo run – *1335*

Visit the taverns for information – *802*

Visit the Mariners' Guild for information – *124*

If you have had enough of Malin's town, then **consult the voyage chart and set sail.**

150

You have been sailing a long time, looking for Estes' treasure and today is a day too far. Your crew are sick of the travel and have lost belief that you will be able to find the treasure. There are rumblings and when you investigate you find even your first officer has turned against you. You've may have been through a lot together, but these crews don't stay loyal for long.

You are thrown overboard, with little more than a "good riddance". As you sink beneath the waves you realise that you have failed to avenge your family, and have missed out on regaining your former life. At least you don't have long to contemplate this before you sink far below the waves.

Bad luck. Next time you need to be slicker, or maybe find a different crew. Either way, start again at *1*

151

Do you have the codeword **Calm** – *210*

If not, continue below

You walk along the jungle path, sweating in the sun, and you can hear rushing water. As you round a corner in the path, you see a small, turbulent lake in front of you, the water swirling this way and that, the choppy water seemingly impossible to cross. In the water, on a small rock that juts out of the crazy surging lake, sits a casket, lying open and with golden treasure inside. You can see straps attached to the casket, clearly to allow you to carry the treasure while in the water, if you can reach it. Estes truly was very precious about his treasure.

You set down the rest of your possessions and step up to the water in front of you. You can see that the water flows in different currents, but each seems to be so random. You see a small branch fall into the water halfway across from the overhanging jungle, and it is sent one way and then the other, forward, and then back. There is definitely a pattern to the flow but can you understand it, and more importantly can you last in the water.

Do you have the codeword **Myra** – *939*

If not, continue below.

In order to do this task, you realise that you will need to be able to take a breather if you cannot go directly to the rock from the side you are on. If you have a pole with you that may be able to find the bottom of the maelstrom and give you a chance to get a breather. Although, you don't know how deep anywhere is so you will not know where you can get a breather until you make an attempt. Otherwise, it will be a manic swim, and then you will need to get back again.

Is this something you can do? It seems like a risky business.

Do you

Take on the Waters of Myra – *480*

Decide this is not for you and head back down the jungle path - *236*

152

You take out the Bodach sword and swoosh it through the water at a crab creature. But the sword passes clean through the creature, and you are nipped on the arm by a claw and drop the sword. **Untick the codeword Bodach Sword.** You forgot it's for spirits, not physical creatures when used by a human. What now?

Do you have the following codewords and wish to use the items

Spear – *271*

Orange Algae – *576*

Green Plant – *609*

Eye Charm – *1382*

If not, or you choose not to try them, you need to swim back to your vessel before the creatures get any closer.

If your vessel is in the shallows – *632*

If not, and it is anchored further out – *672*

153

The woman is rather striking in a way and the eyes seem to capture the attention of any admirer of the painting. It also bears the legend "Lady Argyle". It is small though and you can hide it on your person. If you take it, tick the codeword **Argyle.**

Go to *1400*

154

The gypsy ignores you at first until you sit down. With dark eyes, she watches you carefully before she runs a hand through her long black hair and gives a forced laugh. But she says nothing until another pirate comes across and interrupts, saying that the gypsy had told him to return at this time.

"I'm sorry," says the gypsy, "but it looks like someone got here before you."

With that, they disappear off to the rear of the tavern and you realise that if you look like a pirate, you'll be treated like one.

What now? If you haven't already,

Approach the bar – *669*

Walk over to the single pirate – *838*

Go over to watch the pirate playing the mouth organ – *1421*

Or leave – *1112*

155

The whiskey and ale stalls are packed with slaves, traders, and gentle folk. It seems everyone likes their drink of choice, and you walk among the various stalls wondering what to look for or do. As you walk you see a young slave girl getting beaten by her master. Most people walk on by, but you feel for her, lying on the dirt as she is kicked. Should you get involved? Do you have other business you could conduct here?

If this is your third stall visited in the market, note the number of this section, and then go to *1336*

Otherwise, do you

Intervene for the slave girl – *290*

Have a bottle of whiskey you could trade – *487*

Or do you

Approach the jewellery stall – *1158*

Go to the provisions stalls – *1368*

Or return to the street – *496*

156

Reduce your time by 1.

If your time is in the following gaps (32-28 or 12-08), then go to *1037*.

If your time is in the following gaps (47-38), then go to *1128*.

If neither of these apply, continue at the plain text below

You creep up to the building and to the single wooden door. You feel exposed as you stand there and wonder if you should just pull at the door and enter the building to get cover. It would be madness to stand here, but what's inside?

Do you

Hide where you are – *1197*

Route through the open gate – *519*

Creep East – *1435*

Go North – *1393*

Listen at the door – *1011*

Open the door and enter the building – *680*

<u>157</u>

Reduce your time by 1. Stepping forward you reach a wooden wall with something on it. There is also a wooden wall on your right but there is clear water to the left.

Do you

About turn and step forward – *44*

Turn left and walk forward – *663*

Examine the wall before you – *33*

<u>158</u>

You smile as the vessel clips away from the creature and you turn to fire a broadside at it. It has just raised itself slightly above the surface and you seize your chance.

Is your vessel's firepower

Heavy or very heavy – *592*

Light or Moderate – *1345*

None – *389*

<u>159</u>

You arrive at a small pool with three channels routing into it. There are exits to the northeast, southeast and southwest, all with wide channels.

Do you

Sail northeast– *144*

Route southeast – *881*

Go southwest – *1043*

160

The alley is heavily in shadow, and you are nervous about entering. You think you can see someone leaning up against the wall of a building, dressed in boots and a long-coat but you are not sure of any further details. There's cart half blocking the alley and that will force you towards the dark stranger. You know that beyond the alley is a place that many of the sea adventurers visit but you don't know what it is.

Do you

Approach the stranger – **498**

Try to walk calmly past the stranger through the alley – **724**

Forget this and return to the street – **496**

161

Reduce your time by 1.

You slide down into the tunnel and find it's as bad as the smell that came from it. Your hands touch damp walls with white mildew, at least that's what you hope it is, the light being so poor. You must walk slowly due to the lack of light, but you find yourself at an end wall quite quickly. You feel a trapdoor above and wonder where it leads.

Do you

Push open the trapdoor – **909**

Wait for a moment listening – **795**

Or if you think you should leave it alone, continue below

You retreat along the tunnel and exit back in the message room, covering up the trapdoor again with the rug. Now, do you

Look at the desk – **206**

Look at the other rug – **565**

Try to open the safe – **1288**

Decide this is a bad idea and return outside – **174**

162

There is a stirring outside the window, and you realise that the patrol has come back. One of them is pointing out the open shutters to the other. You freeze.

Do you have the codeword

Stowed – *450*

Nocturne – *1146*

163

You get hit by a dart and fall to the floor. When you wake up you are in the same room and have managed to drag yourself back to where you started on this floor. You don't realise now, but will when back at the ship, that a day has passed since you collapsed. **Add 1 day to your voyage chart. Go to *843***

164

Having crossed the line of green blood you note that the walls of the hall seem to be changing and you are now standing in a room with 3 doors. Above one door is a shield, above another is a spider and over the third is a pirate flag. The room is quite barren with a wooden floor, and you are not sure how it has come to be. Regardless you are here now. You listen but cannot hear anything else. What will you do?

Go through the spider door – *388*

Go through the shield door – *874*

Go through the pirate flag door – *1091*

Remain here – *1074*

165

You sail away and the Brigantine doesn't follow, obviously uninterested in what you have to offer.

Continue the voyage at **654**

166

Go to **238**

167

Reduce the Hot Strip by 1. If this places you on a Fire spot add 20 to this section's number and go there for the walls have moved. There are walls of fire to the south and west. You can route north or east from your current location.

Do you

Go East – **485**

Go North – **320**

168

Reduce the Hot Strip by 1. If this places you on a Fire spot add 20 to this section's number and go there for the walls have moved. There are walls of fire to the north and east. You can route south or west from your current location.

Do you

Go West – **456**

Go South – **969**

<u>169</u>

You bend down and pull back the rug revealing a wooden trapdoor with a large brass ring which is what caused the ripple in the rug. You try it gently and the trapdoor seems to open easily. Below is a dark tunnel and you struggle to see what's along it.

Do you

Enter the tunnel beneath – *240*

Decide against this and replace the trap door and rug. If so, do you then

Look at the desk – *1167*

Look at the other rug – *366*

Try to open the safe – *1289*

Decide this is a bad idea and return to Timmers, saying you should get back to the ship pronto – *351*

<u>170</u>

You step onto the pillar with the cliff edge just before you. There are pillars behind you and diagonally to your rear left. **Tick the codeword Rosary if you haven't already**.

Do you step

Forwards on to the cliff – *294*

Backwards – *142*

Diagonally backward right – *166*

171

Reduce your Island Time Chart by 1

You leave the cliffs behind and reach a fork in the path, wondering which way to go. You can take either fork, or you could always head out into the jungle off the path.

Do you go

Left – *224*

Right – *677*

Strike out into the Jungle – *1347*

Turn around back the way you came – *1366*

172

You wander along the path, wishing you had a bottle of wine, and reach a junction. Which way now?

Left – *707*

Right – *1230*

Turn back – *328*

173

Go to *1394*

174

Reduce your time by 1.

If your time is in the following gaps (52-48) and you are not hidden, then go to *1037*. If you are hidden, you see a guard on his patrol and must remain hidden until he clears the area. Reduce your time by 6. Now continue at the plain text below

If your time is in the following gaps (22-18) and you are not hidden, then go to *1128*. If you are hidden, you see a guard on the enclosing wall patrolling and must remain hidden until he clears the area. Reduce your time by 6.

If neither of these apply, continue at the plain text below

You can see a path before you leading up to a hut which is unguarded. It is close to the wall but otherwise it looks very unassuming. The hut is small but could certainly contain an office of some sort. It is dark around it though, with only a single brand alight.

Do you

Hide where you are – *455*

Route South-west – *1435*

Creep West – *103*

Sneak North-west – *42*

Try to enter the hut – *337*

175

The weather is rough but not unmanageable. You still feel like you need to be careful, and you see the sails take a battering. At one point you feel the need to lighten the load in the ship and throw 2 provisions overboard. When you clear the storm after two days you assess the damage.

The vessel is in good condition but remove 2 provisions from your vessel's cargo. If you cannot reduce your vessel speed level by 1 due to damage.

Now resume your voyage at *654*

<u>176</u>

Reduce the Hot Strip by 1. If this places you on a Fire spot add 20 to this section's number and go there for the walls have moved. There are walls of fire to the north and south. You can route east or west from your current location.

Do you

Go East– *1455*

Go West – *1303*

<u>177</u>

Reduce your Island Time Chart by 1

You trek along the path, overcome by the amount of green. Suddenly there's a fork in the path, and you wonder which way to go. You can take either fork, or you could always head out into the jungle off the path.

Do you go

Left – *268*

Right – *245*

Strike out into the Jungle – *1283*

Turn around back the way you came – *1111*

<u>178</u>

"If I'm not mistaken that's the galleon of Emmanuel Gonzales." You have no idea who your first officer is talking about, but you want to know more.

If your first officer is

Simon Kilmer, Robert Grimshaw, Diggory Hurst or Timmers – *652*

Martha Downham or Black Robert – *931*

179

Because you have spent time looking at the other papers you have already used some of your time until daylight is gone. Therefore, ignore the instruction to start your island time chart in section *1039* at 100 and instead **start at number 96**. Also note that daylight will run out at number **05,** not **00** as advised in the instructions. After all, Estes realised that the day was shorter here, didn't he?

Return to *1039* and continue with the instructions to set up your island time chart noting this change you have been instructed with.

180

Move Tabetha.

You are in a white walled room, bathed in the strange light, with two doors, one with a picture of a shield above it, and the other with a pirate flag above it.

If Tabetha's number is 23 – *1459*

If Tabetha's number is 10 – **note this number and go to *239***

If Tabetha's number is 12 – **note this number and go to *1029***

Where do you go next?

Through the shield door – *358*

Through the pirate flag door – *867*

Wait here - **return to the top of this section**

181

As you approach the front doors you think that they are open slightly and you delicately try to pry your way inside. Suddenly someone throws the doors open completely and there is a cry to the air, alerting everyone to your presence. You run as hard as you can back to the docks, telling the crew to set sail immediately.

The Treasure of Captain Estes

You must leave Malin's Town immediately, and you may not return for 20 days until the heat dies down, for you cannot be sure your face was not seen.

Consult the voyage chart and set sail for another destination.

182

"We're heavy and can't turn quick. Let it get close and blow it to hell!"

Return to *927* and make your decision.

183

Reduce your Island Time Chart by 1

You trek forward along the path, and everything looks the same. You try to remember if you came this way already because the vegetation all looks so similar. Soon you reach a fork in the path, and you wonder which way to go. To the right you think you hear the sound of the beach. You could always simply strike out into the jungle off the path.

Do you go

Left – *1079*

Right – *1246*

Strike out into the Jungle – *1347*

Turn around back the way you came – *1064*

184

You find the pull of the main current tough to overcome to get to the eddy, but you do it eventually. **Reduce your Waters Strength Chart by 1.** You swim through to the eddy. Go to *866*

185

Do you have the codeword **Crossed** – *1440*

If not, read on.

"Keep it at a distance and use the guns on it. This ship can handle itself!"

Return to *927* and make your decision.

186

You enter an open pool which is very calm. There are two exits from it, northwest and southeast. But as you prepare to sail, your crew start pointing over the side where you see a large turtle swimming about. One of your crew suggests you try and spear it for food or capture it to take to a market. It could be valuable as it is nearly the size of a man.

Do you

Attempt to spear the turtle – *234*

Sail on to the northwest – *606*

Pass on to the southeast – *1263*

187

"We're fast and have heavy firepower, so let's keep it at a distance but blow it to kingdom come!"

Return to *927* and make your decision.

188

The heavy galleon is not difficult to outrun, and you alter heading so the galleon does not know your true course. After a day, you are clear of it and can resume your original course.

Add 2 days to your voyage time. Continue the voyage at *654*

189

You tell your guard to organise a cabin for the person, but to guard them, which causes a muttering among the crew. They look genuinely scared and unhappy with your decision.

Your crew is furious and scared. Lower your crew morale by 2 levels. Tick the codeword Passenger Cabin.

Now continue your voyage at *654*

190

Tick the codewords **Nocturne** and **Jog. Go to *628***

191

You route past jagged rocks and find yourself in a large pool that has four exits. Two of the exits route northwest and southwest along open channels. One routes southeast but it seems very shallow judging by the water, so unless your vessel can operate in the shallows you won't risk this way. A route to the northeast looks wide enough and heads straight to the main formation but you cannot see if it reaches it.

Do you

Sail northwest – *1465*

Route southwest – *1263*

Pass through the shallows to the southeast (vessels that can operate in shallows only) – *244*

Make for the main structure to the northeast – *947* **and note this section's number**

192

You sail into a small opening that has three exits from it. The rocks are spaced here, and you can turn easily. There are exits from the channel to the north, southwest, and southeast. All the channels are wide but the one to the southwest looks like it reaches the main structure, but you cannot be sure.

Do you

Sail north – *1030*

Route southeast – *916*

Make for the main structure to the southwest – *275* **and note this section's number**

193

You remain in silence, listening intently but you can hear no one up above.

Do you

Push open the trapdoor – *1014*

Or if you think you should leave it alone, continue below

You retreat along the tunnel and exit back in the message room, covering up the trapdoor again with the rug. Now, do you

Look at the desk – *1167*

Look at the other rug – *365*

Try to open the safe – *1289*

Decide this is a bad idea and return to Timmers, saying you should get back to the ship pronto – *351*

<u>194</u>

"I require a vessel and a crew," you say brightly.

"And you are paying for this, how?"

Do you have

The codeword **Emerald** or **Promissory Note** – *967*

If not, the man looks at you with disgust. He walks to the door and calls out. Before you can do anything, you are grabbed by the pirates from the front door and thrown out into the street. It appears that you have nothing of value, and you have ended up muddied and bruised.

Continue at *1256* but don't come back to the stone building.

<u>195</u>

Is your first officer

Simon Kilmer – *763*

Robert Grimshaw – *1214*

Diggory Hurst – *102*

Timmers – *932*

Martha Downham – *414*

Black Robert – *1053*

<u>196</u>

In front of the crew, you ball out the ring leaders and you note that the crew do not seem that impressed. Over the next few days, you can see the suspicion amongst your crew.

Reduce your crew by 1 level if you can, if not reduce your speed by 1 level due to lack of crew, until your crew goes up a level. If you can do neither you're in bad enough shape as it is.

Also reduce your crew morale by 2 levels as they now live in fear of each other.

Now continue the voyage at *654*

<u>197</u>

You walk down the path and can hear the sea coming closer. Soon you break from the jungle path onto the small beach where you landed not so long ago. You see the small boat and the sea beyond it. You turn and see the jungle path closing up, vegetation growing over the entrance and when you examine it, you see it is so thick you could never get in again. This place is indeed very strange.

There's nothing left to do except return to your vessel and see if you can get out of here.

If your Island Time Chart shows 8 or above – *695*

If it shows 7 or less – *824*

<u>198</u>

You arrive in the waters around the Birds Paradise, a towering rock formation in the middle of the sea with a myriad of birds nesting on it and flying around it. It is hard to see the rock beneath due to the sheer volume of birds on it but what draws your attention are the many jagged rocks sticking out of the water around the large rock formation.

As foreboding as it looks, this would be a great place to drop treasure or to store anything secret, if you can reach the main structure. Those rocks in front are saying different. Will you be able to find a way in past the wicked formations emerging from the sea? Maybe this is a place best left alone.

Do you

Try to reach the main formation – *800*

Decide this is a bust and go elsewhere – **consult the voyage chart**

199

Go to *832*

200

"A lady hiring a vessel, but why? Who are you?" The man's eyes narrow and you feel uncomfortable.

Do you

Tell him the truth - *481*

Make up a story – *208*

201

Reduce your Waters Strength Chart by 1. The current is pushing you south. However, you think you can reach an eddy that seems to allow a way west. Your foot scrapes the bottom briefly and you think you may be able to drop a pole and take a rest. Do you

Swim West – *266*

Float South – *610*

Drop a pole – **Make a note of this section and go to *694***

202

You wander along the path, leather boots chaffing your ankles, and reach a junction. Which way now?

Left – *891*

Right – *554*

Turn back – *483*

203

Have you encountered the Devil's Sloop before – *697*

If not, read on,

As you sail along on a sunny day with a fresh breeze blowing and a good feeling in your gut, you feel a sudden chill. Looking around at your crew, you fail to understand why this strange cold struck you. You shake it off and then see the skies suddenly become dark and clouds begin to roll. Your crew become panicky, and your first officer looks worried.

The wind becomes stronger, turning into a gale and the sea begins to swirl around your vessel in a fashion you have never seen before. Your vessel begins to spin as it gets caught in a whirlpool, and you see the clouds now descend and engulf your ship making it hard to see more than a few yards.

Most of your crew are now on the floor, quivering wrecks, with many murmuring the words "Devil's Sloop". As if from nowhere, a strange sloop appears beside your vessel, with rotten timbers and sails with large holes ripped through them. Seaweed hangs over its fixtures, and you can see no crew.

"Tribute or die," yells a voice in your head. You try to shake it off but then see blood cascading down the sloop's tattered sails and dripping onto the deck below.

"Do something, Captain," yells a crewman, "for the love of God do something!"

Is Martha Downham your first officer – *1076*

If not, do you

Have codeword **Spanish Priests** – *544*

Have codeword **Holy Man** – *1105*

Decide to go on board the mysterious sloop – *840*

Open fire on the other vessel – *505*

Offer some tribute – *768*

204

You find the pull of the main current tough to overcome to get to the eddy, but you do it eventually. **Reduce your Waters Strength Chart by 1.** You swim through to the eddy. Go to *291*

205

You hand over the note and the man smiles greedily. "Good, good, I can see you are a businesswoman. I have just the vessel for you, a delightful charge with a Captain Timmers running the show. Very good man. Let me escort you to the vessel. I believe Captain Fareham at the garrison is looking for you, so we need to keep you safe. This way my lady."

Untick the codeword Promissory Note.

You take the man's hand and rise from the chair. Outside he calls a carriage, and you are whisked away down the pier to a vessel and the next stage in your adventure. You have your ship and crew, meet them at *691*

206

Reduce your time by 1.

If your time is in the following gaps (52-48) you see a guard on his patrol outside and must remain hidden until he clears the area. Reduce your time by 6. Now continue at the plain text below

You walk around the desk and notice it has a drawer. You pull at it and the drawer comes out, dropping onto the floor. There's some parchment and a brass key that tumbles to the floor.

Do you

Look at the parchment – *476*

Examine the key – *478*

Or replace everything and instead

Check the rug that's slightly lifted – *565*

Look at the other rug – *1356*

Try to open the safe – *1288*

Decide this is a bad idea and return outside – *174*

207

Your gift is accepted by the pirate at the entrance to the pirate King's abode. You are led through several rooms with treasure piled high and many pirates guarding it showing off the pirate king's wealth. As you enter a final room you see a spindly man on a throne with a patch over one eye. He is dressed in a golden coat and leather boats. He's not as you expected him to be but you see a pirate being carried out of the room and you believe he might be dead

You wait for a while but then are called forward by the king. You don't get to speak but he strokes his bearded chin and leans forward to whisper to you.

But what does he whisper.

Roll 1xD100 (2xD10) and add your modifier. Go to the section associated with your result.

00-30 – *287*

31-60 – *528*

61-90 – *660*

91-110 – *1068*

111-160 – *453*

<u>208</u>

You tell a tale of a father who has put you charge of his affairs and is looking to send cargo from this part of the world to England. The man begins to shake his head.

"You lie. I was hoping we could do business, Mary Hastings, but I need to trust those I deal with. Captain Fareham of the garrison, however, has been straight in his affairs, even if I don't agree with them. And he wants you."

He gives a shout, and several men enter the room and handle you roughly, taking you outside before calling the garrison guards in the town to them. You are taken away to the garrison and thrown into prison.

Captain Fareham of the garrison visits you and tells you that he intends to marry you, and he does so in quiet, keeping you locked up in the jail. Fareham now owns your father's lands and keeps you in your cell for the next year. When you don't respond to his advances and wishes to be a passive wife, he has you taken away in the night and disposed of. Your last thoughts are that your family remains unavenged. Try again at **1** and next time try and be more discreet

<u>209</u>

You sail away and the Schooner doesn't follow, obviously uninterested in what you have to offer.

Continue the voyage at **654**

<u>210</u>

You have arrived back at the Waters of Myra which you have already taken the treasure from. Lost, are we? Head back down that jungle path and get about your business – **236**

211

"Diggory Hurst is my Captain."

"Diggory Hurst, the fugitive?" asks the man with the scar. "There's a decent reward on him. Where are you moored?" The man stands up and you hear knives being pulled and the click of a musket. Without waiting, you run from the ale house with several people in pursuit. You race through Malin's Town unable to shake them and eventually run to your vessel, telling Hurst to take her out of the harbour.

When he has done so, he asks you what happened? You tell him the story and he is furious asking how you could be so stupid to say his name in public. He advises that you need to stay low for a while and that you should avoid the main settlements.

For the next ten days on your time chart, you must avoid New Southampton and Fort August, and avoid Malin's Town for the next twenty. Now consult the voyage chart and set sail to a different destination.

212

You slide down the pole and grab any hidden gear before disappearing into the night. That was close, too close and you decide to get out of Malin's Town.

You may not return to the guild as they have decided to put on extra security at night and have also stopped any daytime visitors, when they realised that the room had been entered the following day.

What else shall you do in Malin's Town?

Do you

See to the needs of your vessel and crew – *903*

Try to earn some money by signing up to a cargo run – *1335*

Visit the taverns for information – *802*

If your first officer is Simon Kilmer – *24*

If your First officer is Robert Grimshaw – *737*

If your First officer is Diggory Hurst – *786*

If you have had enough of Malin's town, then **consult the voyage chart and set sail**.

213

"I can offer you some doubloons," you say and watch as the dark-skinned pirate draws her sword.

"Get out before I strike you down. You insult me."

Whoops! You blew that and decide to high tail it out of the tavern. **You may not visit the tavern until you come back to Hell's Deep again.** Once outside you decide what to do next. Do you

Make for the small houses – *1304*

Approach the gambling groups – *1424*

Go to see the fights – *84*

Decide this is not a place you want to explore and return to your vessel - *314*

214

You allow the man to lie in the cargo hold but he is found dead the next day. The infection has also reached your crew and many are infected. You realise you need to act, and in brutal fashion. You throw your infected crewmen overboard, jettison all cargo they have been in contact with, and quarantine the cargo hold areas for 30 days.

Lower your crew morale by 2 levels. Block off 4 sections of your cargo hold for 30 days and remove all the cargo within.

The spread of the plague is finally contained but at a terrible cost. Now continue your voyage at *654*

215

"State your business, wench."

You tell her that you are looking to hire a crew for a voyage in order to gain vengeance on a man who has wronged your family and the woman seems dubious. But she also turns away and gives thought to what you are suggesting. When she turns back you see a scowl across her face.

"Look at you, do you even have the money to hire a crew?"

Do you

Have the codeword **Promissory Note** – *1192*

If not – *1132*

216

"We could route for it, Captain," says your first officer. "We're a match for speed and if we can outmanoeuvre it, we could capture it. There may not be much on board, and it is well manned. Otherwise, we may be able to simply chase it off. Or we could outrun it. It's your call unless you're happy to let us be followed. That would be the quickest option, but I wouldn't be keen on it tailing us."

The Treasure of Captain Estes

You ponder your move as you look at the sleek vessel through your eyepiece. Would an engagement be wise? Would a tail be dangerous?

Do you

Look to engage the Brigantine – *1188*

Want to outrun the Brigantine – *325*

Let the Brigantine tail you – **read on**

As you watch the Schooner it continues course with you, tailing you. It never gets too close, and you wonder what its intentions are but there's little you can do except continue course or change your destination. You now have a Spaniard watching you (Tick codeword **British Tail**).

If you decide to change course, use the voyage chart to determine your voyage length from your original departure point to your new destination. Then **add 2 days to your voyage** for starting off in a different direction.

If you maintain course use your original planned voyage days. Either way, continue the voyage at *654*

<u>217</u>

Tick the codewords **Stowed** and **Pace. Go to *628***

<u>218</u>

Roll 1xD100 (2xD10). For every point of damage you have already done to the sloop add 3 to the result. Check the table below for the result of this round of the sea battle.

00-20 – You get caught with a severe broadside. **Lower your vessel manoeuvrability by 1 level and your vessel speed by 1 level.**

21-40 – A volley lands on deck killing many of the crew. **Lower your crew by 1 level.**

41-69 – A volley blows out some of your canons, but you hit back – **Lower your firepower by 1 level.** But you cause the following damage dependent on your firepower: **Light – 1 point, Moderate – 2pts, Heavy – 3pts, Very Heavy – 4 pts**

70-89 – You land a splendid volley. Note you have done the following damage dependent on your firepower: **Light – 1 point, Moderate – 2pts, Heavy – 3pts, Very Heavy – 4 pts**

90 and up - You catch them cold with a blinding manoeuvre. Note you have done the following damage dependent on your firepower: **Light – 2 point, Moderate – 4pts, Heavy – 6pts, Very Heavy – 8 pts**

If you have caused 8 points of damage overall to the sloop – *1097*

If not

Do you want to continue the battle – *1267*

Do you wish to run – *1196*

219

"I want to see who is in charge. Tell him now that I want to see him."

"You demand?" says one of the pirates. "Nobody demands anything of Black Robert."

Before you can do anything, you are grabbed by both pirates and thrown out into the street. It appears that your threats carry no weight here and you have ended up muddied and bruised.

Continue at *1256* but don't come back to the stone building.

220

The weather is brutal, and you feel like you are going to die. Several of your crew fall overboard trying to keep the sails together and you fear the worst. At numerous times you hear cracks that cause you to think the vessel will break apart. When you clear the storm after two days you assess the damage.

You're in a mess. Lower your Vessel's speed by 3 due to serious sail and structural damage, lower your vessel's manoeuvrability by 2, lower your crew level by 1. Your crew are in a sombre mood for their lost colleagues.

Now resume your voyage at **654**

221

Suddenly your cell is opened and Timmers is thrown in beside you. The fort commander tells you he is no fool and that the pair of you can rot. And you do, for no one comes for you. The only thing worse than the imprisonment is Timmers daily wittering on about how you failed.

Looks like life didn't work out. Try again at *1*

222

The rest of your journey is uneventful, and your crew seems happy with how you dealt with the incident (**Raise Crew Morale by one level**).

Continue the voyage at **654**

223

You feel like your shoulders are coming out of your back as you put everything into the shove. The jailor stumbles backwards, momentarily looks like he's going to right himself but then steps back once more. Diggory grabs him from behind through the bars of his cell and chokes the man around the neck until he collapses on the floor. Diggory quickly grabs the keys on the jailer's belt and unlocks his door. He then lets you out.

"Quick, we need to hurry," implores Diggory.

Escape now at *1371*

224

Reduce your Island Time Chart by 1

You trek along the path, panting for breath in the heat. There's a fork in the path, and you wonder which way to go. You can take either fork, or you could always head out into the jungle off the path.

Do you go

Left – *245*

Right – *1129*

Strike out into the Jungle – *1283*

Turn around back the way you came – *854*

225

The captain of the cargo vessel opens fire on you, and you begin to fight a raging sea battle. It becomes clear that you are not equal to the task and are taking a pounding. Your first officer shuts at you that you are outgunned and must flee, hoping that you will not be pursued.

Do you

Remain and fight – *1272*

Flee the battle – *1399*

The Treasure of Captain Estes

<u>226</u>

You grab some of the purple fruit and toss it away from the man. You watch as the rats ignore it and then you stamp on it. Suddenly they flock to it and the man is left lying in pain. You run over and help him up. He has a grey beard that is in tatters and looks like he used to have some fine clothing that has fallen into some serious disrepair.

Together with the man you run down the mountain, until you are well clear of the rats. He bends over and grabs his breath before beginning to thank you.

"That is most kind, stranger. Thank you. What can I do for you? Please tell me, what is on your heart?"

You tell him you are looking for the treasure of Captain Estes and wonder if he has heard where the captain was last. But the man puts a finger up to your lips.

"The natives here know something for he came this way. But they won't talk to you without a gift. And it needs to be a gift they can use. There is a Kraken Horn in the jungle, located in the temple. They are afraid of what guards it, but they are desperate for it. You see it sends a Kraken back to the deep and we are in Kraken waters. They are not from here but have been kept prisoner by the threat of the Kraken. Get the horn and they can tell you what Estes told them when he met them. Otherwise, don't go near them for they will attack you. I have a treaty with them so I will go there now and heal these rat wounds. Thank you again."

The man descends the mountain, and you follow. Once at the bottom he points to a canopy covered path and tells you the temple where the Kraken Horn resides is in there although he has never been to it. He then disappears into the jungle before you can stop him. **Tick the codeword Parley. You cannot return back up the mountain due to the rats.**

There are two paths away from the mountain, one a canopy covered path to the north, the other a more open topped path to the west, although it is still surrounded by the dense jungle.

Do you

Head north – *435*

Take the path west – *477*

227

The courthouse is as impressive building as you get in the town, and it stands two stories high with impressive wooden pillars at its entrance. Some gallows paint a bleak image before the building. There is a line of guards across the front of it and as you approach you can see them staring at you.

Maybe this is not such a good idea. Or will there be help inside from the local authorities?

Do you

Continue to the courthouse entrance – *1425*

Turn away back to the street - *760*

228

As you pass the fish stalls, you make a leap onto the dusty ground, tumbling before rolling back to your feet and running into the crowd. The smell of fish is strong and the crowd parts as you sprint their way. You look back and cannot see any of the guards, so you slow to a walking pace. With the dust on your smart dress you look a sight and easy to spot, never mind being a familiar face. **Tick the codeword Prominent** on your list and go to *1152* to continue your escape.

229

Do you have any of the following codewords ticked:

Bodach Sword; Noiseless Horn; Johnstone's Confuser; Bird whistle; Eye Charm; Spear; Gold Medallion; Brass key; Bird Chart; Silver Key; Gold Key; Gold Chain; Sextant; Argyle

If so and you wish to part with that item, **untick that codeword** and go to *306*

If not, do you

Leave it to your officer – *1241*

Offer doubloons – *1297*

Decide the price is too high and leave Hells Deep – **Consult the voyage chart and set sail**

230

You are able to set your feet on a sandy seabed as you close in on the island and you can see the cave from the map appear as you get closer. It looks like a narrow entrance, and you wonder just where it goes and what is inside. But as you stare you see a crab-like creature emerge from the cave. You think crab-like because it is the size of a human. Two large claws are before it and you see it turn and start to scuttle sideways towards you.

And then you get an eerie feeling. Glancing right and left, you see more giant crab creatures emerging from the sandy seabed around you. You're trapped and may have to fight your way out.

Do you have the codeword (Go to the first one in the list you have)

Crate Scroll – *441*

Small Crew – *642*

Large Crew – *1299*

If not – *1140*

<u>231</u>

Your sails are unfurled and you are so much quicker than the galleon that you are able to get clear in no time at all, far beyond the reach of its impressive canons. You breathe a sigh of relief but your crew although relieved to be alive are down at the beating they took. **Reduce your crew morale by 1 level. Because you fled in a random direction it takes you time to recover your course. Add 2 days to the voyage time to allow for this.**

Continue the voyage at **654**

<u>232</u>

You tell him you need work, and he simply grins and then laughs.

"No, no, little lady, no you don't. Fancy clothes like that mean someone will come for you and we don't need that hassle. On your way, now."

Do you

Try to see the boss – **405**

Take his advice and return to the main street – **496**

<u>233</u>

Reduce the Hot Strip by 1. If this places you on a Fire spot add 20 to this section's number and go there for the walls have moved. There are walls of fire to the north and east. You can route north or west from your current location.

Do you

Go West – **772**

Go South – **983**

234

You organise a team to gather spears and you hang off the side of the vessel ready to attack the turtle. It glides under your ship before rising to the surface and you throw a mass of spears at it connecting with a fin. It breaks the surface, and you hear it cry out in pain.

Suddenly you are descended upon by birds from above, knocking several of the crew into the water. You thrash above you and pray for the relentless attack and deafening screeching to stop. As the turtle swims away, you find the birds retreat and you assess your losses.

Your sails have been attacked. Reduce your speed by 1 level if possible. Reduce your crew by 1 level if possible.

You have no choice but to sail on. Do you sail

Northwest – *606*

Southeast – *1263*

235

You step onto the pillar and breathe a sigh as it doesn't crumble. The waves crash far below, and you ponder your next move. There is a pillar in front of you and the cliff edge behind you.

Do you step

Forwards – *448*

Step back off the pillar onto the cliff edge behind – *1180*

236

Reduce your Island Time Chart by 1

You trek along the path, leaving the waters behind you. You find a multi-fork in the path, and you wonder which way to go. You can take one of the paths, or you could always head out into the jungle off the path.

Do you go

Left – *407*

Right – *1223*

Straight ahead – *429*

Strike out into the Jungle – *1283*

Turn around back the way you came – *151*

237

Reduce your time by 1. You walk forward and immediately hit a cage that blocks your progress. To your right you are also block by some fallen woodwork. You can turn left to open water though.

Do you

About turn and step forward – *41*

Turn left and walk forward – *458*

238

You step onto the pillar in front, and it crumbles before you. Desperately you reach out, but you cannot grab the pillar beside you, and you fall down into the waters below. Although you thrash to keep yourself above the waves, you are sent smashing into a pillar and blackness takes over.

So near to Estes' treasure but with something missing. Where did you go wrong? You can try again at *1* or you can always reset to the start of this puzzle if you like at *830* (remember to untick the following codewords: Aisle, Pew, Rosary, Transept if ticked). This time make sure you know your path across before you try.

239

You can hear scratching noises through the shield door. Sounds like Tabetha is through that door. You decide to risk that door would be foolish. Return to your noted section and decide which door to go through or to stay put **but you cannot choose the shield door**.

240

You enter the tunnel and find it dark and cold. Little light travels into it and you cannot see the end of it as you grope your way along. It continues for what seems an age and you feel the damp and algae that has formed on the walls. Suddenly you reach the end of the tunnel and think you can hear a voice above you. Everything then goes silent. Your hands reach up and feel the wood of what you believe to be another trapdoor.

Do you

Open the trapdoor above – *904*

Wait for a few moments – *921*

Decide this is a bad plan? If so, you retreat the tunnel and exit back in the message room, covering up the trapdoor again with the rug. Now, do you

Look at the desk – *1167*

Look at the other rug – *366*

Try to open the safe – *1289*

Decide this is a bad idea and return to Timmers, saying you should get back to the ship pronto – *351*

241

You race across to the far side of the room and stand beside the chest. There's a rope above you leading up to another floor. Behind you are the remains of darts on the floor but you don't know if it's a trap that will spring again.

Do you

Examine the chest – **990**

Climb up the rope now above you – **479**

Run back across the room – **421**

242

Which codeword do you have

Human Bait – **393**

Silent Running – **1334**

Johnstone's Confuser – **359**

243

Reduce your time by 1.

If your time is in the following gaps (42-38) you see a guard on his patrol outside and must remain hidden until he clears the area. Reduce your time by 6. Now continue at the plain text below

Well, guess what, they are chairs, some with rather delightful rose patterns on them. And if you want to, you can sit on them. Seriously, they are chairs and you've wasted time looking at them.

Do you

Examine the desks – **994**

Check out the cabinets – **284**

Peruse the charts on the wall – **324**

Or leave the room and return back to tunnel – **693**

244

You route past jagged rocks and find yourself in a large pool that has three exits. Two of the exits route north-northeast and southeast along open channels. One routes northwest but it seems very shallow judging by the water, so unless your vessel can operate in the shallows you won't risk this way. The route to the north-northeast heads straight to the main formation but you cannot see if it reaches it.

Do you

Route southeast – *126*

Pass through the shallows to the northwest (vessels that can operate in shallows only) – *191*

Make for the main structure to the north-northeast – *947* **and note this section's number**

245

You strike out along the path and suddenly there's a blurring in the air. A maniacal laugh starts, and you find everything goes dark for a moment. Your eyesight returns and everything is as it was a moment before. Except it's not. This is not the same piece of path. At least you think it isn't. Everything is just so green. You walk on.

Roll 1xD100 (2xD10) and go to the result below for your next section.

00-19 – *429*

20-39 – *854*

40-59 – *125*

60-79 – *886*

80-99 – *758*

246

You steer in past the rocks watching your bow carefully. It's tight but you believe you can make it. Your first officer warns you that the rocks may narrow here and there and that turning may be an issue, but you are keen to reach the main formation where the birds are gathered. Soon you reach your first decision. Go to *1338*

247

You spy Fort August in the distance and tell your crew to fly the Red Ensign, the flag flown by commercial British vessels. Still some way off, you wonder what the best way is to approach the fort. After all, you are a pirate, and this navy is here to seek your sort out and destroy them. If you just sail in, will you be okay? You decide to consult your first officer.

Is your first officer

Simon Kilmer – *299*

Robert Grimshaw –*302*

Diggory Hurst –*1151*

Timmers –*445*

Martha Downham –*1063*

Black Robert – *19*

If none of these are your first officer – *315*

248

"Well, well, looking for a good time, sir?" asks the man in the rocking chair without lifting his hat. "We have something to suit everyone's taste. Tell me, fine sir, what can we help you with?"

Do you

Say you are looking for a crew and a vessel – *344*

Ask if you can hide for a while – *465*

Ask to go in – *806*

Decide this is a bad idea and return to the main street – *496*

249

The **Check 200** pattern is a way for soldiers at the fort to know when they should be moving around the fort when on sentry duty. Basically, they have different points to be at, arriving at a set time. They move on from each point at "5" time intervals. So if you see them there at time T then they will have moved on to the next location after time T+5. There is also a sweep where the areas are flooded. This occurs at Time 3 to 0. You need to be back out by that time and on your small boat. Make sure you know your time! Now return to *1143* and get ready to infiltrate the fort.

250

Reduce your Waters Strength Chart by 1. You swim through to the eddy. Go to *295*

251

Reduce the Hot Strip by 1. If this places you on a Fire spot add 20 to this section's number and go there for the walls have moved. There are walls of fire to the south and west. You can route north or east from your current location.

Do you

Go East – *552*

Go North – *25*

252

If you have been to Madame Le Vert's before go to **578**

You approach Madame Le Vert's shop with some guards outside. It has various outfits inside that you can see through the windows, from dresses to long-coats. Maybe it's not a good idea that you just walk in. You could look for another way inside if you think there's something of importance in there.

Do you continue to the front door – **822**

Try to see another way in – **1279**

253

"You will reinstate full rations or we will mutiny," says the second officer.

You have had a direct challenge to your authority, and you need to respond. You are not strong enough to win in a hand-to-hand fight, but you need to do something.

Do you

Agree to full rations – **897**

Say you will keep half rations for another week and then lift them – **1264**

Go to embrace the man and then knife him for insubordination – **457**

254

You sail south to the small island off the main one and make way to the large beach, full of smooth white sand and the wisp of greenery beyond. You can see small huts in the distance and as you watch the beach, shadows move beyond the plant life.

Do you

Launch the small boat for the shore – *384*

Fire your canons at the settlement – *3*

Decide to leave the island and

Tell the crew to sail to the north of the island – *468*

Route for the centre of the island – *746*

Decide to set sail - **consult the voyage chart**

255

You grab hold of the drawers on one of the walls, pulling them out and flicking through the contents. As much as you can make out these are charts of waters far away and of little use to you. There are also almanacks containing tide tables, port details and other information of waters around the world but nothing of use to you.

Go to *415*

256

You watch in horror as you cannot get your vessel turned in time and as you desperately fire your canon, they miss the creature rising from the water. Large tentacles sweep upwards before crashing down on the decks and you are dragged straight down to a watery grave. Your vessel never stood a chance, and neither did you.

The waters around New Southampton are deadly, and you have succumbed. You may try again at *1*

257

You stand and watch the temple but then hear a hissing behind you. On the ground are hundreds of snakes and they are slithering towards you, forcing you into the temple. You see the path beyond and maybe you could reach it but you would have to step incredibly lightly over and through the snakes.

Do you

Enter the temple – *1089*

Risk running through the snakes – *644*

258

You are back at the Drops of Daniel and they are exactly as you left them with the challenge complete, and the gold in your possession. How did you get back here? You're wasting time, so turn around and find more treasure. You turn and walk back down the jungle path you took to get here. Go to *1003*

259

The pirate sweeps you away to the rear of the building where you are led in through a cellar door. There are hushed whispers, and you are taken to a small room in the cellar where you are told to sit and wait on an old barrel. The door is locked, and you wait for what seems like an age before a pirate with a large bushy black beard enters and closes the door behind him. You gulp wondering what will happen next.

"Let me see the letter," he says.

You hand it over and watch as he tears the envelope open and reads it. He scratches his beard and then stares at you.

"I'm sorry for your loss, Mary. I heard about what happened to your father, a man to whom I owe a lot. You may not realise but out here you have to keep an uneasy alliance between pirate and landowner and between us, your father and I, made it work. I am Black Robert, the pirate Lord in this place. But tell me, what is it you want?"

"I want Estes," you say.

"Indeed, and so you shall but we need your lands back as well, so this alliance between your family and me may continue. But you shall have your revenge, Mary. Now come, let's see you properly fed and dressed.

You have the pirate Lord on your side. If you have wounds they are tended and cured. **You may remove all wounds from you and ignore any timers regarding their effects.** Now plan your future at *1370*

260

You have treasure, more than enough for the crew, and an abundance for yourself. You are the wealthiest of women and buying back your home and lands is easy. The wealthiest person in any of the world's empires, you have influence and you have seen your family avenged as best you could.

You dominate the area and set up fleets running goods across the world. You can deal with the pirates as well as the British and Spanish empires and you are courted by kings and queens. But you remain on the island, at the home you fled so long ago. You bear many children, and your family is established for generations to come. You are loved and feared, one of the great names in the history books.

Congratulations, you have succeeded and brought honour and justice back to your family. You have succeeded in every way possible. This is the complete victory you sought, the total life change that treasure can bring. Revel in it, for you are one of the greatest adventurers the waves have ever seen!

261

You're not taking any nonsense and you draw your pistol and hold it up to the man's face. He seems impassive, almost at ease and you hear a shot being fired. You fall to the ground and realise that you have been hit in the chest. The big man bends over you laughing and rolls you out into the middle of the street where you slowly pass away. Maybe you were a bit hasty drawing your weapon. You can try again at *1*

262

Standing in the middle of the dusty street, you can see a house on one side with plenty of candles ablaze beyond the half open shutters. You can hear whoops of laughter and some angry voices too, and there is a large gentleman with a scar across his face in front of the door with a large sword hanging from his side. Opposite the house you can see several pirates, swigging at bottles and playing some sort of game in the dust of the ground. Beyond you is the rest of Strangar with plenty of candles and shadows and shouting and the odd cry to chill your bones.

Do you

Look to join the pirate game – *1049*

Approach the house – *1137*

Walk further into Strangar – *1112*

Walk to New Southampton if you haven't been there yet – *1114*

263

You have accepted an offer for a dark run. In the Dark Run Table (*App 13*) write down the three places to visit: The Bird's Paradise, The Abandoned Island, and Hell's Deep. When you visit them, score them off. When you next visit Malin's Town, and all the locations have been visited, go to *1278* (note this down now) and continue from there.

The man has left so what will you do next

The Treasure of Captain Estes

Do you

See to the needs of your vessel and crew – *903*

Try to earn some money by signing up to a cargo run – *1335*

Visit the taverns for information – *802*

Visit the Mariners' Guild for information – *124*

If you have had enough of Malin's town, then **consult the voyage chart and set sail.**

264

You turn and flee, hearing the pirate women coming after you. As you reach your longboat, they jeer at you as you row back to your vessel. Go to *314* to decide your next move. **You may not go to the wild isle again during this visit to Hell's Deep.**

265

You see the bemused look of the crew as you instruct them on how to configure your vessel to sail without noise. Many don't believe you, but you bark your orders at them and watch as they enact your wishes. Quickly, your vessel is rigged, and you tell them all to be quiet.

You sail away with the wind and scan the surroundings for the Kraken. You see it briefly on your port side. Then it's at the aft of your vessel. Then to starboard. And then you see it no more. Being careful you track away from the area before resuming course later that night, you notice how the crew looks at you with admiration and you grin.

Raise your crew morale by 2 levels. Your detour however has cost you 1 day extra, so add that to your voyage time.

Continue the voyage at *654*

266

Reduce your Waters Strength Chart by 1. You swim through to the eddy. Go to *631*

267

"What do you want, sailor? I hope you're not here to waste my time."

You tell her that you are looking to hire a crew for a voyage in order to gain vengeance on a man who has wronged your family and the woman seems quite pleased. But she also turns away and gives thought to what you are suggesting. When she turns back you see a scowl across her face.

"You wish a crew, so I take it you can offer me something to engage them?"

Do you

Have the codeword **Promissory Note** – *1192*

If not – *1132*

268

Do you have the codeword **Bullied** – *423*

If not, continue below.

You break forth from the jungle path onto an impossible plain. You remember seeing it from your vessel and it looked strange then but here amongst the greenery of the jungle you wonder how the place exists. The plain is also squeezed by a sheer set of rock faces which narrow in the middle of the plain to only a few people wide. Beyond the tiny gap you can see with your eyepiece what looks like a casket of treasure in the distance.

As you prepare to simply walk to the far side of the plain, through the gap in the rock formation, you hear the thunderous sound of a stampeding herd. There is dust on the other side of the rock formation, and you see bulls charging through the gap out onto your side of the plain. As they clear the gap they spread off to the right and left, reaching the jungle and then disappearing into the jungle beyond.

You ponder this crazy sight. If you are to get to the casket on the other side of the plain you seem to have little choice on what to do. You can't climb the sheer rock formation and must run the valley it has created to get to the other side of the plain. However, the bulls keep charging down this valley. Your only other option is to enter the jungle as the bulls are doing and see if you can go around the rock formation that way.

As you continue to think on this, you note that the bulls are of different colours. They all have sharp horns but some are white, some brown and some black.

You can't afford to wait any longer and need to either go get this casket or search for another one.

Do you

Try to run the gap – **59**

Route into the jungle to try and go round the rock formation – **923**

Turn around and walk back down the jungle path in search of other treasure – **1145**

269

You rest up waiting to recoup your strength. **For every 3 points you add to your Waters Strength Chart, take 1 off your Island Time Chart. Once refreshed, dive in again.** Do you jump in at the

Most western point – **1201**

Second most western point – **43**

Mid-point of the edge – **1372**

Second most eastern point – **489**

Most Eastern point – **948**

270

Congratulations, you have the treasure chest. You open it as the water drips off it and find a copious number of gems and gold inside. You tell one of your crew to carry it and turn to set off back down the jungle path for there is more to do. Tick the codeword **Calm** and then route down the jungle path to *236*

271

You grab the spear and begin to swing it around under the water. It's hard work, but you can keep the crab creatures at a distance, although you note that if you go towards the cave then they close ranks and there's no way through. An all out attack on them is impossible as there are too many.

You retreat away from the island, back to your vessel. Clearly the crab creatures have an attachment with the island and currently you have no way of penetrating their numbers to get into the cave. Stumped, you decide to set sail to another location.

Set sail for a new destination by consulting the voyage chart.

272

You steal quietly into the barn and hear a gasp as you enter. You see a large group of men tied up and eagerly hoping for release. One coughs and then explains.

"Helps us, please. I am John Darnold, first officer to Diggory Hurst, and soon to be executed or held to ransom. If you release us, I can help you with whatever you need."

"I need a crew," you reply, and the man almost begs you with his eyes.

"I will make sure Captain Diggory assists you, I swear with my life, if you but let us go from here. Please you must hurry. There were more of them in the tavern, and they will return soon."

A tempting offer but do you want a crew that gets caught?

Do you

Accept the offer and release them - **870**

Refuse the offer – **570**

273

You turn on your heel and bolt for the door catching everyone by surprise. As you run, a pirate steps back from a table, you collide, causing you to fall to the floor. As you do so you think something has fallen from you. Not wanting to hang around you run out to the street. Once out in the street you get that feeling that something is missing. **Check your ticked codewords and untick the top item you are carrying. If you are carrying nothing, then you realise it was just a feeling.** Continue now on the street at **1112**

274

Your sails are unfurled, and you are so much quicker than the sloop that you are able to get clear in no time at all, far beyond the reach of its impressive canons. You breathe a sigh of relief but your crew although relieved to be alive are down at the beating they took. **Reduce your crew morale by 1 level. Because you fled in a random direction it takes you time to recover your course. Add 2 days to the voyage time to allow for this.**

Continue the voyage at **654**

275

Your vessel moors next to the main structure, and you swim the short distance to the main rock formation. Above you the birds squawk loudly, and you see a mass of bird droppings all over the rocks around you. There is a wooden door in the rock structure which is closed and has a brass engraved plaque on it. The writing is in Spanish, not one of your languages but you shout back the words to your crew and your first officer finds a crewmate who can translate.

A fool and his gold are easily parted, and you sir, are a fool for entering!

You step back and wonder what you should do and see a rope dangling down the outside of the structure. You could climb the rocks with the aid of the rope but there are so many birds around, many with young, that you are not sure of the wisdom of this idea.

Do you

Enter via the wooden door – *303*

Climb the rock formation with the aid of the rope – *362*

Decide this is a bad idea and leave the Bird's Paradise – **consult your voyage chart**

276

Reduce your time by 1. You step forward and feel a wooden wall which is also on your right. There is, however, clear water on your left.

Do you

About turn and step forward – *517*

Turn left and walk forward – *327*

277

The captain of the cargo vessel opens fire on you, and you begin to fight a raging sea battle. It becomes clear that you are not equal to the task and are taking a pounding. Your first officer shuts at you that you are outgunned and must flee, hoping that you will not be pursued.

Do you

Remain and fight – *1094*

Flee the battle – *1130*

278

You stand and declare that this is your only word, and you see the crew become furious. You realise you have made a mistake as the second officer takes a knife and attacks you. In the ensuing melee as the crew all jump you, you are taken to the edge of the vessel and tossed overboard. You pushed them too far and paid for it, sinking down to Davy Jones' locker. Begin again at *1*.

279

You start up the banks of the river working the opposite way to its descent. You feel the spray as it has numerous drops causing a refreshing spray to hit your face. As you climb you see the wooden chest at the side of the river that you have already opened. You look around but there is no one about.

Do you

Return down the mountain to its foot – *61*

Ignore the chest and climb the mountain – *1205*

280

You march through the jungle, pushing past such dense greenery. As you work hard, you hear a howl like nothing you have ever heard. There is something out there and you can now hear its heavy breathing. This is no creature of stealth and you hear a crashing from your left. As you turn something clawed swipes at you, killing you instantly.

Off the jungle path is a treacherous place and one where you are a stranger and in constant jeopardy. Maybe next time you should stay on safer routes. It's a pity as you had done so well to reach the island. You can try again at *1* or rewind to a point of your choosing, maybe at *499* when you arrived at this island. As for this attempt, it's over!

281

Reduce your time by 1. You walk forward and reach a wooden wall. There's also a wall on your left but clear water is to your right.

Do you

About turn and step forward – *327*

Turn right and walk forward – *517*

282

You see a white flag go up in surrender from the opposite captain and you soon board the vessel. In the hold you find the following: **Roll 1xD100 (2xD10)**

00-25 – **20 provisions and 300 doubloons worth of cargo (6 spaces)**

26-50 – **An empty hold and 400 doubloons**

50-75 – **A hold full of female slaves (if you take them on board increase your crew size by one level. Also raise your crew morale one level and tick the codeword Female Crew. If you cannot take them on board, or choose not to, reduce your crew's morale by one level).**

77-99 – **You find treasure taking up 10 spaces and worth 400 doubloons a space. You may fill up what your cargo can hold.**

You must now decide what to do with the captain of the other vessel. You could leave him adrift with his crew, or you could scupper the vessel and its crew. You find the idea of taking the crew and vessel along with you cumbersome and unpractical. You look at your own crew wondering what they would expect of you and compare that to your own morals.

Do you

Leave the vessel and captain adrift – *717*

Scupper the vessel with the crew and captain on board – *798*

283

You worry that you may not have enough to get clear, and you are right in that the first volley from the brigantine hits you sending wood int the air. But the vessel holds fast, and you are just out of range of the next volley. However, that first volley did serious damage, and your crew are battered.

Reduce your crew morale by 1 level. Also reduce your vessel Storm Handling and Treasure Store by 1 level each as they were damaged in that last volley. Because you fled in a random direction it takes you time to recover your course. Add 2 days to the voyage time to allow for this.

Continue the voyage at **654**

284

Reduce your time by 1.

If your time is in the following gaps (42-38) you see a guard on his patrol outside and must remain hidden until he clears the area. Reduce your time by 6. Now continue at the plain text below

You take a look at the cabinets, most of which are open. At the bottom of one you find a leather-bound set of papers. Opening them up, you can just about see a title saying, "The Empty Chart - a Book of Instruction". May be interesting. **If you want to take these papers, tick the codeword Instruction Book.** Beyond this, you see nothing of potential use.

Do you

Examine the desks – **994**

Look at the chairs – **243**

Peruse the charts on the wall – **324**

Or leave the room and return back to tunnel – **693**

<u>285</u>

Reduce your Waters Strength Chart by 1. The current is pushing you south. However, you think you can reach an eddy that seems to allow a way north but to get there will be incredibly hard work. Do you

Swim North – *893*

Float South – *8*

<u>286</u>

Reduce the Hot Strip by 1. If this places you on a Fire spot add 20 to this section's number and go there for the walls have moved. There are walls of fire to the south and west. You can route north or east from your current location.

Do you

Go East – *929*

Go North – *515*

<u>287</u>

The pirate king leans forward and smiles weakly. "Estes buried his treasure on Hangman's Island but it's hard to get to. Once there he spread out the treasure, and there are five tests to recover it. But who knows what they are."

With a wave of his hand, he dismisses you and you are ushered from his presence and back to your vessel. Who knows how much use that was? The pirate who mans the door to the pirate king's abode advises that you will not be welcome again on this visit. **You may not visit the pirate king again until you return to Hell's Deep on another visit. Go to *1436***

The Treasure of Captain Estes

288

Because you have spent time looking at the parchment map you have already used some of your time until daylight is gone. Therefore, ignore the instruction to start your island time chart in section *1039* at 100 and instead **start at number 99**.

Return to *1039* and continue with the instructions to set up your island time chart noting this change you have been instructed with.

289

You creep down the stairs and get to the corner of the courtyard looking out to a crowd of sellers and soldiers, bartering, and shouting as livestock run amok. This could be perfect for you. Then you hear a shout, a cry has gone up alerting everyone to your escape. There's chaos in the courtyard. Will that be good for escape? You can see the open gates which will lead to your freedom. Or should you retreat to the wall surrounding the garrison, back up the stone steps by the jail. Decide quickly!

Do you

Make a run for the gates – *878*

About turn and run for the wall – *78*

290

What are you wearing

Dressed like a slave in your torn gown – *1232*

Wearing a dress or a long-coat and breeches – *472*

291

Reduce your Waters Strength Chart by 1. The current is terribly strong, and you are swept north. There is nothing you can do except float to *778*

292

Tick the codewords **Nocturne** and **Walk. Go to *628***

293

"I'm sorry," you say, "I have nothing but your goodwill to lean on."

The man grunts. "Goodwill does not pay my bills."

He gives a shout and several men enter the room and handle you roughly, taking you outside before calling the garrison guards in the town to them. You are taken away to the garrison and thrown into prison.

Captain Fareham of the garrison visits you and tells you that he intends to marry you, and he does so in quiet, keeping you locked up in the jail. Fareham now owns your father's lands and keeps you in your cell for the next year. When you don't respond to his advances and wishes to be a passive wife, he has you taken away in the night and disposed of. Your last thoughts are that your family remains unavenged. Try again at *1* and next time try and be more discreet

294

Do you have all four codewords **Aisle, Pew, Rosary** and **Transept** ticked?

If so – *791*

If not – *113*

295

Reduce your Waters Strength Chart by 1. The current is too strong and sweeping you south. Your foot scrapes the bottom briefly and you think you may be able to drop a pole and take a rest. Do you

Float South – *778*

Drop a pole – **Make a note of this section and go to *694***

296

There's a thunderous explosion and the tailing vessel is engulfed in spray and noise. You tell your crew to fire another volley and the same vast barrage sends towers of displaced water into the air.

"Captain, I can see the tentacles. Over by the vessel. I think it's working."

You respond to the Crow's nest hail, and spy with your eye glass towards it. You see long tentacles rip into the air from out of the sea and then lash towards the vessel, one striking it amidships and rendering the mast broken. But you see another tentacle reaching towards you. Just how large is the Kraken? The tentacle lashes out and rips into your hull, causing the contents to spill out.

But you don't look back, telling your crew to give it everything as your vessel glides away from the carnage. There's a part of you that feels a touch responsible for the many deaths behind you, but it was you or them, wasn't it?

Your crew are relieved, raise crew morale by 1 level. However, your vessel is damaged. Two sections of the cargo hold are damaged. These were full of provisions, so delete the provisions and take the sections out of use until you can repair them. Untick either Spanish Tail or British Tail as appropriate.

Now continue your voyage at *654*

<u>297</u>

Reduce your time by 2. If your time is in the following gaps (40-35 or 10-05) then go to *1322*. If not continue below

The flagpole is wooden and rises up to a flag at the top which you struggle to see but can hear flapping above. You wonder if you could climb up and get the flag. Otherwise there's nothing of note here.

Do you

Wait in hiding – *433*

Climb the flagpole – *602*

Look at the wagon – *147*

Move to the North quarter – *1176*

Move to the South quarter – *519*

<u>298</u>

You narrowly avoid disaster and are clear and running in the left channel. Just what happened is hard to tell but an animal passed by close.

If you haven't already, start a timer at 0 in your notes. Now add 1xD10 to it. If the timer is over 30 go to *1378*. If not, continue below.

Roll 1xD100 (2xD10) and check the result below.

00-19 – *1102*

20-39 – *781*

40-59 – *960*

60-79 – *1411*

80-99 – *1274*

<u>299</u>

Simon smiles at you and gives a laugh. "My reputation is not so sullied that I cannot sail in and pick up provisions from the fort. We can land in daylight, but we will not be able to moor alongside through the night. Alternatively, if you want to be more discreet, we can sneak in at night. It depends on what you want to do. Provisions we need to go in during the day, something else, we go at night."

So, what are you looking to do?

Arrive during the day for provisions – *665*

Sneak in during the night – *307*

<u>300</u>

Do you have the codeword **Charlie** – *162*

If not go to *1311*

<u>301</u>

The man glowers at the bottle of whiskey you proffer. He shakes his head and walks to the door calling for other pirates.

"You dare try to bribe someone in the employ of Black Robert. Take him out!"

Before you can do anything, you are grabbed by the pirates from the front door and thrown out into the street. It appears that you have nothing of value, and you have ended up muddied and bruised. **Untick codeword Bottle of Whiskey.**

Continue at *1256* but **don't come back to the stone building.**

302

Robert gives a thoughtful rub of his chin. "If we go during the day, we keep our heads down and only go for provisions. If we do anything else they'll be watching me, and therefore, you. If you think there's anything else worth going in for, we need to do a raid at night. Probably just one or two of us at most. That's the home of the British navy in these parts. You don't fight them here. They'd tear us apart."

So, what are you looking to do?

Arrive during the day for provisions – *665*

Sneak in during the night – *307*

303

You find yourself in a nautical room with a ships wheel on the wall, paintings of various vessels, and a large chest against one wall. There are no candles in the room, but it is lit by the green glow of the walls giving the whole area a ghostly feel. You can see a rope hanging down from an aperture in the ceiling, up to who knows where.

Do you

Climb the rope – *843*

Examine the paintings – *621*

Look at the ship's wheel – *620*

Check out the chest – *889*

Leave the room by the wooden door – *1439*

304

"Hugh Jameson is a friend of mine, we used to sail together with the British before we all got clear. We'll see if he knows anything about Estes' treasure."

You wave a flag signal to the vessel and come alongside. Diggory does the introductions, and you dine on board Jameson's vessel that night. He tells you he knows very little but gives you a whistle which when blown does nothing. **You may tick the code word Bird Whistle if you want to.**

"It scares the birds, which amuses me, but you can have it. I'm sorry I know little else to help you. But take a few extra provisions if you need them. **You may add up to 4 provisions to your cargo hold.**

The next morning you are underway and have left Jameson behind. **Add 1 day to your voyage time for the previous day's slight delay.**

Continue the voyage at **654**

305

You close in on the two pirates with the monkey figure and one of them signals for you to sit down beside them.

"What is that you ask?"

"It is a monkey figurine from the Incas. A major talisman and one I know Blind Tom wants. He's a pirate who knows everyone and everything and the owner of this can trade for information with Tom. He'll tell you everything. We'd go ourselves except we got into trouble with him before when we stole from under his nose. But for a price you can have this and find out his secrets. You look like you have money. Shall we say 3,000 doubloons?"

You sit back and think this sounds tempting. But is it worth it? Are these pirates trustworthy?

If you want to purchase the figurine, deduct 3,00 doubloons from your total and tick the codeword **Monkey.** Either way, your business with the pirates is finished.

Do you

Join the main bar – *594*

Climb up to the adapted poop deck and the two female pirates – *658*

Or leave the tavern and

Make for the small houses – *1304*

Approach the gambling groups – *1424*

Go to see the fights – *84*

Decide this is not a place you want to explore and return to your vessel - *314*

306

"Your gift is well received, my fellow pirate. Now sail inside and enjoy our hospitality. The king is delighted that you join us."

The man turns and signals to vessels that are gathered around the entrance to the islands, and you sail into the small group. Go to *473* to continue your adventure.

307

You wait well off the shores of the fort until darkness descends. You are in luck as the clouds are passing by and the night is particularly dim without even a passing moonbeam lighting up the water. With your first officer, you clamber into a small boat and row quietly towards the shore. As you reach the rocky shoreline, you see a guard patrolling the high inner wall of the fort.

The Treasure of Captain Estes

You gulp at the fort before you and wonder how you will get in. You also wonder where you should explore. Your first officer may be able to help.

Is your First Officer

Simon Kilmer or Robert Grimshaw *–1113*

Diggory Hurst *–625*

Timmers *–748*

Martha Downham or Black Robert or a replacement first officer– *1119*

<u>308</u>

Move Tabetha.

You are in a white walled room, bathed in the strange light, with two doors, one with a picture of a spider above it, and the other with a pirate flag above it.

If Tabetha's number is 8 – *1459*

If Tabetha's number is 2 – **note this number and go to *1287***

If Tabetha's number is 22 – **note this number and go to *1029***

Where do you go next?

Through the spider door – *1174*

Through the shield door – *1397*

Wait here - **return to the top of this section**

309

You grab the handles of the chest and your hands burn. You scream in pain and stumble almost into a wall of fire, but you stagger here and there momentarily lost in your pain. When you recover, you are not sure where you are.

Reduce the Hot strip by 2 and go to *456*

310

The only wall of fire is to the east. You can route south, west or north from your current location.

Do you

Go West – *539*

Go South – *1355*

Go North – *459*

311

You open the doors of "The Dog's Knackers" and realise that this place is rough. Maybe it's the blood on the floor, or the two men fighting in the corner, the numerous ladies giving men attention, or the row of faces at the bar who are staring at you like you don't belong in here.

"Who you sailing with?" asks a man with a scar from ear to ear at the bar.

"Yeah, what Captain has you for his wench?" cries another voice and there's plenty of laughter.

Do you

Beat a hasty retreat to the crossroads – *802*

Tell them you are the Captain – *567*

Cry "Ale for everyone!" – *1277* (further options over the page)

Announce your first officer as the Captain – *557*

Draw your weapon – *736*

Tell them you have good money for information – *93*

312

1 Skull 0 Scales 4 Coins

That's how you do it! **Tick the codeword of your prize, keeping your stake item**, and return to *1060*

313

You notice the figure look up and then says, "Be seeing you later, love," before dipping their head again. You think you can hear a laugh, but you stumble on to the end of the alleyway. Go to *828*

314

What next? Do you

Go to see Blind Tom – *681*

Visit the provisions isle – *334*

Explore the dark isle – *397*

Approach the pirate king – *1348*

Decide you have had enough of Hells Deep and set sail - **Consult the voyage chart and set sail**

315

Your first officer looks at you nervously. "During the day," he says, "we can try to go in for provisions. As for night time…," He looks uncomfortable with the night-time shenanigans but awaits your orders.

So, what are you looking to do?

Arrive during the day for provisions – *665*

Sneak in during the night – *307*

316

You swim for the main deck and diving, you see an empty deck. This makes sense as most things would have floated away. However, the main deck is deeply gorged, by something unknown. You feel uneasy looking at it and decide to return to the mast to get air.

Do you

Swim for the poop deck – *683*

Investigate the forecastle deck – *770*

Or instead

Dive and search the outside of the vessel – *136*

Return to your vessel – *894*

317

Move Tabetha.

You are in a white walled room, bathed in the strange light, with two doors, one with a picture of a schooner above it, and the other with a shield above it. (Note: further options are over the page)

If Tabetha's number is 14 – *1459*

If Tabetha's number is 11 – **note this number and go to 239**

If Tabetha's number is 10 – **note this number and go to 446**

Where do you go next?

Through the shield door – **686**

Through the schooner door – **358**

Wait here - **return to the top of this section**

318

Roll 1D100 (2xD10) to find where the coin actually is. Did you roll?

00-33 – **777**

34-67 – **1308**

68-99 – **46**

319

You approach the gate in the central wall, and it looks to be open. But you had seen guards atop the wall previously. Is there one there now?

Is the time 25-20 – 1343

Otherwise – **42**

320

Reduce the Hot Strip by 1. If this places you on a Fire spot add 20 to this section's number and go there for the walls have moved. There are walls of fire to the north and east. You can route south or west from your current location.

Do you

Go West – **670**

Go South – **167**

321

The only wall of fire is to the south. You can route west, east or north from your current location.

Do you

Go East – *539*

Go West – *1389*

Go North – *1284*

322

You tell your crew to set a course away from the vessel and to your relief it doesn't follow you. You make a course that takes you slightly out of your way to make sure you remain clear of Mary Pearl, but you don't see her vessel again.

Add 2 days to your voyage time for the detour.

Continue the voyage at *654*

323

You've been caught unawares out in the open and have to scramble for cover. Will you be able to find somewhere to hide.

Roll 1xD100 (2xD10)

01-25 – *1117*

26-75 – *1228*

76-00 – *1379*

324

Reduce your time by 1.

If your time is in the following gaps (42-38) you see a guard on his patrol outside and must remain hidden until he clears the area. Reduce your time by 6. Now continue at the plain text below

The charts on the wall show the waters around New Southampton and have the occasional annotation on them. There are a few places highlighted, namely The Bird's Paradise and Malin's Town. There's no indication why they are marked. There is also a chart with no markings on it which may be ready for use although it is held to the wall by a single nail. Maybe it's a joke. There's also a chart of the Bird's Paradise, showing pilotage.

You can take either of the charts with you. Tick the codeword Bird Chart if you take the Bird's Paradise chart, and the codeword Empty Chart if you take the empty chart.

Do you

Examine the desks – *994*

Check out the cabinets – *284*

Look at the chairs – *243*

Or leave the room and return to tunnel – *693*

325

You cry at your crew to let the vessel run at its hardest and you set course away from your foe. For a day it tries to pursue but eventually gets fed up and changes course away from you. You breathe a sigh of relief as do the crew who are delighted by how you handled the situation (**Raise Crew Morale by one level**). You return to your voyage but must **add 2 days extra** to it for this diversion.

Continue the voyage at *654*

326

The rats are everywhere as you continue the voyage, and your crew are not happy about it. You wake in the night as one runs across you, and you wonder if the crew let it in deliberately. The crew are also reporting rations are being destroyed by the hungry rats.

Your rations are now decreasing by 1 every 2 days on top of what you are normally using. Lower your crew morale by 2 levels. However, you haven't lost any time, but what's that on your pillow – ooh, rat poo!

Continue the voyage at *654*

327

Reduce your time by 1. You step forward and feel clear water ahead. On your left you feel a cage while a wooden wall is on your right.

Do you

About turn and step forward – *281*

Walk forward – *157*

328

You wander along the path, thinking someone is following you, and reach a junction. Which way now?

Left – *1191*

Right – *202*

Turn back – *172*

329

"Just looking, eh? Well that comes with a cost!" The pirate searches you at sword point and takes something from you (If you have no ticked items, go to **905**). You are then marched through Strangar to the entrance to the town.

"Look around here, stranger," says the pirate knocking you to the ground. At least you're still alive. **Untick the top item from your inventory, as the pirate now has it. Go to 262**

330

You sprint for the door and are grabbed by one of the soldiers despite your efforts. He eyes you up, before his fellow soldier says they should take you back with them. Your mind is terrified thinking that you could become a slave to these men and all that it would entail. A cry is heard as a man enters the room. You recognise him as Captain Fareham from the garrison and you think you might be saved. But the soldiers have spotted him too and decide you are surplus to requirements. One runs you through with his sword leaving you to slowly bleed out as you see the captain take the pair on. You never see who wins.

You'll need to be cleverer than that. Try again at *1*

331

As you approach the figure, it moves out from the wall but keeps its hat tipped forward. "What have we here? Are you looking for a good time sailor, or for a boat?"

This might be a way in to get vessel to go after Captain Estes. However, you have just met this man and he might not take kindly to a woman looking for a boat. You have a few options to respond with, but which are safe and will get you nearer to Estes.

Do you

Tell the man you are after a good time – *809*

Advise him you are in need of a crew – *1182*

Undo your hair from under your long-coat and tell him you need a boat – *1006*

332

You raise your hand and begin to sing a shanty to the delight of your crew. There's a sigh of relief and then the party continues, and you are handed a bottle of rum.

You wake up 2 days later with a rather jaded but happy crew around you.

Increase your crew morale by 3 levels. However, you have wasted 3 days on the party and recovery which must be added to your voyage.

Now continue the voyage at *654*

333

You flip open the trapdoor and two hands suddenly grab you and haul you up in front of a group of soldiers in their nightwear. You are in a room of bunks and sleeping accommodation but not for long. They immediately arrest you, taking you to the Fort's commander.

You have been caught. What will be your fate as you are taken before the fort's commander? Go to *1358*

334

You visit the provisions isle and enquire about prices and repairs for your vessel. The isle is quiet, and you need to motivate the assembled throng with money. How good the job is looks like it may vary.

You may make repairs here for the appropriate cost, or you can fill up with cargo. Simply check the table below but be aware, there is a cost in time as well as financially. You can trade in doubloons or treasure (use the doubloon equivalent score for your treasure). Once you have decided on your requirements, adjust your Vessel chart as necessary.

The Treasure of Captain Estes

Provisions

- 10 doubloons per provision pack – 1 day to load
- A day's rum for the crew – 2 days cost (1 to acquire, 1 to drink to excess) Lifts crew morale by one level
    - Large crew – 50 doubloons
    - Medium crew – 25 doubloons
    - Small crew – 15 doubloons

Vessel repair

Note you may not repair your vessel higher than its initial level. All days required for each level are added together to get your total repair time.

- Vessel speed
    - Two days for each level increased by
    - 400 doubloons for each level, or gold equivalent
- Vessel Firepower
    - Three days for each level increased by
    - 500 doubloons for each level, or gold equivalent
- Cargo Hold
    - Two days for each level increased by
    - 300 doubloons for each level, or gold equivalent
- Manoeuvrability
    - Four days for each level increased by
    - 400 doubloons for each level, or gold equivalent
- Storm Handling
    - Four days for each level increased by
    - 800 doubloons for each level, or gold equivalent

Having done your deals at the provisions isle and once you have adjusted your vessel chart and your time chart, what are your plans?

Go to see Blind Tom – *681*

Enjoy yourself at the wild isle – *879*

Explore the dark isle – *397*

Approach the pirate king – *1348*

Decide you have had enough of Hells Deep and set sail - **Consult the voyage chart and set sail**

335

Go to *34*

336

You grab a basket of bananas and walk directly to the gate. You notice a soldier staring at you but keep her face hidden behind the basket. Every now and then you peek from behind the basket until you realise, he is not watching anymore. You walk out the gate into the bright sunshine. A trader then gruffly takes the basket off you.

"These are going into the garrison, stupid girl. Just useless. Go on, clear off and don't come back."

You feign a look of hurt before disappearing quickly down the path towards town. As you approach New Southampton, you see another path branching off, one that leads to Strangar, the pirate haven.

Do you

Make for Strangar – *671*

Or head into New Southampton – *1114*

337

Reduce your time by 1.

If your time is in the following gaps (52-48) and are not hidden, then go to *1037*. If you are hidden, you see a guard on his patrol and must remain hidden until he clears the area. Reduce your time by 6. Now continue at the plain text below

If your time is in the following gaps (22-18) and you are not hidden, then go to *1128*. If you are hidden, you see a guard on the enclosing wall patrolling and must remain hidden until he clears the area. Reduce your time by 6. Now

If neither of these apply, continue at the plain text below

You creep up to the building and find the door unlocked. Inside looks like an office but it's dark and hard to see what's there. You will need to enter to see it properly.

Do you

Hide where you are – ***174***

Route South-west – ***1435***

Creep West – ***103***

Sneak North-west – ***42***

Enter the hut – ***1072***

338

You barely overcome the main current to get to the eddy, and you suffer for it. **Reduce your Waters Strength Chart by 2.** You swim through to the eddy. Go to ***1372***

339

You turn asking for everything your vessel has, and the crew respond. Everyone is working hard but the cargo vessel is wise to your move and sails away from you. No matter what you do you don't seem to close the gap and after a day you know you need to call the pursuit off. You return to your voyage but must **add 2 days extra to it** for this diversion.

Continue the voyage at **654**

340

Is your first officer

Simon Kilmer – **409**

Robert Grimshaw – **953**

Diggory Hurst – **1352**

Timmers – **571**

Martha Downham, or you have replaced Martha – **667**

Black Robert – **574**

341

Your first officer looks at you as if you are insane, but you ignore them issuing instructions to the crew about how to plot a course and when to fire. You gulp as you see large tentacles reach up from the sea but tell the helm to stay your course and then wait to give the order to fire.

As the canons ring out, you see the kraken reaching up with its tentacles, but they are always some distance from your vessel. You continue shouting out instructions and watch as the Kraken seems to be getting further and further away. Once you are clear you continue in that direction until nightfall before resuming your course. Your crew looks at you with renewed pride and awe.

Raise your crew morale by 2 levels. Your detour however has cost you 1 day extra, so add that to your voyage time. Continue your voyage at 654.

342

Go to *1254*

343

Reduce your time by 1. As you step forward you find a wooden wall ahead. On your right this wall extends but there is clear water to your left.

Do you

Turn left and walk forward – *899*

About turn and step forward – *90*

344

You tell the man you are looking for a crew to handle a vessel for you and the man eyes you suspiciously.

"This is a place of entertainment, not business. The men in here are not the working type if you understand me. Now beat it before I call Little Annie out. She doesn't take to people in the building unless they are customers."

The man seems friendly but firm, and maybe he's right. Or is he hiding something?

Do you

Insist on entering – *806*

Take his advice and return to the main street – *496*

345

Reduce your time by 1. Stepping forward you reach out and immediately feel a desk in front of you. On your right is a wooden wall. You feel left and there's just water.

Do You

About turn and walk forward – *1248*

Examine the desk – *85*

Turn left and step forward – *1344*

346

Reduce your Waters Strength Chart by 1. The current is pushing you east. However, you think you can reach an eddy that seems to allow a way west but to get there will be incredibly hard work. Your foot scrapes the bottom briefly and you think you may be able to drop a pole and take a rest. Do you

Swim West – *204*

Float East – *80*

Drop a pole – **Make a note of this section and go to *694***

347

You wander along the path, feet deep in mud, and reach a junction. Which way now?

Left – *70*

Right – *612*

Turn back – *639*

348

The charts on the wall interest you, especially an unmarked one of the seas around New Southampton. If you take it tick the codeword, **Empty Chart.**

Go to *415*

The Treasure of Captain Estes

<u>349</u>

Your voyage begins well and you gaze upon blue skies as you race through the water. But after a short time into your passage, you feel the wind ease off, drastically, until there is not a breath to be had. After a day of not moving and the heat on deck becoming unbearable, your crew start to grumble.

Do you sail a Brigantine – *1034*

If not, continue below

You have hit the doldrums and who knows how long you are going to be here. Follow the below instructions to find out.

<u>Day 1</u>

The wind does not change, absent from the sails. The crew are okay but slightly restless.

<u>Day 2</u>

Roll 1xD100 (2XD10)

00-15 The wind has picked up again and you may resume your course. Continue to the Resume voyage section below.

16-99 The crew are becoming more restless and you can hear grumblings

<u>Day 3</u>

Roll 1xD100 (2XD10)

00-20 The wind has picked up again and you may resume your course. Continue to the **Resume voyage section** below.

21-99 The crew are openly arguing with one another, and you give out an extra ration portion to quieten them. **Remove an extra ration from your hold.**

<u>Day 4</u>

Roll 1xD100 (2XD10)

00-25 The wind has picked up again and you may resume your course. Continue to the **Resume voyage section** below.

26-99 The crew have a fight, agitated at each other, in which one section of cargo is lost oversea. **Remove one section of cargo.**

<u>Day 5</u>

Roll 1xD100 (2XD10)

00-35 The wind has picked up again and you may resume your course. Continue to the **Resume voyage section** below.

36-99 One of the crew, delirious, decides to build a makeshift raft for himself which he rips one of the sails for use with. **Reduce your speed by 1 level.**

<u>Day 6</u>

Roll 1xD100 (2XD10)

00-50 The wind has picked up again and you may resume your course. Continue to the **Resume voyage section** below.

51-99 One of your crew accidentally sets off a canon and blows several of the others apart. **Reduce your vessel's Firepower by 1 level.**

<u>Day 7</u>

Roll 1xD100 (2XD10)

00-65 The wind has picked up again and you may resume your course. Continue to the **Resume voyage section** below.

66-99 You fear for the crew and order extra rations. **Delete 1 ration from your cargo.**

<u>Day 8</u>

Roll 1xD100 (2XD10)

00-75 The wind has picked up again and you may resume your course. Continue to the **Resume voyage section** below.

76-99 The crew in delirium decide to cover themselves in whatever they find in the hold. In the **process 25% of your cargo is ejected overboard.**

<u>Day 9</u>

Roll 1xD100 (2XD10)

00-85 The wind has picked up again and you may resume your course. Continue to the **Resume voyage section** below.

86-99 One of the crew in a mad delirium drills a hole in the vessel. This causes a submerging of the vessel to the degree that part of your rudder is used to effect repairs, **reducing your vessel's manoeuvrability by 2 levels.**

<u>Day 10</u>

Roll 1xD100 (2XD10)

00-95 The wind has picked up again and you may resume your course. Continue to the **Resume voyage section** below.

96-99 Delirium overtakes all of you and you see an island in the distance. Every member of the crew sees a land of plenty with beautiful inhabitants welcoming you. **As a result you all jump overboard and die beneath the waves, but what a happy way to go!** You can start again at *1.*

<u>Resume Voyage Section</u>

Resume your course now but **add on the number of days you were in the doldrums to the voyage time.**

Continue the voyage at *654*

350

You place the key in the lock, and although it fits, it doesn't turn.

Return to *1289* and make another choice.

351

Timmers is waiting outside, and you tell him you should go but he insists on waiting and sending a message as that was your cover. You agree and he completes his task once the clerk returns from his lunch. Your heart's still racing as you both walk casually back to your vessel and then set sail as if nothing had happened. But did you discover what you wanted? Have you seen all you need to see?

Do you

Wish to sneak into the fort at night – *307*

Sail elsewhere - **consult the voyage chart and set sail.**

352

You take the stone steps up to the wall and are just reaching the top when you hear a cry from outside, alerting everyone to your escape. You see guards beginning to react on the wall and you wonder if your escape route will be compromised. The gates are still currently open in the courtyard, but you are not sure if that way will be any quicker now. Which way will you go?

Do you

About turn and run for the gates – *878*

Race onto the wall the wall – *78*

353

You turn and run for the dressing room as the shop door opens. You throw a hat from a shelf onto the floor in front of the guard. He steps on it and seems to lose his balance.

How lucky are you?

This lucky – *72*

Or this lucky – *1015*

354

"How can I help you, love?" asks the barmaid.

You ask if she knows anything about the local area of New Southampton as you will be sailing around the waters.

"Not me, but you can wake old Jake there, he knows plenty for a bottle of something. Or you can try the merchants there but most of them have never sailed the seas. They just make business deals and stay on land."

She goes back to her bar, and you wonder should you follow her advice.

Do you

Talk to the merchants – *598*

Wake the napping figure – *28*

Leave the tavern and return to the crossroads – *802*

355

It seems like an age but one day your first officer walks into the cells and tells you to be quiet as the guard opens your cell door. You are escorted to the dock and then to your vessel under an armed guard. Only when your vessel sets sail does your first officer tell you it has cost all of your resources to get you out. The crew are not happy.

Remove all your treasure from your stores and half of your provisions. If you had no treasure, reduce your provisions down to half and remove 8 more. Reduce your crew morale by 3. You're alive but not by much. You have also lost 5 days, reduce your time chart by 5.

Now consult the voyage chart and set sail for your next destination.

356

If you have been to the garrison – *922*

If not read on,

As you lie in the dust, two soldiers on horseback approach in the night and one looks at you with intent, he seems to confer with the other and one quickly dismounts and picks you up, throwing you over his shoulder. You are taken back to the island garrison where you are stripped of all weapons and shown to a room. Soon you are joined by a Captain Fareham, the head of the garrison and an admirer of yours you are familiar with. He shows you to a room and you fall asleep after all the drama. **If you have not already, tick the codeword Prominent** and go to *1031*

357

You produce a bottle of whiskey from within your jacket and the big man takes it, pulling out the cork and downing a slug. **Untick the codeword Bottle of Whiskey.**

"It's good," he says, and takes another dram. "Seeing as you have been so generous, I guess you can meet the boss. Come with me." The man laughs and turns to the doors which are already opening. Follow the man inside to *16*

358

Move Tabetha.

You are in a white walled room, bathed in the strange light, with two doors, one with a picture of a spider above it, and the other with a schooner above it.

If Tabetha's number is 10 – *1459*

If Tabetha's number is 4 – **note this number and go to *1287***

If Tabetha's number is 23 – **note this number and go to *446***

Where do you go next?

Through the spider door – *714*

Through the schooner door – *180*

Wait here - **return to the top of this section**

359

It seems strange but the book explaining Johnstone's Confuser might be your best option. It details a pattern of shots that are designed to confuse the Kraken. Captain Johnstone was an eccentric, but he died old, so maybe he was an eccentric who knew what he was talking about.

If you want to follow what Johnstone says – *341*

If not return to *368* and choose again.

<u>360</u>

The guard steps aside obviously taking you for a gentleman and you browse the shop. There are various weapons available, and you ask what you can afford with the items you have, rather than with money. The weaponsmith suggests that a bottle of good whiskey, for example Mackenzie, or a Promissory note, may get you a secreted knife, a standard knife, or for both you can have a Pistol.

If you wish to purchase any items, then untick those you are paying with and tick those you are gaining. As a reminder you can have

A **Secreted Knife** or a **Standard Knife** in exchange for a **Bottle of Mackenzie Whiskey** or a **Promissory Note**.

Or

A **Pistol** in exchange for a **Bottle of Mackenzie Whiskey** AND a **Promissory Note**

Make your trades and then return to the street at *1009*

<u>361</u>

"Jolly good! You look like a spritely fellow. Now where are those blasted forms. The ledger was here only this morning. Blast it, humbugged by my own efficiency. I shall retire to the next room and discover the ledger. Remain here, and don't touch anything."

He walks off to a door you didn't come in by and smiles. "I think you'll be splendid." He exits closing the door behind him.

The room is empty save yourself and you may be able to search the room. However, you don't know when he will return. Do you

Wait for the return of Lord Buffington – *604*

Decide to explore – ***676***

362

Do you have the codeword **Bird Whistle** – *401* If not, continue below.

You grab a hold of the rope and begin to climb up but as soon as you gain any height, several birds begin to flock together and swoop down, pecking at you with strong beaks. You swing your free arm at them, but it is no use and soon they cause you to lose grip and you tumble down the rock. You land heavily and the crew take you back to the vessel where you spend 2 days recovering. **Add 2 days to your voyage chart**. Once you feel like standing again, you return to the base of the formation and ponder your next move.

Do you

Enter via the wooden door – *303*

Decide this is a bad idea and leave the Bird's Paradise – **consult your voyage chart**

363

The tavern is a chaotic place, built from the wreckage of vessels. It has various levels made from decks of scuppered boats and you see the tell-tale work of Spanish, English and Dutch craftsmen. There is rigging from ships, carvings of fairy-tale creatures and women hung by tables and crates with upturned rum barrels. The whole scene is however one of laughter and banter, with the occasional fight breaking out and knives drawn.

As you look about, three different groups draw your attention. On the lowest deck are two pirates with a small monkey figure on the table before them. There are a long line of pirates talking at the main bar section of the tavern while on a higher adapted poop deck stands two female pirates. They have dark eyes, and one is dark skinned while the other appears to be as fair skinned as you have seen. You notice that many of the men stay well clear of them.

Do you

Approach the pirates with the monkey figure – *305*

Join the main bar – *594*

Climb up to the adapted poop deck and the two female pirates – *658*

Or leave the tavern and

Make for the small houses – *1304*

Approach the gambling groups – *1424*

Go to see the fights – *84*

Decide this is not a place you want to explore and return to your vessel - *314*

364

The doctor lays you down on a table and begins to attend to your wounds. It's rough and ready and sore but it'll work. **You are no longer in danger of succumbing to your wounds. Untick one of a pistol, a promissory note, or a bottle of whisky from your codewords.** Having been patched up you return to the street, grateful for the doctor's work. Go to *1256*

365

Timmer's seems a bit agitated, but he agrees to your wish and soon you are accompanying him up to the encircled centre of the fort. The hour is close to lunch and as you approach the gate, the soldiers on guard stare at you with a suspicious glare. Timmers steps forward and tells them you wish to use the message hut. They give way and you see several buildings, all of stone with wooden shutters. They sit in pairs side by side, and three deep, but with a path running up the centre of them and branching paths leading off to the buildings.

The Treasure of Captain Estes

"You can see the armoury on the left," says Timmers, "and a number of barracks." The middle building on the left is the naval intelligence office, and just off to the side of it is a very small building that you cannot see at present. That is where we go by the path on the left."

"How do we get into the Intelligence office?" you ask.

"Well, we could walk up and knock but I doubt that will work. When the lunch hour occurs, we may be able to access the tunnels they use between the message building and the intelligence office. I don't know how many tunnels there are, but I know they exist because at night or if under attack, they like to use them. The man who supervised their building told me so."

Soon you have arrived at the message service building and Timmers leads you inside announcing to the clerk that he has a message to send. As he writes out a letter, you look around the small room.

You can see a wooden desk with a satchel sitting on it. Inside the bag are letters and scrolls, all under the watchful eye of a young clerk. He looks barely older than you and has spectacles through which he peers like a hawk. He doesn't wear a naval or soldier's uniform and you believe he must be a private citizen. He's also tapping his foot like it's been cursed to dance along to some unheard tune.

"There you go," says Timmers.

"Thank you," says the clerk and takes the letter, placing it inside the satchel. He then stands waiting for you to leave.

"But I have another one to write," says Timmers.

"Not over my lunch you haven't. Here, take the pen and ink, and take some parchment outside. You can sit and write it there, and I'll take it from you when I return."

Timmers nods, accepts the writing materials and together you both step outside and sit in the grass beside the small building.

"I'll tell the guard you're here," says the clerk, "just don't go away from here. And if you leave, use the path you came up on."

"Of course," says Timmers, "but we'll just be here."

You watch the clerk close the wooden door behind him but not before he takes the satchel and places it in a safe and locks it with a key. He then steps out of the office and closes the door but you note he doesn't lock it.

"Did you see that?" says Timmers. "You can go in and try to find the tunnel. But be quick as they won't all be at lunch for long."

You don't hang about and open the door once the clerk is completely out of sight. The wall around this central compound has guards on top but they all seem to be looking out to sea, and if you are honest, they look bored.

Inside the office you see the desk of the clerk and the safe. On the floor are two rugs at each end of the small office. One seems to be raised slightly but that may be because the rug has shifted slightly underfoot. Otherwise, it's a pretty bland office. There's a stool but no other furniture.

Do you

Look at the desk – *1167*

Check the rug that's slightly lifted – *169*

Look at the other rug – *366*

Try to open the safe – *1289*

Decide this is a bad idea and return to Timmers, saying you should get back to the ship pronto – *351*

366

This rug is slightly smaller and seems to be sitting trim to the floor. You pull it back revealing a trapdoor but with a finger hole punched to allow it to be lifted. Below is a dank passage, smelling of mildew and stale air. You wonder where this goes, is this one of the tunnels?

Do you

Enter the tunnel – **859**

Or replace the trapdoor and rug and then

Look at the desk – **1167**

Look at the other rug – **366**

Try to open the safe – **1289**

Decide this is a bad idea and return to Timmers, saying you should get back to the ship pronto – **351**

367

You're not going to take this lying down and you throw a punch at the man's stomach. He barely flinches before punching you hard in the face and you black out.

When you wake up, you are in the hold of a ship, and you cower form the men around you. It seems you are now their slave, and your fine dress is long gone replaced with bare rags. It's no life for the daughter of a plantation owner and you'll probably succumb to fever or illness in a few years without seeing any daylight. This is possibly the worst ending you can imagine. Try again at **1**

368

The day is cloudy but at least that stops the sun beating down upon your crew, sapping their energy. All around seems peaceful and your vessel is making way across a mild swell, sails bracing in the wind. This seems like a good time to go below but the Crow's nest shouts down to you.

"Captain, something on the port side. Looked like a tentacle of some sort."

The crew looks to you, clearly frightened and you see one mouth the word Kraken; the beast that lies below, multi-tentacled and capable of taking down a whole galleon. You wonder what your best option is for waylaying the creature for your first officer says you will not defeat it.

Do you have the codeword **Spanish Tail** or **British Tail** – *462*

Otherwise, read on

You can try to outrun the creature though you know it to be quick – *1155*

It's been said if you feed it, the Kraken sometimes stays away from a ship – *1451*

You could try and defend yourself from it – *927*

Or do you have one of the codewords **Human Bait**, **Silent Running** or **Johnstone's Confuser** – *242*

369

You hand over the bottle of whiskey and the man takes a look at it, thinking. "This is a fine whiskey but nowhere near the price of a crew and ship. Captain Fareham at the garrison is looking for you and I was going to hand you to him for a price but I think you could do with a break. I'll keep the bottle and also keep quiet. Now go Mary Hastings and keep a low profile."

Untick the codeword Bottle of Mackenzie Whiskey.

You sit in shock but then stir yourself to your feet and even manage to give the man a kiss on the cheek to keep him sweet. Go back to the pier at *117* and decide your next move.

370

You have passed out from your wounds and now lie dead on the island. No doubt you will be robbed and maybe even thrown aside if you start to smell. Whatever they do to you will not be your problem as your only choice is to return to *1* and start again.

371

If this is at least the second item you have examined then roll 1xD100 (2xD10,) and consult the table below

2nd item	3rd item	4th item
00-39 – *959*	00-59 – *959*	00-89 – *959*
40-99 – **read on**	60-99 – **read on**	90-99 – **read on**

The charts on the wall show the waters around New Southampton and have the occasional annotation on them. There are a few places highlighted, namely The Bird's Paradise and Malin's Town. There's no indication why they are marked. There is also a chart with no markings on it which may be ready for use although it is nailed to the wall by a single nail. Maybe it's a joke. There's also a chart of the Bird's Paradise, showing pilotage.

You can take either of the charts with you. Tick the codeword Bird Chart if you take the Bird's Paradise chart, and the codeword Empty Chart if you take the empty chart.

Do you

Examine the desks – *1239*

Check out the cabinets – *1405*

Look at the chairs – *120*

Or leave the room and return back to tunnel – *558*

372

You try to swim/run away from the creatures, but they are too quick for you. You are grabbed and feel a claw breaking your leg, followed by another. Soon you drown and are released form the pain.

Well, you gave it a good go but next time you'll need better protection. Try again at *1*

373

Your quartermaster asks you to come to the provisions store and he doesn't look very happy. You ask if people have been stealing from them but he shakes his head saying they are all there, but many have gone rotten and he needs to do a proper stocktake. You wonder how much you have lost.

Roll a 1xD100 (2xD10). Check the number below to see how much of your provisions you have lost.

00-20 – **2 provisions**

21-40 – **6 provisions**

41-60 – **10 provisions**

62-80 – **4 provisions**

81-00 – **14 provisions**

Remove the rotten provisions from your vessel chart. Now continue your voyage at *654*

374

The galleon comes alongside you and the first officer of the warship examines your vessel with his large crew. You are powerless to stop him. Then he looks at you with an outraged eye.

"We have reports of a captain matching your description who scuppered one of our vessels, killing nearly all the crew. Such filth must be eradicated from these seas."

Before you can respond, you are run through with a sword and your body is thrown overboard to a watery grave. You don't know what becomes of the crew, and your family is never avenged in any respect. Your tale ends here, like many a vicious pirate. Try again at *1*, and maybe be less ruthless and notorious.

375

Reduce the Hot Strip by 1. If this places you on a Fire spot add 20 to this section's number and go there for the walls have moved. There are walls of fire to the south and west. You can route north or east from your current location.

Do you

Go East – *788*

Go North – *1443*

376

You worry that you may not have enough to get clear, and you are right in that the first volley from the sloop hits you sending wood into the air.

Reduce your crew morale by 1 level. Also reduce your vessel Storm Handling and Treasure Store by 1 level each as they were damaged in that last volley.

The sloop is too quick and catches you up. Return to *1267* and continue the fight.

377

Roll 1D100 (2xD10) to find where the coin actually is. Did you roll?

00-33 – *850*

34-67 – *573*

68-99 – *46*

378

You place the key in the lock, and it doesn't even begin to fit.

Return to *1289* and make another choice.

379

You order a large compliment of crew to go with you and you see them prepare quickly. They are armed with cutlasses and knives for no pistols will survive the passage under the sea in a working order. **Tick the codeword Large Crew.** Together you dive into the water and strike out for the cave.

Continue at *230*

380

Go to *34*

381

You cry at your crew to let the vessel run at its hardest and you set course away from your foe. For a day it tries to pursue but eventually gets fed up and changes course away from you. You breathe a sigh of relief as do the crew who are delighted by how you handled the situation (**Raise Crew Morale by one level**). You return to your voyage but must add 2 days extra to it for this diversion.

Continue the voyage at *654*

382

Reduce your time by 1.

If your time is in the following gaps (57-53 or 42-38, then go to *1037*.)

You try the door and find it locked. By pushing it at the top, middle, and the bottom, you determine it has three bolts across it. You're never going to open it quietly. You could take a charge at it but that's going to be noisy.

Do you

Hide where you are – *103*

Route South – *1435*

Creep East – *174*

Go North – *42*

Sneak West – *1393*

Charge the door – *1135*

383

You pluck up your courage and walk on into the jungle along a curiously cut out path. It winds here and there, and you have several small creatures scuttle across your path before you see a pit of snakes to the side of the path. They are in a deep recess and cannot escape but you feel you could easily reach down and grab them if you wanted, like they are being kept in a form of storage.

You walk on and a clearing comes upon you where a temple stands with pillars all around and seems to be disused. However, you can smell some kind of incense, cloy and claggy. Behind you the path seems to be foggy, almost disappearing from view. You should be bathed in sunshine but instead you feel a heaviness in your head and heart.

Do you

Enter the temple – *656*

Return on the path – *53*

Wait and see what happens – *257*

384

With a small crew you set sail for the island, over the choppy water. Do you have the codeword **Parley** – *1161*. If not, read on,

As you approach the beach you see a large number of what looks like natives coming out of their huts. They hold up muskets and are armed with swords and cutlasses. As soon as you step from the small boat they aim their weapons at you.

Do you

Attack them with your crew – *978*

Try to speak to them – *1401*

Return to your vessel and fire your cannons at them – *1078*

Return to your vessel and leave the natives in peace – *1441*

385

You see a brown bull running directly at you and a white bull in the left channel. You are in the right channel. What will you do?

Stay right – *783*

Go to the middle – *547*

Go to the left channel – *392*

386

Reduce your time by 2. If your time is in the following gaps (55-53, 35-33, 24-23 or 04-02) then go to *810*. If not continue below

Hey, this stinks. It's the latrines and there's some wooden seat tops leading down to the cesspits below. You recoil at the smell and wonder what you bothered looking here for. But then something catches your eye on the edge of the drop inside one of the toilets. Or does it?

 Do you

Wait in hiding – *519*

Reach into the latrine – *406*

Investigate a slum – *847*

If you haven't already

Move to the west quarter – *493*

Move to the east quarter – *678*

Leave the fort for your vessel – *535*

387

Reduce your time by 2. If your time is in the following gaps (46-41 or 16-11) then go to *1126*. If not continue below

As you approach the standing bovine animals, you hear a loud moo break out and there is some shuffling of hooves. The smell of manure is strong but there's little else here for the animals are simply corralled for the night. Unless you like cows, this has been pointless.

Do you

Wait in hiding – *1418*

Look at the sheep – *780*

Go to the gate – *319*

Move to the West quarter – *493*

Move to the East quarter – *678*

388

Move Tabetha.

You are in a white walled room, bathed in the strange light, with one door with a picture of a pirate flag above it.

If Tabetha's number is 20 – *1459*

If Tabetha's number is 9 – **note this number and go to *1029***

Where do you go next?

Through the pirate flag door – *1074*

Wait here - **return to the top of this section**

389

Did you spot your mistake? You have no guns. You cannot prevent the creature coming closer and it rips into your vessel with its long tentacles, smashing timber and flinging crew overboard. You are mercifully saved from a slow drowning as a tentacle slams you against the mast instantly ending your life. But your mistake has cost you and your crew.

The waters around New Southampton are deadly, but that was plain silly. You may try again at *1*

390

You lift the gold chain off the monkey and pocket it. Well, that was easy. **Tick the codewords Monkey and Gold Chain.** You retreat back down the path, leaving the statue behind. Go to *1066*

391

You push open the hatch door, but no light comes through. Stepping forward you find no floor beneath you, and you sink down. Desperately you swim back up, but the hatch has closed and there are no handles on the inside. You drown in a frenzy of panic until the water in your lungs gives you peaceful sleep.

You got trapped in a deadly maze. Tough luck but you can try again at *1,* or begin at the start of this puzzle at *1211*

392

Everything happens so quickly, and a bull smashes you backwards knocking you to the ground and then you scramble as quick as you can back to the plain clear of any more bulls. You're back where you started but you have been winded and feel groggy. **Take 4 off your Island Time Chart while you recover**.

If you want to try and run the gap again – *59*

You could try and go through the jungle and around the rock formation – *923*

Alternatively you can leave the plains back down the jungle track – *1145*

393

You were told that you can sacrifice crew to the Kraken, that if sufficient bodies are sent overboard the creature will feast and spare the vessel. It's a dark place to go to but do you have another option.

If you want to enact this idea – *132*

If not, return to *368* and choose again.

394

The only wall of fire is to the north. You can route south, east or west from your current location.

Do you

Go East – *772*

Go South – *1387*

Go West – *1444*

395

You wander over to the barn and watch the pirate lying asleep before the door. He seems to mutter in his sleep and occasionally stirs briefly but he has not seen you in the dim light. A wine bottle lies at his feet, and you see it's empty. Listening intently, you can hear noises inside the barn; there are low whispers and some quiet conversations. A door in the barn lies slightly ajar.

Do you

Enter through the door – *1092*

Pick up the wine bottle – *1301*

Wake the pirate – *913*

Or decide to return to the street – *1112*

396

You are in a round room where you can see a wooden chest beside you with the rope above that you climbed down. Between you and the other side of the room is nothing, but you can see small holes in the wall pointed right at where you would cross. This may be a trap! There is another rope on the far side which disappears below maybe to another floor, but you'll have to cross over to use it.

Do you

Examine the chest – **990**

Climb back up the rope – **479**

Run across the room – **421**

397

You approach the dark isle in your small boat and on stepping ashore find that a mist has enveloped the island. You are on a sandy beach with a large green jungle before you but can see beyond the greenery to the top of a stone structure. It is not that far away and cannot be, for the isle was small when you viewed it from your vessel.

You can make out a small path through the jungle and approach the entrance feeling like something is wrong. There is sand but there should be sun, for there was on your vessel. Instead, there is the feeling of a dank cellar about you, a dullness in the light and a stench begins to filter out from the jungle.

You reach the small path and see a sign before you. It reads, "Temple of …" but the name has been scratched off. Across from you on a wooden post is a small bell about the size of your head hanging limply. As you go to step past it, it begins to ring of its own accord, making you stop for a moment. Is this a good idea?

Is Martha Downham your first officer – **963**

Do you

Continue – **383**

Return to your vessel – **1227**

398

You approach the bar and see the barman frowning at you. "There are two types of women that come in here. One type sells themselves for money, and I'm guessing you are not of that sort. The other type is generally trouble. I won't have trouble here. I'll not serve you unless the men are happy that you're here."

With that, he turns away and you are left standing, eyes of the clientele on you. What now?

Do you

Try to sit with one of the portly men – *869*

Ask if anyone knows your first officer – *340*

Decide to leave and return to the crossroads – *802*

399

You wander along the path, desperate for a sign of anything not green, and reach a junction. Which way now?

Left – *664*

Right – *1414*

Turn back – *48*

400

Roll 1xD100 (2xD10). For every point of damage you have already done to the brigantine add 3 to the result. Check the table below for the result of this round of the sea battle.

00-20 – You get caught with a severe broadside. **Lower your vessel manoeuvrability by 2 levels and your vessel speed by 1 level.**

21-49 – A volley lands on deck killing many of the crew. **Lower your crew by 1 level.**

50-69 – A volley blows out some of your canons, but you hit back – **Lower your firepower by 1 level.** But you cause the following damage dependent on your firepower: **Light – 1 point, Moderate – 2pts, Heavy – 3pts, Very Heavy – 4 pts**

70-89 – You land a splendid volley. Note you have done the following damage dependent on your firepower: **Light – 1 point, Moderate – 2pts, Heavy – 3pts, Very Heavy – 4 pts**

90 and up - You catch them cold with a blinding manoeuvre. Note you have done the following damage dependent on your firepower: **Light – 2 point, Moderate – 4pts, Heavy – 6pts, Very Heavy – 8 pts**

If you have caused 18 points of damage overall to the brigantine – *645*

If not

Do you want to continue the battle – *145*

Do you wish to run – *992*

401

You grab the rope and begin to climb. As you do so, many birds begin to take flight and form up, flying in to peck at you, trying to knock you off the cliff. You draw your bird whistle and blow it hard which sends the birds into a frenzy. They whirl around here and there, but away from you, allowing you to climb up the rope to where there is an opening in the rock. Above here, the rock formation looks too dangerous to climb so you decide to enter through the opening. Go to *479*

402

You call out to retreat and to turn the vessel but there's seems to be a struggle to get clear. You see the sloop now coming alongside at point blank range and volley after volley is fired into your vessel. The mast falls and then you feel the vessel begin to tilt. Soon it is sinking in the water. You try to flee over the side, but an errant pistol shot hits you between the shoulder blades and you fall to the deck. As the blackness invades your view, you know you are defeated.

Make sure you pick a fight you can win! You can try again at *1*.

403

You've been caught unawares out in the open and have to scramble for cover. Will you be able to find somewhere to hide.

Roll 1xD100 (2xD10)

01-25 – *829*

26-75 – *1228*

76-00 – *1379*

404

Compass Map (map for use with special compass) – *716*

Bird Chart (Pilotage for Birds Paradise) - *1082*

Gold Chain (Chain from monkey statue) - *1244*

Sextant (stolen sextant) - *1309*

Argyle (picture of Lady argyle) - *454*

405

You tell him you'll enter anyway and a voice from behind the doors shouts, "Back off, lady." The voice is female and shrill. The doors open and a woman standing only five feet tall dressed in a gown with her hair tied up glares at you. In her hand is a musket pointed at you.

"Go on, lady. You heard him. I don't give two warnings."

Do you

Push on towards the doors – *839*

Reach for a weapon – *1331*

Take his advice and return to the main street – *496*

<u>406</u>
Reduce your time by 2. If your time is in the following gaps (55-53, 35-33, 24-23 or 04-02) then go to *810*. If not continue below

You put your hand inside and…, that's not what you thought it might be, in fact it's…, well, you know. You find a barrel of water and quickly wash your hand. Yuk!

Do you

Wait in hiding – *519*

Investigate a slum – *847*

If you haven't already

Move to the west quarter – *493*

Move to the east quarter – *678*

Leave the fort for your vessel – *535*

<u>407</u>
Reduce your Island Time Chart by 1

You trek along the path, ever so tired. There's a fork in the path, and you wonder which way to go. You can take either fork, or you could always head out into the jungle off the path.

Do you go

Left – *982*

Right – *1088*

Strike out into the Jungle – *1283*

Turn around back the way you came – *1115*

408

Reduce your time by 1.

If your time is in the following gaps (32-28 or 12-08), then go to *1037*.

If your time is in the following gaps (47-38), then go to *1128*.

If neither of these apply, continue at the plain text below

As you stand at the door, you can hear snoring, and not just a single person. There's the odd creak as well but generally snoring.

Do you

Hide where you are – *1197*

Route through the open gate – *519*

Creep East – *1435*

Go North – *1393*

Open the door and enter the building – *680*

409

"Ah yes, excellent chap," says a rotund gentleman quaffing some ale. "Come sit down, and we can talk about the sea." You take a seat beside the man who orders some ale for you. You drink slowly listening to the man's chatter and are interested when he talks about the Brid's paradise.

The Treasure of Captain Estes

"There is a malevolent force in there, one that delights in tempting a person before spoiling their hopes. And, of course, the entire place is covered in birds which is why everyone calls it the Bird's Paradise but if you check the charts, they all say Brid's Paradise. You need a bird whistle if you go there. Good for keeping the blighters at bay. If you can find one of course. I'm sure there's an example of one in the Mariner's Guild. In the offices of course, you don't leave that sort of thing just lying around."

The man continues for a while before nodding off under the effects of his ale. At this point you politely take your leave, returning to the crossroads. Go to *802*

<u>410</u>

You reach the sailor as he finishes narrating a tale about a battle with a Spanish galleon and how he bested it with a small sloop he had at the time. Despite being outgunned, he had sunk the vessel with a half dead crew and an unfavourable wind.

As he quietens, you approach him and ask if he has a crew for hire. He says that he does, the same crew he was talking about although now he commands a much larger vessel currently moored just off the bay.

You tell him you wish to hire a vessel and ask how much his price would be.

"Do you by chance have a Promissory note of reasonable value? Failing that we could start with a bottle of whiskey."

Do you

Have a **Bottle of Whiskey** and wish to give it to him as payment – *701*

Have a **Promissory Note** and wish to give it to him as payment – *67*

Decide to ignore the sailor – return to *117* and choose another option

New Southampton Port

411

Roll 1D100 (2xD10) to find where the coin actually is. Did you roll?

00-33 – *777*

34-67 – *573*

68-99 – *911*

412

How fast is your vessel?

Very Slow or Slow – *39*

Moderate, Fast, or Very fast – *1059*

413

You take a drink to the pirate and tell him you are interested in this compass he talks of. Immediately he puts his fingers to his lips and tells you to shush.

"Who told you?" he says.

"You did."

"Did I? Well keep it quiet. The bird's will never forgive us if we give away their secret." He touches his nose and gives you a theatrical wink. "You'll need a chart to get to the main rock. Lost ours in a fight with Estes. Always hated the Portuguese even if they are pirates! As for those two up there," he says pointing to the two female pirates on the poop deck, "never trust them! Never!"

You think on this knowledge as he passes out in front of you, clearly having drunk too much. Did you learn something? Is there somewhere you should go? What next?

Do you

Approach the pirates with the monkey figure – *305*

Climb up to the adapted poop deck and the two female pirates – *658*

Or leave the tavern and

Make for the small houses – *1304*

Approach the gambling groups – *1424*

Go to see the fights – *84*

Decide this is not a place you want to explore and return to your vessel - *314*

414

"Help," says Martha, "I thought you were stronger than that. Let's see how you settle this!"

No help there then. She is a pirate after all. Return to *763* and choose another option.

415

You have searched in Lord Buffington's room but when will he return? Can you leave it any longer?

If you wish to cease looking at the room's items, sit down and go to *604*

If you wish to search for another item continue below:

Roll 1 xd10 and follow the result below

0-3 go to *7*

4-6 go to *461*

7-9 go to *846*

416

Reduce your time by 1. Bravely you walk on and bump into some crates up ahead. To your left there's a wooden wall. On your right is clear water.

Do you

About turn and step forward – **588**

Turn right and walk forward – **541**

Examine the crates – **85**

417

You grab hold of the drawers on one of the walls, pulling them out and flicking through the contents. As much as you can make out these are charts of waters far away and of little use to you. There are also almanacs containing tide tables, port details and other information of waters around the world but nothing of use to you.

Go to **1400**

418

"If I'm not mistaken that's the schooner of Aron Jeboe." You have no idea who your first officer is talking about, but you want to know more.

If your first officer is

Simon Kilmer or Robert Grimshaw – **634**

Diggory Hurst, Timmers, Martha Downham, Black Robert – **995**

419

You wait in your vessel as Robert goes into Malin's Town to find your contact and give him the good news. He returns alone and has in his hands a piece of parchment. It has details on how to complete the "Drops of Daniel" whatever that is. **Tick the codeword Drop.** Now decide if you should stay in Malin's Town or depart.

Do you

See to the needs of your vessel and crew – *903*

Try to earn some money by signing up to a cargo run – *1335*

Visit the taverns for information – *802*

Visit the Mariners' Guild for information – *124*

If you have had enough of Malin's town, then **consult the voyage chart and set sail.**

420

The weather is brutal, throwing the vessel here and there on the waves but you are confident in your crew and your ship. You feel sick as the ship is tossed here and there but you note that it is holding well except that your sails have taken some damage. When you clear the storm after two days you assess the damage.

You've done very well all things considering. Lower your Vessel's speed by 1 due to sail damage but raise your crew's morale by 2 levels, for they are grateful to be alive.

Now resume your voyage at *654*

421

You run quickly across the room but you hear a swish as you do so. Small darts fire out from the walls and you desperately try to avoid them. But are you quick?

Roll 1xD100 (2XD10) and check the result below

01-25 *6*

26-50 *163*

50-75 *37*

76-00 *438*

422

You wander along the path, feeling a strange chill in the air, and reach a junction. Which way now?

Left – *1357*

Right – *76*

Turn back – *664*

423

You have arrived back at the plains where the bulls still run but you have the treasure. Why are you here? Turn around and leave on the jungle path. Go to *1145*

424

You give the order to sail clear of the Kraken and fire everything at it. It seems like a risk, but you are up against it now. You watch as the vessel cuts through the water and you try to get broadsides to a creature that only occasionally comes above the water, and then only with its tentacles.

Is your vessel

 Very fast or Fast – *158*

Moderate, slow or very slow – *1107*

425

You give it everything, but this man is heavy. He stumbles backwards but stops well short of Diggory's arms. He yells at you before stomping off back to his room at the start of the cells. Shortly after Captain Fareham arrives and his face looks like thunder. The Captain knows the value to him of your father's lands although they have been ransacked and he forces you to become part of his plan and you are married in private.

He now owns your father's lands and keeps you locked up for the next year. When you don't respond to his advances and wishes to be a passive wife, he has you taken away in the night and disposed of. Your last thoughts are that your family remains unavenged. Try again at *1* and remember enemies are everywhere, even those people who help.

<u>426</u>

"I have the great Timmers on board," you say and watch as the bald man's face turns sour.

"And what has he done? A stooge of the British." **Tick codeword Flop.** Unless you have something else you are going to have to pay or leave.

Do you

Decide you have an item you can offer to prove your worth – *229*

Offer doubloons – *1297*

Decide the price is too high and leave Hells Deep – **Consult the voyage chart and set sail**

<u>427</u>

You desperately breathe the clear air, but you still smell like you are smoking.

If you have ticked the codeword **Fire Chest**, you celebrate a job well done and now need to leave this place and search for more treasure or get back to your vessel. **Reduce your Island Time Chart by 5.** Go back down the path you entered this clearing by at *1193*

If you haven't found the treasure here, **reduce your Island Time chart by 5.**

You can re-enter but you will need to rest up and cool down before re-entering. If you choose to do so, **reduce your Island Time Chart by another 5** and then return to *127* and try again.

If you decide to leave, then simply go back down the path you entered this clearing by at *1193*

428

"No," you cry, "we shall not!"

Suddenly your vessel is raised up to a great height and then dropped back to the ocean. Martha is spun round by many spectres, white and wispy but all snatching at her with wispy claws. She cries out before being dumped on the ground.

And suddenly, everything is as it was, the sun shining, the steady wind in your sails, but Martha is a mass of cuts and blood.

"You crossed me girl," she spits. "I will remember that."

Tick the codeword Crossed. Your vessel is damaged with torn sails and structural cracks. Lower the vessel speed by 2 levels. Lower your crew morale by 1 level. Lower your vessel treasure store by 2 levels, removing any damaged cargo.

Now continue your voyage at *654*

429

Reduce your Island Time Chart by 1

You trek along the path, and note the greenery seems to swim, becoming a blur in your eyes. You try to remember if you came this way already. Soon you reach a fork in the path, and you wonder which way to go. You can take either fork, or you could always head out into the jungle off the path.

Do you go

Left – *1246*

Right – *1064*

Strike out into the Jungle – *1283*

Turn around back the way you came – *1079*

430

You emerge on deck to see a man and a woman of your crew holding hands and looking at you expectantly.

"Captain, I request that you do me the favour of marrying this delightful woman to me."

Do you

Agree -*494*

Tell them to get back to work – *1024*

431

You walk forward into the darkness and realise it is a true darkness. As you walk you feel a wind at your back pushing you forward and you start to stumble. You are pitching along and cannot stop yourself.

Do you have pole in front of you – *49*. If not, read on.

You stumble with an unrelenting wind behind you. Suddenly the ground beneath you vanishes, realised by you as your feet find nothing and you fall. It is only a few moments before the ground comes up and hits you hard.

Guess he wasn't born there then. Such a pity as you had got so far.

You can reset to the start of this puzzle at *1366* if you want or start all over again at *1*. That was a long haul, and you did so well, just not well enough.

432

You tell the crew it will be better if they stay on board while you scout ahead as you are unsure just how the land lies beneath the sea. With that you dive into the water for the cave.

Continue at *230*

433

Reduce your time by 2. If your time is in the following gaps (40-35 or 10-05) then go to *1322*. If not continue below

You wait in the shadows seeing no one move.

Do you

Wait in hiding – *678*

Check out the flagpole – *297*

Look at the wagon – *147*

Move to the North quarter – *1176*

Move to the South quarter – *519*

434

You cross the line of green blood, and you hear the maniacal laugh of the old hag again and you gulp. Was this a bad idea? Is a Kraken horn worth it?

You are about to enter a deadly game where you will be hunted by Tabetha while searching for the Kraken Horn. There are only two outcomes. You are caught by Tabetha (note this is not the preferred option!) or you find the Kraken Horn (better option!)

When you start, you will decide where you move, and you will need to explore and find the horn. However, Tabetha moves too, although you don't know where, but you may hear her. When Tabetha moves you will be asked to consult a table (in the back of the book). Tabetha has a number (starting with 1) which will change with each move you make. Each time you move to a new entry, you will be instructed when to move Tabetha. You then consult Tabetha's table and roll 1xD100 (2xD10) and look at the table to generate a new number for Tabetha. Note this number and continue with the entry.

Enter the deadly game now at *164*

435

You wander along the path which is long and canopy covered, shirt soaking wet from the humidity, until you reach a junction. Which way now?

Left – *328*

Right – *707*

Turn back – *1230*

436

"Well that's a change of plans. I'll escort you down, my lady."

You haven't much choice as the man begins to walk and you descend the stone steps together until you reach the courtyard. Across the dusty yard you see the large double gates. They are open and you see traders coming and going with a few guards watching them carefully. There is a relaxed air about the place, and you see baskets of fruit and vegetables, and some casks among the goods being exchanged.

"Well, they don't appear ready for you, my lady." Of course they are not, as you are here under false pretences. You need to think up something.

Do you

Run for the gates – *1101*

Ask the guard to see what's happening about your transport – *1133*

437

You run as hard as you can up the stairs towards your father's study where you saw him die, hungry for revenge on the evil Estes who killed your father. As you reach the hallway before the door, you see a Spanish soldier exit and turn and throw a blazing brand into the room. You can smell the smoke coming from the room already and you wonder if it will be safe inside. The soldier descends the other stairs appearing to flee the house.

Do you

Enter the room – *1095*

Decide you could burn alive in here and instead return to kitchen to escape, as the armoury is likely to be too risky with this fire – *898*

438

You see the darts fly out and fall to the floor scrabbling back the way you came. You stand up and see the darts now lying around but are unsure if the trap will fire again. Go to *843*

439

"I'm here on business of my Captain," you say and wait for the reply from the door man.

"Well, you see, Lord Buffington doesn't like a lack of respect. If I was you, I'd tell them I want to join the guild to get inside properly and then say you came from your Captain. Otherwise, I'd be risking my own neck letting you in."

You thank him for his advice and wonder what to do next. Do you

Tell him you wish to join the guild – **726**

Offer a bribe to gain access – **1310**

Or

Come back at night in an attempt to gain access when the building is closed – **742**

See to the needs of your vessel and crew – **903**

Try to earn some money by signing up to a cargo run – **1335**

Visit the taverns for information – **802**

If you have had enough of Malin's town, then **consult the voyage chart and set sail.**

440

"Look at you," says the man, "what does a mere slave like you want here? If you want work, we have enough of your type here at the moment. So, unless you have some other sort of business, then get out of here."

He looks quite threatening and you wonder if you should annoy him. Have you anything to sweeten the deal? Or do you simply ask for what you want?

Do you

Have the codeword **Bottle of Whiskey** and wish to use it – *1044*

Tell him his boss will see Mary Hastings – *1194*

Charge the man with a weapon – *1125*

Return to the street – *262*

441

Do you have both codewords **Green Plant** and **Spear** – *1327*

If not, do you have codewords

Small Crew – *642*

Large Crew – *1299*

If not – *1140*

442

Move Tabetha.

You are in a white walled room, bathed in the strange light, with three doors, one with a picture of a spider above it, one with a schooner above it, and the other with a shield above it.

If Tabetha's number is 16 – *1459*

If Tabetha's number is 18 – **note this number and go to *239***

If Tabetha's number is 21 – **note this number and go to *1287***

If Tabetha's number is 22 – **note this number and go to *446***

(if none of these apply turn over page)

Where do you go next?

Through the spider door – *1203*

Through the schooner door – *446*

Through the shield door – *502*

Wait here - **return to the top of this section**

<u>443</u>

Reduce the Hot Strip by 1. If this places you on a Fire spot add 20 to this section's number and go there for the walls have moved. There are walls of fire to the north and south. You can route east or to the west is clear air and your crewmates.

Do you

Go East– *1200*

Go West and step out– *427*

<u>444</u>

"Captain, my apologies for interrupting you," says the cabin boy, "but the duty watch keeper has found someone. A stowaway. But they have kept them out of the way of the rest of the crew, saying that you need to see this person."

You swing your legs out of bed and tell the cabin boy to wait outside while you quickly dress. He then leads you down into the hold and into a small cargo hold where you see a dark figure in the corner, guarded by one of your crew.

As you get close to the figure it begins to shriek and you see a pair of dark limbs and white eyes looking back at you. You try to communicate but the figure doesn't seem to know any English, or French, or even Portuguese.

"I suggest we throw this person overboard," says the guard, "the crew will think that they are a bad omen. Someone strange."

You don't know what to make of the person and you consider what to do with them.

Do you

Throw them overboard – *767*

Stow them away in the hold – *1431*

Give a small cabin on the vessel – *189*

445

Timmers looks quizzically at you. "During the day," he says, "we can happily go in for provisions, even ashore, such is my standing. I'm not sure why you want to go in at night, as if caught it'll ruin my standing but if that's what you want, we can do that as well." He looks uncomfortable with the night-time shenanigans but awaits your orders.

So, what are you looking to do?

Arrive during the day for provisions – *665* **and tick codeword Decent Chap**

Sneak in during the night – *307*

446

You can hear scratching noises through the schooner door. Sounds like Tabetha is through that door. You decide to risk that door would be foolish. Return to your noted section and decide which door to go through or to stay put **but you cannot choose the schooner door.**

447

You take the item from your bag and hand it over and the guard takes it from you but continues to block your path. "Street, please," he says. **Untick the item on the codeword list.** You seem to have little choice. Or do you?

Do you

Make a scene, calling him a pig – *516*

Return to the street as suggested – *1009*

448

Go to *238*

449

With a prayer, you fire the canons and see the smoke floating across the air. Have you hit the creature, for it was closer this time. There's a thrashing in the water and the creature seems to dive. Your crew stares at the water and you wait to hear another spotting but there's nothing. You cautiously get the crew to resume your voyage, but you keep a sharp lookout. After an hour you believe it is gone and you continue your voyage.

Your crew are relieved. Raise your crew morale by 2 levels. But you have taken damage. Reduce your vessel speed by 1 level, and your vessel manoeuvrability by 1 level. Also reduce your crew by 1 level. Adjust your voyage time as necessary.

Now continue your voyage at *654*

450

You left items at the foot of the pole, and you realise that one of the patrol is waiting there. You can't leave that way. You try to leave the room, but every other door is locked. Soon, some patrol members open the door, and you are grabbed and searched. **If you have the following codewords untick them: Argyle, Sextant. If you have an Empty Chart, they don't remove it from you as it looks like an ordinary chart.**

You are taken off to the local cells for 5 days before being released to your vessel. Cross off 5 days from your time chart and then immediately leave Malin's Town. You may not return here for 30 days.

Consult the voyage chart and set sail for another destination.

451

You wander down the steps and find a musty air below the surface. You appear to be inside great stone hallways which beam with an ethereal light, green lighting your way even though you know not where it has come from. As you walk on, you see a ghostly figure appearing before you and you find yourself routed to the spot. It is a fair maiden, dressed in the lightest of fabrics and you watch as she floats towards you.

"Welcome, my sweet," she says in the voice of an angel. "You have entered the lair of Tabetha, the mother of all arachnids, the weaver of the web of destruction and the devourer of all those who disturb her sleep. Many years ago, she was blinded by Captain Estes, sailing his first vessel, Margarite, when he tried to steal her tapestry of silk which depicts the end of the world. No human hand may hold it, but he dropped his Kraken horn as she fought with him. It lies within undisturbed."

"What's a Kraken horn?" you ask.

"When the beast rises, you cannot stop it, but with this horn you can send it back to the deep. Tabetha keeps it as payment for losing her eyesight to the dreaded Captain, but you may come for it."

The figure turns away for a moment, and when it turns back you see the most frightful face of a hag you have ever seen looking back at you.

"If you come for it, she comes for you!" The hag now wails with laughter and produces a knife from thin air which she cuts her wrist with. Her blood drips green and she lets it fall in a line across the hallway.

"Enter now and the game begins. Can you escape except with your life. Where she roams is up to her, but you won't hear her come, you'll simply die, wrapped up in her latest web."

The hag vanishes but the line of blood remains. Behind you are the steps back up to the light and the dense jungle beyond. Ahead, who knows what, but also a kraken horn, left by Estes. Is it worth it?

Do you

Retreat to the surface – *862*

Cross the line of green blood – *434*

452

You sail into a small opening that has three exits from it. The rocks are spaced here, and you can turn easily. There are exits from the channel to the northeast, northwest, and east-northeast. All are wide channels so where next?

Do you

Sail northeast– *126*

Route northwest – *1338*

Go east-northeast – *1118*

453

The pirate king leans forward and smiles weakly. "Estes buried his treasure on Hangman's Island but it's hard to get to. Once there he spread out the treasure, and there are five tests to recover it. I know how to complete one of them." He details out how to complete the Waters of Myra. **Tick the codeword Myra.**

With a wave of his hand, he dismisses you and you are ushered from his presence and back to your vessel. Who knows how much use that was? The pirate who mans the door to the pirate king's abode advises that you will not be welcome again on this visit. **You may not visit the pirate king again until you return to Hell's Deep on another visit. Go to *1436***

454

You send for your offering, and it is brought before Tom who touches it carefully, examining it. He smiles and a child takes your offering away.

"Only in retreat will you clear the field."

You wonder what Tom is on about, but you make sure to note what he says. **Tick the codeword Charge**.

What now?

Do you want to offer another gift - *1416*

Or do you take your leave of Tom and

Visit the provisions isle – *334*

Enjoy yourself at the wild isle – *879*

Explore the dark isle – *397*

Approach the pirate king – *1348*

Decide you have had enough of Hells Deep and set sail - **Consult the voyage chart and set sail**

455

Reduce your time by 1.

If your time is in the following gaps (52-48), you see a guard on his patrol and must remain hidden until he clears the area. Reduce your time by 6. Now continue at the plain text below

If your time is in the following gaps (22-18), you see a guard on the enclosing wall patrolling and must remain hidden until he clears the area. Reduce your time by 6.

If neither of these apply, continue at the plain text below

You hide and see no one approaching. All is quiet and you are in cover.

Do you

Hide where you are – *174*

Route South-west – *1435*

Creep West – *103*

Sneak North-west – *42*

Try to enter the hut – *337*

456

The only wall of fire is to the south. You can route east, west or north from your current location.

Do you

Go West – *1217*

Go East – *168*

Go North – *1403*

457

"Yes, I see your point," you say to the second officer getting close to him. "But we must all make sacrifices."

With that you stab him with a small dagger you have hidden in the palm of your hand. He collapses on the deck, and you slit his throat to make sure he's dead.

"Get that filth off my vessel," you cry and glare at the crew.

Is your first officer Timmers, or Robert Grimshaw – *1341*

If not, read on

Your first officer commends your action but tells you it will upset the crew and not to do it too often. You can tell over the coming days as although they obey your commands quickly, they seem to watch you closely. **Reduce your crew morale by 2 levels.** Now continue at *654*

458

Reduce your time by 1. Stepping forward you run into a wooden wall. On your left you can feel some crates and on your right is clear water.

Do you

About turn and step forward – *986*

Turn right and walk forward – *562*

Examine the crates – *605*

459

Reduce the Hot Strip by 2. If this places you on a Fire spot add 20 to this section's number and go there for the walls have moved. There are walls of fire to the north, west, and east, so you route south from your current location. Go to *310*

460

You approach the man, and he glares out from under his hat.

"Look, lady, your husband isn't here. Neither is your father, or any other man you're looking for. You're in luck because I'm a gentleman but anyone else in here I can't vouch for, so do the smart thing and go back to the main street and the shops. Classy woman like you shouldn't be here."

Do you

Heed his advice and return to the street – *496*

Tell him you are looking to hire a crew – *871*

Tell him you are looking for work – *232*

461

You hear a sound just outside the room and race back to your seat. Go to *604*

462

You spin round with your glass and think about the vessel behind you. It's been tailing you but maybe you can put it to go use. Surely, the Kraken will not mind which vessel it goes for. The other vessel is fast but maybe if you can cause a mass of noise around it, you could make the Kraken go there instead. It's either that or another option at *368*. If you choose to continue with this plan read on. Otherwise return to *368* (If you have a vessel firepower of **None,** you cannot use this option, so return to *368*.)

You turn the vessel to give a good broadside in the direction of the tailing vessel and advise your cannoneers to get as much length on their shots as possible. Every cannon fires, and a barrage of cannonballs emerge from a billowing of smoke and noise to race off in the direction of the tailing ship. But will it work?

The Treasure of Captain Estes

Roll 1D100 (2xD10). Check the result against the chart below.

Your vessels Firepower	Result	Section to go to
Very Heavy	50-99	*943*
Very Heavy	20-49	*296*
Very Heavy	00-19	*1285*
Heavy	75-99	*296*
Heavy	00-74	*1285*
Moderate	85-99	*296*
Moderate	50-84	*1285*
Moderate	00-49	*917*
Light	90-99	*1285*
Light	00-89	*917*

<u>463</u>

You sit back in the coach and await your arrival at Madame Le Vert's shop. As the carriage pulls up a tall, elegant woman in her late fifties approaches you and gives an over-the-top welcome. As you take her hand in helping you down from the carriage, you note that the guards are simply waiting on their horses. Of course, it would be indiscreet for them to watch you being fitted.

On entering the shop, you note the large collection of dresses and gowns on one side of the shop, but on the other, there are long-coats and breeches, boots and hats, everything a working man in this town could want.

Madame Le Vert begins to show you her latest collection and you try to feign interest in them as you ponder on your escape from the guards outside. Madame Le Vert asks if you wish to try any of the dresses on and you absentmindedly pick one and take it through to the small room at the rear of the shop.

Once the door is closed, you scan the tiny dressing room and see a window up high. It is shuttered and certainly not wide in aperture, but you believe you could squeeze through. There are also a small number of wine bottles on the floor in the corner along with some boxes. Plans form in your mind.

Do you

Use the boxes to climb up to the window and try to squeeze through – *731*

Take a wine bottle and then sneak up on Madame Le Vert in an attempt to incapacitate her with it – *1013*

Lie on the floor with the wine bottles, empty them and pretend to be drunk, so you can then lure Madame Le Vert inside to incapacitate her – *796*

464

You cannot stop yourself but you manage to take the pole and swing it sideways, jamming it into the rock. The wind howls and you stay flat as you crawl your way back to the entrance. The wind does not abate until you are back at the junction. You breathe a sigh of relief, but you are faced with the same choice minus your pole.

Remove the circle around your chosen pole and untick the codeword. You may choose another pole to use if you have one. If so, circle that codeword and continue.

What will you do now?

Walk and enter

Yellow – *1333*

Grandeur – *522*

Margarite – *1391*

Or crawl and enter

Yellow – *342*

Grandeur – *815*

Margarite – *1254*

Or do you beat a hasty retreat – *34*

465

The man stands up and you realise you've said the wrong thing.

"We don't want no trouble, if you understand me, so clear off back to the street and we'll forget about it. You understand me stranger?"

Do you

Insist on entering – *1415*

Take his advice and return to the main street – *496*

466

You narrowly avoid disaster and are clear and running in the middle of the gap. Just what happened is hard to tell but an animal passed by close.

If you haven't already, start a timer at 0 in your notes. Now add 1xD10 to it. If the timer is over 30 go to *1378*. If not, continue below.

Roll 1xD100 (2xD10) and check the result below.

00-19 – *98*

20-39 – *1323*

40-59 – *139*

60-79 – *123*

80-99 – *551*

467

"I need a vessel and crew," you say confidently.

"You'll need to wait inside," says the pirate, "but you'd better need it for good reason."

You wonder what that statement is about, but you walk on in as the door is opened for you. Continue at *684*

468

Tick the codeword North Beach. Your crew takes your vessel round to the north of the island and you see a small beach where the small boat can reach shore. You strike out in your little boat and arrive through the surf without incident, landing on the sand. Ahead of you are three paths into the jungle like vegetation and you realise that to travel outwith these routes is impossible due to the density of the plant life. You'll need to follow one of the paths or turn around. But which one?

Which path do you follow

Left hand path – *1275*

Middle path – *137*

Right hand path – *844*

Or you can get back in you small boat and return to your crew and choose another option at *1386*

469

The brass sextant is of excellent quality and has the legend Lord Buffington inscribed on the side. If you take it, tick the codeword **Sextant.**

Go to *1400*

470

Do you have the codeword **Rock – *1070***. If not, read on.

You enter a room with a curtain of water in the middle of the room. You cannot understand how it can be there, but it is. As you watch it, the water changes from blue to green and then to a silver over a period of time. Above you is a rope going up, and below is another rope going down.

Do you

Enter the water – *1168*

Climb up the rope – *756*

Climb down the other rope – *843*

471

The pirate stares at you, wondering what you are doing here. He glowers at his friend who shakes his head.

"Lady, it is only because you are a lady that I am not throwing you out into the street. Now please leave for you have no business here."

Do you

Tell him you want a vessel – *1225*

Ask for Duncan Mackenzie (only if you have codeword **Letter Duncan Mackenzie**) – *720*

Offer the pirate a bribe – *1314*

472

You tell the man to stop being so harsh to the girl and suddenly you have a crowd watching. He looks a little shaken and slowly backs down before you can help the slave girl back to her feet. As you do so she smiles before going back behind her stall.

If you have the codeword **Prominent** – *868*

Otherwise

As you go to leave the girl sneaks a bottle of whiskey into your hand. You look at it and see the label, Mackenzie whiskey. (Tick the codeword **Bottle Mackenzie Whiskey**) As you go to put it away a man taps you on the shoulder.

"Can I see that whiskey?"

Do you tell him politely, no – *58*

Engage the man in conversation – *512*

Leave the bottle and steal away to the street – *817*

<u>473</u>

You sail into the middle of the islands where you moor your vessel alongside a few others. The bald man bows to take his leave of you but then points out the five islands that surround you.

"If you require provisions then please head to the provision isle where you can fill your ship and see to repairs. For words with the king simply go to his throne isle but do not go there lightly. For a good time go to the wild isle. The dark isle is available for worship. And beside us is the barge of Blind Tom who may not see anything, but he knows all. Enjoy our kingdom."

You watch him leave and then think about what you need here. Do you

Go to see Blind Tom – *681*

Visit the provisions isle – *334*

Enjoy yourself at the wild isle – *879*

Explore the dark isle – *397*

Approach the pirate king – *1348*

Decide you have had enough of Hells Deep and set sail - **Consult the voyage chart and set sail**

474

You see a guard atop the wall and take cover waiting until they have continued further along to the east. **Reduce your time by 6. Go to *1197***

475

Do you have the codeword **Ellie** – *162*

If not go to *1311*

476

Reduce your time by 1.

If your time is in the following gaps (52-48) you see a guard on his patrol outside and must remain hidden until he clears the area. Reduce your time by 6. Now continue at the plain text below

There's plenty of scribbling but most of the writing is unintelligible. One scrap of paper says that the noiseless horn is in the 2nd drawer for collection. It is signed by a Captain Drummond, naval Intelligence. Otherwise, there's nothing else of note.

Do you

Examine the key – *478*

Or replace everything and instead

Check the rug that's slightly lifted – *565*

Look at the other rug – *1356*

Try to open the safe – *1288*

Decide this is a bad idea and return outside – *174*

<u>477</u>

You walk the muddy path with dense vegetation on either side until you reach a tiny beach. If you have the codeword **Middle**, you see your vessel just off the island and your small boat on the beach. If not, there's no small boat, and this really is a path to nowhere and you'll need to retrace your steps.

Do you

Walk the muddy path back towards the mountain – *601*

If you have the codeword **Middle,** take your small boat to your vessel – *1386*

<u>478</u>

Reduce your time by 1.

If your time is in the following gaps (52-48) you see a guard on his patrol outside and must remain hidden until he clears the area. Reduce your time by 6. Now continue at the plain text below

The key is made of brass and is very simple. It might be for a safe or a door but you cannot be sure. **If you take the brass key, tick the codeword Brass Key (see what I did there!).** If you haven't already you can

Look at the parchment – *476*

Or you can instead replace everything and

Check the rug that's slightly lifted – *565*

Look at the other rug – *1356*

Try to open the safe – *1288*

Decide this is a bad idea and return outside – *174*

The Treasure of Captain Estes

<u>479</u>

You stand in a dark room with a door behind you and two ropes, one descending and one ascending. In the room is a shrine with a picture of Captain Estes hanging over a chest in one corner. The candles of the shrine are lit and are burning with an eerie green glow. You can see nothing else in the room.

Do you

Climb up the rope – **470**

Descend a rope – **843**

Examine the shrine further – **108**

Leave by the door – **920**

<u>480</u>

You are standing on the edge of the jungle before the waters, and it is a sheer drop into the water. You believe if you can get back to the edge your friends can pull you out, but there will be no relief around the edges of the waters otherwise. Once in, you are in until you reach the rock, or your friends can pull you out.

In your mind you break the pool up into sections, five across and six deep. The rock you need to get to is four sections away in the middle of the pool. Otherwise, it's all just churning water.

Use *the Waters of Myra map at App 16* to assist with your view of the waters. All positions and directions of current will be referenced to the nominal north on the grid. You will need to watch your strength as you negotiate the waters. To do this use the Waters Strength chart which starts at 10 and goes down to zero. Do not let it reach zero! You will be out of strength and at the mercy of the waters. You realise that to go with the current will probably take 1 of your strength to move a square. To swim against the current may take a lot more (Hint, opposite the current will take more than perpendicular to the current).

Get ready to jump in! You walk along the edge and wonder what is the best place to enter the waters but in truth you cannot tell what currents lie below. So, you may as well choose at random where to enter.

One last point. If you have any of the codewords **Green Pole, Red Pole,** or **Blue Pole**, you may select one of these poles, and one only, to enter the water with. Ring the codeword to indicate you have made this choice.

Do you enter at the

Most western point – *1201*

Second most western point – *43*

Mid-point of the edge – *1372*

Second most eastern point – *489*

Most Eastern point – *948*

481

You tell the man all about the attack on your home and of your desire for revenge which he listens to intently and you realise he's not just a gawking fool.

"Terrible business, just terrible, Miss Hastings. And I get it, I do but we have to make a profit here. You do understand. Do you have some way of funding this, expedition, shall we say?"

Do you

Have a **Promissory Note** to give the man – *205*

Have a **Bottle of Mackenzie Whiskey** – *369*

Threaten him with a **Pistol** – *762*

Say you have nothing to give – *293*

482

You yell at the crew to go down to the hold and throw some provisions overboard. As you drift away from the floating provisions, a crewman asks if they have thrown enough overboard. You tell them yes and watch as the Kraken begins to feed on what you have thrown into the sea. But it doesn't feed for long.

A tentacle sweeps across the deck, throwing many overboard. Another one rips your mainsail and then pulls down the mast. Then, with amazing speed tentacles rise on all sides of the deck until the creature drags the vessel straight down, drowning everyone on board.

The waters around New Southampton are deadly, and you have succumbed. You may try again at *1*

483

If you have the codeword **Closed** – *23.* If not, read on

You reach the end of the path and find a temple before. It is open with many columns and seems to be declining somewhat. You can see another path into the jungle on the other side. What do you do?

Explore the temple – *805*

Skirt round the temple and walk along the other path – *1329*

Retreat along the path you came on – *202*

484

Roll 1D100 (2xD10) to find where the coin actually is. Did you roll?

00-33 – *850*

34-67 – *573*

68-99 – *46*

485

Reduce the Hot Strip by 1. If this places you on a Fire spot add 20 to this section's number and go there for the walls have moved. There are walls of fire to the south and east. You can route north or west from your current location.

Do you

Go West – *167*

Go North – *969*

486

Reduce your time by 1.

If your time is in the following gaps (52-48) you see a guard on his patrol outside and must remain hidden until he clears the area. Reduce your time by 6. Now continue at the plain text below

You place the key in the lock, and although it fits, it doesn't turn.

Return to *1288* and make another choice.

487

You decide to take the bottle of whiskey you have to the traders and see if you can get a price for it. As you start to show it, many shake their head but then a man approaches from one of the stalls.

"Now that is a special bottle of Mackenzie whiskey which only I sell around here and it only goes to Hastings the plantation owner. Terrible business, but I think you saw that first hand. It's Mary, isn't it?"

He looks tall and strong and has a scarred, if kind, face. His hand touches your shoulder, and you wonder if he can be trusted.

Do you reply

No – *589*

Yes - *36*

The Treasure of Captain Estes

<u>488</u>

You grab several cups, prized by your mother, and throw them at the soldiers. They turn and draw their swords, angry but not affected greatly by your efforts. That didn't work and your path to the door is now blocked by sword wielding soldiers. You'll not be able to grab any of the other possible weapons and your choices seem limited as your heart pounds realising you could be facing a quick death.

Do you

Run for the door anyway, hoping to slip past the Spanish soldiers – *330*

Turn and flee up the stairs despite the footsteps coming from that direction – *115*

<u>489</u>

Reduce your Waters Strength Chart by 1. Ignore this if you have just jumped in. The current is forcibly pushing you back to the edge. However you think you can reach an eddy that seems to allow a way north but to get there will be incredibly hard work. Do you

Swim North – *1149*

Yell at your friends to pull you out – *1056*

<u>490</u>

"Looks like Jameson's Brigantine, a privateer. Sharp enough man, but workable with. We may be able to trade, or we can fight?"

Do you

Order your crew to sail towards the pirate ship, preparing to attack – *586*

Decide to keep your distance and stay away – *165*

Approach the vessel looking to trade – *1005*

491

Move Tabetha.

You are in a white walled room, bathed in the strange light, with a door with a picture of a schooner above it.

If Tabetha's number is 1 – *1459*

If Tabetha's number is 19 – **note this number and go to *446***

If not,

Where do you go next?

Through the schooner door – *1213*

Wait here – return to the top of this section

492

You grit your teeth and decide to turn and face the creature. But you see such a horror before you as her hair has turned to snakes and they race at you. She laughs as they strike and you crumple to your knees. You don't know what darkness this is, but you rue the day you found it. As your mind goes black, you pray for a way out, but none comes.

You have died in one of the darkest places in this ocean. Sometimes you must simply flee from evil. Your tale has ended but you can try again at *1*.

493

Reduce your time by 2. If your time is in the following gaps (52-47 or 22-17) then go to *1377*. If not continue below

You are standing amidst supplies and rations in the west quarter, with boxes stored up high. You can see barrels of biscuits and stacks of fruit. There are some scrolls in leather sitting on top a barrel and other papers at the rear of a small hut.

In the north quarter, you can see horses and livestock at rest in pens. To the south, you can see servant slums and latrines.

Do you

Wait in hiding – *926*

If you haven't already

Look at the scrolls on top the barrel – *1332*

Investigate the papers in the hut – *77*

Move to the north quarter – *1176*

Move to the south quarter – *519*

<u>494</u>

You say you would be delighted to the excited cries of the crew. In a quickly arranged ceremony, you give the woman to her man in marriage. As the ceremony ends a crewman shouts out that they should all celebrate, and then turns to you.

"What do you think, Captain, a celebration?"

Do you

Agree – *29*

Tell them there's no time – *1294*

<u>495</u>

You find the pull of the main current tough to overcome to get to the eddy, but you do it eventually. **Reduce your Waters Strength Chart by 1.** You swim through to the eddy. Go to *1108*

496

You are in the main street with a dark alley on one side which looks foreboding, and the market on the other side. The market has stalls of fish, meat, and vegetables as well as material and other wooden items. The day is hot, and the market is busy with bustling crowds.

Further into town will be the courthouse and Madame Le Vert's store. Alternatively, the road out from New Southampton is available leading to Strangar but it's a long walk.

Do you

Go to the market – *1152*

Enter the dark alley – *160*

Walk further into New Southampton – *1166*

Leave the town and make the journey to Strangar – *671*

497

The crew are happy with their share of the cargo. You have enough left to buy a small dwelling and some land where you can start again. You can work the land and have a reasonably comfortable life. Your escapades have taught you how to look after yourself and you live in relative peace. Eventually, a decent man comes your way, and you settle down together. Your children are born, and you view the future with optimism as you tell them the tales of the their grandparents.

Your lands may yet be recovered, your name avenged, but it will be achieved by your children. For you, life is a happy domesticated family home. Your adventuring days are done but at least you have a happy ending.

498

You approach the stranger whose face remains in shadow. But what are you wearing?

Are you

Still in your dress to go shopping – *952*

Dressed like a slave in your torn gown – *1319*

Wearing a long-coat and breeches – *331*

499

You sail for Hangman's Island and arrive at the latitude and longitude your compass, or bearings, led you to on the chart. Although there's nothing on the chart in that location except endless sea, you find your vessel quickly surrounded by fog that is so thick you have no idea of your direction except for your compass. You keep the vessel on the course to steer so that you arrive at the exact point on the chart and bring your vessel to as much of a halt as you can.

Sitting in the fog, you hear the muttering of your crew, wondering what foul environment you have taken them into. There's no wind in your sails but you feel as if the vessel is moving quickly, and you start to hear birds and the crash of the sea on rocks. Your vessel slows and then the fog drifts away. A vista of a small island is revealed with foreboding rocks around it, along with choppy waters. The waters seem unnaturally stirred for the wind is calm.

You send out a scout team in the small boat and await their return. The island seems to be heavily vegetated, but you cannot see an easy route onto the island due to the vicious rocks surrounding it. You believe there is a plain of some sort and you think you can see animals there. There is also a high peak as well as some sheer cliffs.

The small boat party return excitedly telling you about a small beach landing on the other side of the island. You tell the helm to make for it, but he says he cannot. There is no wind in the sails, but the helm says it is more than that. He takes you to the edge of your vessel and points down at the sea. It is pushing your boat hard on that side. He next asks you to look over the other side and you see the vessel is being pushed in again by the sea, effectively holding it in position.

There is some sort of witchcraft happening here, or a strange phenomenon, but either way you will need to free the vessel. You see no option other than exploring the island and seeing if you can find a way out of the vessel's predicament as well as Estes' treasure.

You take a few crew in the vessel's small boat and are rowed round to the other side of the island. Sure enough, there is a tiny beach where you ground the small boat and jump off into the sand. You see a small hut a hundred yards from where you have beached and wonder what is in there. There is one path off the beach into what looks like jungle. In the sand are three wooden poles.

Do you

Strike out for the path – *1039*

Investigate the hut – *1395*

Look at the poles – *703*

500

Hiding behind a rock you can see a sentry walking out from a gate from where he walks along the beach for a few minutes and then returns. The gate remains open this whole time and you think this might be a way into the fort. You can wait for the sentry to repeat the action, or you could try and climb the walls, though there are sentries up there too.

Do you

Run and climb the wall – *1144*

Wait for the sentry and then enter via the gate when they come back out- *1317*

<u>501</u>

If you have the Codeword **Ratcatcher** ticked – *1404*

If not, continue below

You come up on deck to see the crew running around after rats. They are spearing them and hitting them with whatever they can but there seems to be so many.

"Captain, they are everywhere! We cannot live with this."

Do you

Order everyone to do a concentrated effort to get them off the vessel – *71*

Tell the crew to get on with it as there's no time to stop and sort the problem out – *326*

<u>502</u>

Move Tabetha.

You are in a white walled room, bathed in the strange light, with two doors, one with a picture of a spider above it, and the other with a schooner above it.

If Tabetha's number is 18 – *1459*

If Tabetha's number is 5 – **note this number and go to *1287***

If Tabetha's number is 16 – **note this number and go to *446***

Where do you go next?

Through the spider door – *1052*

Through the schooner door – *442*

Wait here - **return to the top of this section**

<u>503</u>

There's plenty of scribbling but most of the writing is unintelligible. One scrap of paper says that the noiseless horn is in the 2nd drawer for collection. It is signed by a Captain Drummond, naval Intelligence. Otherwise, there's nothing else of note.

Do you

Examine the key – *863*

Or replace everything and instead

Check the rug that's slightly lifted – *169*

Look at the other rug – *366*

Try to open the safe – *1289*

Decide this is a bad idea and return to Timmers, saying you should get back to the ship pronto – *351*

<u>504</u>

The man grimaces as you approach and blocks your path. "You need some sort of payment to get in here, sailor," he says, and places his hand on his sword. You look beyond wondering if there's a crew behind those doors. One thing is certain you won't find out unless you can get past this brute.

Do you

Try to run past him – *973*

Have the codeword **Pistol** and wish to use it – *261*

Have the codeword **Bottle of Whiskey** and wish to offer it – *357*

Return to the street – *262*

505

"Get up," you cry at your crewman, "and blast that sloop to Kingdom Come!"

You see your crew rise to go below deck but before they reach the hold ladders, spectres sweep over from the sloop, terrible and white with maniacal laughter. The scrambling crew are scooped up and taken to the sloop in obvious pain. The rest of the crew drop to the deck and refuse to move, faces pinned to the wooden boards.

"You dare to attack the Devil's Sloop," says an unseen voice. "And no tribute being offered. Then I will take tribute."

You stare in horror as various spectres fly from the sloop onto your vessel and start grabbing your crew. Your crewmates scream as you see the spectres cut at them with ghostly knives which still seem to damage flesh. You don't see if they are still alive as your crewmates are taken back to the sloop, but you hear the sounds of devouring and of crew screaming wildly.

"Next time, tribute!" The spectre flies back to the sloop and the wind becomes steady, filling the sails in a gentle fashion, while the sun returns to the sky.

You look around you at white faces, shocked and confused, eyes wide in terror. A head count tells you how many crew you have lost. **Reduce your crew by 2 levels if you can and crew morale by 3 levels.** The crew are keen to get underway and return to your voyage as quick as you can, wondering what you have just seen.

Now continue your voyage at **654**

506

Your crew gets excited as you order your vessel to engage the galleon before you. As you draw closer to the galleon, you see so many cannons aimed at you, that you realise you will have to outmanoeuvre it consistently or you will perish. Or at least you'll end up in a destructive tete-a-tete.

Is your vessel manoeuvrability

Great or Good – *774*

Reasonable – *1318*

Poor or Lacking -*587*

507

You cry to the crew to let the vessel run as fast as she can as you race for the Schooner. But you are up against a trained crew who use the weather and the sea magnificently. After a day they are gone from sight. You return to your voyage but must **add 2 days extra to it** for this diversion.

Continue the voyage at *654*

508

You reach for the gold. As you do so, the chest falls away as does a section of the wall. They swing back and down creating an opening to the outside of the rock formation. The floor you stand on tilts up, forcing you to fall forward and out of the rock formation and down to the water below.

You are knocked unconscious on impact and the next thing you know you are on your vessel, attended to by your first officer. You've lost two days from the fall, but will you go back to the formation as you are still moored beside it? **Add 2 days to the voyage chart.**

Do you

Return to the rock formation – *1439*

Decide this is a bad idea and leave the Bird's Paradise – **consult your voyage chart**

<u>509</u>

Reduce your Island Time Chart by 1

You trek along the path, head hung low in the heat. This path seems to never end. Suddenly there's a fork in the path, and you wonder which way to go. You can take either fork, or you could always head out into the jungle off the path.

Do you go

Left – *984*

Right – *830*

Strike out into the Jungle – *1283*

Turn around back the way you came – *550*

<u>510</u>

As you exit the room you almost bump into a face you know. Captain Fareham is an officer at the garrison and has been at your mansion many times. In his late thirties, you know he has had eyes on you as a potential wife and could be a route to safety.

"Mary, thank God you are alive. I saw your father and thought they had got to you as well. Come now, quickly and I'll get you to the garrison. You'll be safe with me."

Captain Fareham is probably correct, you will be safe with him in the protection of the garrison. From there you could plan your next steps. But he is a powerful figure and may seek to simply take whatever's left of your father's lands for himself by taking you for his wife. You know you'll get little say in the matter now your father is gone. It's a risk but one that may pay off in the short term.

Do you

Accept the Captain's offer – *1031*

Run away from him down the stairs to the kitchen (the armoury would be too dangerous in the fire) – *898*

511

Is your vessel's manoeuvrability

Poor or Lacking – *277*

Reasonable, Good or Great – *134*

512

"That's a Mackenzie," says the man. "There's only me who deals that whiskey over here and there's only one man of note who drinks it. You're not Hasting's girl are you?"

Do you

Say no and leave the man – *589*

Tell him you are – *36*

513

Go to *141*

514

You flip open the trapdoor and two hands suddenly grab you and haul you up in front of a group of soldiers. You are in a room of bunks and sleeping accommodation but not for long. A soldier immediately arrests you, taking you to the Fort's commander. Timmers is brought in too and speaks eloquently about a mere misunderstanding, but the Commander is not happy. Thanks to Timmers you can walk away from the fort, **but half of your treasure and your provisions have been removed from your vessel. Delete these now. If you have no treasure, remove three quarters of your provisions. The brass key if you have it is removed from you. Untick the codeword brass key.**

Timmers is angry with you as his reputation at the fort is ruined and your crew are annoyed at the loss of treasure and provisions. **Lower your crew morale by 1 level. Tick the codeword Caught.**

You are told to leave the fort immediately and you set sail. But where are you going?

Do you

Wish to sneak into the fort at night – *307*

Sail elsewhere - **consult the voyage chart and set sail.**

515

Reduce the Hot Strip by 1. If this places you on a Fire spot add 20 to this section's number and go there for the walls have moved. You can see fire to the north and to the west.

Do you

Go South – *286*

Go East – *1444*

516

"You pig, how dare you obstruct me, kindly get out of my way and stop manhandling me."

The man does not move and merely points to the street. If you have the codeword **Prominent**, go to *976*

Otherwise, it seems you have little choice but to follow his advice. Pulling a weapon at the weaponsmith's may leave you outgunned. **Tick the codeword Prominent** and go to the street at *1009*

517

Reduce your time by 1. You step forward and feel clear water ahead. On your left you touch a wooden wall while there is fallen wood blocking the way to your right.

Do you

About turn and step forward – *276*

Walk forward – *1162*

518

Because you have spent time looking at the parchment map and then the other papers you have already used some of your time until daylight is gone. Therefore, ignore the instruction to start your island time chart in section *1039* at 100 and instead **start at number 95**. Also note that daylight will run out at number **05,** not **00** as advised in the instructions. After all, Estes realised that the day was shorter here, didn't he?

Return to *1039* and continue with the instructions to set up your island time chart noting this change you have been instructed with.

519

Reduce your time by 2. If your time is in the following gaps (55-53, 35-33, 24-23 or 04-02) then go to *810*. If not continue below

You are in the south quarter with the slum shacks for the labourers and with the latrines at the walls. All is quiet and you can sneak around if you wish. You could examine the latrines or maybe infiltrate the slums. There is also a gate at the foot of the outer wall.

Do you

Wait in hiding – *133*

If you haven't already

Investigate a slum – *847*

Take a look at the latrines – *386*

Move to the west quarter – *493*

Move to the east quarter – *678*

Leave the fort for your vessel – *535*

520

Reduce the Hot Strip by 1. If this places you on a Fire spot add 20 to this section's number and go there for the walls have moved. There are walls of fire to the north and east. You can route south or west from your current location.

Do you

Go West – *744*

Go South – *757*

521

You yell at the crew to go down to the hold and throw some provisions overboard. As you drift away from the floating provisions, a crewman asks if they have thrown enough overboard. You tell them, no, to throw some more over but not too much as you need to also eat. The Kraken feeds on the provisions but its attention is not kept for long and as you try to sail away, a tentacle comes out and rips a hole in the side of your vessel followed by another one cracking against the hull. You see part of your aft deck smashed as a tentacle comes down.

And then nothing. As your vessel pulls away from the black murky mass under the water, you see the creature feasting on what would have been sustaining your crew.

With a sigh of relief, you steer well clear of where the Kraken was spotted but resume course later that night.

Your crew are delighted at surviving. Raise crew morale by 1 level. However, the vessel is badly damaged. Reduce your vessel speed by 2 levels. Lower your vessel manoeuvrability by 1 level. Remove 10 provisions from your hold (or all your provisions if you have less than 10). The hold areas containing those provisions are now unusable until you can effect repairs. Reduce your vessels Storm Handling by 1 level. Add 1 day to your voyage time for your diversion.

Now continue your voyage at *654*

522

Go to *1333*

523

The galleon comes alongside you and the first officer of the warship examines your vessel with his large crew. You are powerless to stop him. Then he looks at your first officer with an outraged eye.

"It's you. Pirate scum, murderer of men, women, and children. Run them all through, all of them."

Before you can respond, you are run through with a sword and your body is thrown overboard to a watery grave. You don't know what becomes of the crew, and your family is never avenged in any respect. Your tale ends here, like many a vicious pirate. Try again at *1*, and maybe pick a more pleasant first officer.

524

Roll 1D100 (2xD10) to find where the coin actually is. Did you roll?

00-33 – *777*

34-67 – *573*

68-99 – *46*

525

You sail into a small opening that has three exits from it. The rocks are spaced here, and you can turn easily. There are exits from the channel to the west, southwest, and south. All are wide channels so where next?

Do you

Sail west– *698*

Route southeast – *1380*

Go north – *938*

526

You wander along the path and reach a junction with three paths off it. Which way now?

Left – *73*

Middle – *5*

Right – *1050*

Turn back – *26*

527

Go to *632*

528

The pirate king leans forward and smiles weakly. "Estes buried his treasure on Hangman's Island but it's hard to get to. You need the Devil's Compass to find the place. I think they might have one on the dark isle." He laughs maniacally.

With a wave of his hand, he dismisses you and you are ushered from his presence and back to your vessel. Who knows how much use that was? The pirate who mans the door to the pirate king's abode advises that you will not be welcome again on this visit. **You may not visit the pirate king again until you return to Hell's Deep on another visit. Go to *1436***

529

Your cargo hold has little treasure in it. After all this journey there is a pittance to show for your efforts. You give the command to sail for New Southampton, but your crew does not heed you. Instead, they grab you and place you in the small boat abandoning you on the sea.

You meet another vessel coming the other way. It is a pirate vessel, but the captain takes a liking to you. However, you are forced to pledge allegiance to him, and cook, clean and care for him in every way. This takes a toll on your young body and after a few years, you find yourself a poor replica of the girl who left New Southampton to regain her fortune.

To top it all, the vessel is attacked one day, and you die protecting your captain from other pirates.

Life wasn't a total disaster, but it was far from the dreams you had when you first fled your home. So much for high adventure and success!

530

Go to **431**

531

You step onto the pillar, and it feels a bit slippery. There are pillars diagonally in front of you to your left and right, and a pillar to your right and one behind you.

Do you step

Diagonally forward right – **68**

Diagonally forward left – **1429**

To your right – **238**

Backwards – **754**

532

You grab the pot on the stove, feeling the handle burning into your skin, but you manage to twist and throw it at the back of the soldiers. They scream in pain, and you drop the pot, running for the door. By the time they have reacted you are out into the fields surrounding your mansion. As you sit in the dark you watch the mansion burn to the ground and the Spanish forces are slowly repelled by soldiers from the New Southampton garrison. Go to **647**

533

You are fortunate as you are beside cover and hide straight away. Go to **1293**

534

Your voyage starts well, and you seem to be making steady progress to your destination. Alone in your chart room, you become aware of a commotion up on deck and you decide to investigate.

Roll 1xD100 (2xD10) and go to the result below

- 00-20 – *1454*
- 21-40 – *769*
- 41-60 – *1407*
- 61-80 – *430*
- 81-00 – *501*

535

The gate in the outer wall can be opened from the inside and you do so quickly, running out to the shore and climbing into your waiting boat. You have got away with it, safe back on your vessel, but was it worth it?

Take an extra day off your time chart. Now consult your voyage chart and set sail for the next destination.

536

You stand still and wait for someone to come out. After a moment, a tall pirate emerges with a pistol and looks at his colleague on the ground. Without a word he puts 2 and 2 together and fires at you catching you on the shoulder. You run off, howling in pain towards the edge of town. Your leg is bleeding badly though, and you feel faint. You need a Doctor, and fast! If you don't find one within 4 entries, you must go to *370*. Return now to *262* **and remain clear of the barn.**

537

Move Tabetha.

You are in a white walled room, bathed in the strange light, with two doors, one with a picture of a spider above it, and the other with a shield above it.

If Tabetha's number is 6 – *1459*

If Tabetha's number is 11 – **note this number and go to *1287***

If Tabetha's number is 3 – **note this number and go to *239***

Where do you go next?

Through the spider door – *686*

Through the shield door – *608*

Wait here - **return to the top of this section**

538

You shout to the crew to get ready to attack the vessel before them and you lift your eye piece. In the ocular, there is a tall white woman wearing nothing at all. Your eyes swim and you think she has several snakes beside her. Putting the eye piece down, you see your crew in a trance-like state and you know it's wrong, but you cannot act against it. You want to shout orders to tell them to stop but you cannot say a word, instead standing totally still as your vessel is brought alongside and boarded.

"Don't worry," whispers the woman from the vessel suddenly in your ear, "I won't harm you. Instead, I'll give you a gift." She places a leather strap necklace over your head and the next thing you know, the crew and you are out on the sea sailing along again.

"Captain," shouts a crewman, "all the treasure is gone." **If you had no treasure half of your provisions are missing. Remove all your treasure or half of your provisions, whichever is appropriate.**

You wonder what to do but there's nothing to do for the square-rigged ship is nowhere in sight. You settle down to continue your voyage and look at the necklace you have been given. There's an eye on it, a gold one. You think about taking the necklace off but you can't. You even ask a crewman to do it for you and then just cannot begin, like some sort of mental block or curse. **Tick the code word Eye Charm.**

There's nothing left to do but continue the voyage at *654*

539

You are clear of all walls of fire and can route in any direction. Do you

Go East – *310*

Go West – *321*

Go North – *648*

Go South – *1236*

540

You see a Spanish Flag on a Schooner vessel, one of the quickest going. "Blast," you cry out. You know that it has a lot of the options here, and now it seems to be following you.

Is your vessel *Very Fast* – *593*

If not, read on

As you watch the Schooner it continues course with you, tailing you. It never gets too close, and you know that if you turn to it, it can outrun you before tailing again at a distance. You wonder what it's intentions are but there's little you can do except continue course or change your destination. You now have a Spaniard watching you (Tick codeword **Spanish Tail**).

If you decide to change course, use the voyage chart to determine your voyage length from your original departure point to your new destination. Then **add 2 days to your voyage** for starting off in a different direction.

If you maintain course use your original planned voyage days. Either way, arrive at your destination:

New Southampton – *1466*

The Wreck of the Marie Saratoga – *968*

The Abandoned Island – *1154*

Fort August – *247*

Malin's Town – *580*

Bird's Paradise – *198*

The Pirate Den at Hell's deep – *17*

<u>541</u>

Reduce your time by 1. Stepping forward you run into a large barrel blocking your progress. To your left and right is open water.

Do you

About turn and step forward – *1381*

Turn right and walk forward – *1252*

Turn left and walk forward – *237*

<u>542</u>

You hit her hard on the head with the bottle which smashes causing Madame Le Vert to scream loudly. The sound of breaking glass was so loud, and you look at the men's clothing longingly as a good disguise. However, there are shouts from the guards outside asking if everything is alright.

Do you

Reach for the men's clothing and then try to escape out of the dressing room window – *1392*

Bluff a response to the guards outside to prevent them from entering – *887*

Simply make a run for the dressing room window to escape – *353*

543

You yell at the crew to go down to the hold and throw provisions overboard. As you drift away from the floating provisions, a crewman asks if they have thrown enough overboard. You tell them, no, to throw lots more over. The Kraken feeds on the provisions as you sail away from it. By the time its attention returns to you, your vessel is long gone.

Your crew are delighted at surviving. Raise crew morale by 2 levels.

Now continue your voyage at *654*

544

You remember the Spanish Priests you have in the hold, and you tell a crewman to get them on deck quickly. You see the horror on their faces, but one of their number begins to hold up an ornate cross at the sloop and speaks in Latin. The winds grow in strength so that your vessel shakes and strange wispy spectres race around your vessel, causing your crew to run below decks. But the main priest holds his cross aloft and continues his mantra against the sloop.

Gradually the wind subsides, and the sloop vanishes before your eyes. A moment later the sun is shining, and a steady wind is now propelling the vessel across the sea as if nothing ever happened. You look at the priest who seems to appear older now than he did before. He simply nods at you and returns to the cargo hold. Your heart is still pounding, and you wonder what other strange evil lurks on these waters.

Now continue your voyage at **654**

545

You wander along the path and reach a junction. Which way now?

Left – **1234**

Right – **20**

Turn back – **750**

546

Your sails are unfurled, and you are so much quicker than the brigantine that you are able to get clear in no time at all, far beyond the reach of its impressive canons. You breathe a sigh of relief but your crew although relieved to be alive are down at the beating they took. **Reduce your crew morale by 1 level. Because you fled in a random direction it takes you time to recover your course. Add 2 days to the voyage time to allow for this.**

Continue the voyage at **654**

547

Everything happens so quickly, and a bull smashes you backwards knocking you to the ground and then you scramble as quick as you can back to the plain clear of any more bulls. You're back where you started but you have been winded and feel groggy. **Take 5 off your Island Time Chart while you recover.**

(Continue over page)

If you want to try and run the gap again – *59*

You could try and go through the jungle and around the rock formation – *923*

Alternatively you can leave the plains back down the jungle track – *1145*

548

Reduce the Hot Strip by 1. If this places you on a Fire spot add 20 to this section's number and go there for the walls have moved. There are walls of fire to the west and east. You can route south or north from your current location.

Do you

Go North – *1420*

Go South – *775*

549

0 Skull 2 Scales 3 Coins

Wow, that's a win! **Tick the codeword of your prize, keeping your stake item**, and return to *1060*

550

Reduce your Island Time Chart by 1

You trek along the path, your feet feeling weary. There's a fork in the path, and you wonder which way to go. You can take either fork, or you could always head out into the jungle off the path.

Do you go

Left – *690*

Right – *125*

Strike out into the Jungle – *1283*

Turn around back the way you came – *509*

551

You see a black bull running directly at you and a white bull on your left running. You are in the middle channel. What will you do?

Go right – *1047*

Stay in the middle – *466*

Go left – *1165*

552

Reduce the Hot Strip by 1. If this places you on a Fire spot add 20 to this section's number and go there for the walls have moved. There are walls of fire to the south and east. You can route north or west from your current location.

Do you

Go West – *251*

Go North – *1389*

<u>553</u>

In the kitchen, two Spanish soldiers are facing away from you. You can also see a pot on the boil over the fire and there are several cups on the side as well as a large kitchen knife. The mansion sounds like it is falling apart so act quickly. The door is beyond the soldiers and your only escape.

Do you have the following codewords and wish to use,

A **Pistol** – *998*

A **Standard Knife** – *961*

A **Secreted Knife** – *1164*

Or do you

Throw some cups at them – *488*

Grab the pot and throw its contents over them – *532*

Take the knife and stab the soldiers with it – *138*

Just make a run for it – *651*

<u>554</u>

You wander along the path, feeling dejected at all the greenery, and reach a junction. Which way now?

Left – *728*

Right – *89*

Turn back – *727*

555

You trudge along the path, feeling a blackness on your soul and reach a junction. Which way now?

Left – *347*

Right – *1004*

Turn back – *776*

556

You scream at the crew to get gunpowder barrels and drop them over the side. As they surround the vessel, floating like a deadly circle, you see the creature below your vessel and tentacles start to rise form the sea. You shout at the crew to throw flaming brands onto the barrels.

As the first one explodes you realise how close they are to the vessel. Part of your hull is blown away and then another. There are the screams of your injured crew and others who scream no more. You struggle to give the order to stop blowing the barrels as your vessel is pounded from your own weapons. You never know if the kraken gets you as a nearby explosion sends you into the mast and everything goes black. That may be a small mercy.

The waters around New Southampton are deadly, but you managed to stop yourself! You may try again at *1*

557

Simon Kilmer – *849*

Robert Grimshaw – *1085*

Diggory Hurst – *211*

Timmers – *833*

Martha Downham – *1434*

Black Robert – *734*

558

You leave the room and close the trapdoor, returning to the message station. Once there you close the trapdoor there and cover it with the rug. **You may not return down this tunnel again.**

Now, do you in the message station

Look at the desk – *1167*

Look at the other rug – *365*

Try to open the safe – *1289*

Decide this is a bad idea and return to Timmers, saying you should get back to the ship pronto – *351*

559

Reduce your time by 3. You search the desk and a wad of what you think is parchment seems to float by your face. Your hands scurry over the compartments until one hand lights on a scroll. (If you have found this before the desk is merely empty).

Take it if you wish and tick the code word Desk Scroll if you do. Also, do you put it in your breeches, shirt or teeth to hold it as you need your hands free? Record your choice now in your notes.

You stand now with the desk at your back. On your left you feel a wooden wall, on the right and ahead you find clear water.

Do you

Walk forward – *1248*

Turn right and walk forward – *1344*

560

You wander along the path, wondering of there is anything in life but path, and reach a junction. Which way now?

Left – **555**

Right – **564**

Turn back – **613**

561

Roll 1xD100 (2xD10). For every point of damage you have already done to the sloop add 3 to the result. Check the table below for the result of this round of the sea battle.

00-35 – You get caught with a severe broadside. **Lower your vessel manoeuvrability by 1 level and your vessel speed by 1 level.**

36-60 – A volley lands on deck killing many of the crew. **Lower your crew by 1 level.**

61-80 – A volley blows out some of your canons, but you hit back – **Lower your firepower by 1 level.** But you cause the following damage dependent on your firepower: **Light – 1 point, Moderate – 2pts, Heavy – 3pts, Very Heavy – 4 pts**

81-90 – You land a splendid volley. Note you have done the following damage dependent on your firepower: **Light – 1 point, Moderate – 2pts, Heavy – 3pts, Very Heavy – 4 pts**

91 and up - You catch them cold with a blinding manoeuvre. Note you have done the following damage dependent on your firepower: **Light – 2 point, Moderate – 4pts, Heavy – 6pts, Very Heavy – 8 pts**

If you have caused 8 points of damage overall to the sloop – **1097**

If not

Do you want to continue the battle – **1267**

Do you wish to run – **1196**

562

Reduce your time by 1. You step forward and run into a wooden wall. The wall is also on your left, but you feel something there. On your right you find clear water.

Do you

About turn and step forward – *663*

Turn right and walk forward – *44*

Examine the left hand wall – *33*

563

You resist the temptation and Madame Le Vert stands and says that she agrees with you, that the dress needs a little adjusting. She suggests you re-enter the dressing room where she can make a quick alteration with being walked in on by any customers.

You invite her to walk ahead of you and once you have closed the door behind you, you stand as she assumes the same position she was in before at your feet. This time you do strike her on the head and the bottle shatters. You listen carefully but there seems to be little response from outside despite a groggy Madame Le Vert, moaning on the floor.

You quickly step into the main shop and acquire a full outfit of breeches, boots, shirt, long-coat and hat, before organising the boxes in the dressing room and climbing out of the small window. It's a squeeze but you make it out to the alley outside and then to the street. You tip your hat to cover your face and get ready to plot your next path. **Tick the codeword Incognito.** Go to *1166*

564

You wander along the path, praying for a glimpse of the sea, and reach a junction. Which way now?

Left – *20*

Right – *750*

Turn back – *1234*

565

Reduce your time by 1.

If your time is in the following gaps (52-48) you see a guard on his patrol outside and must remain hidden until he clears the area. Reduce your time by 6. Now continue at the plain text below

You bend down and pull back the rug revealing a wooden trapdoor with a large brass ring which is what caused the ripple in the rug. You try it gently and the trapdoor seems to open easily. Below is a dark tunnel and you struggle to see what's along it.

Do you

Enter the tunnel beneath – *857*

Decide against this and replace the trap door and rug. If so, do you then

Look at the desk – *206*

Look at the other rug – *1356*

Try to open the safe – *1288*

Decide this is a bad idea and return outside – *174*

<u>566</u>

As you wait to see what he will say a trapdoor opens beneath you and you fall into a chute which makes you tumble out of the barge and into the waters around it. As you surface, a few children are laughing at you from the barge. Indignant, you swim to your vessel to dry off and decide your next course of action.

Go to see Blind Tom again – *681*

Visit the provisions isle – *334*

Enjoy yourself at the wild isle – *879*

Explore the dark isle – *397*

Approach the pirate king – *1348*

Decide you have had enough of Hells Deep and set sail - **Consult the voyage chart and set sail**

<u>567</u>

"I am the Captain!" you declare, and some snigger but others look at you for confirmation until a man with a rich black beard and a missing leg stands up on crutches and looks you up and down.

"And what sort of Captain are you? Have you any trophies or tales? We don't take kindly to charlatans."

Do you have any of the following codewords ticked:

Bodach Sword   **Noiseless Horn**

Bird Whistle   **Eye Charm**

Spear   **Gold Medallion**

Gold Chain

If so – *55*

If not – *1342*

568

You see a black bull running directly at you and a white bull in the middle channel. You are in the right channel. What will you do?

Stay right – *392*

Go to the middle – *1165*

Go to the left channel – *298*

569

If you have the codeword **British Tail** – *1099*

Otherwise, read on.

Out on the open water all seems well until you hear a cry from the crow's nest above. "Ship ahoy! Captain, I can see a vessel on the horizon."

"That's all good and well," you cry, "but what are we up against." There are numerous types of vessels out here and you might be facing a lightening quick schooner or a heavy gunned galleon. You grab your scope and peer out towards the vessel. You eye widens as you see your foe.

Roll 1xD100 (2xD10). Check the result below and go to that entry.

00 to 40 – *540*

41 to 80 – *655*

81 to 99 – *32*

570

You tell John Darnold that you don't require a crew that gets themselves in this sort of situation but that he can help you escape back to the street. You untie the crew who flee out of Strangar making such a noise that the other pirates in the tavern race after them briefly, allowing you to return to the street without anyone seeing you. Having refused a vessel, you had better find one elsewhere. Return to *1112* **and make your next choice remaining clear of the barn.**

571

Go to *409*

572

Reduce the Hot Strip by 1. If this places you on a Fire spot add 20 to this section's number and go there for the walls have moved. There are walls of fire to the west and east. You can route south or north from your current location.

Do you

Go North – *958*

Go South – *925*

573

No, it's in the middle cup, so you lose your stake. Hope you didn't bet too much. Want another try? If so whose game

Look to join the one-legged pirate's game – *1181*

Engage in the stumpy pirate's game – *1316*

Play in the female pirate's game – *618*

If not go to *64*

574

Go to *667*

575

You wander along the path, music playing in your mind to keep the loneliness at bay, and reach a junction. Which way now?

Left – *750*

Right – *1234*

Turn back – *20*

576

You take out the orange algae with its spongy texture and wave it in front of the creatures. One scuttles forward and snatches it out of your hand with a large claw. It moves the algae to what you presume is its mouth and the algae disappears. That didn't work.

Do you have the following codewords and wish to use the items

Spear – *271*

Green Plant – *609*

Eye Charm – *1382*

Bodach Sword – *152*

If not, or you choose not to try them, you need to swim back to your vessel before the creatures get any closer.

If your vessel is in the shallows – *632*

If not, and it is anchored further out – *672*

577

You sweep the straw away and find a small silver key under it. **If you want to take the key, tick the codeword Silver Key. Reduce your time by 1.** What will you do now?

Do you

Wait in hiding – *433*

Investigate the flagpole – *602*

Move to the North quarter – *1176*

Move to the South quarter – *519*

578

You must be an idiot to return to a scene of destruction such as this. The guards are on the lookout for you, and you have simply walked straight into their hands. You are instantly arrested and taken to the garrison where you are taken before Captain Fareham.

He tells you that he intends to marry you, and he does so in quiet, keeping you locked up in the jail. Fareham now owns your father's lands and keeps you in your cell for the next year. When you don't respond to his advances and wishes to be a passive wife, he has you taken away in the night and disposed of. Your last thoughts are that your family remains unavenged. Try again at *1* and next time try and be more discreet.

579

Before you can go any further a hand grabs you and throws you roughly back to the dockside. "Get out slave, the master will not want a disturbance from the likes of you.

You rub your sore body but get back up. It appears you are not welcome here. Go to *117* and decide your next move.

<u>580</u>

You sail into the port of Malin's Town on a warm day at one of the busiest ports in the area. Here, goods are traded in the commercial hub of the New Southampton seas. There are all sorts of vessels occupying the harbour, including those of the English Navy but they are not the dominant force here. Rather the Mariners' Guild who have impressive offices in the centre of town. There is also a lively market, a smithy and joinery for ships repairs, chandlers for other vessel purchases, and of course, alehouses and taverns for entertainment.

There are lots of things to do in Malin's Town and you need to decide what you want to do first.

Do you

See to the needs of your vessel and crew – *903*

Try to earn some money by signing up to a cargo run – *1335*

Visit the taverns for information – *802*

Visit the Mariners' Guild for information – *124*

If your first officer is Simon Kilmer – *24*

If your First officer is Robert Grimshaw – *737*

If your First officer is Diggory Hurst – *786*

If you have had enough of Malin's town, then **consult the voyage chart and set sail.**

<u>581</u>

Do you have the codeword **Trap**, if so – *83*. If not, read on.

As you walk along the path, eyes blurred from the endless jungle, you swoon a little and feel your right foot begin to fall in front of you. You are suddenly pitched into a deep trap, and you scrabble with your hands which slows your fall down the deep trap. However, you hit your head before you land. When you wake you see that the trap is deep, but you can climb up the tree roots. However, you have no idea how long you have been in here.

Roll a D100 (or 2xD10)

00-35 You have only been out for a few minutes

36-79 You have been out for a day. Mark off 1 day from your voyage chart.

80-99 What a hit to the head. You've lost two days. Mark off 2 days from your voyage chart.

You climb up with difficulty out of the pit, disorientated about how you entered. **Tick codeword Trap**. There are two ways you can go but you don't know which one you came in by. Do you

Go this way – *116*

Or try this way – *38*

582

"If I'm not mistaken that's the square-rigged ship of Mary Pearl." You have no idea who your first officer is talking about, but you want to know more.

If your first officer is

Simon Kilmer, Martha Downham or Timmers – *981*

Otherwise – *1296*

583

The only wall of fire is to the north. You can route south, east or west from your current location.

Do you

Go East – *826*

Go South – *1303*

Go West – *766*

584

You place something on the shrine from your inventory. **Untick the item from your inventory now.** The howl stops and the flames on the candles all blow out. You see the chest at the shrine has opened and you can see an incredible amount of gold doubloons. With these you could upgrade your ship, your crew, or simply retire!

Do you

Take the doubloons – *1265*

Leave the chest alone and

Climb up the rope – *470*

Descend the other rope – *843*

Leave by the door – *920*

585

You run over to the closet as fire races around the room. Inside are a pair of breeches and a long-coat. Decide if you want to put them on as you need to be quick. If so, **tick the codeword Long-coat**. Either way, the room is burning too fast for any further searching and you cough due to the smoke as you exit the room.

Go to *510*

586

Your crew gets excited as you order your vessel to engage the galleon before you. As you draw closer to the brigantine, you see so many cannons aimed at you, that you realise you will have to outmanoeuvre it consistently or you will perish. Or at least you'll end up in a destructive tete-a-tete.

Is your vessel manoeuvrability

Great or Good – **400**

Reasonable – **965**

Poor or Lacking -**999**

587

Roll 1xD100 (2xD10). For every point of damage you have already done to the galleon add 3 to the result. Check the table below for the result of this round of the sea battle.

00-39 – You get caught with a severe broadside. **Lower your vessel manoeuvrability by 2 levels and your vessel speed by 1 level.**

40-69 – A volley lands on deck killing many of the crew. **Lower your crew by 1 level.**

70-85 – A volley blows out some of your canons, but you hit back – **Lower your firepower by 1 level.** But you cause the following damage dependent on your firepower: **Light – 1 point, Moderate – 2pts, Heavy – 3pts, Very Heavy – 4 pts**

86-99 – You land a splendid volley. Note you have done the following damage dependent on your firepower: **Light – 1 point, Moderate – 2pts, Heavy – 3pts, Very Heavy – 4 pts**

100 and up - You catch them cold with a blinding manoeuvre. Note you have done the following damage dependent on your firepower: **Light – 2 point, Moderate – 4pts, Heavy – 6pts, Very Heavy – 8 pts**

If you have caused 24 points of damage overall to the galleon – *1001*

If not

Do you want to continue the battle – *761*

Do you wish to run – *87*

588

Reduce your time by 1. You step forward and feel a wooden wall on your left. There is clear water ahead and to your right.

Do you

About turn and step forward – *416*

Turn left and walk forward – *1339*

Walk forward – *343*

589

You shake your head and the man looks at you quizzically but he lets you go. You disappear into the crowd and look for your next move.

Do you

Approach the jewellery stall – *1158*

Go to the provisions stalls – *1368*

Or return to the street – *496*

590

"Captain, my apologies for interrupting you," says the cabin boy, "but the duty watch keeper has found something. A stowaway of sorts."

The cabin boy leads you to the cargo bay where you see a rotund man in a monk's habit.

"Take pity on me, for I fled a terrible ordeal. I seek to return to New Southampton but please simply keep me on board until then and I'll work for you."

Your First Officer takes you to one side and explains that many of the crew will see action against a holy man as bad luck and he suggests you keep the man on board, but by all means, make him pay for his passage.

You tell the holy man he will keep the decks clean, and the cargo holds too. The man kneels before you and then kisses your hand, thanking you for your kindness.

The crew think they are blessed with a holy man on board. Raise your crew morale by 1 level. Tick the codeword **Holy Man.**

Now continue your voyage at *654*

591

You pull the Promissory Note out and hand it to the man who keeps an arm locked on you. He looks at it and laughs before hauling you inside the doors to meet Little Annie. You are held against your will, working in the brothel and live out a short but miserable life. When your end comes due to a violent customer, it is at least a merciful release. Try again at *1* and stay away from places such as this.

592

You send a volley at the creature and try to peer through the copious smoke from your canon. You can see thrashing in the deep and you believe you have hit it with all you've got. The creature retracts the appendages it has above the surface and the sea becomes eerily silent. Your crew stares at the water and you wait to hear another spotting but there's nothing. You cautiously get the crew to resume your voyage, but you keep a sharp lookout. After an hour you believe it is gone and you continue your voyage.

Your crew are relieved. Raise your crew morale by 2 levels.

Now continue your voyage at *654*

<u>593</u>

"We could route for it, Captain," says your first officer. "We're a match for speed and if we can outmanoeuvre it, we could capture it. There may not be much on board. Otherwise, we may be able to simply chase it off. Or we could outrun it. It's your call unless you're happy to let us be followed. That would be the quickest option, but I wouldn't be keen on it tailing us."

You ponder your move as you look at the sleek vessel through your eyepiece. Would an engagement be wise? Would a tail be dangerous?

Do you

Look to engage the Schooner – *1054*

Want to outrun the Schooner – *381*

Let the Schooner tail you – **read on**

As you watch the Schooner it continues course with you, tailing you. It never gets too close, and you wonder what its intentions are but there's little you can do except continue course or change your destination. You now have a Spaniard watching you (Tick codeword **Spanish Tail**).

If you decide to change course, **use the voyage chart to determine your voyage length from your original departure point to your new destination. Then add 2 days to your voyage for starting off in a different direction.**

If you maintain course use your original planned voyage days. Either way, arrive at your destination:

New Southampton – *1466*

The Wreck of the Marie Saratoga – *968*

The Abandoned Island – *1154* (More options over the page)

Fort August – *247*

Malin's Town – *580*

Bird's Paradise – *198*

The Pirate Den at Hell's deep – *17*

594

You swan up to the main bar and order a drink to listen to the conversation and boasting that's going on. You eavesdrop on such fanciful tales but are almost stopped in your tracks when you hear talk of a compass that can direct you to Captain Estes treasure. The pirate who tells of it has one eye and a mouth that has a large scar running just under it. He appears to be drunk and raving, but he also seems sure of himself when challenged.

Do you

Talk directly to him – *413*

Continue to listen in on his ramblings – *599*

Ignore his chatter and try a different part of the tavern

Approach the pirates with the monkey figure – *305*

Climb up to the adapted poop deck and the two female pirates – *658*

Or leave the tavern and

Make for the small houses – *1304*

Approach the gambling groups – *1424*

Go to see the fights – *84*

Decide this is not a place you want to explore and return to your vessel – *314*

595

Reduce your Waters Strength Chart by 1 unless you have just jumped in. The current is pushing you west. However, you think you can reach an eddy that seems to allow a way north but to get there will be incredibly hard work. Equally hard seems the eddy to the south. One thing that is impossible is to swim east and reach the rock. Do you

Swim North – *1295*

Float West – *1083*

Swim South – *118*

596

Reduce the Hot Strip by 1. If this places you on a Fire spot add 20 to this section's number and go there for the walls have moved. There are walls of fire to the north and east. You can route south or west from your current location.

Do you

Go West – *1123*

Go South – *1150*

597

Taking a bottle from the boxes, you peer into the main shop from the dressing room until you see Madame Le Vert is alone. You sneak up behind her and bring the bottle down hard on her head and it smashes, causing Madame Le Vert to scream loudly. The sound of breaking glass was so loud, but you look at the men's clothing in the shop longingly as a good disguise. However, there are shouts from the guards outside asking if everything is alright.

Do you

Reach for the men's clothing and then try to escape out of the dressing room window – *1392*

Bluff a response to the guards outside to prevent them from entering – *887*

Simply make a run for the dressing room window to escape – *353*

598

You approach the merchants and ask if you can sit with them. They part and let you sit among them. After ordering an ale you listen as they talk about the price of goods and weather prospects for various crops. But then one says, they heard a rumour that Captain Estes left directions to his treasure in the barracks at Fort August.

"If you go into the centre of the fort from the southwest, the barrack hut you require is the second one up."

You nod sagely as they go back to more details about cargo they have previously carried. Bored you turn to the man by the fire, but he has left. The barmaid also seems busy, so you decide to try elsewhere.

You cannot return to the Malin's Town Alehouse. You return to the crossroads to plan your next place to visit – *802*

599

You stare into your drink as you hear the pirate tell of the Spanish fort across from New Southampton, and then of the day he attacked and destroyed the harbour at Strangar. Clearly the man is raving and a complete drunk. You realise you need to ignore anything he is saying. What next?

Do you

Approach the pirates with the monkey figure – *305*

Climb up to the adapted poop deck and the two female pirates – *658*

Or leave the tavern and

Make for the small houses – *1304*

Approach the gambling groups – *1424*

Go to see the fights – *84*

Decide this is not a place you want to explore and return to your vessel - *314*

600

Reduce your time by 5. Anything you were holding in your teeth is gone. Untick that item. You reach out and immediately feel a desk on your left. Ahead is a wooden wall. You feel right and behind and there's just water.

Do You

About turn and walk forward – *1344*

Examine the desk – *85*

Turn right and step forward – *1248*

601

The vegetation around you is so dense and the path is long but you force yourself to walk on, seeing the mountain rising high above you. It is not long before you have reached the impressive fixture and realise that it is not as large as you thought. There is a river running down its side which will give you purchase to climb along its banks but otherwise the mountain is also covered in dense foliage. There is a path running around the mountain which shows you another path covered by a canopy leading north from the mountain.

Do you

Climb the mountain – *1177*

Take the canopy covered path – *435*

Retrace your steps – *477*

602

You climb the flagpole, driving your legs and arms up the pole until you can reach the flag. You look down to see every guard in front of every house looking at the idiot holding on for dear life in the most prominent place in the fort. As you descend you are surrounded by guards with rifles and swords. You have been caught. Go to *1358*

603

You swim for the mast that sticks above water and clamber onto it looking down at the vessel. From up above the water, you can see the poop deck, the main deck and the forecastle deck to the fore of the ship. They are all underwater and you will have to swim to examine them. You give a thumbs up to your first officer to indicate you are okay and choose your next action.

Do you

Swim for the poop deck – *683*

Dive for the main deck – *316*

Investigate the forecastle deck – *770*

Or instead

Dive and search the outside of the vessel – *136*

Return to your vessel – *894*

604

As you sit, you hear Buffington's footsteps getting closer and suddenly he barges in. You notice he is wearing an entirely different set of glasses.

"Can you believe it, I had on Adamson's glasses, no wonder I couldn't see. But you're still here, you're still…, blast it, sir, you are not a sir. You are a woman, and a woman has no place on a vessel, and no place in this guild! Robert! Get this wench out of here! Blast it, how did she get in?"

Robert strides quickly into the room and grabs you by the arm wheeling you out and taking you straight to the front doors and the town outside.

"Sorry," he says "but that was so funny." You see his friend laughing with him, and clearly you have been set up. **You cannot return to the Mariner's Guild in daylight as your womanly face is known.**

Do you

Come back at night in an attempt to gain access when the building is closed – *742*

See to the needs of your vessel and crew – *903*

Try to earn some money by signing up to a cargo run – *1335*

Visit the taverns for information – *802*

If you have had enough of Malin's town, then **consult the voyage chart and set sail.**

605

Reduce your time by 3. You search the crates but can find no opening. You now have your back to the crates. Ahead and right is clear water, but you feel a wooden wall on your left side.

Do you

Walk forward – *562*

Turn right and walk forward – *986*

606

You sail along until you reach a break in the channel where you can turn. It has two exits including the one you entered by: northeast and southeast.

Do you

Sail northeast – *1465*

Route southeast – *186*

607

You shout out in English and panic as the door opens. A guard casts his eye around the room, instantly sizing up the situation. He grabs and binds your hands, telling the others to help Madame Le Vert. You are taken back to the garrison to Captain Fareham who is livid.

The Captain knows the value to him of your father's lands although they have been ransacked and he forces you to become part of his plan and you are married in private. Fareham now owns your father's lands and keeps you locked up for the next year. When you don't respond to his advances and wishes to be a passive wife, he has you taken away in the night and disposed of. Your last thoughts are that your family remains unavenged. Try again at *1* and remember enemies are everywhere, even those people who help.

608

Move Tabetha.

You are in a white walled room, bathed in the strange light, with two doors, one with a picture of a pirate flag above it, and the other with a schooner above it.

If Tabetha's number is 3 – *1459*

If Tabetha's number is 7 – **note this number and go to *1029***

If Tabetha's number is 6 – **note this number and go to *446***

Where do you go next?

Through the pirate flag door – *1179*

Through the schooner door – *537*

Wait here - **return to the top of this section**

609

You take out the green plant and wave it in front of the crab creatures. As they get close you see them recoil but they are snatching at it. Maybe if you had something longer with which to use it at a distance from yourself

Do you have the codeword **Spear** – *1327*

If not, the creatures rip the green plant form you and throw it away. **Untick the codeword Green Plant.** You are back at square one.

Do you have the following codewords and wish to use the items

Spear – *271*

Orange Algae – *576*

Eye Charm – *1382*

Bodach Sword – *152* (More options over the page)

If not, or you choose not to try them, you need to swim back to your vessel before the creatures get any closer.

If your vessel is in the shallows – *632*

If not, and it is anchored further out – *672*

610

Reduce your Waters Strength Chart by 1 unless you have just jumped in. The current is pushing you west. However, you think you may be able to swim up an eddy to the south and clamber onto the rock in the middle of the waters. Do you

Float West – *1087*

Swim South for the rock – *971*

611

You walk round and over to the doors set into the ground which are broken. You open them but it is dark inside. Slowly you creep forward but then something bites hard into your leg. And then something else. You kick out with all your might but the bites continue and so you explode out of the broken doors to the outside. Unfortunately, as you kick a rat off you, you cause so much commotion that the patrol starts running your way. There is a cry to the air, alerting everyone to your presence. You run as hard as you can back to the docks, telling the crew to set sail immediately.

You must leave Malin's Town immediately, and you may not return for 20 days until the heat dies down, for you cannot be sure your face was not seen.

Consult the voyage chart and set sail for another destination.

612

You follow the path and find yourself on a beach. When you turn back around you see the vast jungle vegetation before you and three paths leading back into the green mass. If you have the codeword **North Beach**, you see your vessel lying off the beach and your small boat clear of the surf on the sand.

Do you take the

Left hand path – *1275*

Middle path – *137*

Right hand path – *844*

Or if you have the codeword **North Beach** you can get back in your small boat and return to your crew and choose another option at *1386* **(Untick North Beach if you do so)**

613

You wander along the path and reach a junction with three paths off it. Which way now?

Left – *1033*

Middle – *422*

Right – *105*

Turn back – *560*

614

You peer into the main shop from the dressing room until you see Madame Le Vert is alone and you sneak up behind her. You try to grab her, but she struggles, calling out to the guards outside. Realising you are in trouble, you bolt for the dressing room and the window. But she has seen your face. If you don't have the codeword **Prominent, tick it now**. You land in the alley and run to the end of town to mingle with the crowd. Go to *1009*

615

Reduce the Hot Strip by 1. If this places you on a Fire spot add 20 to this section's number and go there for the walls have moved. There are walls of fire to the south and west. You can route north or east from your current location.

Do you

Go East – *790*

Go North – *687*

616

The man looks at you and then stands up, checking you up and down.

"Are you one of ours? Or have you run from your master, girl? Not that it matters. You'll be ours now."

He reaches forward and grabs you by the arm, dragging you closer to the doors behind him. Clearly, he sees you as an opportunity to get a slave in his employ.

Do you have the codeword and want to use

A **Standard Knife** – *970*

A **Pistol** – *853*

A **Bottle of Whiskey** to appease him – *657*

A **Promissory Note** to appease him – *591*

Or try to free yourself – *1048*

617

You sail into a small opening that has three exits from it. The rocks are spaced here, and you can turn easily. There are exits from the channel to the west, east, and southwest. All are wide channels so where next?

Do you

Sail west– *1349*

Route east – *938*

Go southwest – *916*

618

"Here comes an idiot," says the female pirate, openly mocking you. She points to the three cups in front of her. "Do you want to play? I can take a stake up to 600 Doubloons. Place your money down and we will start."

The other pirates look at you expectantly. If you want to play, make a note of how many doubloons you are placing as your stake. Now go to *719*.

If you decide it isn't worth the gamble, then return to *1424* and pick a different option.

619

You don't hesitate but fire a shot into the man's belly. He recoils back to the wall but the noise echoes around the alley and suddenly people are coming from everywhere towards you. If you have the codeword **Prominent** go to *880*.

If not, you run hard into the crowd which initially parts until the mass arriving is so large that you manage to blend into the crowd. You have had to run up into town, so you are now up near the docks. Add the codeword **Prominent** to your list and note that you may no longer enter the alley as it will not be safe. Go to *1009*

620

You approach the ship's wheel and feel a sudden chill in your bones. You could swear the room just got darker and then you hear a laugh. Someone speaks in Spanish but you cannot understand what they say except for "Tu Meurte!" - Your Death. But the laugh at the end makes you feel like someone is looking over your shoulder. You find yourself unable to move as the ship's wheel begins to rotate quickly and the laughter continues.

And then it all stops. Did you imagine it? Is this place haunted? You step back from the wheel and wonder. What now?

Do you

Climb the rope – *843*

Examine the paintings – *621*

Check out the chest – *889*

Leave the room by the wooden door – *1439*

621

You glare at the paintings, showing fantastic Spanish galleons from the past in a tasteful style. They remind you of the English galleons you saw occasionally at New Southampton. One has a picture of a man with a blue beard and has carved below it, Estes. Otherwise, they just hang there as paintings do.

Do you

Climb the rope – *843*

Look at the ship's wheel – *620*

Check out the chest – *889*

Leave the room by the wooden door – *1439*

The Treasure of Captain Estes

The pirate women are delighted and share their bearing with you, taken from Seagull's Peak , and the map they have acquired. Tick the codewords, **Bearing D, Empty Chart** and **Girlfriends.**

The rest of the tavern have seen you make a deal with the female pirates and now no one will talk to you in the tavern, as they seem scared of you. **You can no longer enter the tavern as it is pointless. Go to *314*** and decide your next move.

623

The pirate sweeps you away to the rear of the building where you are led in through a cellar door. There are hushed whispers, and you are taken to a small room in the cellar where you are told to sit and wait on an old barrel. The door is locked, and you wait for what seems like an age before a pirate with a large bushy black beard enters and closes the door behind him. You gulp wondering what will happen next.

The pirate stares at you for a moment before he speaks.

"I'm sorry for your loss, Mary. I heard about what happened to your father, a man to whom I owe a lot. You may not realise but out here you have to keep an uneasy alliance between pirate and landowner and between us, your father and I, made it work. I am Black Robert, the pirate Lord in this place. But tell me, what is it you want?"

"I want Estes," you say.

"Indeed, the pirate from where God only knows,and so you shall but we need your lands back as well, so this alliance between your family and me may continue. But you shall have your revenge, Mary. Now come, let's see you properly fed and dressed.

You have the pirate Lord on your side. If you have wounds they are tended and cured. **You may remove all wounds from you and ignore any timers regarding their effects.** Now plan your future at *1370*

624

You find the pull of the main current tough to overcome to get to the eddy, but you do it eventually. **Reduce your Waters Strength Chart by 1.** You swim through to the eddy. Go to *201*

625

Diggory gives you a smile. "Remember what I have told you, there's a set time for the guard patrol and they will also have a sweep periodically, at least every hour. You need to move between the guards when they are elsewhere, so keep your eyes peeled. There is a message station and somewhere an intelligence room where all the good stuff is kept. You need to find the message station because there's always some underground route from one to the other and the intelligence room will be locked up tight in the middle of barracks. You don't want to be there. So, head for the main walled area in the middle of the fort. Also, I can't be sure but I think they work on a check 200 pattern for their moving on around the fort on patrol."

Tick the codeword Check 200. You nod and look at the walls before you. Go to *1143*

626

Your voyage starts off in a rather mundane fashion with nothing unusual occurring, nor any vessels being seen. However, as you sleep one night, there comes a knock at your door.

Roll a 1xD100 (2xD10,). Check the result below for your next section.

00-20 – *444*

21-40 – *834*

41-60 – *892*

62-80 – *653*

81-00 – *590*

627

You watch your crew with pride as they give everything they have, and your vessels races away like the wind itself. But behind you, you see the murky mass of the creature still maintaining pursuit. The wind remains strong, and you feel the gap growing but a long tentacle flicks out pulling at your sails. One rips but the effort seems to have exhausted the creature and it drops away.

With a sigh of relief, you steer well clear of where the Kraken was spotted but resume course later that night.

Your crew are delighted at surviving. Raise crew morale by 1 level. However, the sail is badly damaged and will affect your vessel handling. Lower your vessel manoeuvrability by 1 level. Add 1 day to your voyage time for your diversion.

Now continue your voyage at **654**

628

Roll 1xD100 (2xD10) dice and consult the chart below to tick the corresponding codeword.

If you have the codeword Pace move down two sections, if you can, below your result and note that codeword instead. (If you cannot move two sections but can move down one, do that instead.)

If you have the codeword Jog move down one section, if you can, below your result and note that codeword instead.

00-19   **Anna**

20-39   **Barbara**

40-59   **Charlie**

60-79   **Debbie**

80-99   **Ellie**

Now continue below

You climb the pole and arrive adjacent to the shutters and find them easy to open. You then climb into the room beyond. Although it is dark you can make out a vast wooden desk. Also in the room are a series of charts on the wall, a brass sextant on a shelf, a portrait of a rather stunning looking woman in an evening gown and a set of large drawers hugging the wall closest to you. You need to be quick so where will you search?

Do you

Search the desk – *1224*

Look at the charts – *469*

Examine the sextant – *153*

Go to the portrait – *417*

Check out the drawers – *741*

629

You continue to wax lyrical about your exploits and try to embellish on what you have already said. Suddenly the pale-skinned pirate draws her weapon and stabs you straight through the heart. You tried to bluff a deadly pirate in their own den, and it's failed. **Your tale is done. Return to *1* to start again.**

630

This is a tricky manoeuvrer, and you'll need to first turn the ship in close quarters to the creature before blasting it. You shout the order to turn the vessel as the Kraken comes close – at least what you can see of it above the water. Get this wrong and you are in trouble.

Is your vessel's manoeuvrability

Great or Good – *692*

Reasonable – *1183*

Poor or Lacking – *256*

631

Reduce your Waters Strength Chart by 1. The current is terribly strong, and you are swept west. There is nothing you can do except float to *1461*

632

You get back onto your vessel without further incident and are somewhat disappointed. Clearly the crab creatures have an attachment with the island and currently you have no way of penetrating their numbers to get into the cave. Stumped, you decide to set sail to another location.

Set sail for a new destination by consulting the voyage chart.

633

You have treasure, more than enough for the crew, and plenty for yourself. You are a wealthy woman and buying back your home and lands is easy. Although not the wealthiest person on the island you have influence and you have seen your family avenged as best you could.

The treasure does not last forever but you make sensible investments and run several successful vessels bringing many goods to the area from far overseas. Your adventures have gained you contacts and wisdom, and life is good.

Congratulations, you have succeeded and brought honour and justice back to your family. You have won. But there are greater victories if you dare to try again. More treasure to be won and more power and influence to achieve. Try again at *1* if you dare, or will you simply bask in your current victory?

634

"Aron is a friend of mine, we have sailed these parts together. We'll see if he knows anything about Estes' treasure."

You wave a flag signal to the vessel and come alongside. Your first officer does the introductions, and you dine on board Jeboe's vessel that night. He tells you he knows very little but gives you a key, shaped like a dolphin on the handle. **You may tick the code word Dolphin Key if you want to**.

"I came across it when taking down an old Spanish vessel last month but you can have it. I'm sorry I know little else to help you. But take a few extra provisions if you need them. **You may add up to 4 provisions to your cargo hold.**

The next morning you are underway and have left Jeboe behind. **Add 1 day to your voyage time for the previous day's slight delay.**

Continue the voyage at **654**

635

"If I'm not mistaken that's the Brigantine of Hugh Jameson." You have no idea who your first officer is talking about, but you want to know more.

If your first officer is

Diggory Hurst – **304**

Otherwise – **490**

636

So, what tales do you have to tell? Do you have any of the following codewords?

Bodach Sword: Eye Charm: Spear: Gold Medallion: Brass key: Silver Key: Gold Chain: Sextant

If so – *804*

If not but you want to spin a tale anyway – *901*

If this has been a bad idea, then you apologise and take your leave of the women with the rest of the tavern watching a boaster who had nothing to tell. You leave the tavern and decide not to come back for a long time. **You may not visit the tavern until you come back to Hell's Deep again. Go to *314***

637

You walk through the horn door and find yourself suddenly above ground standing in the middle of the temple. Before you is the fair maiden you saw originally before she turned into a hag. She bows before you and lifts her hands in which there is a horn.

"Take it, for you have won this in honest battle. When you blow it, the fearsome Kraken will return to the depths leaving you free to travel where you want."

You reach forward and take the kraken horn from her. **Tick the codeword Kraken Horn.** As you take hold of the horn she vanishes before your eyes. You look around the temple but there's nothing to see, no way back down to the hall you just left. **Tick the codeword Closed.**

Not much to do except leave this place with your prize. You check the sun and realise you can go north - *202* or south - *1329* along a jungle path. Choose now.

638

Are you

Dressed like a slave in your torn gown – *47*

Wearing a dress or a long-coat and breeches – *10*

639

You wander along the path, sweat on your brow, and reach a junction. Which way now?

Left – *1004*

Right – *776*

Turn back – *347*

640

The woman is rather striking in a way and the eyes seem to capture the attention of any admirer of the painting. It also bears the legend "Lady Argyle". It is small though and you can hide it on your person. If you take it, tick the codeword **Argyle.**

Go to *415*

641

Roll 1xD100 (2xD10) and check the result below.

00-19 – *98*

20-39 – *1323*

40-59 – *139*

60-79 – *123*

80-99 – *551*

642

You stare as the crab creatures get closer and then hear a commotion in the water behind you. Spinning around you see your crewman in the water having been upended from the small boat. The crab creatures are tearing into them, and you fear they may be lost. It looks like you are on your own. **Lose 2 crew morale as your crew on the vessel would have seen their crewmates taken down.**

Go to *1140*

643

The weather is rough but not unmanageable. You still feel like you need to be careful, and you see the sails take a battering. At one point you feel the need to lighten the load in the ship and throw 2 provisions overboard. When you clear the storm after two days you assess the damage.

The vessel is in good condition but remove 2 provisions from your vessel's cargo. If you cannot, reduce your vessel speed level by 1 due to damage.

Now resume your voyage at *654*

644

You need to act and do so quickly by high stepping it back through the snakes, lifting your knees high as they strike out at you. You think you are clear until on manages to sink fangs through your boots. You yell in pain but continue to run with the creature still attached to your flesh. At the beach you forsake the small boat instead swimming back to your vessel where you are hauled on board. Your first officer cuts the snake's head from its body but removing the head is much more difficult.

When it does finally become free you slip into a fever and are confined to your cabin for over five days, taking only a little water and bread. You shiver and see monstrous hallucinations of snakes and darkness. Finally, after you break free of the sweats and shivers you realise that you have been ill for ten days. **Mark off ten days on your time chart.** Fortunately, the crew has recovered your small boat.

You decide you will not return to the dark isle, ever, but there may still be places to explore at Hell's Deep. **You may not return to the dark isle for the rest of your adventure.** So what next?

Go to see Blind Tom – *681*

Visit the provisions isle – *334*

Enjoy yourself at the wild isle – *879*

Approach the pirate king – *1348*

Decide you have had enough of Hells Deep and set sail - **Consult the voyage chart and set sail.**

645

You fire another volley of canon fire and see the Brigantine slowly begin to sink. Crew are abandoning it and you desperately come alongside before it sinks into the sea. You find a dead Captain Jameson on deck and his crew are in no mood to defend themselves further. You don't have long to gather his stores though.

What you can gather is dependent on your crew size. It is also dependent on your cargo hold. Check what you can take from the Brigantine on the chart below. Then place it in your hold up to your capacity. Note you cannot throw any of your cargo out to make room, there isn't time.

Your Vessel's Crew	Cargo you can take
Large	**10 units of treasure worth 1000 doubloons each**
Medium	**10 units of treasure worth 1000 doubloons each**
Small	**5 units of treasure worth 1000 doubloons each**

Continue the voyage at *654*

646

You flip the trapdoor above you open and reach up with your hands to pull yourself through. As you do so you hear a shout. Desperately you drop and reach for the edges of the trapdoor closing it above you. You then sprint along the dark of the tunnel, your hands tracing the wall as you hear voices behind you and the trapdoor opening again.

You reach the trapdoor in the messages office and climb up into the darkness, eyes squinting. But there's no time for any pause and you close the trapdoor and cover it quickly with the rug. You then run out of the messages office and hear shouts and cries from nearby buildings.

A small group of soldiers round the larger buildings beyond the messages office and they yell out at you.

"You there, what are you doing?"

You have been caught. What will be your fate as you are taken before the fort's commander? Go to *1358*

647

By dawn the house is burnt to the ground, but the garrison soldiers are in charge. You can see Captain Fareham, an officer at the garrison who has been at your mansion many times. In his late thirties, you know he has had eyes on you as a potential wife and could be a route to safety. He's taking charge and you know he will look after you if you go to him now. From there you could plan your next steps. But he is a powerful figure and may seek to simply take whatever's left of your father's lands for himself by taking you for his wife. You know you'll get little say in the matter now your father is gone. It's a risk but one that may pay off in the short term.

Your other options are riskier. You could head into New Southampton, but you have no money on you and without your father, you will have little say in what other people do. On the other hand, making for Strangar, the illegal port, may bring you opportunities to go after Estes but at what cost and danger.

Do you

Go to Captain Fareham and ask for his help – *1315*

Walk into New Southampton – *1114*

Head for Strangar – *671*

648

Reduce the Hot Strip by 1. If this places you on a Fire spot add 20 to this section's number and go there for the walls have moved. There are walls of fire to the west and east. You can route south or north from your current location.

Do you

Go North – *30*

Go South – *539*

649

Roll 1D100 (2xD10) to find where the coin actually is. Did you roll?

00-33 – *777*

34-67 – *573*

68-99 – *46*

650

"Dear Mary Hastings, your father was a dear friend of mine, although he did keep it quiet for various reasons. I was distraught when Estes killed your father and have pondered nothing more than vengeance for him. My name is Martha Downham, known as the Bloody Mistress of the Sea, and a scourge to all who cross me. I have a vessel and a crew at the docks but was wondering if you had been grabbed by Captain

Fareham of the garrison. But no, you are here and together we shall seek Estes out! Come with me and we shall gain back what he took from your father. What say you?"

Now there's an offer. Do you

Accept – *1042*

Look somewhat panicked and refuse – *1069*

<u>651</u>

This is a bold risk but just maybe it'll work. You simply put your head down and run for the door. You are past the soldiers before they can react and you race out into the darkness of the fields beyond. But you can hear they are in pursuit. The crop fields are a short way off but you may not make it before they catch you. You could shout, hoping someone hears you.

Do you

Run – *1226*

Shout – *112*

<u>652</u>

"Emmanuel Gonzales is a most feared pirate captain, a born killer and one who doesn't deal with other pirates. He may have much on his galleon, but it will be hard to overcome, and he will have numbers on that vessel. He may have information about Estes but who knows?"

Do you

Order your crew to sail towards the pirate ship – *506*

Decide to keep your distance and stay away – *188*

653

"Captain, my apologies for interrupting you," says the cabin boy, "but the duty watch keeper has found something. A stowaway of sorts."

You are taken to the rear of a hold area and see a number of cats, which purr lightly. The duty watch keeper has taken the liberty of feeding them.

"I thought we could keep them on board and keep the rat population down."

You nod your approval and decide to keep the cats on board. **Tick the codeword Rat Catcher.**

Now continue your voyage at **654**

654

Arrive now at your destination, marking off your voyage time:

New Southampton – **1466**

The Wreck of the Marie Saratoga – **968**

The Abandoned Island – **1154**

Fort August – **247**

Malin's Town – **580**

Bird's Paradise – **198**

The Pirate Den at Hell's deep – **17**

Or if you think you know where you really want to go and either have:

Codeword **Devil's Compass** and one of the following codewords **Bearing A, Bearing B, Bearing C** or **Bearing D**

Or if you have three out of four of the following codewords:

Bearing A, Bearing B, Bearing C or **Bearing D**

Then go to **499.**

655

You see a Spanish flag on the vessel but it's a cargo vessel, a square-rigged ship, slower than most vessel. There may be items of worth on board and it doesn't look heavily armed either. You can see it already turning away from you. It's a distraction but one that may prove profitable.

Do you

Turn to engage the Vessel – *412*

Ignore the vessel – *1120*

656

Do you have the codeword **Darkness** – *1325*. If not, read on.

You walk slowly into the temple and before your eyes the jungle beyond becomes ablaze. Maybe it's the incense that did it or maybe this is for real but either way, you can feel the heat of the fires and see before a woman who is half sea creature and half human. Her black hair seems to have a life of its own reminding you of the snake pit.

You stand in terror as she wields a knife before you and approaches. You see that blood drips from the knife already and her mouth seems to salivate as she casts her eyes over you.

"Another one for sacrifice, another one to join us. Will you join me? Lay your throat open and join me."

The woman reaches a hand to your cheek and gently starts to coax your head backwards. She's going to cut your throat, you can sense it. Do you run, do you strike out? Can you even? Or do you feel ready to be a sacrifice?

Do you

Tilt your head back and let happen what will happen – *1089*

Push at her and run – *933*

657

You pull out your bottle of whiskey and offer it to him. As he relaxes, you quickly bring the bottle down on his head, smashing it but knocking him to the floor. The doors begin to open but you don't look back, running to the alley and then the street beyond. **Untick the codeword Bottle of Whiskey**. Continue your adventure on the main street at *496*

658

You find the cobbled together stairs that lead up to the poop deck that almost acts as a separate floor in the tavern and climb to the higher floor. As you step onto the deck, you can see the two female pirates stare at you. They are the only ones on the deck, and you noticed that the male pirates stay well clear of them.

The darker skinned pirate stands and comes toward you as if you have disturbed their peace. The two women clearly have no issues being among the men, and almost have a place of respect.

"And why do you deserve to be on our deck?" asks the pirate before you.

Do you

Take off your hat and let your hair unfurl to show you are a woman – *1351*

Tell them a tale of your adventures – *636*

Offer some money – *213*

Or apologise, leave the deck and

Approach the pirates with the monkey figure – *305*

Join the main bar – *594*

Or leave the tavern and

Make for the small houses – *1304*   (further options over the page)

Approach the gambling groups – *1424*

Go to see the fights – *84*

Decide this is not a place you want to explore and return to your vessel - *314*

659

Reduce your time by 1.

If your time is in the following gaps (22-18), you see a guard on his patrol and must remain hidden until he clears the area. Reduce your time by 6. Now continue at the plain text below

If your time is in the following gaps (57-53 or 17-13), you see a guard on the enclosing wall patrolling and must remain hidden until he clears the area. Reduce your time by 6.

If neither of these apply, continue at the plain text below

You keep to the shadows, but no one comes. What will you do now?

Do you

Hide where you are – *785*

Route South – *1393*

Creep East – *42*

Approach the building before you to break in – *1271*

660

The pirate king leans forward and smiles weakly. "Estes buried his treasure on Hangman's Island but it's hard to get to. I do have one bearing though from the abandoned Tower." He passes you a piece of paper. **Tick the codeword Bearing A.**

With a wave of his hand, he dismisses you and you are ushered from his presence and back to your vessel. Who knows how much use that was? The pirate who mans the door to the pirate king's abode advises that you will not be welcome again on this visit. **You may not visit the pirate king again until you return to Hell's Deep on another visit. Go to *1436***

661

The spectre speaks.

"You have disgraced the Master and mock his unholiness. Failure is not tolerated. You have no place among us."

The spectre vanishes as the fog thins. For a moment, you stand in the sunshine of the day. Your crew stand, relieved that they are free of the Devil's Sloop.

Then, without warning, your vessel plunges straight down to the depths, all hands sucked into the wake of the descending vessel. You see your crewmates slowly die before you become a drowned captive of the deep sea too.

Some decisions in life come back to haunt you, and yours certainly did.

662

Do you have ticked the code word **British Hunted** – *374*

Otherwise, the vessel routes towards you and you know you cannot outrun it.

Is your first officer Martha Downham or Black Robert or Diggory Hurst – *523*

If not, the galleon comes alongside you and the first officer of the warship, examines your vessel with his large crew and you are powerless to stop him. **He takes 50% of your cargo for his troubles** but he lets you carry on in your voyage. You breathe a sigh of relief when the galleon departs.

You return to your voyage but must **add 1 day extra to it** for this diversion.

Continue the voyage at *654*

663

Reduce your time by 1. You step forward and run into some crates. On your right you feel a wooden wall but there is clear water to your left.

Do you

About turn and step forward – *562*

Turn left and walk forward – *986*

Examine the crates – *605*

664

You wander along the path and reach a junction with three paths off it. Which way now?

Left – *105*

Middle – *560*

Right – *1033*

Turn back – *422*

665

You sail into the harbour at Fort August on a sunny morning with a strong breeze blowing. You see careful stares from guards on the walls and plenty canon that could be fixed upon you if you step out of line. Your first officer is smiling but you can see they are a little nervous.

If you have the codeword Spanish Tail, untick it, as a Spanish vessel will never follow you into a British fortification. If you have the codeword British Tail, untick it, as they follow you in but moor alongside and begin to unload crew and replenish.

Your first officer takes you to the British quartermaster who governs what can be bought and sold at Fort August. **If Timmers is your first officer,** you may also take advantage of any repair services to bring your vessel up to scratch but beware how many days repairs take.

You can trade in doubloons or treasure (use the doubloon equivalent score for your treasure). Peruse the deals below and advise your quartermaster what is required. Once you have decided, adjust your Vessel chart as necessary.

Provisions

- 5 doubloons per provision pack – 1 day to load
- A day's rum for the crew – 2 days cost (1 to acquire, 1 to drink to excess) Lifts crew morale by one level
    - Large crew – 50 doubloons
    - Medium crew – 25 doubloons
    - Small crew – 15 doubloons

Vessel repair

Note you may not repair your vessel higher than its initial level. All days required for each level are added together to get your total repair time.

- Vessel speed
    - One day for each level increased by
    - 300 doubloons for each level, or gold equivalent
- Vessel Firepower
    - Two days for each level increased by
    - 500 doubloons for each level, or gold equivalent
- Cargo Hold
    - One day for each level increased by
    - 200 doubloons for each level, or gold equivalent
- Manoeuvrability

The Treasure of Captain Estes

- o   Two days for each level increased by
- o   300 doubloons for each level, or gold equivalent
- Storm Handling
  - o   Two days for each level increased by
  - o   500 doubloons for each level, or gold equivalent

Having done your deals at Fort August and once you have adjusted your vessel chart and your time chart, it's time to set sail once again. Where are you going?

Do you have the codeword **Decent Chap** – *1100*

To sneak ashore at night – *307*

If you have had enough of Fort August, then **consult the voyage chart and set sail**.

666

The bottles before you are a motley collection but maybe you could use them as a weapon. You try to see the labels in the firelight, and one strikes you as a certain favourite of your fathers. The label reads Mackenzie, and you believe it is a whisky of some sort. You remember your father standing at the window on dark nights sipping this drink, and even holding it up to toast someone unknown. If you wish to take this bottle, **tick the codeword Bottle Whiskey Mackenzie.** The room is now fully ablaze, and you are starting to choke. Exit quickly to *510*

667

"The pirate!" cries a man as soon as you mention your first officer's name. You see others suddenly reach for swords and you can see a clear path to the door, so you run for your life. As you reach the crossroads panting you realise that was a rather dumb move. You need to remember just where you are. **You cannot come back into the Admiral's Whiskers. Go to *802***

668

Tick the codewords **Stowed** and **Jog. Go to *628***

669

As you approach the bar the punters turn to look at you.

Are you wearing

Your torn gown – *109*

A dress – *1169*

A long-coat – *15*

670

Reduce the Hot Strip by 1. If this places you on a Fire spot add 20 to this section's number and go there for the walls have moved. You can see fire to the north and to the west. To the south is clear air and your crewmates, while there is a clear route to the east.

Do you

Go South – *1428*

Go East – *320*

671

It is night time when you arrive at Strangar, the other side of the island from New Southampton. The path leading to it is a dusty track and you traipse into the hole of a place, wary of everything around you. Considering it is the middle of the night, the place is still alive and you can hear laughter and raucous amusement from up ahead. You have only heard rumours about this place but they are enough to make you not want to be here. You steel yourself, knowing what you must do: get a ship and a crew and get after Estes.

The Treasure of Captain Estes

As you enter Strangar you get long hard looks from several pirates, but no one approaches. Maybe they know not to invite trouble and you may just be that. Stepping on you decide you will need to search every nook and cranny to get yourself the best crew you can. That's if any of them can be trusted.

You are at the entrance to Strangar, step on and find your crew at **262**

672

You have a very long swim back to your vessel and the crab creatures are following. If you are quick enough and can get out of the shallows you may be able to escape as they seem to operate only on the seabed. As they are all around it will not be easy.

Roll 1xD100 (2xD10)

00-33 – **372**

34-67 – **851**

68-99 – **527**

673

Move Tabetha.

You are in a white walled room, bathed in the strange light, with one door with a picture of a spider above it.

If Tabetha's number is 24 – **1459**

If Tabetha's number is 17 – **note this number and go to 1029**

Where do you go next?

Through the spider door – **1106**

Wait here - **return to the top of this section**

674

0 Skull 0 Scales 5 Coins

Well, this game is easy. **Tick the codeword of your prize, keeping your stake item**, and return to *1060*

675

You raise your weapon and ask the man where Captain Estes is, but the man simply continues to whittle away at the stick. Off to your right you hear the click of a musket, and you slowly lower your weapon. You walk slowly away, knowing **you cannot return to this pier**. Make your next decision at *117*

676

There is Lord Buffington's desk to explore. Or you could look at the large set of drawers. Maybe the brass sextant takes your fancy, or the picture of the woman, or do the charts on the wall grab your fancy? What will you look at?

The desk – *1305*

Brass Sextant – *1446*

The picture of the woman – *640*

The drawers – *255*

The charts – *348*

677

Reduce your Island Time Chart by 1

You trek along the path, staring at the dense jungle around you. There's a fork in the path, and you wonder which way to go. You can take either fork, or you could always head out into the jungle off the path.

Do you go

Left – *245*

Right – *758*

Strike out into the Jungle – *1283*

Turn around back the way you came – *937*

678

Reduce your time by 2. If your time is in the following gaps (40-35 or 10-05) then go to *1322*. If not continue below

You are in the accommodation block with many buildings, many of which are labelled as residences of officers. There are guards at many doors, and you won't be able to go close to the houses without being seen. You wonder what you can achieve here. There is a flagpole in the centre of the quarter with no one nearby. There's also a small wagon lying along one of the paths, again unattended. Beyond these items, everything else looks like trouble.

In the north quarter, you can see horses and livestock at rest in pens. To the south, you can see servant slums and latrines.

Do you

Wait in hiding – *433*

Check out the flagpole – *297*

Look at the wagon – *147*

Move to the North quarter – *1176*

Move to the South quarter – *519*

679

You see a white bull running directly at you and it doesn't look like it will move to avoid you. You are in the right channel. What will you do?

Stay right – *1047*

Go to the middle – *466*

Go to the left channel – *298*

680

You open the door and walk into a dark room with a candle on the far side. You can see a number of bodies lying on beds and several are waking as the cool air enters the room.

"Oi, you," comes a shout and suddenly you are becoming the subject of rapidly opening eyes. It's a guards' barracks! You turn to flee but one of them has already got to the door and you are grabbed and then jumped on by many more guards.

You have been caught. What will be your fate as you are taken before the fort's commander? Go to *1358*

681

You take your small boat to the barge of Blind Tom and find it manned by teenagers and younglings. There are no adults on board, and you wonder where it is you have come to. A small child, maybe six or seven, welcomes you and asks that you accompany her. She leads you down below and then through the barge to the aft end. As you walk along you see hand drawn pictures of cats, a sword held by a ghost, a double pointed arrow, a picture of a Lady, a man standing by the sea where a mermaid swims off as he blows a horn, a man looking at the stars with a device as he sails, a large chicken with three wings, a long spear pointing out of the sea, a multitude of plants under the sea with many different colours, a canon, and finally a large group of children around a bearded man with his eyes plucked out.

The Treasure of Captain Estes

The child opens a door into a cabin in the aft section and you see an old man in a white beard. Children are feeding him, and you realise he has no eyes. However, he hears your approach and asks,

"Who do you bring me, my child?"

"Travellers like you were. Friends," says the child now addressing you, "Tom has seen so much, and he may offer you information for a price. You must offer him something and he will either accept it and furnish you with information, or he will have you removed from the boat. You may always return but Tom does not see so beware he may often give you the same information, such is his way."

What will you do? Do you have something to offer Tom?

Do you have any of the following codewords:

Ratcatcher: Monkey: Bodach Sword: Noiseless Horn: Johnstone's Confuser: Eye Charm: Spear: Orange Algae: Green Plant: Gold Medallion: Compass Map: Bird Chart: Gold Chain: Sextant: Argyle

If so go to *1416*

If not, do you offer doubloons – *1021*

If you have nothing to offer, or decide you don't wish to offer anything, then you should return to your vessel escorted by the child off the barge. Return to *473* and make another decision.

You yell at the crew to retreat and watch as the vessel slips to the aft of the galleon which allows you a run to freedom as the galleon tries to turn its broadside to you and launch volleys as you retreat. Your vessel now has a chance but is it quick enough to avoid what will be brutal volley after brutal volley?

Is your speed

Very Fast or Fast – *231*

Moderate – *1290*

Slow or Very Slow – *1427*

683

You dive swimming towards the poop deck and find that the helm has been broken off halfway up the wheel. The thick wood has been cracked by some external force. The deck has also been gorged, deep marks that run here and there. Something strange has happened here because you doubt any normal vessel would suffer this type of damage.

There's something shiny at the far corner of the deck and swimming over you see a medallion on a gold chain. It has a pentagram hanging from the chain, encircled in gold and you wonder if it could be worth something or of use.

If you take the medallion tick the code word Gold Medallion.

You realise you are short of air and decide to surface to the mast again. Having caught your breath make your next move.

Do you

Dive for the main deck – *316*

Investigate the forecastle deck – *770*

Or instead

Dive and search the outside of the vessel – *136*

Return to your vessel – *894*

684

Inside the building you are shown to a small room where a small man sits in his shirt sleeves. He has a small pair of spectacles and looks over a ledger of some sort. You sit for a long while as he ignores you until he suddenly looks up and pierces you with his gaze.

"State your business!"

Do you

Announce you want a vessel and crew – *194*

Tell the man who you are – *623*

Offer him a bottle of whiskey (if you have one) – *301*

685

Nervously, you get up from the table and walk outside the tavern and linger close to the dark shadows away from the dimly burning lanterns. You stand there for several minutes, watching drunken pirates come and go, until someone taps you on the shoulder. You jump and turn to see the gypsy woman. She is holding a pair of breeches, a long-coat and a hat, along with some boots.

"Now the boots are mine but the other items are from a rather disappointed fellow behind the tavern who thought he was in for a night of fun with me. He'll come to in an hour or two so don't be about here when he does."

You thank her and change into the clothing, feeling like you are less conspicuous. When you have dressed, you go to thank her again but the gypsy woman has gone. It's time to move on and get a crew. **If you wish change into the new clothing and note this. Otherwise, leave it right here.**

Leave the centre of Strangar and

Walk further into Strangar – *1256*

Make for the entrance of Strangar – *262*

686

Move Tabetha.

You are in a white walled room, bathed in the strange light, with three doors, one with a picture of a spider above it, one with a schooner above it, and the other with a pirate flag above it.

If Tabetha's number is 11 – *1459*

If Tabetha's number is 19 – **note this number and go to *1287***

If Tabetha's number is 14 – **note this number and go to *446***

If Tabetha's number is 6 – **note this number and go to *1029***

Where do you go next?

Through the spider door – *1213*

Through the schooner door – *317*

Through the pirate flag door – *537*

Wait here - **return to the top of this section**

687

Reduce the Hot Strip by 2. If this places you on a Fire spot add 20 to this section's number and go there for the walls have moved. There are walls of fire to the north, west, and east, so you route south from your current location. Go to *615*

688

You run directly to the flames and feel the scorching heat. You throw your arms up as you enter them and feel a wild pain coursing across your body. But the flames fall away, and you see the path from the temple back to the beach and run for all you are worth, hearing a laugh from behind you.

The Treasure of Captain Estes

At the beach, you forsake the small boat instead, swimming back to your vessel where you are hauled on board. You slip into a fever and are confined to your cabin for over three days, taking only a little water and bread. You shiver and see monstrous hallucinations of fire and darkness. Finally, after you break free of the sweats and shivers you realise that you have been ill for five days. **Mark off five days on your time chart.** Fortunately, the crew has recovered your small boat.

You decide you will not return to the dark isle, ever, but there may still be places to explore at Hell's Deep. **You may not return to the dark isle for the rest of your adventure.** So what next?

Go to see Blind Tom – *681*

Visit the provisions isle – *334*

Enjoy yourself at the wild isle – *879*

Approach the pirate king – *1348*

Decide you have had enough of Hells Deep and set sail - **Consult the voyage chart and set sail.**

<u>689</u>

Opening the chest, you see a gleaming stack of gold doubloons inside. You consider their weight and reckon you could get them back to the ship. As you reach forward, you hear a laugh from somewhere echoing around the room. You feel somewhat unsettled but that gold is right before you.

Do you

Take the gold – *131*

Close the lid of the chest and instead

Climb the rope – *843*

Examine the paintings – *621*

Look at the ship's wheel – *620*

Leave the room by the wooden door – *1439*

690

Reduce your Island Time Chart by 1

You trek along the path, and everything seems to be a mass of green. There's a fork in the path, and you wonder which way to go. You can take either fork, or you could always head out into the jungle off the path.

Do you go

Left – *245*

Right – *81*

Strike out into the Jungle – *1283*

Turn around back the way you came – *789*

691

You walk along the dock until you see a rather pompous man aboard a vessel who looks down at you at first. You are introduced to him, and he suddenly becomes very interested in you.

"Ah, my dear Mary, so delighted to meet you. My name is Captain Timmers but you can call me Timmers. And this vessel you are so taken by is a Dutch Fleut, the Paradise. I am told you wish to retrieve things that are yours. Terrible business these last days with your father, shocking. I will be delighted to assist in the recovery of your fortune, for a small fee of course. Please, welcome on board."

The next few days you stay on board hidden away from the people of New Southampton and Timmers sends out scouts to ascertain the whereabouts of Captain Estes. During this time you are introduced to ship procedures and also given a pirate's outfit to wear including a tri cornered hat. It seems an age before any reports of Estes come back.

While you wait, it's time to fill in your vessel chart with the details of your vessel and crew. Look for the chart at the rear of the book. You may photocopy this for ease of use. Fill it in now.

The Treasure of Captain Estes

First Officer: Timmers

Vessel: Paradise - Dutch Fleut

Speed: Moderate

Firepower: Heavy

Treasure store: Large

Shallows: No

Manoeuvrability: Great

Storm Handling: Good

Crew: Medium

Initial Provisions: 18 sections

Doubloons: 500

Timmers approaches your room onboard one day and has a look of dashed bad luck on his face.

"Mary, I'm sorry but Estes is dead. He ran into the British and was jolly well hammered somewhere near New Southampton. My informant states the cad left his treasure on an island in the vicinity of New Southampton. They call it the Dark Land, and it's not a place the locals like with their superstitious mumbo jumbo. I've been around these parts long enough to know that it's a pile of nonsense and any right-thinking person knows he has simply buried the spoils of his efforts on a small island that is hard to navigate to."

"So, I have nothing," you say, "unless I chase this treasure."

"Well dash Mary, I guess that's the case exactly."

"Well then, when do we start? And where should we go?"

"I have no definitive sightings of Estes before his last battle which was southeast of New Southampton. If you look at this chart, Mary, there are six places in the general locale where he could have been before he died and which may be able to shed light on his travels, and where the island is. Once you have examined them all, give the crew orders of where to sail to."

Check the *chart of New Southampton at App 02* to help you in your decisions. You may photocopy it for use with this book. Turn now to section *1276* to learn about the six locations and about sailing around New Southampton, and then to make your first decision as captain!

692

You tun the vessel quickly and gasp as large tentacles surround your vessel. But this was the plan, and you are in position to dispatch a deadly load. You give the order to fire!

Is your Firepower

Very Heavy or Heavy – *808*

Moderate – *773*

None or Light – *1463*

693

Reduce your time by 1.

You leave the room and close the trapdoor, fumbling down the passage and returning to the hut. **You may not return down this tunnel again.** Once there, you close the trapdoor and cover it with the rug.

If your time is in the following gaps (52-48) you see a guard on his patrol outside and must remain hidden until he clears the area. Reduce your time by 6. Now continue at the plain text below

Now, do you in the hut

Look at the desk – *206*

Look at the other rug – *565*

Try to open the safe – *1288*

Decide this is a bad idea and return outside – *174*

694

Did you select a pole (indicated by a codeword) to enter the water with? Which one of these codewords was it.

Red Pole – *99*

Green Pole – *872*

Blue Pole – *1002*

If you have none, return to the section you noted as you have no useable poles.

695

You take the small boat back to your vessel and clamber on board. The crew lift what treasure you have gathered and you ponder how to leave this cursed island.

Go to *725*

696

If your first officer is Martha Downham or Black Robert or Diggory Hurst, your crew are disgusted with your actions and are grumbling. **Reduce your crew morale by one level.**

If your first officer is Simon Kilmer, Robert Grimshaw or Timmers, your crew approve of your actions. **Increase your crew morale by one level.**

Now resume your voyage but you must **add 2 days extra to it** for this diversion.

Continue the voyage at *654*

<u>697</u>

Have you acquired the following codewords since your last encounter

Spanish Priests or **Holy Man** – *704*

Or is Martha Downham your first officer – *1186*

Or if you already had **Spanish Priests** or **Holy Man** during your first encounter – *945*

Otherwise read on

A familiar mist surrounds your ship after black clouds form and the sea begins to swirl as before when you last saw the Devil's Sloop. You know what this means, and you hear the words in your head "Tribute". You freeze on deck wondering what tribute will be asked for this time.

Roll 1xD100 (2xD10). Read the result below and then remove the indicated cargo.

00-20 – **All your treasure. If you have no treasure, then half your cargo hold is suddenly destroyed and will require repair.**

21-40 – **Half of your provisions.**

41-60 – **Twenty crewmates. Reduce your crew by 1 level. Reduce your crew morale 2 levels.**

61-80 – **Three days of worship. You remain bowed before the sloop for three days. These must be added to your voyage time, and your crew morale is lowered by 1 level.**

81-00 – **Half your treasure and half of your provisions. If you have no treasure, then half your cargo hold is suddenly destroyed and will require repair.**

You see the day return to normal after your tribute is offered, the sun again shining and the wind blowing steadily in your sails, the sloop nowhere in sight. But you feel haunted, will that dammed sloop never leave you alone. Now continue your voyage at **654**

698

You sail into a small opening that has three exits from it: East, west, and southwest. The southwest exit is described as awkward by your first officer and will require a vessel with at least good manoeuvrability that can operate in the shallows. The other channels look wide and passable.

Do you

Sail west– **1349**

Route east – **525**

Go southwest (only vessels with Good/Great manoeuvrability and which can operate in the shallows) – **1118**

699

"Lost? Well, no one will miss you then." The pirate stabs you and lets you fall from the quay into the water. Pain races through your body and you try to struggle in the water but cannot keep your head above the lapping tide. It's a watery grave for you in Strangar. Still, you're not the first to suffer that. Try again at **1** and be more careful.

700

You see a brown bull running directly at you and it doesn't look like it will move to avoid you. You are in the right channel. What will you do?

Stay right – *783*

Go to the middle – *392*

Go to the left channel – *298*

701

The sailor looks delighted with the **bottle of whiskey (Untick the codeword)** and he tells you to wait here while he goes to get his crew for introductions. You stand waiting for twenty minutes before you hear a cry from out on the water. Turning around you see the sailor on a small rowing boat, the open bottle of whiskey to his lips, giving you a toast. As he does a flurry with his hand as a way of a bow, he overbalances and falls into the water.

From behind you, you hear someone say, "I see Captain Courageous has robbed another poor sod of a bottle. Total con man, and a drunkard."

You slump your shoulders having wasted the whiskey but there's nothing for it but to look again. Go to *117* and choose another option.

702

You walk forward into the darkness shaking as you do so. As you walk you feel that same wind at your back pushing you forward, and you start to stumble. You stumble along unable to stop yourself. But the floor remains, solid beneath your feet.

Up ahead you see daylight again and you emerge out into the cool sunlight with yet more branching paths and another post and a board. This time it reads

'Who was my hero pirate as I grew up?'

The Treasure of Captain Estes

You look up above the dark entrances back into the cliffs and see three answers:

Once more dear friends! Do you walk the path that leads to

Bluebeard – *721*

Yellowbeard – *65*

Redbeard – *1361*

Or do you turn around and forget these crazy questions to head back down to the jungle path – *335*

703

You see three poles in the sand, as if thrust deep into it. One is marked with a blue band, one a green band and another a red band. They look as if they could be handled, and maybe even pulled out. You can see no danger around them but maybe it's lurking.

Do you pull out the

Green banded one – *739*

Red banded one – *835*

Blue banded one – *883*

None of them and instead

Strike out for the path – *1039*

Investigate the hut – *1395*

704

A familiar mist surrounds your ship after black clouds form and the sea begins to swirl as before when you last saw the Devil's Sloop. You know what this means, and you hear the words in your head "Tribute". You freeze on deck wondering what tribute will be asked for this time.

Who is in the cargo hold?

Spanish Priests – *544*

Holy Man – *1105*

705

You barely overcome the main current to get to the eddy, and you suffer for it. **Reduce your Waters Strength Chart by 2.** You swim through to the eddy. Go to *291*

706

Reduce your Waters Strength Chart by 1. The current is pushing you south. However, you think you may be able to swim up an eddy to the east. Do you

Float South – *285*

Swim East – *1295*

707

If you have the codeword **Closed** – *23.* If not, read on

You reach the end of the path and find a temple before you. It is open sided with many columns and seems to be declining somewhat. You can see another path into the jungle on the other side. What do you do?

Explore the temple – *805*

Skirt round the temple and walk along the other path – *202*

Retreat along the path you came on – *1329*

708

"So, you've come back to join then. Jolly good. This way then." Before you can react, you are swept inside the Guild Building and you decide you'd better go along with this. Go to *811*

709

Reduce your time by 1. You step forward and feel clear water in front of you. This is also true on your left but on your right is a large barrel blocking your progress.

Do you

About turn and step forward – *1252*

Turn left and walk forward – *1381*

Walk forward – *237*

710

When you are asked to roll the dice in the very next section add 50 to the result up to a maximum result of 99. Now go to *1017*

711

As you approach the gypsy woman stares at you. Are you wearing

Your torn gown – *13*

A dress – *100*

A long-coat – *154*

<u>712</u>

Reduce the Hot Strip by 3. If this places you on a Fire spot add 20 to this section's number and go there for the walls have moved. You are surrounded by fire. There is nothing you can do but wait for the walls to move. **Reduce the Hot Strip down to the next Fire spot and add 20 to this section's number and go there.**

<u>713</u>

You seem to go through your doubloons quickly with a number of pirates stepping forward and when you get back to the vessel you see that your new crew is there. **Increase your crew size by 1 as long as the vessel has room. If not, you have wasted money on a new crew that cannot come with you.**

What now?

Go to see Blind Tom – *681*

Visit the provisions isle – *334*

Go back to the Wild Isle – *879*

Explore the dark isle – *397*

Approach the pirate king – *1348*

Decide you have had enough of Hells Deep and set sail - **Consult the voyage chart and set sail**

714

Move Tabetha.

You are in a white walled room, bathed in the strange light, with a door with a picture of a pirate flag above it.

If Tabetha's number is 4 – *1459*

If Tabetha's number is 10 – **note this number and go to *1029***

Where do you go next?

Through the pirate flag door – *358*

Wait here – **return to the top of this section**

715

Reduce your time by 1. You step forward and feel clear water ahead. On your right you touch a wooden wall while there is fallen wood blocking the way to your left.

Do you

About turn and step forward – *1162*

Walk forward – *276*

716

You send for your offering, and it is brought before Tom who touches it carefully, examining it. He smiles and a child takes your offering away.

"The island you seek requires a chart and three bearings to locate. Or a mystic compass can show you the way on an empty chart."

You wonder what this all means. Could he be talking about where Estes has hidden his treasure?

What now?

Do you want to offer another gift - *1416*

Or do you take your leave of Tom and

Visit the provisions isle – *334*

Enjoy yourself at the wild isle – *879*

Explore the dark isle – *397*

Approach the pirate king – *1348*

Decide you have had enough of Hells Deep and set sail - **Consult the voyage chart and set sail**

717

If your first officer is Martha Downham or Black Robert, your crew are disgusted with your actions and are grumbling. **Reduce your crew morale by one level.**

If your first officer is Simon Kilmer, Robert Grimshaw or Timmers, your crew approve of your actions. **Increase your crew morale by one level.**

If your first officer is Diggory Hurst, the crew seem unphased by your actions.

Now resume your voyage but you must **add 2 days extra to it** for this diversion.

Continue the voyage at *654*

718

There's not a sound as you walk past, the figure barely moving. You try not to stare and instead walk quickly past. Go to *828*

719

The pirate places a coin into the central cup of three and turns them all upside down. Her hands then become a blur as the cups are moved around at pace before being reset in a line.

"Now call," says the pirate, indicating you should choose the left cup, the middle cup or the right cup.

Do you choose

Left – *484*

Middle – *318*

Right – *411*

720

"I want to see Duncan Mackenzie," you say holding the letter up in front of you. The pirates look at each other uncertainly before one steps forward and looks to put his arm around you.

"You need to come with me. We don't mention that name here. If people hear that name, then Black Robert will not be happy."

The man encroaches upon you, but you have a chance to run before he reaches you. Is it safe to go with him?

Do you

Go with him – *259*

Run – *908*

721

Once more you walk forward into the darkness shaking as you do so. As you walk you feel that same wind at your back pushing you forward, and you start to stumble. But thankfully, the floor remains, solid beneath your feet.

Up ahead you see daylight again and you emerge out into the cool sunlight but there is no branching path, merely a treasure chest filled with gems and coins. Congratulations you have the treasure of the Winds of the World, including to your delight, the Cross of Cadiz!

Tick the codeword Still. Reduce your Island Time Chart by 8, to take account of how long you have taken with this challenge.

Time to get moving. You take the chest back to your crewmates and you all return down the mountain and to the jungle path you came from. Go to *171*

722

"I have the great Martha Downham on board," you say and watch as the bald man bows before you.

"Please enter into our stronghold. The king is delighted that you join us."

The man turns and signals to vessels that are gathered around the entrance to the islands, and you sail into the small group. Go to *473* to continue your adventure.

723

You stand as the soldiers frisk you, and one produces the brass key you found in the message office from your pockets. He immediately arrests Timmers and you, taking you to the Fort's commander. Timmers speaks eloquently about a mere misunderstanding, but the Commander is not happy. Thanks to Timmers you can walk away from the fort, **but half of your treasure and your provisions have been removed from your vessel. Delete these now. If you have no treasure, remove three quarters of your provisions. Untick codeword Brass Key.**

The Treasure of Captain Estes

Timmers is angry with you as his reputation at the fort is ruined and your crew are annoyed at the loss of treasure and provisions. **Lower your crew morale by 1 level. Tick the codeword Caught.**

You are told to leave the fort immediately and you set sail. But where are you going?

Do you

Wish to sneak into the fort at night – *307*

Sail elsewhere - **consult the voyage chart and set sail.**

724

You try to casually walk past the figure in the shadows and hold your breath as you pass by.

Are you

Still in your dress to go shopping – *952*

Dressed like a slave in your torn gown – *313*

Wearing a long-coat and breeches – *718*

725

You stand on your deck wondering how to leave this cursed island, but a thick fog begins to surround your vessel. You hear waves begin to crash up against your vessel and it pitches to starboard, then violently to port. You wrap your arm around a nearby rope and hang on for your life.

You are unsure how long this fog lasts for but when your vessel stops its violent lurching, the fog begins to dissipate. You wonder where you are and take a spyglass to discover your location. On the horizon is an island, an extremely large. Tentatively you set sail for it. As you get closer, you realise you are just south of the port of New Southampton.

You are close to where it all started, and your home is in sight. This is the end of the journey for now, but do you have what you need to regain your life? It's time to count your treasure.

Do you

Have the codeword **Darkness** – *1340*

Have the codeword **Girlfriends** – *1062*

If not, read on

It is time to count up your treasure so check your cargo hold. Add up the monetary value of all your treasure and cargo. The following treasure is worth these amounts:

Treasure of Drops of Daniel: 100,000 doubloons

Treasure of Waters of Myra: 300,000 doubloons

Treasure of Wall of Fire: 200,000 doubloons

Treasure of Winds of the World: 500,000 doubloons

Treasure of Bulls of the Plain: 200,00 doubloons

Once you have added up your treasure, check the table below and go to the assigned section

Total Treasure (in Doubloons)	Section
0	996
1-3,000	821
3,001-5,000	529
5,001-50,000	747
51,001-99,999	497
100,000-299,999	633
300,000-499,999	954
500,000-999,999	1222
1,000,000 or more	260

Pirate on the rigging as a rival pursues!

<u>726</u>

Do you have the codeword **Decline – 708**. If not, read on.

"Join the guild, eh? Well, you look like a reasonable fellow so we will get you inside and see what the Master Mariner makes of you."

"Master Mariner?" you query.

"Yes, Lord Hugo Buffington, a qualified Master Mariner, and current head of the guild here in Malin's Town. But you'd better have your credentials with you, he doesn't suffer fools gladly. If you want to still apply, please step inside."

Do you

Enter – *811*

Decide that this is a bad plan and decline. If you do so **tick the codeword Decline.** Now what next? Do you

Come back at night in an attempt to gain access when the building is closed – *742*

See to the needs of your vessel and crew – *903*

Try to earn some money by signing up to a cargo run – *1335*

Visit the taverns for information – *802*

If you have had enough of Malin's town, then **consult the voyage chart and set sail.**

<u>727</u>

You wander along the path, resisting the urge to skip, and reach a junction. Which way now?

Left – *483*

Right – *891*

Turn back – *554*

728

You wander along the path and reach a junction with three paths off it. Which way now?

Left – *422*

Middle – *105*

Right – *560*

Turn back – *1033*

729

You feel like you have been in the cell for months when one night your first officer suddenly turns up and releases you from your cell. You march past dead bodies, obviously their work, and you are smuggled back onto your vessel, sitting out in the bay. The crew however are not happy, and your first officer tells you it has taken them 15 days to get you out.

Reduce your crew morale by 4 levels. You're alive but not by much. You have also lost 15 days, reduce your time chart by 15 and your provisions accordingly.

Now consult the voyage chart and set sail for your next destination.

730

"Excuse me," you say, "do you know where I can acquire a vessel with a crew?"

"Hut back there," says the man, pointing at the hut you saw previously. The man doesn't lift his head but resumes his whitling. He seems very uninterested in you.

Do you

Offer him a **Bottle of Whiskey** – *813*

Threaten him with a weapon for information – *675*

Go to the hut – *753*

Return to the front of the docks – *117*

<u>731</u>

You tell Madame Le Vert that you need a few moments and begin to place the wooden boxes on top of each other allowing you to reach the small window. Pulling back the shutters, you find it a real squeeze but manage to haul yourself through to the outside, where you drop into the alley at the rear of her shop. You are still in your dress and are sweating profusely with the effort in what is now a hot sun as you make for the main street.

Tick the codeword Prominent, if not already ticked, on your list and go to *1166* to continue your escape.

<u>732</u>

You grab the handles of the chest and your hands burn. You scream in pain and stumble almost into a wall of fire, but you stagger here and there momentarily lost in your pain. When you recover, you are not sure where you are.

Reduce the Hot strip by 2 and go to 648

<u>733</u>

Add a modifier of 10 when asked in the next section. Go to *207*

734

"Black Robert is my Captain."

There is a sudden hush over the assembled drinkers. The barmaid steps forward and invites you into the rear room asking what it is you need. When you tell her you are looking for information, she gathers some of the local drinkers who spend time answering your questions. You get several good titbits of information.

"Beware Brid's Paradise, for Brid, a malevolent spirit resides inside. It is a spirit of tricks, tempting you before leaving you empty."

"The Mariner's Guild found something of Estes', but they keep it in the back offices. It has to do with his treasure."

"There are crab people around the Abandoned Island. I have seen them."

You thank them all for the information and take your leave back to the crossroads at *802*

735

Reduce the Hot Strip by 2. If this places you on a Fire spot add 20 to this section's number and go there for the walls have moved. There are walls of fire to the north, south, and east, so you route west from your current location. Go to *826*

736

You draw your sword which causes many other swords to be drawn. You then hear a click and turn to see the barmaid pointing a musket at you.

"Leave now, or die!"

You decide that living is better and slowly walk away. **You cannot return to "The Dog's Knackers" in the future. Go to** the crossroads at *802*

737

"While we are here in Malin's Town, I have a contact who could help us get some money. Or maybe even some information. Let me go to town."

You wait while Robert disappears, and he comes back a few hours later with a gentleman in tow. In your Captain's quarters, over rum, he tells you how Estes has buried his treasure on an island that is hard to locate. He can offer no help in finding it but he knows that the island has several trials to be overcome in order to reach the treasure. He can obtain information about one of these trials if you are prepared to commit a *dark run* for him. This is contraband goods. There are three drop-off points: Fort August, The Marie Saratoga, and Hell's Deep. If you do this and then return to Malin's Town, he will have the information. He looks nervous as he asks if you will accept.

Do you

Accept – *779*

Reject the offer – *1104*

738

Reduce the Hot Strip by 2. If this places you on a Fire spot add 20 to this section's number and go there for the walls have moved. There are walls of fire to the north, west, and south, so you route east from your current location. Go to *1236*

739

You pull out the green banded one and it comes away fairly easily. You can see very little markings on it except for a coarsely drawn creature. Does it have legs or fins, it's hard to tell. **Tick the codeword Green Pole.** What next?

Do you pull out the

Red banded one – **835**

Blue banded one – **883**

Neither of them and instead

Strike out for the path – **1039**

Investigate the hut – **1395**

740

You cannot miss the anger on your first officer's face as you tell them you wish to avoid and encounter. However, they tell the crew to set a new heading and you pull away from the vessel you sighted. They follow you but eventually lose you in the dark of the night.

If you sail a galleon, add 3 days to your voyage time, if a Brigantine, add 2 days. Also lower your crew morale by 1 level, as your first officer tells them how weak you are.

Continue the voyage at **654**

741

The charts on the wall interest you, especially an unmarked one of the seas around New Southampton. If you take it tick the codeword, **Empty Chart.**

Go to **1400**

742

You return to the Guild in the dead of night and find this area of Malin's Town to be extremely quiet, if not quite dead. However, the guild are not daft and have a patrol operating around the building. You decide to sit a while and watch to see if you can gain any ideas about how to infiltrate the building. Most shutters seem locked up tight except one on the first floor which is near the top of a hanging post. It would be an exposed climb but doable. There are also the front doors which are slightly ajar, but the patrol passes by regularly. There is also a half-broken set of doors in the ground just before the building.

The patrol seems to take little interest in the shutters on the first floor or in the broken doors. What will you do to gain access?

Do you

Try to go up the hangman's pole to the first-floor shutters – *1172*

Approach the front doors – *181*

Enter the broken doors into the ground – *611*

743

As you reach up for the chain, you hear a screech, and thundering from the jungle. Suddenly a swoop of monkeys race in, carrying you away and you have no idea where you are going. Eventually they dump you on a jungle path. **Tick the codeword Monkey.** You get up battered and bruised and unsure of your surroundings. You walk down your current path but where are you?

Roll 1xD100 (or 2xD10). Check your result below

00-19   go to *422*

20-39   go to *70*

40-59   go to *202*

60-79   go to *545*

80-99   go to *73*

744

Reduce the Hot Strip by 1. If this places you on a Fire spot add 20 to this section's number and go there for the walls have moved. There are walls of fire to the north and south. You can route east or west from your current location.

Do you

Go East– *520*

Go West – *27*

745

Your vessel sails so slowly, and you see the inevitable as the sloop turns broadside to you. The first volley obliterates your mast. The second sends great shards of wood flying from the deck. The third lands on you and you are gone. Fortunately, you don't see or hear the suffering as Gonzales sinks your vessel.

Make sure you pick a fight you can win! You can try again at *1*.

746

Your crew sail your vessel to the middle of the island where you are put ashore to a tiny beach via the small boat. **Tick the codeword Middle.** Standing on the sand, you see a path cut through the jungle before you. It had a muddy base and looks to be shrouded by impenetrable jungle. You can stand here all day beneath the dark, overcast skies, or get on.

Do you

Strike out on the path – *601*

Return to your vessel and choose a different path – *1386*

747

You examine the cargo hold and the crew are not ecstatic about your haul, but they are content to sail to New Southampton and take their meagre share.

However, you do not have enough to restart your life and regain your home, not by a long way. Instead, you find service running a trading vessel which at least brings you an income. Life isn't comfortable but you have food in your belly, and usually somewhere warm to sleep. It could have been a lot worse. And there's always the hope for new adventures.

748

Timmers is frowning and looks extremely worried. "This is not a good idea so listen carefully. As I have said before, go to the message station, the small hut, and there will be some sort of access from there to the intelligence building. Don't go near the barrack buildings as all the soldiers will be asleep in those. That's all in the middle of the fort inside the inner walled area. The patrol is set up on a check 200 pattern, so move wisely."

Tick the codeword Check 200. You nod and look at the walls before you. Go to *1143*

749

You turn this way and that as you run around the inner section of the fort... and walk straight into the guard who is patrolling the area. You're out of breath and he has a pistol pointed at your head. Oh dear, looks like you are out of luck.

You have been caught. What will be your fate as you are taken before the fort's commander? Go to *1358*

750

Do you have the codeword **Well** – *1036*. If not continue below.

The path ends in a small clearing at the centre of which is a well. There is a rope hanging down from the well head, but you cannot see how far it goes down such is the blackness below. There is a handle for winding up the well rope, but should you risk bringing up what is down below? Otherwise, the clearing is empty save for the mud beneath your feet.

Do you

Wind up the well rope – *1051*

Decide it is not worth the risk, turn around and retreat down the path – *545*

751

You sidle up to one of the pirates and he offers you a drink. He asks where you are from, and you keep evading his questions but tell him you need to get a ship to take you after some treasure. He seems to think it's all a brag, but he tells you that if you'll walk out with him, he can take you to a vessel. It might not be the fastest, but he says it is good for sneaking around.

Do you

Take the pirate up on his offer – *848*

Or decide to check out the rest of the tavern instead and

Talk to the gypsy woman – *711*

Walk over to the single pirate – *838*

Go over to watch the pirate playing the mouth organ – *1421*

Or leave – *1112*

752

Your crew is made up of female slaves you found in the hold of the Spanish cargo vessel, and you yell at them to do whatever they can to distract the male crew. You watch as the women first try to simply slap the men or yell at them. You tell them they need to use more of their feminine charms, and you see the women become more amorous with the men. Gradually they begin to lead them below deck where the women keep them in amorous embraces, distracted from the mermaids.

It takes a day of this and having all the hatches and doors to the main deck locked before the mermaids give up realising that they have lost the battle for the men. You breathe a sigh of relief as you unlock the hatches, but you realise it will take another while before you can get everyone back to their jobs on deck.

You have lost 2 days sailing due to the distraction, so add 2 days to the voyage time. However, you have a very happy crew. Raise the crew morale by 3 levels.

Now continue your voyage at **654**

753

You enter the hut and see a rotund gentleman in a fancy hat sitting behind a wooden desk with several scrolled papers lying across it. The room is bare except for a few bottles lying here and there. He grunts as you approach before looking up at you.

Are you

In a dress – **930**

Disguised in a slave outfit – **579**

Wearing a long-coat – **1139**

754

You step onto the pillar and breathe a sigh as it doesn't crumble. The waves crash far below, and you ponder your next move. There is a pillar in front of you and the cliff edge behind you.

Do you step

Forwards – *531*

Backwards – *1045*

755

"If you want to hire a vessel then I need to know why, and you'll need money." Again, the man has not raised his eyes.

Do you

Place a **Promissory Note** on the table – *934*

Tell him who you are - *481*

Decide to leave – *117*

756

You are in a round room with a chest in the middle of the room. There is nothing else in the room and yet there is an eerie glow of green that seems to light the area dimly. As you approach the chest, you hear laughter, mocking and which cuts through you like a knife. The wind picks up and you can hear a howling.

Do you

Open the chest – *1432*

Leave the room by the rope – *470*

757

Reduce the Hot Strip by 1. If this places you on a Fire spot add 20 to this section's number and go there for the walls have moved. There are walls of fire to the south and west. You can route north or east from your current location.

Do you

Go East – *1403*

Go North – *520*

758

Reduce your Island Time Chart by 2

You trek along the path, and it seems such a long stretch. Eventually there's a fork in the path, and you wonder which way to go. You can take either fork, or you could always head out into the jungle off the path.

Do you go

Left – *245*

Right – *910*

Strike out into the Jungle – *1347*

Turn around back the way you came – *1433*

759

"How do you know me?"

The sailor looks away. "Your mother when she was younger travelled to America and came into child with my father. They managed to conceal my birth from others, and she returned to England but my father then took a wife and stated I was from that union. That is as much as I know from my adopted mother. My father died before I came of age. You are my half-sister, and I have sought you out but could not reveal the truth of the matter until I met you in person. But I have watched you from afar whenever I landed in New Southampton.

"But come, Mary, we have no time, give me the cross."

He looks sincere but is he really a conman.

Do you

Throw him the cross – *1018*

Refuse to help him and await your fate – *884*

760

Do you have the codeword **Prominent** – *96*

If not

Are you in a long-coat and breeches – *1324*

If not continue below

You turn away but someone has spotted you and they think they know who you are. One of the guards shouts and pursues you to the street, causing many people to look. You have to run to the far end of town to escape but you have been noticed. **Tick the codeword Prominent** to your list and continue at the far end of town at *1009*

761

Is your vessel manoeuvrability

Great or Good – *774*

Reasonable – *1318*

Poor or Lacking -*587*

762

You don't like the man and decide you can bend him to your will with a little coercion. You take out your pistol and point it at the man. As you do so you hear a click of another pistol being cocked.

"Miss Hastings, I have been in this business since before you were born and I never work alone. Kindly lower the pistol or my man will shoot. He's just outside the window in case you were wondering."

You lower your pistol, and he takes it off you (**Untick the codeword Pistol**). He then searches you. If you have no items in your inventory, then go to *918*. If you have any items, **untick them** as the man has taken them all from you. A pair of strong hands take you and throw you out of the hut back onto the pier. Continue now at *117*

763

"Well," says Simon, "you need to put the foot down. Watch this."

He strides into the middle of the deck and casts a dirty look at the rest of the crew and in particular your second officer. He draws his cutlass and swings around pointing it at the crew.

"The Captain has made a decision; since when did we have a debate on the matter. Now all of you back to work, unless anyone wants to challenge me right here and now, but understand, you will see the ocean floor before I'm done."

The crew take a step back and Simon smiles as they disperse. You see how they look at you though and you wonder if you have made the right move here. You can tell over the coming days as although they obey your commands quickly, they seem to watch you closely. **Reduce your crew morale by 2 levels.** Now continue at *654*

764

"I have the great Simon Kilmer on board," you say and watch as the bald man's face turns sour.

"And what has he done? He's hardly struck a blow that we have heard of. If that is the best you have then you must pay." **Tick codeword Flunk.** Unless you have something else you are going to have to pay or leave.

Do you

Decide you have an item you can offer to prove your worth – *229*

Offer doubloons – *1297*

Decide the price is too high and leave Hells Deep – **Consult the voyage chart and set sail**

765

You shout at the crew to cut out the nonsense and get back to work. They moan and groan, but do as you ask. In a matter of minutes you are back underway as you would like.

Decrease your crew morale by 1 level. However, you have wasted no time.

Now continue the voyage at *654*

766

Reduce the Hot Strip by 1. If this places you on a Fire spot add 20 to this section's number and go there for the walls have moved. You can see fire to the north and to the west. To the south is clear air and your crewmates, while there is a clear route to the east.

Do you

Go South – *890*

Go East – *583*

767

You order the guard to get a hold of them and take them above board before throwing into the sea. The person cries out, all arms and legs swinging crazily, and it sounds like you are being cursed. But there's a cheer from the crew as the person is dropped into the sea.

Raise your crew morale 2 levels. Tick the code word Passenger Overboard.

Now continue your voyage at *654*

768

You decide you are out of your depth and need to comply with the voice. You wonder what tribute to offer and decide to throw some cargo over to the sloop. You order the crew to go below and take some cargo, but you hear the voice in your head telling you how much to give.

Roll 1xD100 (2xD10). Read the result below and then remove the indicated cargo.

00-20 – **All your treasure. If you have no treasure, then half your cargo hold is suddenly destroyed and will require repair.**

21-40 – **Half of your provisions.**

41-60 – **Twenty crewmates. Reduce your crew by 1 level. Reduce your crew morale 2 levels.**

61-80 – **Three days of worship. You remain bowed before the sloop for three days. These must be added to your voyage time, and your crew morale is lowered by 1 level.**

81-00 – **Half your treasure and half of your provisions. If you have no treasure, then half your cargo hold is suddenly destroyed and will require repair.**

You see the day return to normal after your tribute is offered, the sun again shining and the wind blowing steadily in your sails, the sloop nowhere in sight. But you feel haunted, as if you will never be the same again. Now continue your voyage at **654**

769

You come on deck to see several crew seem to be missing. Your First Officer tells you that there has been a fight, a large one and that many of the crew have been dispatched overboard. You ask who started it and he points to two men.

"Rundle and Cole, they are the ring leaders. What should we do with them?"

Do you

Keel haul them – **1390**

Have a stern word – **196**

Throw them in the brig – **1292**

770

You swim over to the forecastle deck which is empty but deeply gorged by you know not what. There is a brass plaque on the deck, broken but it reads "first capture, Victory". You can see the hatches to the forecastle and wonder can you open them.

Do you

Try to open the hatches – **1211**

Or instead

Return to the mast – *603*

Dive and search the outside of the vessel – *136*

Return to your vessel – *894*

771

As you wait to see what he will say a trapdoor opens beneath you and you fall into a chute which makes you tumble out of the barge and into the waters around it. As you surface, a few children are laughing at you from the barge. Indignant, you swim to your vessel to dry off and decide your next course of action.

Go to see Blind Tom again – *681*

Visit the provisions isle – *334*

Enjoy yourself at the wild isle – *879*

Explore the dark isle – *397*

Approach the pirate king – *1348*

Decide you have had enough of Hells Deep and set sail - **Consult the voyage chart and set sail**

772

The only wall of fire is to the north. You can route south, east or west from your current location.

Do you

Go East – *233*

Go South – *30*

Go West – *394*

773

You wonder if you have enough firepower as the creature looms on all sides of your vessel, tentacles raised high. Fire and find out.

Roll 1xD100 (2xD10)

00-49 – *808*

50-99 – *1463*

774

Roll 1xD100 (2xD10). For every point of damage you have already done to the galleon add 3 to the result. Check the table below for the result of this round of the sea battle.

00-19 – You get caught with a severe broadside. **Lower your vessel manoeuvrability by 2 levels and your vessel speed by 1 level.**

20-39 – A volley lands on deck killing many of the crew. **Lower your crew by 1 level.**

40-59 – A volley blows out some of your canons, but you hit back – **Lower your firepower by 1 level.** But you cause the following damage dependent on your firepower: **Light – 1 point, Moderate – 2pts, Heavy – 3pts, Very Heavy – 4 pts**

60-79 – You land a splendid volley. Note you have done the following damage dependent on your firepower: **Light – 1 point, Moderate – 2pts, Heavy – 3pts, Very Heavy – 4 pts**

80 and up - You catch them cold with a blinding manoeuvre. Note you have done the following damage dependent on your firepower: **Light – 2 point, Moderate – 4pts, Heavy – 6pts, Very Heavy – 8 pts**

If you have caused 24 points of damage overall to the galleon – *1001*

If not

Do you want to continue the battle – *761*

Do you wish to run – *87*

<u>775</u>

Reduce the Hot Strip by 1. If this places you on a Fire spot add 20 to this section's number and go there for the walls have moved. There are walls of fire to the south and west. You can route north or east from your current location.

Do you

Go East – *925*

Go North – *548*

<u>776</u>

You wander along the path, feet now dragging, and reach a junction. Which way now?

Left – *564*

Right – *613*

Turn back – *555*

<u>777</u>

No, it's in the left cup, so you lose your stake. Hope you didn't bet too much. Want another try? If so whose game

Look to join the one-legged pirate's game – *1181*

Engage in the stumpy pirate's game – *1316*

Play in the female pirate's game – *618*

If not go to *64*

778

Reduce your Waters Strength Chart by 1. The current is pushing you east. However, you think you may be able to swim up an eddy to the north. Do you

Float East – *285*

Swim North – *250*

779

You have accepted an offer for a dark run. In the Dark Run Table (*App 13*), write down the three places to visit: Fort August, The Marie Saratoga, and Hell's Deep. When you visit them, score them off. When you next visit Malin's Town, and all the locations have been visited, go to *419* (note this down now) and continue from there.

The man has left so what will you do next

Do you

See to the needs of your vessel and crew – *903*

Try to earn some money by signing up to a cargo run – *1335*

Visit the taverns for information – *802*

Visit the Mariners' Guild for information – *124*

If you have had enough of Malin's town, then **consult the voyage chart and set sail.**

780

Reduce your time by 2. If your time is in the following gaps (46-41 or 16-11) then go to *1126*. If not continue below

You hear a loud bleat as you approach and there's a general migration towards you from the sheep in the pen. One tries to reach for your coat and have a nibble. Other than this distraction, there's nothing else here of note.

Do you

Wait in hiding – *1418*

Look at the cows – *387*

Go to the gate – *319*

Move to the West quarter – *493*

Move to the East quarter – *678*

781

You see a black bull running directly at you and it doesn't look like it will move to avoid you. You are in the left channel. What will you do?

Stay left – *298*

Go to the middle – *1047*

Go to the right channel – *783*

782

You rip the bedgown of its frills leaving a tunic-like outfit which reaches to your shins. From a piece of the ripped fabric, you fashion a crude belt and set off for the hallway. At first it is easy to move about, most of the soldiers casting you a look and maybe staring for a while but it's from attraction not suspicion. You can handle that.

Carefully you make your way to the courtyard of the garrison that leads to the front gates. They are open and you see traders coming and going with a few guards watching them carefully. There is a relaxed air about the place, and you see baskets of fruit and vegetables, and some casks among the goods being exchanged.

If you are going to escape, then you need to go out that gate.

Do you

Just walk out the gate – *907*

Grab a basket of fruit and walk out the gate – *336*

Grab a cask and walk out of the gate – *1438*

783

You narrowly avoid disaster and are clear and running in the right channel. Just what happened is hard to tell but an animal passed by close.

If you haven't already, start a timer at 0 in your notes. Now add 1xD10 to it. If the timer is over 30 go to *1378*. If not, continue below.

Roll 1xD100 (2xD10) and check the result below.

00-19 – *679*

20-39 – *1346*

40-59 – *700*

60-79 – *385*

80-99 – *568*

784

As the man holds you tight you pull your knife and press it against his stomach. "Back off, or die," you say in a steely whisper that surprises even you. The man gently lets go and slumps back to the wall.

"Easy lady, easy. No harm done here."

You watch him closely as you make your way down the alley to its end. Go to *828*

<u>785</u>

Reduce your time by 1.

If your time is in the following gaps (22-18) and you are not hidden, then go to *1037*. If you are hidden, you see a guard on his patrol and must remain hidden until he clears the area. Reduce your time by 6. Now continue at the plain text below

If your time is in the following gaps (57-53 or 17-13) and you are not hidden, then go to *1128*. If you are hidden, you see a guard on the enclosing wall patrolling and must remain hidden until he clears the area. Reduce your time by 6.

If neither of these apply, continue at the plain text below

You can see before you the shadow of a large building with a single person wooden door. There appears to be no one on guard.

To the south you can see a similar building to what is before you while to the east there is another building and further beyond, although the dark makes it hard to see.

Do you

Hide where you are – *659*

Route South – *1393*

Creep East – *42*

Approach the building before you to break in – *1271*

<u>786</u>

"While we are here in Malin's Town, I have a contact who could help us get some money. Or maybe even some information. Let me go to town."

You wait while Diggory disappears, and he comes back a few hours later with a gentleman in tow. In your Captain's quarters, over rum, he tells you how Estes has buried his treasure on an island that is hard to locate. He can offer no help in finding it, but he knows that the island has several trials to be overcome in order to reach the treasure. He can obtain information about one of these trials if you are prepared to commit a *dark run* for him. This is contraband goods. There are three drop-off points: New Southampton, The Abandoned Island, and Hell's Deep. If you do this and then return to Malin's Town, he will have the information. He looks nervous as he asks if you will accept.

Do you

Accept – **845**

Reject the offer – **1249**

787

Roll 1D100 (2xD10) to find where the coin actually is. Did you roll?

00-33 – **777**

34-67 – **1308**

68-99 – **46**

788

Reduce the Hot Strip by 1. If this places you on a Fire spot add 20 to this section's number and go there for the walls have moved. There are walls of fire to the north and south. You can route east or west from your current location.

Do you

Go East– **803**

Go West – **375**

789

Reduce your Island Time Chart by 1

You trek along the path, ever so tired. There's a fork in the path, and you wonder which way to go. You can take either fork, or you could always head out into the jungle off the path.

Do you go

Left – *125*

Right – *509*

Strike out into the Jungle – *1283*

Turn around back the way you came – *690*

790

The only wall of fire is to the East. You can route south, west or north from your current location.

Do you

Go West – *615*

Go South – *1065*

Go North – *1150*

791

You step onto the cliff edge and feeling relief at the solid rock beneath your feet. Quickly you grab the treasure chest, finding it a struggle, but light enough to carry back across the pillars to your crew. **Tick the codeword Gold A. Tick off 10 steps on your Island Time Chart for the time you spent doing this puzzle. Tick the codeword Whee.** Your men hoist up the gold and you all set off back on the jungle path you arrived from to see what else you can find on this strange island. Go to *1003*

792

You yell at the crew to go down to the hold and throw provisions overboard. As you drift away from the floating provisions, a crewman asks if they have thrown enough overboard. You tell them, no, to throw plenty more over. The Kraken feeds on the provisions but its attention is not kept for long and as you try to sail away a long tentacle flicks out ripping at your sails. One tears but the effort seems to have exhausted the creature and it drops away.

With a sigh of relief, you steer well clear of where the Kraken was spotted but resume course later that night.

Your crew are delighted at surviving. Raise crew morale by 1 level. However, the sail is badly damaged and will affect your vessel handling. Lower your vessel manoeuvrability by 1 level. Add 1 day to your voyage time for your diversion.

Now continue your voyage at **654**

793

You reply no, but that you would be interested in the whereabouts of Estes' treasure.

"Wouldn't we all," says Lord Buffington, "indeed we all would. But alas I fear there is little information about that in these parts."

You watch as his eyes flick towards the wall before he then sits down. "Well, if there is nothing else, do not let me detain you. But understand you have turned down our offer to join, so let's not see you back here soon."

You nod and are soon escorted from the building by Robert.

You cannot return to the Mariner's Guild in daylight as your refusal to join is known and you will not gain access.

Do you

Come back at night in an attempt to gain access when the building is closed – *742*

See to the needs of your vessel and crew – *903*

Try to earn some money by signing up to a cargo run – *1335*

Visit the taverns for information – *802*

If you have had enough of Malin's town, then **consult the voyage chart and set sail.**

794

You watch your crew with pride as they give everything they have, but your vessel struggles for its best speed. A tentacle comes out and rips a hole in the side of your vessel followed by another one cracking against the hull. You see part of your aft deck smashed as a tentacle comes down.

And then nothing. As your vessel pulls away from the black murky mass under the water, you see a large number of your provisions have fallen from the vessel where the creature struck the hull. The creature seems to be feasting on what would have been sustaining your crew.

With a sigh of relief, you steer well clear of where the Kraken was spotted but resume course later that night.

Your crew are delighted at surviving. Raise crew morale by 1 level. However, the vessel is badly damaged. Reduce your vessel speed by 2 levels. Lower your vessel manoeuvrability by 1 level. Remove 10 provisions from your hold (or all your provisions if you have less than 10). The hold areas containing those provisions are now unusable until you can effect repairs. Reduce your vessels Storm Handling by 1 level. Add 1 day to your voyage time for your diversion.

Now continue your voyage at *654*

795

Reduce your time by 1.

You remain in silence, listening intently but you can hear no one up above.

Do you

Push open the trapdoor – **909**

Or if you think you should leave it alone, continue below

You retreat along the tunnel and exit back in the message room, covering up the trapdoor again with the rug. Now, do you

Look at the desk – **206**

Look at the other rug – **565**

Try to open the safe – **1288**

Decide this is a bad idea and return outside – **174**

796

You empty several wine bottles in the corner, before lying down with the empties and beginning to babble loudly. Madame Le Vert asks if you are alright, but you just babble more. Soon she opens the door and comes close to see if you are alright. You hit her with one of the wine bottles and see her eyes spin as she drops cold to the floor.

You quickly step into the main shop and acquire a full outfit of breeches, boots, shirt, long-coat and hat, before organising the boxes in the dressing room and climbing out of the small window. It's a squeeze but you make it out to the alley outside and then to the street. You tip your hat to cover your face and get ready to plot your next path. **Tick the codeword Incognito.** Go to **1166**

797

You wander along the path and reach a junction. Which way now?

Left – *612*

Right – *639*

Turn back – *70*

798

If your first officer is Simon Kilmer, Robert Grimshaw or Timmers, your crew are disgusted with your actions and are grumbling. **Reduce your crew morale by one level.**

If your first officer is Martha Downham or Black Robert, your crew approve of your actions. **Increase your crew morale by one level.**

If your first officer is Diggory Hurst, the crew seem unphased by your actions.

Tick the codeword Spanish Hunted

Now resume your voyage but you must **add 2 days extra to it** for this diversion.

Continue the voyage at *654*

799

You hear a horn and suddenly the fort is swarming with soldiers. Maybe they saw you or maybe this is part of their security regime but whatever it has caught you out. There's no escaping the flooding of the area with soldiers and you are caught easily.

You have been caught. What will be your fate as you are taken before the fort's commander? Go to *1358*

The Treasure of Captain Estes

<u>800</u>

You circle the formation in your vessel keen to find a way in, but it all looks so very tight and understanding the depth of water below will be key. You can sound the depth beneath you but ahead of you will be impossible unless you have a chart. If you have the keyword **Bird Chart** – *1235*. If not, continue below.

You can see three points of entry into the maze of rocks surrounding the main rock formation and the cries of the birds makes it hard to concentrate on which would be best. The waves are choppy around the rocks too not allowing you to see over them and so your entry point will be a matter of blind luck. The three entry points are to the north, southwest and southeast of the formation.

Do you

Sail into the north entry point – *1260*

Try the southwest entry point – *246*

Take the southeast entry point – *1300*

<u>801</u>

You approach the first branch in the path in trepidation. From your high view point you can see the rest of the island, including the brief plains and lake of some sort in the jungle. As you approach the fork, you feel a cold wind like death approaching and you must force yourself to be steady.

There is a sign at the fork and you read it:

'Where was I born, you vagrant?'

You look at the three openings in the cliff face before you and see there is an answer engraved above each one. One says, *'Barcelona'*, another *'Seville'*, and the last *'God knows'*. It's time to make a choice.

If you have the codewords **Green Pole, Red Pole,** or **Blue Pole**, you can decide to walk with a pole in front of you, but decide which one now by placing a circle around that codeword.

Which opening do you enter?

Barcelona – *431*

Seville – *530*

God knows – *1229*

Or do you beat a hasty retreat – *34*

802

You stroll into town and arrive at a crossroads from which you can see three taverns. One is a high-class establishment and possibly visited by proper ex-navy officer types, called The Admiral's Whiskers. Another looks fairly quiet but not very rough, called the Malin's Town Alehouse. A third is rowdy and located amongst the rougher looking houses, called The Dog's Knackers. What information you can garner at these establishments, who knows? But which will you try if any?

Do you

Visit The Admiral's Whiskers – *966*

Go to The Malin's Town Alehouse – *60*

Wander to The Dog's Knackers - *311*

Or decide this is a bust and go elsewhere in Malin's Town

See to the needs of your vessel and crew – *903*

Try to earn some money by signing up to a cargo run – *1335*

Visit the Mariners' Guild for information – *124*

If your first officer is Simon Kilmer – *24*

If your First officer is Robert Grimshaw – *737*

If your First officer is Diggory Hurst – *786*

If you have had enough of Malin's Town, then **consult the voyage chart and set sail**.

The Treasure of Captain Estes

<u>803</u>

Reduce the Hot Strip by 1. If this places you on a Fire spot add 20 to this section's number and go there for the walls have moved. There are walls of fire to the south and east. You can route north or west from your current location.

Do you

Go West – **788**

Go North – **1250**

<u>804</u>

You proudly tell your tale of how you got your item and when they ask for proof, you send back word to your vessel to bring the item. The women are impressed, and you sit to talk about your life and journey to find Estes' treasure. They say they have also been searching for Estes treasure and have found some details out. He has left bearings to the island he left his treasure on and these have been acquired by various parties. They have acquired one of them and will share it with you if you divide the treasure found with them, half for you and your crew, half for them.

Do you

Agree – **622**

Refuse – **1282**

<u>805</u>

You enter the open plan temple and see amongst the many stone pillars, steps descending beneath the surface. Other than these large stone steps, everything is crumbling and overgrown with vines and foliage. You find the air humid and maybe going beneath the surface would allow you a little respite. What lurks down below you have no idea, but maybe it will have a clue to Estes' treasure?

Do you

Descend the steps – *451*

Decide to move on elsewhere on the abandoned island. You check the sun and realise you can go north - *202* or south - *1329* along a jungle path. Choose now.

806

"We'll need to see some money if you will. No items, no notes, just hard currency if you get me. All up front if you please."

You have a problem as you have no coins to speak of. Do you need to go in? If you do you'll have to force your way in.

Do you

Try to enter – *1415*

Return to the main street – *496*

807

A familiar mist surrounds your ship after black clouds form and the sea begins to swirl as before when you last saw the Devil's Sloop. You know what this means, and you hear the words in your head "Tribute". You freeze on deck wondering what tribute will be asked for this time.

Martha steps forward before you begging her master on board the devil's Sloop for mercy. She is grabbed by white spectral spirits who claw at her. You see her agony, but you can do nothing to help, even if you wanted to. She is thrown to the deck, and you hear cries from below deck. And then as soon as it all started you find yourself amidst sunshine and a steady wind in your sails.

You smile thinking it is only Martha who has been punished but the cabin boy runs up from below deck and yells at you that many of the crew are missing. They were ripped out and away by the spectres. You have paid a heavy price.

Lower your crew by 1 level. Lower your crew morale by 2 levels.

Now continue your voyage at *654*

<u>808</u>

You let loose with all your canon and swear you hear a cry from below the depths. The vast tentacles suddenly fall into the water causing great splashes that drench all above deck. But the creature has fallen, or at least retreated and you give the order to set sail away from the area. After an hour you believe it is gone and you continue your voyage.

Your crew are relieved. Raise your crew morale by 2 levels.

Now continue your voyage at *654*

<u>809</u>

"Well then sailor, head on down the alleyway and tell them Garner sent you. On second thoughts don't, I owe them money. Could be bad for your health." He gives a grin and then slumps back against the wall clearly having finished with you. Continue down the alleyway to *828*

<u>810</u>

You suddenly hear movement. There's a guard afoot, patrolling the area and although you can hear them you are not sure where they are coming from.

Are you in hiding?

Yes – *951*

No – *323*

<u>811</u>

Inside the building is an impressive wooden entrance hall full of paintings of vessels and sailors whom you believe must be quite famous to be hanging here. Across from you is a small wooden counter with a rather officious man sitting behind. He glances at you over a pair of spectacles."

"One to join," grunts the man in the overcoat who has come inside behind you.

"Very good. I believe Lord Buffington has finished lunch and is available for an initial interview. Take him on up but do make sure you knock, Robert. John got him in a terrible mood yesterday just barging in."

"Of course," says Robert.

You are taken up a set of stairs to the upper floor and led to a room at the end of the corridor. There is a brass plaque on the door, reading *Master Mariner Lord Buffington*, and Robert knocks unsubtly on the door.

"Come in," cries a voice form the other side and Robert opens the door, escorting you in.

"One to join," says Robert.

"And their name," says a diminutive man sitting behind a vast wooden desk. Also in the room are a series of charts on the wall, a brass sextant on a shelf, a portrait of a rather stunning looking woman in an evening gown and a set of large drawers hugging the wall closest to you.

"I don't know," says Robert.

"Useless," cries the man behind the desk as Robert leaves the room. "You, sir, you want to join the guild then?"

Do you

Agree – *361*

Say no, but that you would love information on the whereabouts of Estes' treasure – *793*

Say no, but that you are on business from your captain – *1306*

812

You stand inside the outer wall and look around you. You are close to the latrines which you see on the wall close by but to be honest, you can smell them first. There are also accommodations here, little hovels, almost shacks, and you reckon these are for the labourers. At the moment, you cannot see any sentries, but you know they are about.

To your left (the west side of the fort) you can see buildings that seem to be locked up tight but there are barrels nearby and other crates. It may be stores and supplies. To your right (the east side of the fort) you see rather well constructed buildings and flags flying, which may indicate important people. Ahead in the centre of the fort, is a wall which has sentries patrolling the top of it, but you cannot see inside the wall. There is a gate at the foot of the wall.

Do you

Wait where you are – *519*

Move to the west quarter – *493*

Move to the east quarter – *678*

Go to the gate in the wall at centre – *1073*

Leave the fort for your vessel – *535*

813

You offer the bottle of whiskey up to the man and he opens it and takes a swig. He grunts a "Thank you" before placing the bottle behind him. Clearly you are not getting it back. **Untick the codeword Bottle Whiskey Mackenzie**. The man returns to his whitling.

Do you

Threaten him with a weapon for information – *675*

Ask about getting a crew and a vessel – *730*

Leave the rickety pier – *117*

814

The rest of your journey is uneventful, and your crew seems happy with how you dealt with the incident (**Raise Crew Morale by one level**).

Arrive now at your destination, marking off your voyage time:

New Southampton – *1466*

The Wreck of the Marie Saratoga – *968*

The Abandoned Island – *1154*

Fort August – *247*

Malin's Town – *580*

Bird's Paradise – *198*

The Pirate Den at Hell's deep – *17*

815

Go to *1254*

816

You step onto the pillar and feel a slight wobble as the wind blows past you. There are pillars diagonally to your rear right, diagonally to your front right, and directly in front and behind. You can see a small item on the pillar directly before you.

Do you step

Diagonally forward right – *448*

Diagonally backward right – *1307*

Forwards – *238*

Backwards – *1363*

817

You drop the bottle, and the man begins to shout loudly after you. Diving through the crowd you manage to evade the man but plenty of people are now staring at you, and some appear to think you are someone being sought after. Tick the codeword **Prominent** in your list and go to the street at *496* for your next decision.

818

You slink up to the door, standing right beside it. A pirate soon walks out, a pistol before him. You clunk him over the head too and then pull the prone figure to one side. You think about going inside but you hear another noise and wait as another pirate walks out. You clunk him on the head too and this time the bottle smashes. You wait for a breathless minute, looking at the second pirate now lying on the ground. No one else emerges from the barn.

Do you

Enter the barn – *272*

Call it quits and return to the street – *1112*

819

You get hit by a dart and fall to the floor. When you wake up you are in the same room and have managed to drag yourself back to where you started on this floor. You don't realise now, but will when back at the ship, that a day has passed since you collapsed. **Add 1 day to your voyage chart. Go to *843***

820

Reduce your time by 1.

You can hear snoring above you in the room but note that it's intermittent. Is it safe to go up?

Do you

Open the trapdoor – *333*

If not, continue below

You retreat along the tunnel and exit back in the message room, covering up the trapdoor again with the rug. **Reduce your time by 1.** Now, do you

Look at the desk – *206*

Look at the other rug – *1356*

Try to open the safe – *1288*

Decide this is a bad idea and return outside – *174*

821

Your cargo hold has little treasure in it. After all this journey there is a pittance to show for your efforts. You give the command to sail for New Southampton, but your crew does not heed you. Instead, they grab you and place you in the small boat abandoning you on the sea.

You manage to row ashore but struggle to find any food. In the end, you are forced to sell yourself into servitude to be able to eat. You spend your days working long hours for so very little, being beaten and scolded when you do something wrong. Your life is a living hell which your battered body takes leave of in your twenties. So much for high adventure and success! Try again at *1*.

822

What are you wearing as you approach the shop? Are you

In a dress – *1402*

Disguised in a slave outfit – *896*

Wearing a long-coat – *935*

823

The day is somewhat feisty, with a strong breeze blowing and a swell on the sea. You watch your crew working away on deck when you hear the crow's nest shout down to you.

"Captain, pirate flag on the starboard side!"

You race to the side of the ship and take your eye piece, trying to spot the vessel called. You see a black flag and then try to take in the ship. Beside you, your first officer, is doing the same and they say to you,

"I recognise that vessel!" But who is it?

Roll 1xD100 (2xD10). Check the result below and go to that section. If you have been at this section before on a previous voyage and have rolled the same result, roll again until a different result is obtained.

01-20 – *178*

21-39 – *635*

40-59 – *418*

60-79 – *1131*

80-99 – *582*

824

The sun is incredibly low as you enter the small boat with your crewmates and whatever treasure you have taken from the island. You make for your vessel, rowing round to the other side of the island. As you reach your vessel, it is fully dark, and you can hear something in the water. Your necks hairs prick up just as a tentacle grabs hold of the small boat. The boat is flipped within reach of your vessel and your crewmates, and all the treasure hit the water with you.

Desperately you try to grab whatever treasure you can and make for your vessel. But do you make it?

Roll 1xD100 (2xD10) and consult the table below

00-19 – *991*

20-39 – *1257*

40-59 – *69*

60-79 – *1462*

80-99 – *1385*

825

The crew turn and discuss your offer before offering a hand to shake on it. "Know this Captain, if you reduce the rations again, we will throw you overboard."

Well, it's a deal. **You cannot reduce rations below 75% when trying to stretch them.** Continue your voyage at *654.*

826

There is a wall of fire to the south. You can route east or west, or to the north where there is clear air and your crewmates.

Do you

Go East– **735**

Go West – **583**

Go North and step out– **427**

827

Reduce your Island Time Chart by 1

You trek forward along the path, finding it muddy and stopping for the occasional snake. Soon you reach a fork in the path and you wonder which way to go. You could always simply strike out into the jungle off the path.

Do you go

Left – **886**

Right – **183**

Turn back around and go back to the beach – **197**

Strike out into the Jungle – **1347**

828

At the end of the alley is a tall building whose walls are beginning to crumble. At the door sits a man in a rocking chair, face covered by a broad hat. Beyond him are two wooden doors that have seen better days. As he sits there a woman steps out through the doors dressed in no more than a sheet, glares at you and then turns back inside. You see a wooden sign hanging at an angle on the wall. It reads, "Little Annie's". You have heard of this place, somewhere any self-respecting woman would stay away from, a brothel, a place where women sell themselves for money.

You wonder if it's a good idea to go inside. Maybe you can find a crew in this place though, although what sort of a crew, you wonder at.

Do you

Approach the man in the seat – *975*

Walk to the doors and try to open them – *1090*

Return to the main street via the alley - *496*

829

You are fortunate as you are beside cover and hide straight away. Go to *148*

830

You walk further along the jungle path, thick green all around you until you start to hear crashing waves. You creep forward until the path disappears and you find yourself standing on a sea cliff.

If you have the codeword **Drop** – *1313*

If you have the codeword **Whee** – *258*

Before you are several tall rock pillars about a man wide that rise some one hundred feet high. Below them is a churning sea that crashes against the bottom of these pillars. On the far side of the pillars is another ledge and you can see a treasure chest brimming with golden items. These are the Drops of Daniel.

To one side is small wooden post, at the top of which is a wooden board with a piece of parchment nailed to it. Given how windy it is up here you wonder how the notice remains but then this place is strange, or maybe cursed. Still, you want the gold, so you read the parchment.

"To cross the pillars, you must bless yourself before you take the gold. But beware for if you step on the wrong pillar, you will plummet to your death. Know this, I protect my gold, so death to all who come to take it."

Clearly you have to step from pillar to pillar across to the far side and there collect your gold but you see how any fall from a pillar will result in your doom. There are several initial pillars to choose from and you can see that some pillars have items on them. Maybe they are what you will use to bless yourself. You can see where the items are, but the items are so small that you cannot tell what they are.

Look at the diagram at *App 15* which shows your position now and the pillars that are in place before you. You can step out and accept this challenge by going to the section indicated on the initial pillars. Or you can turn around and leave the gold on the far side, forever in Estes' dead hands. Just remember that the note said you would fall to your doom.

Note all descriptions of the pillars when you are on them are given as if you are facing the gold on the far cliff edge.

If it's all too much and you wish to turn back, go to *1003*

<u>831</u>

The only wall of fire is to the west. You can route south, east or north from your current location.

Do you

Go East – *143*

Go South – *1141*

Go North – *1303*

<u>832</u>

You walk forward into the darkness and realise it is a true darkness. As you walk you feel a wind at your back pushing you forward, and you start to stumble. You are pitching along and cannot stop yourself.

Do you have pole in front of you – *1291*. If not, read on.

You stumble with an unrelenting wind behind you. Suddenly the ground beneath you vanishes, realised by you as your feet find nothing and you fall. It is only a few moments before the ground comes up and hits you hard.

Where did you dig that vessel name from? New Southampton Harbour? Such a pity as you had got so far.

You can reset to the start of this puzzle at *1366* if you want or start all over again at *1*. That was a long haul, and you did so well, just not well enough.

<u>833</u>

"Timmers is my Captain," you say. Everyone starts to laugh and shake their heads.

"Timmers is a weak lily-livered fool. God help you. Now get out!"

You see knives being pulled and hear the click of a musket. It's time to leave. Dejected you walk back to the crossroads. **You cannot return to "The Dog's Knackers" in the future. Go to *802***

<u>834</u>

"Captain, my apologies for interrupting you," says the cabin boy, "but the duty watch keeper has found someone. A stowaway."

You're taken to a small, fat man who speaks French. Luckily you do too, and you discover he is running away from his master in New Southampton whose wife he was having an affair with. He was the chef in the house, and you tell him his best option is to become your cook. The man gladly agrees, rather than be thrown overboard and you quickly realise how good he is with food. Your crew are delighted.

Raise your crew morale by 3 levels. Now continue your voyage at *654*

835

You pull out the red banded one and it comes away fairly easily. You can see nothing on it. **Tick the codeword Red Pole.** What next?

Do you pull out the

Green banded one – *739*

Blue banded one – *883*

Neither of them and instead

Strike out for the path – *1039*

Investigate the hut – *1395*

836

You arrive in a clearing and see the monkey statue you saw before but without the gold chain. There is nothing else here and you retreat back down the path. Go to *1066*

837

Reduce your time by 1.

If your time is in the following gaps (37-33 or 07-03), then go to *1037*.

You creep up to the building and to the single wooden door. You feel exposed as you stand there and wonder if you should just pull at the door and enter the building to get cover. It would be madness to stand here, but what's inside?

Do you

Hide where you are – *1435*

Route North – *103*

Creep West – *1197*

Go North-east – *174*

Listen at the door – *1061*

Open the door and enter the building – *680*

838

As you approach the pirate, he sticks his leg out catching the other stool at the table and dragging it close so no one can sit on it. "Go away!" There's no explanation. You can barely see his face but his manner is very abrupt and frankly, he looks severely angry at something.

Do you

Ask him if you can get a ship and crew from him – *1096*

Ask if he knows where you can get a doctor – *1219*

Leave him alone and instead

Approach the bar – *669*

Talk to the gypsy woman – *711*

Go over to watch the pirate playing the mouth organ – *1421*

Or leave – *1112*

839

You storm forward and Annie shoots you in the shoulder. You grab your wound and feel blood on your hand. Turning, you run for the alley and the street. Go to *1156*

840

You draw your cutlass and stride over to the edge of your vessel, preparing to board the sloop. A spectre dressed in the garb of a pirate, complete with boots and tri cornered hat, flies at you from out of the mist. It picks you up by the neck, causing you to drop your cutlass, and then pins you to your own mast.

"You dare to set foot on the Devil's Sloop," it spits. "And with no tribute being offered. Then I will take tribute."

You stare in horror as various spectres fly from the sloop onto your vessel and start grabbing your crew. Your crewmates scream as you see the spectres cut at them with ghostly knives which still seem to damage flesh. You don't see if they are still alive as your crewmates are taken back to the sloop, but you hear the sounds of devouring and of crew screaming wildly.

"Next time, tribute!" The spectre flies back to the sloop and the wind becomes steady, filling the sails in a gentle fashion, while the sun returns to the sky.

You look around you at white faces, shocked and confused, eyes wide in terror. A head count tells you how many crew you have lost. **Reduce your crew by 1 level and crew morale by 2 levels.** The crew are keen to get underway and return to your voyage as quick as you can, wondering what you have just seen.

Now continue your voyage at **654**

841

You wait your moment and as the soldier seems to be at his most relaxed talking to you, you strike him hard across the jaw. He is rocked for a moment but then draws his sword and takes you by the wrist. You are not as strong as you think you are, and the soldier marches you to the cells. Fortunately, he doesn't recognise who you really are. You are roughly led to the cells in the garrison and left on the cold stone floor. Go to **114**

842

The weather is rough, throwing the vessel here and there on the waves but you are confident in your crew and your ship. You feel sick as the ship is tossed here and there but you note that it is holding well except that your sails have taken some damage. When you clear the storm after two days you assess the damage.

You've done very well all things considering. Lower your Vessel's speed by 1 due to sail damage, and you've lost 1 provision through a hole that broke open near the top of the hull.

Now resume your voyage at *654*

843

You are in a round room where you can see a wooden chest on the far side away from you. Between you and it is nothing, but you can see small holes in the wall pointed at where you would cross. This may be a trap! There is another rope above the chest which disappears upwards maybe to another floor, but you'll have to cross over to the chest to use it. There's also the rope beside you that you climbed up from below.

Do you

Run across the room – *1388*

Return back down the rope - *303*

844

The mud path is dense, and you dare not step off it into the thick green plants that lie beyond, fearing that they will close up behind you, trapping you in an endless humid jungle. You hear nothing, no bird life, no animals or insects and everything feels eerie. Sweat rolls down your face as the path now forks before you, left and right. Which way do you go?

Left – *1453*

Right - *526*

Turn back – *612*

<u>845</u>

You have accepted an offer for a dark run. In the Dark Run Table (*App 13*), write down the three places to visit: Fort August, The Marie Saratoga, and Hell's Deep. When you visit them, score them off. When you next visit Malin's Town, and all the locations have been visited, go to *149* (note this down now) and continue from there.

The man has left so what will you do next

Do you

See to the needs of your vessel and crew – *903*

Try to earn some money by signing up to a cargo run – *1335*

Visit the taverns for information – *802*

Visit the Mariners' Guild for information – *124*

If you have had enough of Malin's town, then **consult the voyage chart and set sail**.

<u>846</u>

You suddenly hear a door opening and Lord Buffington is standing there, in new glasses, as you are examining his wares. He is furious and then he notices that you are a woman.

"You are a woman, and a female thief at that. Robert! Get this wench out of here! Blast it, how did she get in?"

Robert strides quickly into the room and grabs you by the arm, wheeling you out before frisking you, and removing any of the items you have found in Lord Buffington's room. He then takes you straight to the front doors and throws you on the street outside.

You cannot return to the Mariner's Guild in daylight as your thieving, womanly face is known.

Do you

Come back at night in an attempt to gain access when the building is closed – *742*

See to the needs of your vessel and crew – *903*

Try to earn some money by signing up to a cargo run – *1335*

Visit the taverns for information – *802*

If you have had enough of Malin's town, then **consult the voyage chart and set sail.**

847

Reduce your time by 2. If your time is in the following gaps (55-53, 35-33, 24-23 or 04-02) then go to *810*. If not continue below

You approach one of the slums and see that the door lies half open. Inside you see a couple sleeping, half exposed with their sheets strewn aside. You see some items on the cheap table beside their bed. There's a bottle of rum and a hairbrush but nothing significant. This has been a waste of time.

Do you

Wait in hiding – *519*

If you haven't already

Take a look at the latrines – *386*

Move to the west quarter – *493*

Move to the east quarter – *678*

Leave the fort for your vessel – *535*

848

You let the pirate escort you from the tavern, an arm around your waist as he takes you to the edge of Strangar and then down to the water's edge. You can see a small boat and are about to tell him he is having a laugh when you feel a blow to the back of the head. When you wake up you are in a wooden cage, in the hull of a ship. You wonder what is happening to you but within a few months you are sold as a slave into a brutal existence. You were in Strangar and took a pirate's word, a mistake that has cost you dear. Try again at *1*

849

"Simon Kilmer's my Captain," you say. There's a bit of commotion as people whisper to each other and then the man with the large scar stands up.

"Kilmer's not welcome here. And neither are you."

You see knives being pulled and hear the click of a musket. It's time to leave. Dejected you walk back to the crossroads. **You cannot announce yourself in "The Dog's Knackers" as a Captain in the future. Go to *802***

850

Yes, it's in the left cup. Double your stake money and get your stake back. Once you've noted that down, do you want to play again? Is so, with whom?

Look to join the one-legged pirate's game – *1181*

Engage in the stumpy pirate's game – *1316*

Play in the female pirate's game – *618*

If not go to *64*

851

With gusto, you strike out to get clear of the creatures, looking for the deeper water. You feel you are going to make it when a claw rips across your body. The wound is superficial, but you drop something you are carrying. **Go down your codeword list and remove the first and third codeword related to an item. Has an (I) after it.**

Go to *632*

852

Do you have ticked the code word **Spanish Hunted** – *1080*

Otherwise, the vessel routes towards you and you know you cannot outrun it.

Is your first officer Martha Downham or Black Robert – *1081*

If not, the galleon comes alongside you and the first officer of the warship, examines your vessel with his large crew and you are powerless to stop him. **He takes 25% of your cargo for his troubles** but he lets you carry on in your voyage. You breathe a sigh of relief when the galleon departs.

You return to your voyage but must **add 1 day extra to it** for this diversion.

Continue the voyage at *654*

853

You pull your pistol, and the man lets go quickly. "I didn't mean anything, I didn't…"

The doors are beginning to open, and you can see a musket coming out of the gap. You quickly turn and run, heading for the alley and the street beyond. Go to *496*

854

Reduce your Island Time Chart by 1

You trek along the path, panting for breath in the heat. There's a fork in the path, and you wonder which way to go. You can take either fork, or you could always head out into the jungle off the path.

Do you go

Left – *677*

Right – *1366*

Strike out into the Jungle – *1077*

Turn around back the way you came – *224*

855

You are searched from head to foot, but the soldiers find nothing of interest. You feel relieved but they watch you suspiciously. Timmers says you need to stay and send the message he was writing otherwise it will look like you were here for some other reason. After the message is given to the clerk when he returns from lunch, Timmers suggests that you leave the fort and the two of you return to the vessel. You set sail but what will you do now.

Do you

Wish to sneak into the fort at night – *307*

Sail elsewhere - **consult the voyage chart and set sail**.

856

You've been hit on the same shoulder and your previous wound has gotten larger and the blood is flowing rapidly. You fall to the ground, but everything is already going dark. You pass out and eventually die on the back streets of New Southampton. Take more care of yourself and try again at *1*

857

Reduce your time by 1.

You enter the tunnel and find it dark and cold. Little light travels into it and you cannot see the end as you grope your way along. It continues for what seems an age and you feel the damp and algae that has formed on the walls. Suddenly you reach the end of the tunnel and think you can hear snoring above you. Everything then goes silent. Your hands reach up and feel the wood of what you believe to be another trapdoor.

Do you

Open the trapdoor above – *646*

Wait for a few moments – *820*

Or

Decide this is a bad plan? If so, you retreat along the tunnel and exit back in the message room, covering up the trapdoor again with the rug. **Reduce your time by 1.** Now, do you

Look at the desk – *206*

Look at the other rug – *1356*

Try to open the safe – *1288*

Decide this is a bad idea and return outside – *174*

858

You seem to go through your doubloons quickly with a number of pirates stepping forward but when you return to the vessel none are there. It seems you've been hoodwinked by pirates, who could guess? You can hear the laughter on the wild isle and decide to steer clear of it.

What now?

Go to see Blind Tom – *681*

Visit the provisions isle – *334*

Explore the dark isle – *397*

Approach the pirate king – *1348*

Decide you have had enough of Hells Deep and set sail - **Consult the voyage chart and set sail**

859

You slide down into the tunnel and find it's as bad as the smell that came from it. Your hands touch damp walls with white mildew, at least that's what you hope it is, the light being so poor. You must walk slowly due to the lack of light, but you find yourself at an end wall quite quickly. You feel a trapdoor above and wonder where it leads.

Do you

Push open the trapdoor – *1014*

Wait for a moment listening – *193*

Or if you think you should leave it alone, continue below

You retreat along the tunnel and exit back in the message room, covering up the trapdoor again with the rug. Now, do you

Look at the desk – *1167*

Look at the other rug – *365*

Try to open the safe – *1289*

Decide this is a bad idea and return to Timmers, saying you should get back to the ship pronto – *351*

860

"I have the great Robert Grimshaw on board," you say and watch as the bald man's face turns sour.

"And what has he done? He's hardly struck a blow that we have heard of. If that is the best you have then you must pay." **Tick codeword Flunk.** Unless you have something else you are going to have to pay or leave.

Do you

Decide you have an item you can offer to prove your worth – *229*

Offer doubloons – *1297*

Decide the price is too high and leave Hells Deep – **Consult the voyage chart and set sail**

861

"It's a good idea," you tell your first officer. "Prepare the small boat."

Tick the code word Small Crew. Soon the small party are ready, and you set for the island, rowing oars pushing the boat over the water. As you get close, you tell the crew to stay in the boat and you dive into the water striking out for the cave.

Continue at *230*

862

It's not worth your life for a horn whoever left it and you run back up the steps your heart pounding. As you do so, the steps close up sealing off the way below. You look around the temple but there's nothing to see, no way back down to the hall you just left. **Tick the codeword Closed.**

Not much to do except leave this place. You check the sun and realise you can go north - *202* or south - *1329* along a jungle path. Choose now.

863

The key is made of brass and is very simple. It might be for a safe or a door but you cannot be sure. **If you take the brass key, tick the codeword Brass Key (see what I did there!).** If you haven't already you can

Look at the parchment – *503*

Or you can instead replace everything and

Check the rug that's slightly lifted – *169*

Look at the other rug – *366*

Try to open the safe – *1289*

Decide this is a bad idea and return to Timmers, saying you should get back to the ship pronto – *351*

864

Reduce the Hot Strip by 2. If this places you on a Fire spot add 20 to this section's number and go there for the walls have moved. You shield the treasure chest for a few moments hoping it will cool down and then grab its handles at the side. Thankfully they are cool. **Tick the codeword Fire Chest** There are walls of fire to the north, west, and east, so you route south from your current location. Go to *321*

865

You seem to go through your doubloons quickly with a number of pirates stepping forward and when you get back to the vessel you see that your new crew is there. **Increase your crew size by 1 as long as the vessel has room. If not, you have wasted money on a new crew that cannot come with you.**

Among the crew is a former navigator of Blackbeard's vessel and he is able to teach you more things about your vessel in terms of handling than you ever thought possible. **Increase your vessel's** manoeuvrability by 1 if possible. (you may increase above the vessel's normal maximum if not at Great) Also increase the vessel's Storm Handling by 1 level.

What now?

Go to see Blind Tom – *681*

Visit the provisions isle – *334*

Go back to the Wild Isle – *879*

Explore the dark isle – *397*

Approach the pirate king – *1348*

Decide you have had enough of Hells Deep and set sail - **Consult the voyage chart and set sail**

866

Reduce your Waters Strength Chart by 1. The current is pushing you east. However, you think you may be able to swim up an eddy to the south. Do you

Float East – *955*

Swim South – *495*

867

Move Tabetha.

You are in a white walled room, bathed in the strange light, with three doors, one with a picture of a spider above it, one with a shield above it, and the other with a schooner above it.

If Tabetha's number is 12 – *1459*

If Tabetha's number is 23 – **note this number and go to 1287**

If Tabetha's number is 2 – **note this number and go to 239**

If Tabetha's number is 15 – **note this number and go to 446**

Where do you go next?

Through the spider door – *180*

Through the schooner door – *874*

Through the shield door – *1174*

Wait here - **return to the top of this section**

868

As you turn to leave the market a hand is placed on your shoulder. You have been gaining attention and now you appear to be surrounded by those who were looking for you. With such a force, you are trapped and are taken away to the garrison and thrown into prison.

Captain Fareham of the garrison visits you and tells you that he intends to marry you, and he does so in quiet, keeping you locked up in the jail. Fareham now owns your father's lands and keeps you in your cell for the next year. When you don't respond to his advances and wishes to be a passive wife, he has you taken away in the night and disposed of. Your last thoughts are that your family remains unavenged. Try again at *1* and next time try and be more discreet.

869

You slide over to a bench and sit down beside one of the portly men, who burps loudly as you sit down. He is heavily overweight and struggles to right himself beside you. You decide to start a conversation.

"Do you by any chance…"

The man grabs you by the hips. "At last a wench," he blurts and then belches. His breath stinks and he is looking at you lecherously. "Sit on my knee like a good girl, time for a bit of fun."

You don't like the sound of that but what will you do?

Do you

Shove him hard – **946**

Tell him you are no wench but a sailor – **135**

Pull your knife on the man – **1298**

Saddle up to the man in an attempt to gain information – **1038**

<u>870</u>

You untie the crew telling John Darnold you will hold him to his word. He is true and after assisting you in escaping from Strangar, he takes you to Diggory Hurst who tells you he will assist you in your quest to find Estes. It will not be easy but now you have a vessel and a crew. Step on to the next part of your adventure at **1460**

<u>871</u>

You tell the man you are looking for a crew to handle a vessel for you and the man nearly falls off his chair laughing.

"You came here to find a crew. Lady, let me save you some time and tell you go to the docks for a crew. The men in here are not the working type if you understand me. Now beat it before I call Little Annie out. She doesn't take to women about the place unless they work here."

The man seems friendly but firm, and maybe he's right. Or is he hiding something?

Do you

Insist on entering – *405*

Take his advice and return to the main street – *496*

872

You push the pole down in the water in an attempt to jam it into the depths but it fails to stick on anything. Wore, it slips from your grasp in the crazy current, and you lose the pole. **Untick the codeword Green Pole**. Now return to your previously noted section.

873

You step onto the pillar and breathe a sigh as it doesn't crumble. The waves crash far below, and you ponder your next move. There is a pillar to your front right or you can turn back.

Do you step

Diagonally forward right – *238*

Step back off the pillar onto the cliff edge behind – *1180*

874

Move Tabetha.

You are in a white walled room, bathed in the strange light, with two doors, one with a picture of a shield above it, and the other with a schooner above it.

If Tabetha's number is 15 – *1459*

If Tabetha's number is 12 – **note this number and go to 239**

If Tabetha's number is 9 – **note this number and go to 446**

Where do you go next?

Through the shield door – *867*

Through the schooner door – *1074*

Wait here - **return to the top of this section**

875

You say the name of your supposed captain and Lord Buffington seems rather dejected. He stands up quickly and then paces about before snorting.

"So, he's unable to come and see me himself. Well, that will never do. Tell him if he wants to do any business with me, he needs to come himself. As for you, I don't want the messenger. Robert!" he shouts. "Get this fool out of here and don't let them back in."

Robert strides quickly into the room and grabs you by the arm wheeling you out to the front doors throws you to the street outside.

You cannot return to the Mariner's Guild in daylight as you are now identified as not worthy.

Do you

Come back at night in an attempt to gain access when the building is closed – *742*

See to the needs of your vessel and crew – *903*

Try to earn some money by signing up to a cargo run – *1335*

Visit the taverns for information – *802*

If you have had enough of Malin's town, then **consult the voyage chart and set sail**.

876

Your shoulder is sore and not getting better. Everything is becoming a little hazy and you feel like you might not last too long. Start the timer box at *App 08* with 15 in it. Every time you turn to a new entry, reduce the timer box by 1. If the timer box reaches zero go to **97. Make a note of this number now**. Return to your previous entry and start the timer from there.

877

Reduce the Hot Strip by 2. If this places you on a Fire spot add 20 to this section's number and go there for the walls have moved. There are walls of fire to the north, west, and east, so you route south from your current location. Go to *1443*

878

You race for the gates but as you enter the courtyard you see them begin to close. You'll never make it. There's a cry and you are spotted. A guard attacks Digory and he blocks magnificently but then he is surrounded and run through with a pike staff. You try to fight but you are grabbed and taken to Captain Fareham. The Captain knows the value to him of your father's lands although they have been ransacked and he forces you to become part of his plan and you are married in private.

He now owns your father's lands and keeps you locked up for the next year. When you don't respond to his advances and wishes to be a passive wife, he has you taken away in the night and disposed of. Your last thoughts are that your family remains unavenged and Diggory died in vain. Try again at *1*.

879

You row the small boat over to an island that appears to be rather raucous. You can see drunken pirates tumbling out of small houses while there is also a large tavern at the centre of the island. You can also see some smaller groups of pirates who appear to be gambling, as well as several fighting rings. The day is hot, and you wonder how the pirates have so much energy. As you step onto the shoreline, you must decide where you go first.

Do you

Make for the small houses – *1304*

Explore the tavern – *363*

Approach the gambling groups – *1424*

Go to see the fights – *84*

Decide this is not a place you want to explore and return to your vessel - *314*

880

People are already looking for you due to your previous actions and when the shot causes such a noise, they soon spot you. You try to escape but you are seized and taken to Captain Fareham who locks you up in one of the cells. In a clever move he forces marriage on you before finding you guilty of the murder of a man in an alley in New Southampton. In doing so he seizes your father's lands and finds you a place on the gallows. It has all gone wrong. Next time don't make such a fuss in public. Try again at *1*

881

The channel narrows so you cannot turn about, and you seem to be routing west and then northeast until you approach a pool. Something seems familiar. Go to *159*

882

You wait until the water is silver and then you step forward. Suddenly the water curtain is behind you, and in front of you is a man on a horse. He is dressed in warm furs and races up to you before throwing a bag at you. You pick it up and see there are doubloons inside. As you look back up the man and his horse are gone, and you are back in the room. The water curtain has turned to rock, but the doubloons are in your hands. **Tick the codeword Rock and add 200 doubloons to your inventory.**

There's nothing else left in this room, save the ropes, so you should move on. Do you

Climb up the rope – *756*

Climb down the other rope – *843*

883

You pull out the blue banded one and it comes away fairly easily. You can see nothing on it. **Tick the codeword Blue Pole.** What next?

Do you pull out the

Red banded one – *835*

Green banded one – *739*

Neither of them and instead

Strike out for the path – *1039*

Investigate the hut – *1395*

884

You don't believe Diggory and turn your back on him, preferring to await your fate. It is not long before Captain Fareham realises where you are and comes to get you. The Captain knows the value to him of your father's lands although they have been ransacked and he forces you to become part of his plan and you are married in private.

He now owns your father's lands and keeps you locked up for the next year. When you don't respond to his advances and wishes to be a passive wife, he has you taken away in the night and disposed of. Your last thoughts are that your family remains unavenged. Try again at *1* and remember enemies are everywhere, even those people who help.

885

"I really don't know what to do, we're not equipped for this."

Return to *927* and make your decision.

886

Reduce your Island Time Chart by 1

You trek along the path, sweat dripping from your forehead into your eyes. Did you come this way already? Soon you reach a fork in the path, and you wonder which way to go. You can take either fork, or you could always head out into the jungle off the path.

Do you go

Left – *830*

Right – *550*

Strike out into the Jungle – *1347*

Turn around back the way you came – *984*

887

You hear the guards outside and quickly go to shout "All's well" to the guards. But do you shout in

English – *607*

French – *1280*

888

You run for your life out onto the path that leads to New Southampton. You can hear the soldiers after you and decide that following this path is a dead giveaway. There's bound to be soldiers in town as well. So you realise that you need to cut across country and away from the civil and decent side of the island. Changing your path, you cut across crop fields until you find the path that leads to Strangar and the pirate haven. Find out what awaits you at *671*

889

You approach the wooden chest, and it appears to have no lock. On the chest are words in Spanish along with the name "Estes". Could this be it? Does it have a clue as to where Estes left his treasure?

Do you

Open the chest - *689*

Leave it alone and instead

Climb the rope – *843*

Examine the paintings – *621*

Look at the ship's wheel – *620*

Leave the room by the wooden door – *1439*

890

Reduce the Hot Strip by 2. If this places you on a Fire spot add 20 to this section's number and go there for the walls have moved. There are walls of fire to the east, west, and south, so you route north from your current location. Go to *766*

891

You wander along the path, confused, and reach a junction. Which way now?

Left – *435*

Right – *1191*

Turn back – *1273*

892

"Captain, my apologies for interrupting you," says the cabin boy, "but the duty watch keeper has found someone. A stowaway."

You are taken to one of your cargo holds where a young man sits in rags. As you get closer you can see he has various legions on his face and his arms are full of cuts and scabs. One of your crew has medical experience and declares that the man has a plague. The infection will spread if you don't act. The crewman recommends that the person be thrown overboard and the cargo around him jettisoned, and the section quarantined for 30 days. Another crewman says, he has seen something like this before and it will probably be alright.

Do you

Follow the first crewman's advice and throw the man overboard – *1170*

Take the second crewman's advice and let the man stay in the cargo hold to recover – *214*

893

You barely overcome the main current to get to the eddy, and you suffer for it. **Reduce your Waters Strength Chart by 2.** You swim through to the eddy. Go to *595*

894

You return to your ship, sodden and wondering what to do next. The island still looks unappealing and barren, and your first officer agrees it is not worth exploring. You may search a part of the Maria Saratoga you haven't already, or you can leave the wreck. The choice is yours.

Do you

Dive and search the outside of the vessel – *136*

Swim to the mast and explore the vessel from the top down – *603*

Or

Set sail for another destination. If so, **consult the voyage chart and set sail!**

895

Reduce the Hot Strip by 2. If this places you on a Fire spot add 20 to this section's number and go there for the walls have moved. You shield the treasure chest for a few moments hoping it will cool down and then grab its handles at the side. Thankfully they are cool. **Tick the codeword Fire Chest** There are walls of fire to the north, south, and east, so you route west from your current location. Go to *831*

896

As you approach one of the guards shouts over to you to clear off. It's a shop for ladies only, not slave girl scum. You turn away angry but know it would be foolish to try and do anything that draws attention.

Do you

Try to see another way in – *1279*

Return to the street – *1166*

897

The crew seems satisfied, and you continue on your voyage. **You cannot reduce rations for another 20 days, or the crew will remove you for your treachery.** Continue to *654*

898

You approach the kitchen and see two Spanish soldiers before you. Both have their back to you, but the door to the outside is beyond them. You'll need to distract or disable them to get past. You can see a pot on the boil over the fire. There are several cups on the side as well as a large kitchen knife. You can hear a sound behind you, someone coming down the stairs, so you'll need to react quickly before the soldiers hear it too.

Do you

Throw some cups at them – *488*

Grab the pot and throw its contents over them – *532*

Take the knife and stab the soldiers with it – *138*

Just make a run for it – *651*

899

Reduce your time by 1. You step forward and reach out around you. On your left you can feel a chair and it seems to be fixed in some fashion, blocking your way. Ahead of you seems clear as does behind, obviously. On your right you can feel some hatch handles and they feel just like the exterior handles of the original hatch you opened.

Do you

Open the hatch to your right and step through – *391*

About turn and step forward – *1330*

Step forward – *345*

900

You call out to the guard telling him that Diggory has stolen your cross. The man shrugs his shoulders and you plead with him, but he ignores you and returns to his duties. Diggory looks annoyed and you wonder if you will get another chance.

It is a half hour later and someone approaches but who is it?

Find out

Here – *1121*

Or here – *1184*

901

You tell a wild tale of how you have vanquished many navy foes as well as exploring great islands. You can see the look of suspicion in the female pirates' eyes and soon they stop you.

"You lie! Show me the evidence! Show me the evidence or I will strike you down!"

Of course do you have no evidence. Do you

Run back to your ship – *264*

Continue your lie – *629*

902

You say you have the right cask in an indignant fashion and try to pick it up again. But it's heavy and as soon as it is on your shoulder you drop it, causing it to crack and a brown liquid runs out. The soldier stares at you.

"You little thief. Trying to take our grog, were you?" He slaps you hard, knocking you to the ground. "It's the cells for you. We don't take kindly to those that steal from us."

You are roughly led to the cells in the garrison and left on the cold stone floor. Go to *114*

903

You visit the harbour marketplace and enquire about prices and repairs for your vessel. Malin's Town is a busy place and has many trained ship builders and repairers all making a good living in the hot sun.

You may make repairs here for the appropriate cost, or you can fill up with cargo. Simply check the table below but be aware, there is a cost in time as well as financially. You can trade in doubloons or treasure (use the doubloon equivalent score for your treasure). Once you have decided on your requirements, adjust your Vessel chart as necessary.

Provisions

- 5 doubloons per provision pack – 1 day to load all packs
- A day's rum for the crew – 2 days cost (1 to acquire, 1 to drink to excess) Lifts crew morale by one level
    - Large crew – 25 doubloons
    - Medium crew – 15 doubloons
    - Small crew – 10 doubloons

Vessel repair

Note you may not repair your vessel higher than its initial level. All days required for each level are added together to get your total repair time.

The Treasure of Captain Estes

- Vessel speed
    - One day for each level increased by
    - 200 doubloons for each level, or treasure equivalent
- Vessel Firepower
    - Two days for each level increased by
    - 400 doubloons for each level, or treasure equivalent
- Cargo Hold
    - One day for each level increased by
    - 150 doubloons for each level, or treasure equivalent
- Manoeuvrability
    - Two days for each level increased by
    - 200 doubloons for each level, or treasure equivalent
- Storm Handling
    - Two days for each level increased by
    - 400 doubloons for each level, or treasure equivalent

Having done your deals at Malin's Town and once you have adjusted your vessel chart and your time chart, what are your plans?

Try to earn some money by signing up to a cargo run – *1335*

Visit the taverns for information – *802*

Visit the Mariners' Guild for information – *124*

If your first officer is Simon Kilmer – *24*

If your First officer is Robert Grimshaw – *737*

If your First officer is Diggory Hurst – *786*

If you have had enough of Malin's town, then **consult the voyage chart and set sail**.

904

You flip the trapdoor above you open and reach up with your hands to pull yourself through. As you do so you hear a shout. Desperately you drop and reach for the edges of the trapdoor closing it above you. You then sprint along the dark of the tunnel, your hands tracing the wall as you hear voices behind you and the trapdoor opening again.

You reach the trapdoor in the messages office and climb up into the daylight, eyes squinting. But there's no time for any pause and you close the trapdoor and cover it quickly with the rug. You then run out of the messages office and hear shouts and cries from nearby buildings. Timmers looks surprised but you sit down beside him, pretending to be eagerly intent on what he is writing.

A small group of soldiers round the larger buildings beyond the messages office and they yell out at you.

"You there, what are you doing?"

"I'm just completing a letter to be sent via the office," says Timmers in a remarkably calm fashion. "Why? What's the matter?"

"We've had intruders. Stand up! We need to search you."

Do you have the codeword **Brass Key** – *723*

If not – *855*

905

"Can't pay the cost. We don't like your sort round here." The pirate stabs you and lets you fall from the quay into the water. Pain races through your body and you try to struggle in the water but cannot keep your head above the lapping tide. It's a watery grave for you in Strangar. Still, you're not the first to suffer that. Try again at *1* and be more careful.

906

Reduce the Hot Strip by 1. If this places you on a Fire spot add 20 to this section's number and go there for the walls have moved. You can see fire to the north and to the west. To the south is clear air and your crewmates, while there is a clear route to the east.

Do you

Step out to the South – *427*

Go East – *1065*

907

You start walking and see a guard taking an interest in you. As you get closer to the gate, he approaches until he cuts you off.

"Who are you?" he asks.

"Anna, just leaving," you say.

"Who's your master, girl?"

"I'm with the vegetable seller."

"No, you're not," says the soldier. "I watched all his girls come in and I don't remember you."

He grabs you forcibly and a commotion begins which attracts the attention of a Lieutenant. He stares at you before instructing the soldier to throw you in the cells to await him later. You are roughly led to the cells in the garrison and left on the cold stone floor. Go to *114*

908

As the pirate reaches for you, you duck and run as hard as you can back to the street. He pursues you, telling you to stop but you dare not, and you eventually lose him in the middle of Strangar. You don't want to go back to that end of town again so continue at *1112,* keeping clear of the far end of Strangar.

909

Reduce your time by 1.

If your time is in the following gaps (42-38) you see a guard on his patrol outside and must remain hidden until he clears the area. Reduce your time by 6. Now continue at the plain text below

You open the trapdoor and find yourself in an office of sorts. It's a stone room but feels cold even compared to the cool night temperature. There are several desks and large cabinets with many drawers. There is a writing desk too, and quite ornate chairs for where you are. You can just about make out charts on the wall. There is a door in the far wall presumably to the outside world.

 Do you

Examine the desks – *994*

Check out the cabinets – *284*

Look at the chairs – *243*

Peruse the charts on the wall – *324*

Or leave the room and return back to tunnel – *693*

910

Do you have the codeword Dampened – *1134*. If not continue below

You can hear the crackling of the fire before you reach it. Walking around a corner in the jungle path, you stand and stare in disbelief. On a blackened soil, you see walls of constantly shifting fire, fierce heat that warns you not to get too close. As you stare into the mesmerizing fire you can see a hint of a casket in the middle. Your heart jumps as this could be a part of Estes' treasure. But how do you get at it?

A sign is erected on a wooden stake, and you read the scrawl carefully.

'These are the walls of fire and the reason I had to replace my first mate. It cost me a lot to hide my casket in there and it will cost you much to get it back out. Look carefully, for the walls move every so often. I hope you burn in this hell!'

You gulp and see the frightened look on your crewmates' faces. This will not be easy and that fire looks like it would burn you to a crisp in an instant.

Do you have the codeword **Walk** – *988*

If not, do you

Want to take on the challenge – *127*

Decide this is a bad idea at the moment and leave back down the jungle path – *1193*

911

Yes, it's in the right cup. Double your stake money and get your stake back. Once you've noted that down, do you want to play again? Is so, with whom?

Look to join the one-legged pirate's game – *1181*

Engage in the stumpy pirate's game – *1316*

Play in the female pirate's game – *618*

If not go to *64*

912

There are great howls of laughter and singing from the tavern which seems to be in full flow. As you approach the doors, they swing open and a pirate sails by you through the air, his mouth bloodied. It seems there may be a degree of roughness inside.

Once you step inside, you see a bar ahead of you which has several pirates sitting on stools and drinking. Behind it is a large woman with a scarf across her face and a couple of other serving girls. A pirate is on your left-hand side playing a mouth organ and suffering jeers and plaudits in equal measure. At the far end of the tavern is a single pirate sitting in the dark at a table and across from him, three tables away, is a gypsy woman on her own. She has bangles on her arms and a red headscarf. Between all these people are various groups of pirates in their own circles.

Do you

Approach the bar – *669*

Talk to the gypsy woman – *711*

Walk over to the single pirate – *838*

Go over to watch the pirate playing the mouth organ – *1421*

Or leave – *1112*

<u>913</u>

You reach down to shake the pirate awake and find a sword pointed at your belly. You slowly step back as the pirate gets to his feet.

"Not everything that lies here is asleep. Nothing doing here. Time to be about your business."

Do you

Walk back to the street with your hands in the air – *129*

Feint to walk away but then run into the barn – *2*

<u>914</u>

You step onto the pillar and breathe a sigh as it doesn't crumble. The waves crash far below, and you ponder your next move. There is a pillar to your right, one diagonally to your right in front, and one diagonally to your left in front.

The Treasure of Captain Estes

Do you step

Diagonally forward right – *754*

Diagonally forward left – *166*

To your right – *1045*

Step back off the pillar onto the cliff edge behind – *1180*

<u>915</u>

Reduce your time by 1.

If your time is in the following gaps (52-48), you see a guard on his patrol and must remain hidden until he clears the area. Reduce your time by 6. Now continue at the plain text below

If your time is in the following gaps (22-18), you see a guard on the enclosing wall patrolling and must remain hidden until he clears the area. Reduce your time by 6.

If neither of these apply, continue at the plain text below

You find cover and remain where you are. You see no one as you wait.

There is a gate out of the enclosed centre of the fort in the wall here, and it is open. To the south are more buildings. To the east is a path and what looks like a small hut. To the west is a large building with no guards outside.

Do you

Hide where you are – *42*

Route South-east – *174*

Creep West – *785*

Sneak north – *103*

Approach the building before you to break in – *1023*

916

You sail along until you reach a break in the channel where you can turn. It has two exits including the one you entered by: northeast and northwest.

Do you

Sail northeast – *617*

Route northwest – *192*

917

You are rather unimpressed as your vessel fires its cannons over toward the tailing vessel. There's a minor ripple in the water and you hold your eyepiece up to see if the Kraken has surfaced over there. But instead, a massive tentacle appears in your eye piece close by. You hear the screams of your crew as the vessel is broken apart by various appendages smashing it. As you jump from one broken piece of deck to another you are then drawn down into the water as the Kraken descends with the vessel in its clutches and you are taken by the drag.

You fight for the surface but to no avail and you drown in the depths of the sea.

The waters around New Southampton are deadly, and you have succumbed. You may try again at *1*

918

"You have nothing to give me to apologise for this insult. You may be aware that Captain Fareham from the garrison is looking for you and he will pay me well, unlike you. It's not personal, Miss Hastings, just business."

He gives a shout and several men enter the room and handle you roughly, taking you outside before calling the garrison guards in the town to them. You are taken away to the garrison and thrown into prison.

The Treasure of Captain Estes

Captain Fareham of the garrison visits you and tells you that he intends to marry you, and he does so in quiet, keeping you locked up in the jail. Fareham now owns your father's lands and keeps you in your cell for the next year. When you don't respond to his advances and wishes to be a passive wife, he has you taken away in the night and disposed of. Your last thoughts are that your family remains unavenged. Try again at *1* and next time try and be more discreet

919

With the Maria Saratoga now below the waves completely, you sail to the barren island and the underwater cave you discovered on the chart from the Saratoga's forecastle. According to the map, the cave entrance is underwater but the seabed slopes in a shallow fashion away from the island so getting the ship close will not be easy.

Is your vessel able to go into the shallows

Yes – *1220*

No – *1058*

920

You open the door and find yourself beside a rope on the outside of the rock formation. The rope leads all the way down but climbs no higher. As you look out you can see hundreds of birds many of which are becoming agitated.

Do you

Close the door and return to the room – *479*

Try to descend the rope – *88*

921

You can hear some footsteps above you in the room but note that they stop. Did they leave the room above, or whatever is up there? Is it safe to go up?

Do you

Open the trapdoor – *514*

If not, continue below

You retreat along the tunnel and exit back in the message room, covering up the trapdoor again with the rug. Now, do you

Look at the desk – *1167*

Look at the other rug – *366*

Try to open the safe – *1289*

Decide this is a bad idea and return to Timmers, saying you should get back to the ship pronto – *351*

922

You have been all over this island and can find no help. You sink into a pit of despair and are found on the ground by a group of wandering pirates. They take you on board their vessel and for the rest of your short life you are their slave girl, running here and there for them and attending to their every need until one day they get bored of you and heave you overboard. You gave it your best, but it was not enough. Try again at *1*

The Treasure of Captain Estes

923

You decide to strike out into the jungle but soon find that you become lost in the mass of greenery around you. You think about turning back but have no idea where the way behind you is. You may even be going round in circles. You need to keep going until you find a way out.

Roll 1xD100 (2xD10). Check the result below and go to the indicated section and cross off the allotted time given from your Island Time Chart.

00-19 – Reduce time chart by 4, go to *1079*

20-39 – *280*

40-59 – Reduce time chart by 9, go to *789*

60-79 – *280*

80-99 – Reduce time chart by 14, go to *177*

924

You feel the strength ebbing from you and are unable to keep your head above water. You sink into the turbulent waters and the maelstrom drives you down where your lungs eventually give up causing you to drown.

So near to Estes' treasure but with something missing. Where did you go wrong? You can try again at *1* or you can always reset to the start of this puzzle if you like at *151*. This time think on where the waters flow and where to take a breather.

925

Reduce the Hot Strip by 1. If this places you on a Fire spot add 20 to this section's number and go there for the walls have moved. There are walls of fire to the south and east. You can route north or west from your current location.

Do you

Go West – *775*

Go North – *572*

<u>926</u>

Reduce your time by 2. If your time is in the following gaps (52-47 or 22-17) then go to *1377*. If not continue below

You wait in the shadows seeing no one move.

Do you

Wait in hiding – *493*

If you haven't already

Look at the scrolls on top the barrel – *1332*

Investigate the papers in the hut – *77*

Move to the north quarter – *1176*

Move to the south quarter – *519*

<u>927</u>

What a bold move, and you need to know how best to approach this. Talk to your first officer quickly, and then come back here and make your decision.

Is your first officer

Simon Kilmer – *1022*

Robert Grimshaw – *187*

Diggory Hurst – *885*

Timmers – *1364*

Martha Downham – *185*

Black Robert – *182*

Now you have their view turn over the page for your options.

Try and hit the Kraken from a distance – *424*

Let the beast come close before opening fire on it – *630*

Drop gunpowder barrels over the side – *556*

928

You cannot stop yourself, but you manage to take the pole and swing it sideways, jamming it into the rock. The wind howls and you stay flat as you crawl your way back to the entrance. The wind does not abate until you are back at the junction. You breathe a sigh of relief, but you are faced with the same choice minus your pole.

Remove the circle around your chosen pole and untick the codeword. You may choose another pole to use if you have one. If so, circle that codeword and continue.

What will you do now?

Walk and enter

Bluebeard – *721*

Yellowbeard – *65*

Redbeard – *1361*

Or crawl and enter

Bluebeard – *342*

Yellowbeard – *815*

Redbeard – *1254*

Or do you beat a hasty retreat – *34*

929

The only wall of fire is to the north. You can route south, west or east from your current location.

Do you

Go West – *286*

Go South – *1200*

Go East – *1387*

930

The man suddenly sits bolt upright, before standing up and racing up beside you. "Madam, please take a seat." He hurries you round the table and into a chair before standing close by. "How may one be of service to you today, dear lady?"

Do you

Tell him you are Mary Hastings, and you wish to hire a vessel to seek out Captain Estes – *481*

Simply ask for a vessel for hire – *200*

Decide you don't like this man and make your apologies and return to the pier – *117*

931

Your first officer spits on the ground. "That dog Gonzales, I owe him one. We should take him on and sink the varmint. They'll be plenty of gold on that vessel, plenty to go around everyone. And it'll be one hell of a fight! What say you, Captain, shall we sink the braggard?"

Do you

Order your crew to sail towards the pirate ship – *506*

Decide to keep your distance and stay away – *740*

932

"I think we can settle this," says Timmers, marching out to the front of the crew. "let's be reasonable, crew, we need to preserve our provisions, so I suggest we keep the half rations in for another week, that's 7 days and then the Captain will agree to not drop them for at least another 30 days. I think that's agreeable.

The crew seem appeased but you're not sure you have got a good deal with this. **You may maintain half rations for another 7 days only. After that for 30 days you must maintain full rations.**

 Now continue your voyage at **654**

933

You desperately throw your arms out, knocking the creature off her balance and you turn to run. Before you are the flames of the jungle at the edge of the temple and there seems to be no way out. From behind you, you hear the creature squeal and know she is coming for you.

Do you

Run through the flames – **688**

Turn and face the creature – **492**

934

"Now that's a start," says the man and looks up at you. You see a gleam in his eye. "now just who are you?"

Tell him the truth - **481**

Make up a story – **208**

935

The guards give a simple nod as you enter Madame Le Vert's shop, and you pass by uninterrupted. Once inside you see a range of long-coats and boots, hats and breeches, but realise you have a number of these disguises anyway. You wait for an opportunity and when the Madame's gaze is averted you grab a hat and walk out of the shop, flopping the hat onto your head and pulling it down as you pass the guards. Probably best not to come back here again. Return to *1166* for your next move.

936

You catch the creature well with your canons, or so you believe peering through the smoke. There's a thrashing in the water and the creature seems to dive. Your crew stares at the water and you wait to hear another spotting but there's nothing. You cautiously get the crew to resume your voyage, but you keep a sharp lookout. After an hour you believe it is gone and you continue your voyage.

Your crew are relieved. Raise your crew morale by 2 levels.

Now continue your voyage at *654*

937

Reduce your Island Time Chart by 1

You trek along the path, panting for breath in the heat. There's a fork in the path, and you wonder which way to go. You can take either fork, or you could always head out into the jungle off the path.

Do you go

Left – *1366*

Right – *224*

Strike out into the Jungle – *1347*

Turn around back the way you came – *677*

The Treasure of Captain Estes

<u>938</u>

You sail into a small opening that has three exits from it. The rocks are spaced here, and you can turn easily. There are exits from the channel to the west, southwest, and south. All are wide channels so where next?

Do you

Sail west– **617**

Route south – **525**

Go southwest – **1349**

<u>939</u>

You remember the advice you were given about how the waters of Myra move. Check out the chart below to see the flows you can expect in order to navigate the waters. The strong currents are indicated with a thick arrow but there are possible other flows that you can get into to swim in another direction, marked with a narrow arrow, although it will take some strength. The places where you can get a breather if you have the blue pole from the beach are also marked with a '**B**'. Mark this section as you can view it at any time. Now return to **151** and decide your next action.

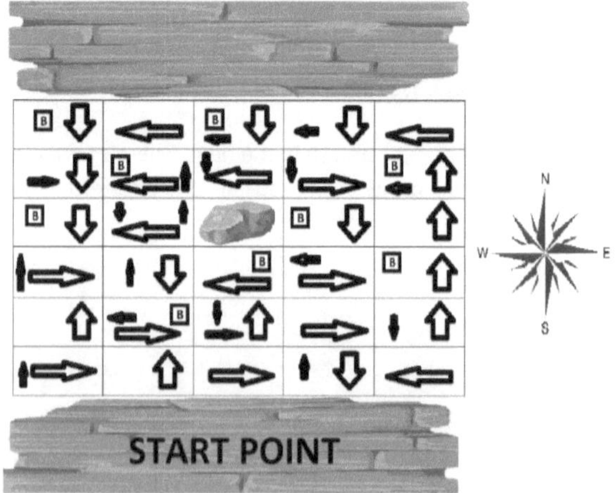

940

Reduce your Island Time Chart by 1

You trek along the path, and you think this path will never end. Suddenly there's a fork in the path, and you wonder which way to go. You can take either fork, or you could always head out into the jungle off the path.

Do you go

Left – *1088*

Right – *1115*

Strike out into the Jungle – *1077*

Turn around back the way you came – *982*

941

You grab some of the wheat grass and throw it down in front of the rats. They stop for a moment and sniff them before starting towards you again This buys you a second and you flee. There are simply too many and you are forced to run down the mountain. As you reach the base of the mountain, you skip over the river and the rats start to lose interest.

Now at the base of the mountain, you grab your breath and decide not to return this way again. **Note you cannot climb the mountain again.**

There are two paths away from the mountain, one a canopy covered path to the north, the other a more open topped path to the west, although it is still surrounded by the dense jungle.

Do you

Head north – *435*

Take the path west – *477*

<u>942</u>

Oh dear, as you pick yourself up from the dirt you see that you are surrounded by many people who have been after you. With such a force, you are trapped and are taken away to the garrison and thrown into prison.

Captain Fareham of the garrison visits you and tells you that he intends to marry you, and he does so in quiet, keeping you locked up in the jail. Fareham now owns your father's lands and keeps you in your cell for the next year. When you don't respond to his advances and wishes to be a passive wife, he has you taken away in the night and disposed of. Your last thoughts are that your family remains unavenged. Try again at *1* and next time try and be more discreet.

<u>943</u>

There's a thunderous explosion and the tailing vessel is engulfed in spray and noise. You tell your crew to fire another volley and the same vast barrage sends towers of displaced water into the air.

"Captain, I can see the tentacles. Over by the vessel."

You respond to the Crow's nest hail, and spy with your eye glass towards it. You see long tentacles rip into the air from out of the sea and then curl around the vessel's masts and deck. With an incredibly powerful contraction, the vessel is torn apart in an instant.

But you don't look back, telling your crew to give it everything as your vessel glides away from the carnage. There's a part of you that feels a touch responsible for the many deaths behind you, but it was you or them, wasn't it?

Your crew are relieved, raise crew morale by 2 levels. Untick either Spanish Tail or British Tail as appropriate.

Now continue your voyage at *654*

944

"You see, Captain, you cut the rations. And it's not good enough. We want more. And if you can't provide them, then we need a new captain."

The second officer is squaring up for a fight, and you're not that strong. A fight is out of the question, as you will lose. You may have other options, however.

Do you

Reinstate full rations – *897*

Pretend to agree with the second officer and then knife him – *457*

Appeal to your first officer for help – *195*

945

A familiar mist surrounds your ship after black clouds form and the sea begins to swirl as before when you last saw the Devil's Sloop. You know what this means, and you hear the words in your head "Tribute". You freeze on deck wondering what tribute will be asked for this time.

As dark clouds roll past and the world begins to feel like there is something coming from another spectral plane, you see an angel sitting on the crow's nest. Then suddenly around you are a host of angels. The crew are weeping with delight as you watch the devil's sloop appear beside you and then suddenly disappear as quickly as it arrived.

You give thanks on your knees and when you open your eyes again, the day is as it was before, a steady wind in your sails and all your crew still on board.

Raise your crew morale by 2 levels. Now continue your voyage at *654*

946

You place both hands on the man's shoulders and push hard. He tumbles back off the bench falling onto his backside before burping loudly. You hear the barman shouting over at you. "Okay, that's enough. I don't think you're welcome here. Time to say goodbye."

You turn around and the barman has a musket aimed at you. The other men in the bar also have hands on swords. You decide this is a good time to retreat and leave the alehouse quickly, back to the crossroads. **You cannot come back into the Admiral's Whiskers. Go to *802***

947

You race along the channel, and you seem to be getting close to the main formation until your vessel becomes grounded. You struggle to free your vessel and can hear some damage as you fight to float it again. You manage it but you may have taken damage.

Roll 1xD100 (2xD10). View the table and adjust your vessel's condition as necessary

01-25 Reduce your vessel's speed by 1 level if possible

26-50 Reduce your vessel's manoeuvrability by 1 level

51-75 Reduce your vessel's storm handling by 1 level

76-00 No damage sustained

You refloat and steer back to the last junction. Return to your noted section and continue. Don't pick the same channel again!!!!

948

The current is brutal and you are swept west. There is nothing you can do except float to *489*

949

You turn asking for everything your vessel has, and the crew respond. Although the cargo vessel is aware of your pursuit, it does not take long to close the gap between you. You wonder if they are up for a fight, and you tell the crew to prepare your canons. It's up to the cargo vessels' captain if they want a fight.

Is your vessel's firepower

None, Light, Moderate – *511*

Heavy, or very Heavy – *134*

950

0 Skull 5 Scales 0 Coins

If ever there was a stalemate, you've managed to find it. **Your stake item remains on your inventory, but you don't gain anything**. Return to *1060*

951

You watch the guard pass by from your hiding place, keeping a track on them, but unable to move freely while they are about. It takes them a while to clear the area as they look here and there. **Remove 6 time.** Finally they are clear but you have had to abort your previous action. Return to *519* and choose again but ignore the time adjustment at that entry this time round.

952

"Well now," says the figure, "what do we have here? A lady out on her own. I think you could be my lucky day. Either you've got some money on you, or we can find another way for you and me to have fun. Let's see some cash lady!"

The figure steps forward and grabs you roughly by the dress. You begin to sweat, in fear of your life or something even worse.

Do you

Have the codeword **Secreted Knife, or Standard Knife** and look to attack the cad - *784*

Have the codeword **Pistol** and draw it on the man – *1398*

Have the codeword **Whiskey Bottle or Promissory Note** and offer it to the man – *993*

Try to fight the man – *367*

953

Go to *409*

954

You have treasure, more than enough for the crew, and plenty for yourself. You are a wealthy woman and buying back your home and lands is easy. Although not the wealthiest person on the island you have influence and you have seen your family avenged as best you could.

The British seek to reach out to you and their protection helps you to manage better investments and keep your interests safe. Your adventures have gained you contacts and wisdom, and life is good. Eventually you asked to be the governor of the island. You are held in great respect, the first female governor in any British territory.

Congratulations, you have succeeded and brought honour and justice back to your family. You have won. But there are greater victories if you dare to try again. More treasure to be won and more power and influence to achieve. Try again at *1* if you dare, or will you simply bask in your current victory?

955

Reduce your Waters Strength Chart by 1. The current is pushing you north. However, you think you can reach an eddy that seems to allow a way west. Your foot scrapes the bottom briefly and you think you may be able to drop a pole and take a rest. Do you

Swim West – *184*

Float North – *1337*

Drop a pole – **Make a note of this section and go to *694***

956

You gulp as through your eye piece you see a British war galleon, armed to the teeth with cannon, one of the most feared sights on the seas.

Is your vessel speed *Very Slow – 662*

Otherwise, your first officer tells you to flee as no good will come from an encounter with this beast of a vessel. You agree and you strike a course away from it, taking a day to be assured you are clear of them and can return to your course.

You return to your voyage but must **add 1 day extra to it** for this diversion.

Continue the voyage at *654*

957

The weather is brutal, throwing the vessel here and there on the waves but you are worried about your crew and your ship. You feel sick as the ship struggles and you hear a significant crack of a mast. When you clear the storm after two days you assess the damage.

You've taken serious damage. Lower your Vessel's speed by 2 and the vessel's manoeuvrability by 1 level due to a broken mast but raise your crew's morale by 1 level, for they are grateful to be alive.

Now resume your voyage at **654**

958

Reduce the Hot Strip by 2. If this places you on a Fire spot add 20 to this section's number and go there for the walls have moved. There are walls of fire to the north, west, and east, so you route south from your current location. Go to **572**

959

You hear footsteps outside and then the office door opens. Standing there is a naval officer.

"Who the devil are you, sir? Guards!"

You turn to run but the officer is alive to your attempts and grabs you. You struggle but guards enter, and you are hauled off to the cells.

When you are brought before the Fort Commander, Timmers speaks eloquently about a mere misunderstanding, but the Commander is not happy. Thanks to Timmers you can walk away from the fort, **but half of your treasure and your provisions have been removed from your vessel. Delete these now. If you have no treasure, remove three quarters of your provisions. Untick codeword Brass Key if you have it.**

Timmers is angry with you as his reputation at the fort is ruined and your crew are annoyed at the loss of treasure and provisions. **Lower your crew morale by 1 level. Tick the codeword Caught.**

You are told to leave the fort immediately and you set sail. But where are you going?

Do you

Wish to sneak into the fort at night – *307*

Sail elsewhere - **consult the voyage chart and set sail.**

960

You see a brown bull running directly at you and it doesn't look like it will move to avoid you. You are in the left channel. What will you do?

Stay left – *1165*

Go to the middle – *466*

Go to the right channel – *783*

961

Go to *138*

962

You barely overcome the main current to get to the eddy, and you suffer for it. **Reduce your Waters Strength Chart by 2.** You swim through to the eddy. Go to *948*

963

Martha has informed you that a dark evil lurks in the temple at the core of the isle for she has been there before. She says that you should enter that temple and take on the power it holds. Return to *397* and decide on your next action.

The Treasure of Captain Estes

<u>964</u>

As you wait to see what he will say a trapdoor opens beneath you and you fall into a chute which makes you tumble out of the barge and into the waters around it. As you surface, a few children are laughing at you from the barge. Indignant, you swim to your vessel to dry off and decide your next course of action.

Go to see Blind Tom again – *681*

Visit the provisions isle – *334*

Enjoy yourself at the wild isle – *879*

Explore the dark isle – *397*

Approach the pirate king – *1348*

Decide you have had enough of Hells Deep and set sail - **Consult the voyage chart and set sail**

<u>965</u>

Roll 1xD100 (2xD10). For every point of damage you have already done to the brigantine add 3 to the result. Check the table below for the result of this round of the sea battle.

00-35 – You get caught with a severe broadside. **Lower your vessel manoeuvrability by 2 levels and your vessel speed by 1 level.**

36-60 – A volley lands on deck killing many of the crew. **Lower your crew by 1 level.**

61-80 – A volley blows out some of your canons, but you hit back – **Lower your firepower by 1 level.** But you cause the following damage dependent on your firepower: **Light – 1 point, Moderate – 2pts, Heavy – 3pts, Very Heavy – 4 pts**

81-90 – You land a splendid volley. Note you have done the following damage dependent on your firepower: **Light – 1 point, Moderate – 2pts, Heavy – 3pts, Very Heavy – 4 pts**

91 and up - You catch them cold with a blinding manoeuvre. Note you have done the following damage dependent on your firepower: **Light – 2 point, Moderate – 4pts, Heavy – 6pts, Very Heavy – 8 pts**

If you have caused 18 points of damage overall to the brigantine – *645*

If not

Do you want to continue the battle – *145*

Do you wish to run – *992*

966

You enter the Admiral's Whiskers and can see that everyone is looking directly at you. It's no surprise as you don't really cut the image of a former naval sailor (after all you are a woman, and the navy doesn't accept women on their vessels). There are several portly naval men lying around with port and ale before them. A young lad is serving and behind the bar a rather smart man is tending. You feel very out of place.

Do you

Try to sit with one of the portly men – *869*

Approach the bar – *398*

Ask if anyone knows your first officer – *340*

Decide to leave and return to the crossroads – *802*

967

The pirate sweeps you away to the rear of the building where you are led in through a cellar door. (**Untick either codeword Emerald or Promissory Note, depending on which you have used.)** There are hushed whispers, and you are taken to a small room in the cellar where you are told to sit and wait on an old barrel. The door is locked, and you wait for what seems like an age before a pirate with a large bushy black beard enters and closes the door behind him. You gulp wondering what will happen next.

The pirate stares at you for a moment before he speaks.

"It's you, Mary. I'm sorry for your loss, Mary. I heard about what happened to your father, a man to whom I owe a lot. You may not realise but out here you have to keep an uneasy alliance between pirate and landowner and between us, your father and I, made it work. I am Black Robert, the pirate Lord in this place. But tell me, what is it you want?"

"I want Estes," you say.

"Indeed, the pirate from where God only knows, and so you shall but we need your lands back as well, so this alliance between your family and me may continue. But you shall have your revenge, Mary. Now come, let's see you properly fed and dressed.

You have the pirate Lord on your side. If you have wounds they are tended and cured. **You may remove all wounds from you and ignore any timers regarding their effects.** Now plan your future at *1370*

968

If you have the code word **Compass Map** – *919*

If you have the code word **Return** – *1147*

Your vessel arrives at the Marie Saratoga wreck on a blisteringly hot morning, sun blazing down, and you find yourself sweating in your long-coat. The wreck is also glistening as it is close to land, a small volcanic island, which sits just north of the wreck. The island is uninhabited which is obvious given that there is no vegetation and bare rock everywhere. It looks bleak and you certainly could not dig into the ground for there is none.

The wreck sits down in the water with just its mast poking out. You realise that you'll need to swim inside it to find all it holds. That's a risk as who knows what lies down below. You look over at the barren landscape and it sends a chill through you.

"Be careful," says your first officer as you strip down to your shirt and breeches, leaving your boots and long-coat on the deck. "Very few people come here, and you can feel why. The whole place has a tangible evil to it."

You nod, very aware of what your first officer is referring to. But Estes may have been here and what better place to hide treasure, the rumours keeping most people away. You may also visit the island but, at the moment, you see no reason. After all it is just rock.

"Wil you dive and search the vessel outside, Captain, or will you go straight inside?"

Well, Captain, do you

Dive and search the outside of the vessel – *136*

Swim to the mast and explore the vessel from the top down – *603*

969

Reduce the Hot Strip by 1. If this places you on a Fire spot add 20 to this section's number and go there for the walls have moved. There are walls of fire to the west and east. You can route south or north from your current location.

Do you

Go North – *168*

Go South – *485*

<u>970</u>

You slash at the man with your knife, cutting his arm and forcing him to release you. You don't look back and run for the alley and the street beyond. Go to *496*

<u>971</u>

You find the pull of the main current tough to overcome to get to the eddy, but you do it eventually. **Reduce your Waters Strength Chart by 1.** You clamber onto the rock.

On the rock, you grab your breath for a moment before taking a look at the chest of treasure you have been seeking. It is filled with precious gems, and you delight in their lustre. However, you still must get back to the edge you jumped in from and your crew. Tick the codeword **Golden 2**

You can rest up if you wish before jumping in. For every 3 points you add to your Waters Strength Chart, take 1 off your Island Time Chart. Once refreshed, strap the chest to your back and dive in again. Do you jump in to the

North – *610*

South – *1083*

East – *1108*

West – *595*

<u>972</u>

"Hi there," you say. "I was wondering if you could help me."

"You stand in line like every other one of you insatiable dogs. Now get out of here while they eat."

You turn and find a brush shoved in your face knocking you back into the sand. Pirates laugh as a large woman keeps hitting you until you leave the area.

"Don't come back!" she says fixing you with an evil eye. **You cannot visit the small houses again during this visit to Hell's Deep.**

Do you

Explore the tavern – *363*

Approach the gambling groups – *1424*

Go to see the fights – *84*

Decide this is not a place you want to explore and return to your vessel - *314*

973

You feint to turn away but then go to run past him. Alas he has you by the collar. He slings you out into the middle of the street before standing over you with his sword. He reaches into your pockets and takes the second item in your inventory. (**Search your codewords for items and remove the second one. If you have only one item, he takes that instead. Untick the item. If you have none, he takes your long-coat, leaving you in your undergarments: count this as a nightgown from now on.**) Continue your adventure at *262*, but you may not return to the house.

974

The weaponsmith's shop has a guard on the door and you can see several gentlemen inside admiring various pistols and knives. You wonder if the weaponsmith will accept a trade for you have no money. And what will you buy anyway? Do you want to enter the shop?

If so, are you

In a dress – *1447*

Disguised in a slave outfit – *1157*

Wearing a long-coat – *360*

Or

Do you want to return to the street – *1009*

975

Are you

Still in your dress to go shopping – *460*

Dressed like a slave in your torn gown – *616*

Wearing a long-coat and breeches – *248*

976

You seem to have attracted a lot of attention with your anger towards the man and you notice that a number of guards have surrounded you. With such a force you are trapped and are taken away to the garrison and thrown into prison.

Captain Fareham of the garrison visits you and tells you that he intends to marry you, and he does so in quiet, keeping you locked up in the jail. Fareham now owns your father's lands and keeps you in your cell for the next year. When you don't respond to his advances and wishes to be a passive wife, he has you taken away in the night and disposed of. Your last thoughts are that your family remains unavenged. Try again at *1* and next time try and be more discreet

977

You hold the pistol up close to the man's belly. "Back off, or die," you say in a steely whisper that surprises even you. The man gently lets go and slumps back to the wall.

"Easy lady, easy. No harm done here."

You watch him closely as you make your way down the alley to its end. Go to **828**

978

You order your crew to charge but almost immediately you are cut down with musket fire. The natives then charge and soon you are in a battle for your life. Your vessel fires on their village which causes panic and allows you to return to your ship.

You will clearly not be welcome back here. Although you have your life, you cannot visit the south island again. If you can, reduce your crew size by 1 level.

Do you

Tell the crew to sail to the north of the island – **468**

Route for the centre of the island – **746**

Decide to set sail - **consult the voyage chart**

979

You take off your hat and shake your hair out at the women and you hear them gasp. They look at you a little in fear and then you hear a voice from behind.

"Girl, get that hair away and sit down quickly."

The Treasure of Captain Estes

Turning you see a large woman who gesticulates for you to do as she says. Once you have done so the woman whispers in your ear.

"Not the place for a female pirate with all these drunk and excitable men about. You would be quite the prize here. However, the pirate king likes a woman who stays true to her colours so make sure you come before him as yourself. But as for now, get out of here."

You thank her and leave the small houses wondering what sort of a life these women have.

Do you

Explore the tavern – *363*

Approach the gambling groups – *1424*

Go to see the fights – *84*

Decide this is not a place you want to explore and return to your vessel - *314*

980

You grab the branches beside the hut and attack the rats with them, but they come at your regardless. They seem to come from everywhere and soon they are jumping on you, even as you thrash them. There are simply too many and you are forced to run down the mountain. But they have gotten to you and ripped your clothing and you have lost some items. **Lose the 2nd[t] and 3rd items from your codewords.** As you reach the base of the mountain, you skip over the river and the rats start to lose interest.

Now at the base of the mountain, you grab your breath and decide not to return this way again. **Note you cannot climb the mountain again.**

There are two paths away from the mountain, one a canopy covered path to the north, the other a more open topped path to the west, although it is still surrounded by the dense jungle.

Do you

Head north – **435**

Take the path west – **477**

981

Your first officer turns to you and says, "Leave well alone, for you don't what you're messing with. She's into that black magic. No one has had a good experience around her."

Do you

Sail away – **322**

Make a course for the square-rigged vessel – **538**

982

Reduce your Island Time Chart by 1

You trek along the path, ever so tired. There's a fork in the path, and you wonder which way to go. You can take either fork, or you could always head out into the jungle off the path.

Do you go

Left – **177**

Right – **245**

Strike out into the Jungle – **1077**

Turn around back the way you came – **940**

983

Reduce the Hot Strip by 2. If this places you on a Fire spot add 20 to this section's number and go there for the walls have moved. There are walls of fire to the east, west, and south, so you route north from your current location. Go to *233*

984

Reduce your Island Time Chart by 1

You trek forward along the path, and everything looks the same. The path is mesmerising. Soon you reach a fork in the path, and you wonder which way to go. To the right you think you hear the beach. You could always simply strike out into the jungle off the path.

Do you go

Left – *183*

Right – *197*

Strike out into the Jungle – *1077*

Turn around back the way you came – *886*

985

You step onto the pillar with a bit of a wobble. There are pillars to your right and left, straight in front, and diagonally to your rear left and right. You can see small items on the pillars diagonally to your rear right and directly in front .

Do you step

To your right – *1136*

To your left – *68*

Diagonally backward left – *448*

Diagonally backward right – *166*

Forwards – *238*

986

Reduce your time by 1. You step forward and run into some fallen woodwork. On your left is a cage blocking your way but to your right is clear water.

Do you

About turn and step forward – *458*

Turn right and walk forward – *41*

987

"No, I want the element of surprise."

This causes some mutterings from the crew but soon you dive into the water and swim steadily towards the island. As you get to the shelf where the seabed rises, you dive under the water.

Continue at *230*

988

You remember the instructions you were given to complete the Walls of Fire and go over them in your head.

'There is but one entrance. When you enter route east, east, north, east, west, north. Then wait for a moment and let things cool. Now route west, north, north, east, and then north to your escape. If you dally though, this plan would be put asunder.'

Note this section as you can return to it anytime during your attempt for advice. Now return to *910* and choose whether you will attempt this challenge or not.

The Treasure of Captain Estes

989

Reduce your time by 1.

If your time is in the following gaps (27-23 or 17-13), then go to *1037*.

If your time is in the following gaps (52-48 or 12-08), then go to *1128*.

If neither of these apply, continue at the plain text below

You creep up to the building and to the single wooden door. You feel exposed as you stand there and wonder if you should just pull at the door and enter the building to get cover. It would be madness to stand here, but what's inside?

Do you

Hide where you are – *1393*

Route South – *1197*

Creep East – *103*

Go North – *785*

Listen at the door – *1011*

Open the door and enter the building – *680*

990

The chest is wooden and has the word "Estes" inscribed into the top. It has no lock and should simply open.

Do you

Open the chest – *508*

Climb up the rope now above you – *479*

Run across the room – *421*

991

You grab hold of one of the treasure caskets as it strikes your foot. Desperately you haul it with you to the vessel and feel the arms of your crew haul you aboard. Soaking you gasp for breath and look around to see who else has been rescued. There are no other crew from the small boat standing there. You realise you have lost all the treasure that was in the small boat. **Adjust this amount now on the Island Time Chart.** There is a silence among the crew but there is little else you can do. Go to **725**

992

This hasn't gone well and getting out of a fight now will be tricky. Let's hope you still have some manoeuvrability and speed.

Is your manoeuvrability

Good, Great or Reasonable – **1163**

Poor or Lacking – **1262**

993

You can feel the sweat pouring down your face as you believe this man may end your life. "I have a gift," you say and pass your item to the man (**Untick the codeword**). He regards it for a moment and then nods with pleasure. "More like it, my lady, now beat it back to the street. Down this alley is no place for you."

You have no choice but to return to the street at **496** minus your "gift".

994

Reduce your time by 1.

If your time is in the following gaps (42-38) you see a guard on his patrol outside and must remain hidden until he clears the area. Reduce your time by 6. Now continue at the plain text below

Each desk is made of stout wood and must have been brought over from European shores for the style and quality smacks of the continent. You race through papers and notes, peering in the darkness but can find very little of note.

Do you

Check out the cabinets – *284*

Look at the chairs – *243*

Peruse the charts on the wall – *324*

Or leave the room and return to tunnel – *693*

995

"Looks like Jeboe's Schooner, a privateer. Sharp enough man, but workable with. We may be able to trade, or we can fight?"

Do you

Order your crew to sail towards the pirate ship, preparing to attack – *1373*

Decide to keep your distance and stay away – *209*

Approach the vessel looking to trade – *52*

996

Your cargo hold has no treasure in it. After all this journey there is nothing to show for your efforts. You give the command to sail for New Southampton, but your crew does not heed you. Instead, they grab you and throw you overboard.

As you descend into the depths, you remember the adventures you had but wish they had been a tad more fruitful! You never see your home restored.

Well that was a long haul to get nowhere. Ready to do it all again. Go to *1* to start again.

997

"I have the great Black Robert on board," you say and watch as the bald man looks impressed.

"The king is delighted that he is with us, a small tribute is customary for one of our greatest sons." **Tick codeword Wanted.** Unless you have something else you are going to have to pay or leave.

Do you

Decide you have an item you can offer to prove your worth – *229*

Offer doubloons – *1297*

Decide the price is too high and leave Hells Deep – **Consult the voyage chart and set sail**

998

You take aim at the soldiers remembering the times your father taught you to fire at bottles. You fire twice, once at each soldier and watch them tumble to the floor. You don't wait to see if they are dead but run out the door to the fields beyond. **Untick the codeword pistol as it is now empty.**

Go to *647*

999

Roll 1xD100 (2xD10). For every point of damage you have already done to the brigantine add 3 to the result. Check the table below for the result of this round of the sea battle.

00-59 – You get caught with a severe broadside. **Lower your vessel manoeuvrability by 2 levels and your vessel speed by 1 level.**

60-89 – A volley lands on deck killing many of the crew. **Lower your crew by 1 level.**

90-99 – A volley blows out some of your canons, but you hit back – **Lower your firepower by 1 level.** But you cause the following damage dependent on your firepower: **Light – 1 point, Moderate – 2pts, Heavy – 3pts, Very Heavy – 4 pts**

100-110 – You land a splendid volley. Note you have done the following damage dependent on your firepower: **Light – 1 point, Moderate – 2pts, Heavy – 3pts, Very Heavy – 4 pts**

111 and up - You catch them cold with a blinding manoeuvre. Note you have done the following damage dependent on your firepower: **Light – 2 point, Moderate – 4pts, Heavy – 6pts, Very Heavy – 8 pts**

If you have caused 18 points of damage overall to the brigantine – *645*

If not

Do you want to continue the battle – *145*

Do you wish to run – *992*

1000

You wander along the path and reach a junction with three paths off it. Which way now?

Left – *560*

Middle – *1033*

Right – *422*

Turn back – *105*

1001

You fire another volley of canon fire and see the galleon slowly begin to sink. Crew are abandoning it and you desperately come alongside before it sinks into the sea. You find a dead Captain Gonzales on deck and his crew are in no mood to defend themselves further. You don't have long to gather his stores though.

What you can gather is dependent on your crew size. It is also dependent on your cargo hold. Check what you can take from the galleon on the chart below. Then place it in your hold up to your capacity. Note you cannot throw any of your cargo out to make room, there isn't time.

Your Vessel's Crew   **Cargo you can take**

Large   **20 units of treasure worth 1000 doubloons each**

Medium   **10 units of treasure worth 1000 doubloons each**

Small   **5 units of treasure worth 1000 doubloons each**

Continue the voyage at **654**

1002

You push the pole down in the water and jam it into the depths. You fling your arms around it and find you are now able to hang on against the flow. You take a breather and rest up waiting to recoup your strength.

Take as long as you need and increase your Waters Strength chart up to any value up to and including 10. For every 3 points you add to your Waters Strength Chart, take 1 off your Island Time Chart. Any fraction of 3 points (i.e. 1 or 2 points over a multiple of 3) also incurs 1 off your Island Time Chart. When ready, return to your previously noted section.

The Treasure of Captain Estes

<u>1003</u>

Reduce your Island Time Chart by 1

You trek along the path, head hung low in the heat. There's a fork in the path, and you wonder which way to go. You can take either fork, or you could always head out into the jungle off the path.

Do you go

Left – *550*

Right – *984*

Strike out into the Jungle – *1347*

Turn around back the way you came – *830*

<u>1004</u>

You wander along the path, the air so still and quiet, and reach a junction. Which way now?

Left – *612*

Right – *575*

Turn back – *1359*

<u>1005</u>

You sail close to the Brigantine under a white flag and are welcomed on board by Captain Jameson. He needs nothing from you but is prepared to sell you provisions at 20 doubloons per provision and he can spare up to 20.

Add provisions to your hold as you see fit, up to 20 provisions at a cost of 20 doubloons each.

After trading, Captain Jameson bids you a farewell and you sail on. Continue the voyage at *654*

<u>1006</u>

You pull your hair out from under your long-coat and you can see the man's face light up. "I am Mary Hastings and I want revenge for my father. I want to hunt down Captain Estes and bring him to death and ruin. I need a boat."

The man laughs. "I get you want vengeance but, really, you are a mere girl."

"Hell hath no fury like a woman scorned," you spit at him, and you see him rear slightly.

"And what of Estes' treasure," he asks.

"Well, those who help me can have their share. Those in my way can sleep together at the bottom of the sea." You're impressed by your own words but underneath you are shaking. You channel every bit of anger and hurt into your face, and you see the man eying you up carefully.

"Well, Mary Hastings, I have a crew who are tired and bored at the brothel, and in need of better fortune. You are clearly angry and determined but have you ever sailed before."

You shake your head. "That's why I need a crew."

The man seems to give thought for a moment and then he simply nods. "Okay, Mary Hastings, we'll see what you have to offer. But the crew will never listen to a Mary Hastings for my men are those on the wilder side of life. So meet me tonight at the last alehouse on the edge of town and I'll take you to our vessel. But it's Mad Mary, you understand. And give no quarter, girl, if you want to be the captain of the vessel. They'll respect determination and order, and a little bit of reward. But go easy on them and you'll end up in the sea or at their whim and pleasure, which is really a poor end for someone so promising."

He seems to have fallen for you in some way and you ask his name.

"Simon Kilmer, former lieutenant in His Majesty's Navy and now a free gentleman on these seas." He takes off his tri-cornered hat and places it on your head. Be the part of a Captain, Mary, for your sake and mine."

Do you

Agree – *1233*

Thank him but politely decline and return to the street – *496*

1007

As you set sail you feel a stiff wind building up behind you and at first you fear a storm. But the clouds roll overhead and the sea chops, but the predicted storm does not arrive and instead you find yourself being boosted along.

- For voyages of 1 or 2 days you see no noticeable difference
- For voyages of 3 to 4 days you can **cut 1 day off your voyage length**
- For voyages of 5 to 7 days you can **cut 2 days off your voyage length**
- For voyages of 8 and over days you can **cut 3 days off your voyage length**

Continue the voyage at *654*

1008

You wander along the path and reach a junction with three paths off it. Which way now?

Left – *26*

Middle – *73*

Right – *5*

Turn back – *1050*

1009

You are in the far end of town and can see the docks with various vessels, some unloading, some ready to sail and others apparently lounging in the hot sun. Opposite the docks is the weaponsmith's store with two angry looking men standing at the door. New Southampton stretches back towards the garrison and looks busy in the glaring sun.

Do you

Go to the weaponsmiths – **974**

Make for the docks – **117**

Route back into town – **1166**

1010

Reduce your time by 1.

If your time is in the following gaps (37-33 or 07-03), you see a guard on his patrol and must remain hidden until he clears the area. Reduce your time by 6. Now continue at the plain text below

You keep to the shadows, but no one comes. What will you do now?

Do you

Hide where you are – **1435**

Route North – **103**

Creep West – **1197**

Go North-east – **174**

Approach the building before you to break in – **989**

Beware the Mermaid's Call!

1011

Reduce your time by 1.

If your time is in the following gaps (27-23 or 17-13), then go to *1037*.

If your time is in the following gaps (52-48 or 12-08), then go to *1128*.

If neither of these apply, continue at the plain text below

As you stand at the door, you can hear snoring, and not just a single person. There's the odd creak as well but generally snoring.

Do you

Hide where you are – *1393*

Route South – *1197*

Creep East – *103*

Go North – *785*

Open the door and enter the building – *680*

1012

The pirate narrows his eyes and points with his sword to the building opposite the docks.

"You need to see Cortez. That way and don't dilly dally about it."

You feel like you have no option looking at his drawn sword and you walk quickly back up the steps and to the building opposite. Go to *1109*

1013

"Are you ready, madam," asks Madame Le Vert from the shop and you tell her you are, as you pick up a bottle and hold it behind your back. You open the dressing room door, and the shop owner compliments you on how you look. Stepping out into the shop, you pretend to take a stumble and say that the dress is maybe a little long.

The Treasure of Captain Estes

"I shall fix it for you," says Madame Le Vert, and bends down to adjust the dress. The back of her head is an easy target.

Do you

Hit her with the bottle – *542*

Wait for a better opportunity - *563*

1014

You open the trapdoor and find yourself in an office of sorts. It's a stone room but feels welcomingly cool compared to outside's stifling midday heat. There are several desks and large cabinets with many drawers. There is a writing desk too and quite ornate chairs for where you are. On the walls are many charts of the area with some ringed areas. There is a door in the far wall which makes you uneasy as it could open at any moment.

 Do you

Examine the desks – *1239*

Check out the cabinets – *1405*

Look at the chairs – *120*

Peruse the charts on the wall – *371*

Or leave the room and return back to tunnel – *558*

1015

The guard slips on the hat backwards falling to the floor and as you run into the dressing room, his fellow soldiers entering the shop trip over him and a mess of long-coats, breeches, shirts and hats fall on the soldiers.

You desperately throw the wooden boxes in the dressing room on top of one another before climbing and squeezing through the small window. You feel a hand nearly grab your foot, before a cry comes from the guard. The boxes must have given way.

You drop into the alley at the rear of Madame Le Vert's shop. You are still in your dress and are sweating profusely with the effort in what is now a hot sun as you make for the main street.

Tick the codeword Prominent, if not already ticked on your list and go to *1166* to continue your escape.

1016

You peer through the smoke and wonder if you have hit the creature. As the fog of war clears you see the creature close to you and an appendage slams down on your vessel causing it to tip and several crewmen fall overboard. But the tentacle fails to hold onto the vessel, and you manage to sail away from the creature and aim another broadside at it.

Roll 1xD100 (2xD10)

00-49 – *1328*

50-99 – *449*

1017

It's pot luck what crew is here and who'll you will attract but here goes. **Roll 1xD100 (2xD10) and check the result below**

00-19 – *858*

20-39 – *713*

40-59 – *865*

60-79 – *11*

80-99 – *1259*

The Treasure of Captain Estes

<u>1018</u>

You throw the cross throught the bars of your cell and into Diggory's cell. He grabs the item and stretches up the window that sits high up in his cell. He really is quite gangly and stretches as tall as any person you have seen.

The light reflects off the cross and you realise some sort of signal is sent but you don't know quite how. Diggory then jumps and pulls himself up to the window, looking out for some sort of signal in return.

The process takes several minutes before Diggory smiles at you. "It is done, and they are sailing for the bay below the garrison. We need to make our move. Call the guard and look to seduce him but make him back towards my cell. Can you do that?"

You nod and softly call for the guard. An overweight guard arrives, and you see the cell keys hanging from his belt. The man is disgusting, and you brace yourself for what must be done.

Do you

Invite him into your cell in an attempt to steal his keys – *1040*

Try and draw him close to your cell before pushing him backwards towards Diggory's cell – *1456*

Tell the guard that Diggory has your cross and you want it back – *900*

<u>1019</u>

It was a long way up and you take a breather before waking back to the jungle path. **Cross off 3 from your Island Time Chart.** Now go to *171*

1020

"Yes, I see your point," you say to the second officer getting close to him. "Walk with me and we'll discuss further."

You walk over to the port side of the vessel and lean over the rail pointing at something. As he bends to look down, you grab his legs and toss him over before he has time to react.

"That's where all dissenters on my vessel end up," you cry and glare at the crew.

Is your first officer Timmers, or Robert Grimshaw – *1341*

If not, read on

Your first officer commends your action but tells you it will upset the crew and not to do it too often. You can tell over the coming days as although they obey your commands quickly, they seem to watch you closely. **Reduce your crew morale by 2 levels.** Now continue at *654*

1021

Decide how many doubloons you will offer Tom and write it down. Now go to *4*

1022

"I've never dealt with a Kraken personally, but we're light and have very little firepower, we need to run!"

If you want to take Simon's advice - *1155* **(but when making the instructed check on the table, reduce your vessel's speed by 1 level as you have wasted some time.)**

Otherwise return to *927* and make your decision.

The Treasure of Captain Estes

1023

You try to sneak up to the building but the guard on the door is making this difficult. When he leaves the door to walk around the building, you find the door to be both stout and locked. **Reduce your time by 2.** This looks like a bust.

If your time is in the following gaps (52-48), then go to *1037*.

If your time is in the following gaps (22-18), then go to *1128*.

If neither of these apply, continue at the plain text below

There is a gate out of the enclosed centre of the fort in the wall here, and it is open. To the south are more buildings. To the south-east is a path and what looks like a small hut. To the west is a large building with no guards outside.

Do you

Hide where you are – *915*

Route South-east – *174*

Creep West – *785*

Sneak north – *103*

1024

Your crew are not happy at what they see as a Captain shirking her duties and they are in a foul mood.

Decrease your crew morale by 1 level.

Now continue the voyage at *654*

1025

Roll 1D100 (2xD10) to find where the coin actually is. Did you roll?

00-33 – *777*

34-67 – *573*

68-99 – *46*

1026

You mingle in with the other customers but notice little that can help you. It's a hard decision between doing nothing so as not to arouse anyone's suspicions about yourself and actually getting on with what you need to do. But you need to do something.

Do you

Try to steal a jewel – *638*

Try the provisions stall – *1368*

Look at the whiskey and ale stalls – *155*

Or return to the street – *496*

1027

You find the pull of the main current tough to overcome to get to the eddy, but you do it eventually. **Reduce your Waters Strength Chart by 1.** You swim through to the eddy. Go to *1127*

1028

Nervously you walk to the rear room and await the bar maid coming in to see you. As she enters she looks at you fiercely and grabs you by your gown.

"What are you doing coming in here dressed like that. These men will want only one thing from you. Lucky for you I was here. Now out the back and round to the street and don't let me see you back in here. Understand?"

You nod profusely and then run out the back and round to the street. That was a lucky escape. Go to the street at *1112*

1029

You can hear scratching noises through the pirate flag door. Sounds like Tabetha is through that door. You decide to risk that door would be foolish. Return to your noted section and decide which door to go through or to stay put **but you cannot choose the pirate flag door**.

1030

You sail into a small opening that has three exits from it. The rocks are spaced here, and you can turn easily. There are exits from the channel to the northwest, south, and southeast. All are wide channels except to the northwest which is narrow and will require a vessel with good manoeuvrability. Where now?

Do you

Sail south– *192*

Route northwest (only vessels with good manoeuvrability) – *144*

Go southeast – *1349*

1031

You awake in a bed within a stone room and with a pitcher of water beside you on a small wooden table. There is a blanket over you and the sunlight is breaking through gaps in the wooden shutters of the room.

You remember being brought to the garrison last night, but you were utterly exhausted. Captain Fareham had seen you to your room before any wounds you had received were cleaned thoroughly by a maid and you were allowed to sleep. (**If you have the codeword Shoulder Wound, untick it**).

You are provided with a clean dress and then shown to an inner room in the garrison to have breakfast with the captain. The servants provide a breakfast of bread and cheese with a little fish, and you eat hungrily. As they clear away the wooden plates you see Captain Fareham begin to cough and then stand before approaching you.

"I've been giving some thought to your situation, Mary Hastings, and I think I have the perfect solution to your problems. Clearly with the death of your father you are in too traumatised a state to think clearly so I will act for you. In order for your father's estate, such that remains, to stay as yours, you will clearly need a man of strength beside you, one who can fend off anyone who would seek to take advantage of a mere woman such as yourself."

"I fail to see myself as a mere woman," you reply.

"Indeed, you are quite beautiful, a delicate flower blossoming in the wind. But beware there are those who would pull you from the ground."

You go to argue but the Captain waves a hand in your face.

"No, sweet Mary, don't be brave. Be glad, for I shall marry you and provide this protection. I am quite a prize according to the ladies at home. Now we need to make arrangements and be wed tomorrow before anyone else can lay claim on the estate. You shall go to New Southampton today acquire suitable attire for a woman soon to be my wife. So, to your room, Mary, and you shall be escorted to town."

You go to argue but Captain Fareham takes you by the wrists. "I know it is a shock, but this is for you, so be quiet and thankful. Do you understand, Mary?" His tone is threatening, and you see little point in arguing now. Instead, you meekly bow your head and then slink off to your room, escorted by a maid.

Alone in your room you think through your options. You could try and escape the garrison now while everyone believes you to be in shock.

The Treasure of Captain Estes

Alternatively, you could wait until you get into New Southampton and then sneak off to find better options than a marriage to Captain Fareham. Of course, you could marry him..., you shake your head in disgust. You are your mother's daughter and no man like Fareham deserves you.

Do you

Try to escape now – *1110*

Wait until New Southampton before making your escape – *1452*

1032

You see a British flag but it's a red ensign, not a military vessel. Instead, it's a cargo vessel, a Dutch Fleut, slower than most vessels. There may be items of worth on board and it doesn't look heavily armed either. You can see it already turning away from you. It's a distraction but one that may prove profitable.

Do you

Turn to engage the Vessel – *1231*

Ignore the vessel – *1075*

1033

You wander along the path, whistling as you go, and reach a junction. Which way now?

Left – *89*

Right – *727*

Turn back – *728*

1034

You wonder what should be done but Martha takes you below to see rows of oars stored in the hold (if Martha has been replaced then your new first officer takes you).

"The joy of the Brigantine," she says, "is that you can row it as well as sail with the wind. Sure it will be slower but at least we will get moving."

Soon the oars are deployed and your crew begins to row clear of the pressure system you are currently lying in. After a while the wind picks up again and you begin to sail on towards your destination.

If your crew is medium or large, you lose only 1 day to the lack of wind. If your crew is small, you lose 2 days. Add these lost days to your voyage time.

Continue the voyage at *654*

1035

You watch the crew jump to their task as they try to get the vessel moving quickly. But it is clear the creature is quicker. A tentacle sweeps across the deck, throwing many overboard. Another one rips your mainsail and then pulls down the mast. Then, with amazing speed, tentacles rise on all sides of the deck until the creature drags the vessel straight down, drowning everyone on board.

The waters around New Southampton are deadly, and you have succumbed. You may try again at *1*

1036

You arrive in a small clearing and remember this is where the well was that you wound up the empty map from. There's nothing more here for you so you retreat along the path. Go to *545*

1037

As you wander round this area, you hear someone coming. They must be close for those footsteps are loud. You scramble for cover but have find none, so you have to run to stay clear of them. In the dark you don't know where you are going and in truth you're not sure where they are.

Roll 1xD100 (2xD10).

00-20 – *749*

21-99 – *1175*

1038

You saddle up to the man, ignoring his stinking breath and let him cuddle you tight, and then a little more. He tells you all about how magnificent a sailor he was and many other tales that are clearly made up. Soon he says he can tell you more in his room. At this point, you know to leave, feeling very sullied and annoyed to have put yourself through that degrading nonsense to gain nothing. If you ever meet him outside, you'll teach him a lesson.

You walk back to the crossroads – ***802***

1039

You approach the jungle warily and see a muddy path before you that twists away into the thickness of jungle vines and plants. Certainly leaving the path would be a struggle but possible.

Do you have codewords

Notes and **Wayfinder** – ***518***

Only **Notes** – ***179***

Only **Wayfinder** – ***288***

If not, continue below

Look at the *Island Time Chart at App 14*. Mark your starting point on this chart as 100. As you move you will be advised to reduce the chart by a certain number. Cross off your used time when you are told.

The chart indicates how long you think you will have until night falls on the island and it might not be a good idea to be in the jungle when night falls if this jungle is like any other you have come across.

At the bottom of the chart is a box to write down any treasure you find on this island. You will be advised what to write if and when you find any treasure.

Now step forward along the path to *827*

1040

You are repulsed by the guard, but you say are prepared to give him whatever he wants in return for some food and better care while in the cell. Gently, you coax him inside and coil yourself around him as he falls for your feminine charm. With your free hand you take the dangling keys from his belt as you kiss him, throwing them across the hallway of the cells where they are caught by Diggory. You only have to suffer the jailer's attentions for another few moments before Diggory frees himself and then enters your cell, grabbing the man from behind and knocking him out.

"Good work," says Diggory, "but we need to go."

Escape now at *1371*

1041

Add a modifier of 60 when asked in the next section. Go to *207*

The Treasure of Captain Estes

Martha Downham is a fearsome captain and has the men of her crew well under her heel. You have been on her vessel for less than a day in the Strangar harbour but already she has it ready to sail.

"Now we need to find Estes," she tells you, "for he's a tricky sort and we don't want to sail in the wrong direction after him. But let me send out scouts to do that, for all authorities seek me, while you take in this vessel. The Lady Fortune is a Brigantine, well armoured and like the wind. We can also hide easily in the shallows and sail the heavy seas. Look her over for you shall guide us."

Martha dresses you in pirate garb complete with a cutlass and explains to you how her vessel runs over the next week while you wait for news of Estes.

While you wait, it's time to fill in your vessel chart with the details of your vessel and crew. Look for the chart at the rear of the book. You may photocopy this for ease of use. Fill it in now.

First Officer: Martha Downham

Vessel: Lady Fortune - Brigantine

Speed: Fast

Firepower: Heavy

Treasure store: Moderate

Shallows: Yes

Manoeuvrability: Good

Storm Handling: Moderate

Crew: Medium

Initial Provisions: 10 sections

Doubloons: 1000

Martha calls you to the map room one day with a serious look on her face.

"Mary, I'm sorry but the varmint, Estes, is dead. He ran into the British and was sunk somewhere near New Southampton. My informant states Estes left his treasure on an island in the vicinity of New Southampton called the Dark Land. Now beware for dark spirits surround that island and you'll need to know your witchcraft to succeed there. Many will tell you the island doesn't exist but neither does anywhere until you find it. It is lost though and we'll need to shake down many a person to find its location."

"So, I have nothing," you say, "unless I chase this treasure."

"With treasure you have everything."

"Well then, when do we start? And where should we go?"

"I have no definitive sightings of Estes before his last battle which was southeast of New Southampton. If you look at this chart, Mary, there are six places in the general locale where he could have been before he died and which may be able to shed light on his travels, and where the island is. Once you have examined them all, give the crew orders of where to sail to."

Check the *chart of New Southampton at App 02* to help you in your decisions. You may photocopy it for use with this book. Turn now to section *1276* to learn about the six locations and about sailing around New Southampton, and then to make your first decision as captain!

1043

The channel narrows so you cannot turn about, and you seem to be routing east and then northwest until you approach a pool. Something seems familiar. Go to *159*

The Treasure of Captain Estes

1044

You produce a bottle of whiskey, and the big man takes it, pulling out the cork and downing a slug. **Untick the codeword Bottle of Whiskey.**

"It's good," he says, and takes another dram. "Seeing as you have been so generous, I guess you can meet the boss. Come with me." The man laughs and turns to the doors which are already opening. Follow the man inside to *16*

1045

You step onto the pillar and breathe a sigh as it doesn't crumble. The waves crash far below, and you ponder your next move. There is a pillar to your left, one in front and the cliff edge behind you. **Tick the codeword Pew if you haven't already.**

Do you step

Forwards – *754*

To your left – *914*

Step back off the pillar onto the cliff edge behind – *1180*

1046

Reduce the Hot Strip by 1. If this places you on a Fire spot add 20 to this section's number and go there for the walls have moved. There are walls of fire to the south and east. You can route north or west from your current location.

Do you

Go West – *1455*

Go North – *1142*

1047

Everything happens so quickly, and a bull smashes you backwards knocking you to the ground and then you scramble as quick as you can back to the plain clear of any more bulls. You're back where you started but you have been winded and feel groggy. **Take 3 off your Island Time Chart while you recover.**

If you want to try and run the gap again – *59*

You could try and go through the jungle and around the rock formation – *923*

Alternatively, you can leave the plains back down the jungle track – *1145*

1048

The man is too strong and pulls you inside the building. You are held against your will, working in the brothel and live out a short but miserable life. When your end comes due to a violent customer, it is at least a merciful release. Try again at *1* and stay away from places such as this.

1049

You look at the pirates gathered around in a circle in the dust at the far side of the street. A lantern lights up the ground and you can see several dice on the ground. As you watch, the pirates seem to be rolling dice that have three images on each one. The first is that of a skull, the second a set of scales, and the last some coins. The aim seems to be to throw the dice and achieve the coins. As you watch you believe that achieving the coins gains you something from whoever has bet against you.

There are ten pirates playing the game, all drinking heavily from wine bottles and the mood seems jovial. Maybe you could gain something from them.

If you wish to play – *1178*

If not return to the street – *262*

1050

You wander along the path, singing as you go to keep the loneliness at bay, and reach a junction. Which way now?

Left – *581*

Right – *1071*

Turn back – *1008*

1051

You take a hold of the handle and it turns easily and you see a bucket coming up from below. It is a standard wooden pail, and when it reaches the lip of the well, you grab it and look inside. The bucket is dry but you see some rolled parchment inside.

Opening the scroll, you see it is a chart with some crude markings on it showing the island of New Southampton and some other local features but it is devoid of detail. Will it be of use? If you want to pocket it, **tick the codeword Empty Chart.**

There's nothing else here so you let the bucket drop and leave the clearing back to the path behind you. Go to *545*

1052

Move Tabetha.

You are in a white walled room, bathed in the strange light, with two doors, one with a picture of a pirate flag above it, and the other with a shield above it.

If Tabetha's number is 5 – *1459*

If Tabetha's number is 18 – **note this number and go to *1029***

If Tabetha's number is 7 – **note this number and go to *239***

Where do you go next?

Through the pirate flag door – *502*

Through the shield door – *1179*

Wait here - **return to the top of this section**

1053

"Help," yells Black Robert, so loud the crew can hear him. "You're meant to be a pirate, leading us to treasure. Deal with it yourself."

Your crew are mocking you now, laughing at you. **Reduce crew morale by 2 levels.** Return to *763* and choose another option.

1054

You turn your vessel towards the Schooner making a direct line for it. As soon as you make a move towards it, the vessel turns and races fast in the water away from you.

Do you

Pursue – *507*

Resume your course – *222*

1055

Your father's desk is a mess of papers, and you quickly scan them as best you can. You can see many dockets relating to cargo, but two items grab your eye. There is a promissory note from a bank in England to the tune of a thousand pounds. Another letter to a Duncan Mackenzie requests that he look after Mary if the worst comes. It is unsealed and looks to have been written very recently. If you want pocket these **in your inventory, tick the codewords Promissory note and Letter Duncan Mackenzie.**

The fire is spreading fast, and you start to choke. Quickly step outside the room to *510*

1056

Reduce your Island Time Chart by 5 to indicate the time spent trying to get to the rock and back.

You are back on the edge of the waters as your friends have pulled you out. If you have the codeword **Golden 2 – *270*.** If not, continue below.

The treasure remains at the centre of the waters but that took some effort. You can try again, you can rest up, or you can leave the waters. Note it might take a bit before you feel ok to re-enter the waters. If you lost a pole in the water, or simply wish to change pole, as long as you have any of the following codewords ticked, **Green Pole, Red Pole** or **Blue Pole**, you may circle one of the codewords to indicate which pole you are taking into the water with you.

Do you

Leave the waters and go back down the jungle path you in by – *236*

Rest up before entering the water again – *269*

Re-enter the water again. If so choose where to enter and jump in

Most western point – *1201*

Second most western point – *43*

Mid-point of the edge – *1372*

Second most eastern point – *489*

Most Eastern point – *948*

1057

As you stand on the deck looking out to sea, you notice storm cloud up ahead and with the way the wind is changing you fear a storm is on the way. There's no way to predict what it will be like but to avoid it will mean a 6-day detour/delay. You wonder how much time you have to waste. You can see the crew is unsettled knowing they may be entering the storm.

Do you

Ride the storm -*95*

Take the delay – *1098*

<u>1058</u>

You set anchor a fair distance from the shore, but you are confident you can swim it with ease. Your first officer is more sceptical about your idea to go to the cave alone.

"You don't know what dangers lie ahead so you should take a crew in the small boat. They can also row you close, and you can take pistols too."

If you take the small boat anyone out there will see you easily. If you swim in alone, you may be able to move about undetected more easily. That's if the island is even inhabited which you doubt.

Do you

Want to take crew with you – *861*

Tell the crew to stay on board – *987*

<u>1059</u>

You turn asking for everything your vessel has, and the crew respond. Although the cargo vessel is aware of your pursuit, it does not take long to close the gap between you. You wonder if they are up for a fight, and you tell the crew to prepare your canons. It's up to the cargo vessels captain if they want a fight.

Is your vessel's firepower

None to Light – *1216*

Moderate, Heavy, or very Heavy – *282*

The Treasure of Captain Estes

<u>1060</u>

"Okay stranger, we have a ranking system so you understand, tells you what you can bet." The pirate shows you a scrap of parchment and you see the following table

Stake	Prize
Knife	Pistol
Pistol	Bottle of Whisky
Bottle of Whisky or Emerald	Promissory Note
Body Part	Any prize

In order to play, ring the **item** in your codeword list, or note you have chosen a body part. Then roll the dice at *1412*. If you have finished playing or have no items left to trade, then leave the game for the street at *262*

<u>1061</u>

Reduce your time by 1.

If your time is in the following gaps (37-33 or 07-03), then go to *1037*.

As you stand at the door, you can hear snoring, and not just a single person. There's the odd creak as well but generally snoring.

Do you

Hide where you are – *1393*

Route South – *1197*

Creep East – *103*

Go North – *785*

Open the door and enter the building – *680*

1062

You made a deal with some lady pirates. That means that when you add up your treasure, you must half your final amount. You got plenty of information from them, but it was at a price.

Now return to **725** and remember to half your final amount when told to add up your treasure.

1063

Martha raises an eyebrow. "We go at night. I'm wanted by them, do you hear, and you'll go alone."

So, that's that. Looks like your choice is made for you. Go to **307** to sneak in during the night.

1064

Reduce your Island Time Chart by 1

You trek forward along the path, and everything looks the same. The path is mesmerising. Soon you reach a fork in the path and you wonder which way to go. To the left you think you hear the sound of the beach. You could always simply strike out into the jungle off the path.

Do you go

Left – **197**

Right – **886**

Strike out into the Jungle – **1283**

Turn around back the way you came – **183**

1065

The only wall of fire is to the south. You can route east, west or north from your current location.

Do you

Go West – *906*

Go East – *1428*

Go North – *790*

1066

You wander along the path, perspiring, and reach a junction. Which way now?

Left – *727*

Right – *728*

Turn back – *89*

1067

"I'm sorry," you say, "but I'm not sure."

The guard steps forward and grabs the cask off you. "Oh no, that's a full one. You're meant to take the empty ones out there."

"I'm so sorry," you say, "they are all so heavy to me."

"I'm sure," he says, quite taken with you. "I'll fetch you an empty one." The soldier places the full cask to one side and walks over to a small wagon, picking up another cask. He returns and hands it to you. You place it on your shoulder finding it much more manageable.

"Thank you," you say and smile, before walking out through the gate. Once out of his sight, you drop the cask and quickly walk down the road to New Southampton. As you approach the town, you see another path branching off, one that leads to Strangar, the pirate haven.

Do you

Make for Strangar – *671*

Or head into New Southampton – *1114*

1068

The pirate king leans forward and smiles weakly. "Estes buried his treasure on Hangman's Island but it's hard to get to. Once there he spread out the treasure, and there are five tests to recover it. I know how to complete one of them." He details out how to complete the Walk of Fire. **Tick the codeword Walk.**

With a wave of his hand, he dismisses you and you are ushered from his presence and back to your vessel. Who knows how much use that was? The pirate who mans the door to the pirate king's abode advises that you will not be welcome again on this visit. **You may not visit the pirate king again until you return to Hell's Deep on another visit. Go to *1436***

1069

Martha Downham seethes as she looks at you. "What, you have no call for adventure? You turn me down, in my house, in my port? Get out for you are no daughter of your father. And don't think of staying in this town. See her to the edge of Strangar."

Oops, you seem to have blown that completely. The big man from the front door, takes you by the arm and marches you out of the house and out of Strangar before throwing you onto the dust and leaving you there in the middle of the night.

If you have not visited New Southampton yet, walk there now at *1114*

If you have been to New Southampton already – *356*

1070

You enter a room with a curtain of rock in the middle of the room. It is still impenetrable. Above you is a rope going up, and below is another rope going down.

Do you

Climb up the rope – **756**

Climb down the other rope – **843**

1071

You wander along the path, mud over your feet, and reach a junction. Which way now?

Left – **664**

Right – **1357**

Turn back – **76**

1072

Reduce your time by 1.

Inside the office you can just about make out a desk and a safe. On the floor are two rugs at each end of the small office. One seems to be raised slightly but that may be because the rug has shifted slightly underfoot. Otherwise, it's a pretty bland office. There's a stool but no other furniture.

Do you

Look at the desk – **206**

Check the rug that's slightly lifted – **565**

Look at the other rug – **1356**

Try to open the safe – **1288**

Decide this is a bad idea and return outside – **174**

1073

You approach the gate in the central wall, and it looks to be open. But you had seen guards atop the wall previously. Is there one there now?

Is the time 45-40 or 5 and below – *474*

Otherwise – *1197*

1074

Move Tabetha.

You are in a white walled room, bathed in the strange light, with three doors, one with a picture of a spider above it, one with a shield above it, and the other with a pirate flag above it.

If Tabetha's number is 9 – *1459*

If Tabetha's number is 20 **– note this number and go to *1287***

If Tabetha's number is 15 **– note this number and go to *239***

If Tabetha's number is 13 **– note this number and go to *1029***

Where do you go next?

Through the spider door – *388*

Through the shield door – *874*

Through the pirate flag door – *1091*

Wait here - **return to the top of this section**

1075

The Dutch Fleut is more than happy at your decision and is soon out of sight. The rest of the voyage is uneventful if rather cloudy.

Continue the voyage at *654*

The Treasure of Captain Estes

<u>1076</u>

Martha Downham holds a hand up to you. She strikes down the crewman who cried out to you.

"There will be no love of God here," she cries. "We need to bless my master. Quick, take some of the crew and throw them overboard, down to the welcoming horde. Feed them, feed them quick!"

Do you

Grab crew and begin throwing them overboard – *110*

Refuse, drawing your cutlass on Martha – *428*

<u>1077</u>

You push out into the jungle and force your way through past several pieces of vegetation. Soon there is no sight of the path but neither does the vegetation in front of you ease up. Eventually you come across a path again, but you have no idea where you are or how long it took you to get here. You're not even sure you are in the same part of the jungle you started in. This place is strange beyond belief, maybe even magical, or cursed!

You strike back out on the path again but where are you?

Roll 1xD100 (2xD10) and go to the result below. Deduct the time indicated from your Island Time Chart and then go to your next indicated section to see where you end up.

00-19 – Reduce time chart by 6, go to *1079*

20-39 –*280*

40-59 – Reduce time chart by 8, go to *789*

60-79 –*280*

80-99 – Reduce time chart by 12, go to *177*

1078

You return to your vessel but give the command to open fire on the village. You see huts go on fire and the land becomes devasted around the settlement. After letting the dust settle, you spy the land and see the utter devastation you have caused. But there is no one there. They must have fled. You take the small boat ashore with some crew but all you find is the wreck of a village. If they had anything of value, it's gone.

You've made sure this place is no longer worth visiting. You may no longer return to the south of the island for it's just a wasteland. So, what's next?

Do you

Tell the crew to sail to the north of the island – **468**

Route for the centre of the island – **746**

Decide to set sail - **consult the voyage chart**

1079

Reduce your Island Time Chart by 1

You trek along the path, and you think this path will never end. Suddenly there's multiple forks in the path, and you wonder which way to go. You can take one of the paths, or you could always head out into the jungle off the path.

Do you go

Left – **1223**

Right – **407**

Straight ahead – **151**

Strike out into the Jungle – **1347**

Turn around back the way you came – **429**

The Treasure of Captain Estes

1080

The galleon comes alongside you and the first officer of the warship examines your vessel with his large crew. You are powerless to stop him. Then he looks at you with an outraged eye.

"We have reports of a captain matching your description who scuppered one of our vessels, killing nearly all the crew. Such filth must be eradicated from these seas."

Before you can respond, you are run through with a sword and your body is thrown overboard to a watery grave. You don't know what becomes of the crew, and your family is never avenged in any respect. Your tale ends here, like many a vicious pirate. Try again at *1*, and maybe be less ruthless and notorious.

1081

The galleon comes alongside you and the first officer of the warship examines your vessel with his large crew. You are powerless to stop him. Then he looks at your first officer with an outraged eye.

"It's you. Pirate scum, murderer of men, women, and children. Run them all through, all of them."

Before you can respond, you are run through with a sword and your body is thrown overboard to a watery grave. You don't know what becomes of the crew, and your family is never avenged in any respect. Your tale ends here, like many a vicious pirate. Try again at *1*, and maybe pick a more pleasant first officer.

1082

You send for your offering, and it is brought before Tom who touches it carefully, examining it. He smiles and a child takes your offering away.

As you wait to see what he will say a trapdoor opens beneath you and you fall into a chute which makes you tumble out of the barge and into the waters around it. As you surface, a few children are laughing at you from the barge. Indignant, you swim to your vessel to dry off and decide your next course of action.

Go to see Blind Tom again – *681*

Visit the provisions isle – *334*

Enjoy yourself at the wild isle – *879*

Explore the dark isle – *397*

Approach the pirate king – *1348*

Decide you have had enough of Hells Deep and set sail - **Consult the voyage chart and set sail**

1083

Reduce your Waters Strength Chart by 1 unless you have just jumped in. The current is brutal, and you are swept west unable to reach the rock in the middle of the water. Your foot scrapes the bottom briefly and you think you may be able to drop a pole and take a rest. Do you

Float West – *285*

Drop a pole – **Make a note of this section and go to *694***

1084

Your father's personal armoury is behind a secret panel in the hallway where you have been hiding, and you slip in, unnoticed. The walls have a small number of armaments, and you can see your father's pride and joy, his double-barrelled pistol. He had shown it to you on many occasions and even let you fire it at bottles outside in his weaker moments. You always believed this was due to his lack of a male heir with whom to bond.

You can also see a tiny blade for secretion on a person, razor sharp but very hard to see. There is also a standard knife and a sheath which will attach to your leg to hold it.

Suddenly you hear a crash, and the wall of the room begins to sink. It holds momentarily, but you realise it will give way soon. You can't equip all weapons and will have to pick just two. Alternatively, don't equip any. **Tick any 2 of the following codewords: Pistol, Standard knife, Secreted knife.**

Having equipped your weapons of choice, the roof falls forcing you out of the room. Standing in the hallway, you see the stairs are now on fire and that way is blocked. You make for the kitchen. Go to *553*

1085

"Robert Grimshaw is my Captain," you say. There's a bit of commotion as people whisper to each other and then the man with the large scar stands up.

"Grimshaw can go to hell. And so can you."

You see knives being pulled and hear the click of a musket. It's time to leave. Dejected you walk back to the crossroads. **You cannot announce yourself in "The Dog's Knackers" as a Captain in the future. Go to *802***

1086

You call out to retreat and to turn the vessel but there's seems to be a struggle to get clear. You see the galleon now coming alongside at point blank range and volley after volley is fired into your vessel. The mast falls and then you feel the vessel begin to tilt. Soon it is sinking in the water. You try to flee over the side, but an errant pistol shot hits you between the shoulder blades and you fall to the deck. As the blackness invades your view, you know you are defeated.

Make sure you pick a fight you can win! You can try again at *1.*

1087

Reduce your Waters Strength Chart by 1. The current is pushing you west. However, you think you can reach an eddy that seems to allow a way north. Your foot scrapes the bottom briefly and you think you may be able to drop a pole and take a rest. Do you

Swim North – *266*

Float West – *706*

Drop a pole – **Make a note of this section and go to *694***

1088

Reduce your Island Time Chart by 1

You trek forward along the path, and things are becoming bland. You try to remember if you came this way already because the vegetation is all the same. Soon you reach a fork in the path, and you wonder which way to go. You can take either fork or you could always head out into the jungle off the path.

Do you go

Left – *1064*

Right – *1079*

Strike out into the Jungle – *1077*

Turn around back the way you came – *1246*

1089

You tilt your head back and are then horrified as she slits your throat. At once you gasp for air but the lack of it doesn't affect your awareness of what is happening. It's like a dark stain is coming over your every limb. You feel disembodied as you find yourself standing in a ring of fire with the creature before you.

The Treasure of Captain Estes

"You are mine and you shall have the treasure. Let nothing stand in your path, kill all. And then bring the spoils back to me."

She produces a compass and hands it to you. As you open it you see it is pointing already, but not north.

"Find the map it needs, and you will have Estes' treasure. Do not return until you have my treasure."

Tick the codeword Devil's Compass.

Suddenly you are alone on the beach of the isle beside your small boat. You take it back to your vessel and ponder what to do next. **You cannot return to the dark isle again on this adventure until you have found the treasure.** What next?

Go to see Blind Tom – *681*

Visit the provisions isle – *334*

Enjoy yourself at the wild isle – *879*

Approach the pirate king – *1348*

Decide you have had enough of Hells Deep and set sail - **Consult the voyage chart and set sail.**

1090

As you step forward, a voice from behind the doors shouts, "Back off." The voice is female and shrill. The doors open and a woman standing only five feet tall dressed in a gown with her hair tied up glares at you. In her hand is a musket pointed at you.

"Go on, back to the street with you. You heard me. I don't give two warnings."

Do you

Push on towards the doors – *839*

Reach for a weapon – *1331*

Take her advice and return to the main street – *496*

<u>1091</u>

Move Tabetha.

You are in a white walled room, bathed in the strange light, with two doors, one with a picture of a spider above it, and the other with a shield above it.

If Tabetha's number is 13 – *1459*

If Tabetha's number is 9 – **note this number and go to *1287***

If Tabetha's number is 17 – **note this number and go to *239***

Where do you go next?

Through the spider door – *1074*

Through the shield door – *1106*

Wait here - **return to the top of this section**

<u>1092</u>

You walk up to the door and are about to enter in when the pirate, who was apparently asleep, suddenly jumps up behind you pushing a sword into your back. You freeze immediately and he gives a little grunt.

"Nothing in there for you. Time to be about your business."

Do you

Walk back to the street with your hands in the air – *129*

Feint to walk away but then run into the barn – *2*

<u>1093</u>

"Look at you, you certainly do need a doctor," he sneers, "but they don't come cheap." He points to one of the boats and motions for you to go on board. You are taken into the depths of the vessel where in a candlelit room you see a small man with glasses. He stares at you and then notices your wounds.

"Oh, you are in need of repair, aren't you? But it'll cost you. I want at least one of the following: a **Bottle of Whisky**, a **Pistol**, or a **Promissory Note**. Do you have one of these?"

Well, do you have any of these codewords ticked?

If you do – *364*

If not -*1350*

1094

Your first officer shakes their head but carries out your orders as cannon balls rip your vessel apart. As the battle becomes more and more of a lost cause, you eventually give the order to sail away and pray the cargo vessel does not follow. It takes a while before you can see clear distance between you through the smoke and you are able to assess the damage.

Reduce your vessel speed by 2 levels. Reduce your crew by 2 levels. Reduce your Firepower by 2 levels. Reduce your Treasure store by 2 levels due damage. 50% of your cargo is destroyed. Reduce your crew morale by 2 levels.

You return to your voyage but must **add 1 day extra to it** for this diversion. **Also, your new voyage time is that of your new reduced speed.**

Continue the voyage at *654*

1095

You skip around fire as you enter the room, and you pull up short as you see your father's body on the floor. He looks so still. You shake your head, trying to clear it as smoke fills your nostrils. You'll not have long to act, and you need to think what to do. You could simply leave and try to escape. There is your father's impressive desk which you could search. You could look at your father's small collection of bottles of drink. Or you could open his large closet to see what's inside. Whatever you do you need to do it quickly.

Do you

Leave the room – **510**

Examine the closet – **585**

Check out the bottles – **666**

Rifle through the desk – **1055**

1096

The man looks at you for a moment with your request.

"I've just lost my brother and my crew and my vessel and you came and ask me that. Are you an idiot or just evil?"

You don't get a chance to answer as the pirate grabs you by the scruff and hauls you to the door, throwing you to the ground outside.

"Come back inside and I'll kill you!"

As he returns inside, you brush the dust from your clothes and decide you need to move on.

Do you

Approach the barn – **395**

Walk further into Strangar – **1256**

Make for the entrance of Strangar – **262**

The Treasure of Captain Estes

1097

You fire another volley of canon fire and see the sloop slowly begin to sink. Crew are abandoning it and you desperately come alongside before it sinks into the sea. You find a dead Captain Rodriguez on deck and her crew are in no mood to defend themselves further. You don't have long to gather her stores though.

What you can gather is dependent on your crew size. It is also dependent on your cargo hold. Check what you can take from the galleon on the chart below. Then place it in your hold up to your capacity. Note you cannot throw any of your cargo out to make room, there isn't time.

Your Vessel's Crew	Cargo you can take
Large	**5 units of treasure worth 500 doubloons each**
Medium	**5 units of treasure worth 500 doubloons each**
Small	**3 units of treasure worth 500 doubloons each**

Now continue your voyage at **654**

1098

You avoid the storm, never knowing just how bad it would have been. **Add 6 days to your voyage time.** Now continue at **654**

1099

You've been extremely fortunate for the sea is often a busy place. However, this voyage has gone peacefully, and you have encountered neither a living nor a dead soul anywhere on the water and now your destination is in sight. Your crew are pleased by this as well. (**Raise crew morale by 1 level**).

Continue the voyage at **654**

<u>1100</u>

With Timmers as your first officer, you certainly do enjoy a freedom at the harbourside of the fort. Above you may be the main settlement with its large walls and canons peering out but there is a friendliness in your dealings. Timmers points out the encircled centre of the fort, surrounded by a stone wall with guards stationed there permanently. You ask what's in there and he advises that it is mostly barracks for soldiers, around a central intelligence building from where all navy business is conducted. Inside he suspects is the Major's office and records of all orders and dealings they have. Of course, it would be busy during the day. Across from it is a small room from where messages are taken to be sent on vessels returning to other lands.

You ask if it would be more difficult to infiltrate at night and he looks horrified, but he agrees it would, for you would have no reason to be there. He could get you to the message station quite easily. He also suggests that lunch would be a good time to visit as the offices empty.

If the British know anything about Estes treasure it will be in these offices. This may be your best chance to try and infiltrate them. However, it is risky. You could try at night.

Do you

Ask Timmers to take you up to the Messages office at lunch – **365**

Decide to leave the harbour and instead infiltrate the fort at night – **307**

Or

If you have had enough of Fort August, then **consult the voyage chart and set sail.**

<u>1101</u>

You bolt for the gates without warning, and it takes the soldier a moment to catch on. But he calls to the guards on the gate, and they close in on you. There is some commotion, and it brings the attention of Captain Fareham. You are escorted to your room and a guard is placed at your door, blocking all escape. Fareham has seen you are unwilling to go along with his plans and doesn't let down his guard as you are married in private.

He now owns your father's lands and keeps you locked up for the next year. When you don't respond to his advances and wishes to be a passive wife, he has you taken away in the night and disposed of. Your last thoughts are that your family remains unavenged. Try again at *1* and remember enemies are everywhere, even those people who help.

1102

You see a white bull running directly at you and it doesn't look like it will move to avoid you. You are in the left channel. What will you do?

Stay left – *547*

Go to the middle – *466*

Go to the right channel – *783*

1103

"I have the great Diggory Hurst on board," you say and watch as the bald man's face considers this.

"We have heard some reports but generally a minor thorn in the side of the British. His efforts are noted but you will still have to pay." **Tick codeword Rumour.** Unless you have something else you are going to have to pay or leave.

Do you

Decide you have an item you can offer to prove your worth – *229*

Offer doubloons – *1297*

Decide the price is too high and leave Hells Deep – **Consult the voyage chart and set sail**

<u>1104</u>

The man is disappointed and so is Robert. **You cannot accept this offer in the future.** Return to *580* and make your next decision.

<u>1105</u>

You remember the holy man in the cargo hold and call for a crewman to get him, but the man has already come up on deck. He stands in the middle of the fog that has now formed, despite the crazy wind, and you see his eyes are set on the sloop.

"Fiend, depart from here. I tell you depart from here."

A spectre, decked out in pirate garb, appears on your deck in front of the holy man and raises up a cutlass that seems to exist only in a gaseous state. For as the spectre swings it almost wisps through the air and as it reaches the holy man, he holds a cross up which the cutlass gets stuck on. The holy man holds up a hand to the spectre's forehead.

"I command you gone. Back to the sea in the name of Christ."

The spectre suddenly flies backwards but drops the gaseous sword as it does so. The fog dissipates and the wind becomes steady, filling the sails in a gentle fashion, while the sun returns to the sky. Everyone on deck breathes a huge sigh of relief and looks at the holy man who simply bends down to pick up the gaseous sword.

As he touches it, it turns into a solid cutlass, and he brings it over to you.

"Captain, I have no need of such trifles. It will however help defend you against such evil ghosts. It will only attack that which you are not. Let me show you."

The holy man swings the cutlass at you, his habit billowing as he does so, and the blade runs right at your neck, where it simply passes through. You feel like your head should be falling from your neck and you are in shock, but you are also uninjured. The crew have leapt forward to defend you, but you put up a hand for them to hold.

The Treasure of Captain Estes

"You see captain, it will not attack flesh if we hold it but it will attack that which is spirit. For them it attacks us. It is the sword of a Bodach, as they would say in my country. It is now yours, use it well. Forgive me," he says handing you the cutlass, "but I must return to my prayers." With that, the holy man returns to his place in the cargo hold. **Tick the codeword Bodach sword.**

 Now continue your voyage at *654*

1106

Move Tabetha.

You are in a white walled room, bathed in the strange light, with two doors, one with a picture of a shield above it, and the other with a pirate flag above it.

If Tabetha's number is 17 – *1459*

If Tabetha's number is 24 – **note this number and go to *1029***

If Tabetha's number is 13 – **note this number and go to *446***

Where do you go next?

Through the pirate flag door – *673*

Through the schooner door– *1091*

Wait here - **return to the top of this section**

1107

You try to get some distance between you and the creature, but the vessel just isn't quick enough. Soon, there's a tentacle on your bow bringing the vessel to a grinding halt. Then follows an even larger tentacle crashing down through the middle of the ship. Soon you feel your vessel being dragged down into the water and as you try to swim clear you are pulled down with it. Try as hard you might you drown fighting for your life.

The waters around New Southampton are deadly, and you have succumbed. You may try again at *1*

<u>1108</u>

Reduce your Waters Strength Chart by 1 unless you have just jumped in. The current is brutal, and you are swept south unable to even get near the rock in the middle of the waters. Your foot scrapes the bottom briefly and you think you may be able to drop a pole and take a rest. Do you

Float South – *285*

Drop a pole – **Make a note of this section and go to *694***

<u>1109</u>

As you approach the building, you look at its stonework and realise that this was a permanent fixture long before the pirates took the town of Strangar over. When the island was reached by the British, this was the main port and this building was the first place of authority. It is ironic that it seems to now be the main place of authority amongst the pirates.

At the door of the building are two pirates, both with cutlasses and they seem to be eyeing you with suspicion. Maybe this is a mistake as these guys don't seem to be pleased to see you.

Do you

Want to return to the street – *1256*

Approach the pirates at the door. If so, are you wearing

A long-coat – *1396*

Your torn gown – *1457*

A dress – *471*

1110

There is no time like the present to escape, and besides, Fareham may decide to escort you to New Southampton. You are going to have difficulty in getting about the garrison though, a place of soldiers and few ladies of note. Your long flowing blonde hair and white if tanned skin will be a dead giveaway. There is a white bedgown in the room which you could adjust and make yourself look like a white slave. If you have the codeword **Long-coat,** you could wear that and try to walk out the front gate. Or you could simply sneak about, pretending you are lost if caught.

Do you

Rip the bedgown and pretend to be a slave – *782*

Dress in the long-coat – *1210*

Stay in your dress and sneak about – *1242*

1111

Reduce your Island Time Chart by 1

You trek along the path, sweat dripping from your brow. There's a fork in the path, and you wonder which way to go. You can take either fork, or you could always head out into the jungle off the path.

Do you go

Left – *177*

Right – *245*

Strike out into the Jungle – *1077*

Turn around back the way you came – *940*

1112

You are in the heart of Strangar and all around you is chaos. Drunken pirates roam the streets, some with women in their arms, some getting robbed as they are too drunk to protect themselves. Others grimace at you and you don't feel safe.

On one side of the street is a low barn with a pirate asleep in front of the door, a bottle of wine lolling around at his feet. There is little light outside the barn, but everyone seems to be avoiding it. On the other side of the street is a tavern which is in full flow, and you can hear screams and laughs from inside as well as music.

Behind you is the entrance to Strangar which seems quieter. Ahead is the docks area, and it appears to be busy but with less noise and more of a focus to what is going on.

Do you

Approach the barn – *395*

Enter the tavern – *912*

Walk further into Strangar – *1256*

Make for the entrance of Strangar – *262*

1113

Your first officer wishes you good luck on this mission. "I'll be here waiting but don't get caught. Remember what I've told you about the place, there's a message station which is a small hut. Beyond that there must be some sort of intelligence building, somewhere they store their intel. That'll be in the most heavily fortified place inside the walls."

You nod and look at the walls before you. Go to *1143*

The Treasure of Captain Estes

<u>1114</u>

You walk into the main street of New Southampton which is bustling on another hot day. The sun beats down and you can see wagons being pulled, large quantities of wheat and fruit piled high as well as garments and material. To your right is the large market, a torrent of noise but a place to purchase or maybe even steal. On your left you see business premises which have shut doors but between the buildings is a dark alleyway.

If you have the codeword **Shoulder Wound** go to *876,* **but note this section's number.**

Depending on what you are wearing you may need to get off the street quickly. Remember you are not entirely unknown here, having been in town with your father on numerous occasions. However, that also brings you the knowledge of the main street. Further up will be the courthouse and Madame Le Vert's clothes shop for those with money. Beyond that will be the docks and the weaponsmith.

As you stroll along you recall your goal of getting hold of Captain Estes and having your revenge. The town appears to be quiet so the Spanish must have left, which means you will need a vessel and a crew to go after Estes.

You are adjacent to the market and the dark alley. What are your plans for your time in New Southampton?

Do you

Enter the dark alley – *160*

Walk over to the market – *1152*

Continue along the street – *1166*

<u>1115</u>

Reduce your Island Time Chart by 1

You trek along the path, weary and grumpy. You find multiple forks in the path, and you wonder which way to go. You can take one of the paths, or you could always head out into the jungle off the path.

Do you go

Left – *429*

Right – *151*

Straight ahead – *1223*

Strike out into the Jungle – *1347*

Turn around back the way you came – *407*

<u>1116</u>

"Come here," he says, "you need help. I can get you it. Go to the docks and ask at the farthest pier for Jalibert. Tell him Albert sent you. He'll fix you up." **Tick the codeword Jalibert**

You realise the wound needs help as you still feel very weak. Best to get it sorted. Head for the docks at *117*

<u>1117</u>

You are fortunate as you are beside cover and hide straight away. Go to *951*

<u>1118</u>

You sail into a small opening that has two exits from it: northeast and west-southwest. The northeast exit is described as awkward by your first officer and will require a vessel with at least good manoeuvrability that can operate in the shallows. The other channel looks wide and passable.

Do you

Sail west-southwest – *452*

Go northeast (only vessels with Good/Great manoeuvrability and which can operate in the shallows) – *698*

1119

Your first officer looks at you. "Good luck and don't get caught or killed. I've no idea where any useful information would be. It's not like they would ever let me within a hundred miles of this place. But it will probably be in the most protected place."

You nod and look at the walls before you. Go to *1143*

1120

The Spanish Square-rigged vessel is more than happy at your decision and is soon out of sight. The rest of the voyage is uneventful if rather cloudy.

Continue the voyage at *654*

1121

As the footsteps approach you throw a prayer up to the sky and pray it's the guard. You almost blurt out in excitement when you see it's him. But you need to act quick before he disappears again.

Do you

Invite him into your cell in an attempt to steal his keys – *1040*

Try and draw him close to your cell before pushing him backwards towards Diggory's cell – *1456*

1122

You wait until the water is green and then step forward. Suddenly the curtain of water is behind you, and you are in the clouds. Several birds fly around you, and you watch as they form the shape of an island before they make a equilateral cross with a "N" at the top. Suddenly, the clouds are gone, as are the birds and you are back in the room and the water curtain has turned to rock. **Tick the codeword Rock.**

There's nothing else left in this room, save the ropes, so you should move on. Do you

Climb up the rope – *756*

Climb down the other rope – *843*

1123

Reduce the Hot Strip by 1. If this places you on a Fire spot add 20 to this section's number and go there for the walls have moved. There are walls of fire to the south and west. You can route north or east from your current location.

Do you

Go East – *596*

Go North – *27*

1124

If your first officer is Simon Kilmer, Robert Grimshaw or Timmers, your crew are disgusted with your actions and are grumbling. **Reduce your crew morale by one level.**

If your first officer is Martha Downham or Black Robert or Diggory Hurst, your crew approve of your actions. **Increase your crew morale by one level.**

Tick the codeword British Hunted

Now resume your voyage but you must **add 2 days extra to it** for this diversion.

Continue the voyage at *654*

1125

You're not taking any nonsense and you draw your weapon and hold it up to the man's face. He seems impassive, almost at ease and you hear a shot being fired. You fall to the ground and realise that you have been hit in the chest. The big man bends over you, laughing, and rolls you out into the middle of the street where you slowly pass away. Maybe you were a bit hasty drawing your weapon. You can try again at *1*

1126

You suddenly hear movement. There's a guard afoot, patrolling the area and although you can hear them you are not sure where they are coming from.

Are you in hiding?

Yes – *1190*

No – *1362*

1127

The current is brutal and you are swept east. There is nothing you can do except float to *1312*

1128

Standing where you are you hear a voice asking another guard to investigate something he can see. You realise it's a guard on the inner wall who must have seen you. You need to get out of here fast. But where is the supporting guard coming from. You don't know and you run of blindly, desperate to get away from this area.

Roll 1xD100 (2xD10).

00-20 – *749*

21-99 – *1175*

1129

Reduce your Island Time Chart by 1

You trek along the path, and everything seems to be a mass of green. There's a fork in the path, and you wonder which way to go. You can take either fork, or you could always head out into the jungle off the path.

Do you go

Left – *789*

Right – *245*

Strike out into the Jungle – *1077*

Turn around back the way you came – *81*

1130

You see that the battle is lost and order a retreat. The other captain clearly didn't want this battle either as they are happy to let you sail away. Once clear of all the smoke and confusion, you are able to assess the damage to your vessel.

The Treasure of Captain Estes

Reduce your vessel speed by 1 level. Reduce your crew by 1 level. Reduce your Firepower by 1 level. Reduce your Treasure store by 1 level due damage. 25% of your cargo is destroyed. Reduce your crew morale by 1 level.

You return to your voyage but must **add 1 day extra to it** for this diversion. **Also, your new voyage time is that of your new reduced speed.**

Continue the voyage at *654*

1131

"If I'm not mistaken that's the sloop of Sarah Rodriguez." You have no idea who your first officer is talking about, but you want to know more. "Sarah is quite the talk of the seas now. She runs fast and hits hard, but no one knows what she is really looking for." As you watch, you see that her vessel is making a direct line for you. It looks like a fights coming as you don't think you can match her speed.

"We'd better prepare for a fight," says your first officer and you nod in agreement.

Your crew gets excited as you order your vessel to engage the sloop before you. As you draw closer to the sloop, you see few canons aimed at you, and you realise it's incredibly manoeuvrable.

Is your vessel manoeuvrability

Great – *218*

Good or Reasonable – *561*

Poor or Lacking -*1255*

1132

"You come here with nothing to purchase your crew. You waste my time. Get out! Throw this scoundrel to the dogs!"

You are grabbed by several men and lifted off the ground and shown the door. You wince as they throw you out into the middle of the street. After a moment when you gather your bearings, you stand up and dust yourself down, ready to look for another vessel and crew. **You may not return to the house**. Go to *262* and continue your adventure.

1133

You ask the soldier to see what is happening with your transport and he tells you to wait right here as the courtyard haggling is not fit for a lady. No sooner is he gone than you make a move for the gate, walking along as if you own the place. A guard asks politely if he can help, and you tell him you just want a little air and will not stray from the garrison wall.

As soon as you are through the gates you walk briskly, never looking back on the path to New Southampton. As you approach the town, you see another path branching off, one that leads to Strangar, the pirate haven.

Do you

Make for Strangar – *671*

Or head into New Southampton – *1114*

1134

You have wandered back to the fire walls which are now just a sorry black residue. You have this treasure so turn around and walk back to the last junction and find some more. Go to *1193*

1135

You take several steps backwards before charging at the door, throwing your shoulder at it. You slam hard against it, and the sound of you hitting the door reverberates around the inner wall of the fort. You fall to the floor, an ache in your shoulder and are momentarily stunned. When you manage to raise yourself, you find a guard holding a pistol to your head.

You have been caught. What will be your fate as you are taken before the fort's commander? Go to *1358*

1136

You step onto the pillar with a sigh of relief. There are pillars directly behind and to your left. **Tick the codeword Transept if you haven't already**. You can see small items on the pillars diagonally to your front left and directly behind.

Do you step

To your left – *985*

Backwards – *166*

1137

You approach the house with laughter in the air, filtering through the shutters. As you get closer the large gentleman approaches you.

Are you

In a dress – *1245*

In a long-coat – *504*

In a night gown, even if it's cut to look like a slave – *440*

<u>1138</u>

You open the desk scroll and you see a chart on the parchment. It shows an island and on that island is marked an opening with the word cave. But the cave is indicated as being underwater. There's also a warning about being prepared. At the top of the map is the legend, The Devil's Compass.

The island in the map matches the barren one beside the Maria Saratoga. Your first officer agrees, and they suggest you could sail to this underwater cave and explore.

If this sounds like a plan – *919*

If not, the island still looks unappealing and barren, and your first officer agrees it is not worth otherwise exploring beyond the chart's information. The wreck is now fully underwater and shifting, making it too dangerous to go back to. I guess you're out of luck here.

Set sail for a new destination by consulting the voyage chart. Tick the code word Compass Map

<u>1139</u>

The man raises his head slowly. "Yes." He seems to be disinterested and you'll need to grab his attention.

Tell him you are Mary Hastings, and you wish to hire a vessel to seek out Captain Estes – *481*

Simply ask for a vessel for hire – *755*

Decide you don't like this man and make your apologies and return to the pier – *117*

The Treasure of Captain Estes

<u>1140</u>

It looks like you are in for a fight, or maybe you have something else that might help. Do you want to try something else.

Do you have the codeword and wish to use the following items

Spear – *271*

Orange Algae – *576*

Green Plant – *609*

Eye Charm – *1382*

Bodach Sword – *152*

If not, or you choose not to try them, you need to swim back to your vessel before the creatures get any closer.

If your vessel is in the shallows – *632*

If not, and it is anchored further out – *672*

<u>1141</u>

Reduce the Hot Strip by 1. If this places you on a Fire spot add 20 to this section's number and go there for the walls have moved. There are walls of fire to the south and west. You can route north or east from your current location.

Do you

Go East – *1250*

Go North – *831*

1142

Reduce the Hot Strip by 2. If this places you on a Fire spot add 20 to this section's number and go there for the walls have moved. There are walls of fire to the north, west, and east, so you route south from your current location. Go to *1046*

1143

You are about to enter a timed part of the book. The time starts at 60 and you will be instructed when to reduce the number. You can use the timer at *App 09* at the rear of the book, or you use your own notes to keep track of the time spent. Note that if the time reaches 0 you should go to *799*. If you have the codeword **Check 200** go to *249*. Otherwise, or if you have already been there, go to *500*.

1144

You run for the wall and begin to climb but it is hard going. You have to work hard and by the time you reach the top, the sentry has returned below, and another is above on the wall. You hang onto the wall, sweating in the warm night, wondering if you'll be seen. Luckily, you manage to blend in, and they return to their sentry routes. You climb up onto the wall and climb down the rear of it into the fort.

Reduce the time by 4 for this effort. Continue at *812*

1145

Reduce your Island Time Chart by 3

You trek along the path, leaving the plain behind, and everything seems to be a mass of green. There's a fork in the path, and you wonder which way to go. You can take either fork, or you could always head out into the jungle off the path.

Do you go

Left – *245*

Right – *1111*

Strike out into the Jungle – *1283*

Turn around back the way you came – *268*

1146

You watch from the window and see the patrol route towards the front doors of the guild. You quickly slide down the pole and grab any hidden gear before disappearing into the night. That was close, too close, and you decide to get out of Malin's Town before the town is searched for any stolen goods.

You may return to Malin's Town after 5 days when any searches will have stopped. You may not return to the guild however as they have decided to put on extra security at night and have also stopped any daytime visitors.

Consult the voyage chart and set sail for another destination.

1147

You have returned to the wreck and see that it is still underwater. The island looks as barren as ever and you wonder why you came back here. Your crew are wondering too as there's nothing to do. **Lower your crew morale by 2 levels.**

Set sail for a new destination by consulting the voyage chart.

1148

You draw your weapons and race at the rats, but they come at your regardless. They seem to come from everywhere and soon they are jumping on you, even as you slice some of them apart. There are simply too many and you are forced to run down the mountain. But they have gotten to you and ripped your clothing and you have lost some items. **Lose the 1st and 4th items from your codewords.** As you reach the base of the mountain, you skip over the river and the rats start to lose interest.

Now at the base of the mountain, you grab your breath and decide not to return this way again. **Note you cannot climb the mountain again.**

There are two paths away from the mountain, one a canopy covered path to the north, the other a more open topped path to the west, although it is still surrounded by the dense jungle.

Do you

Head north – **435**

Take the path west – **477**

1149

You barely overcome the main current to get to the eddy, and you suffer for it. **Reduce your Waters Strength Chart by 2.** You swim through to the eddy. Go to **1127**

1150

Reduce the Hot Strip by 1. If this places you on a Fire spot add 20 to this section's number and go there for the walls have moved. There are walls of fire to the west and east. You can route south or north from your current location.

Do you

Go North – **596**

Go South – **790**

1151

Diggory almost bursts out laughing. "At night of course. The crew and I are very well known here and frankly, don't want to be seen."

Looks like your choice is made for you. Go to *307* to sneak in during the night.

1152

The market contains many stalls and is full of all kinds of people looking to buy and sell. Some are surrounded by servants and are looking at the more expensive stalls of jewellery and expensive meats and fruit. Others look like the work horses of society and are fetching basic vegetables and provisions for their masters. All is hustle and bustle. You note three areas of interest: the jewellery stalls, the provisions stalls and the whiskey and ale stalls.

Do you

Approach the jewellery stall – *1158*

Go to the provisions stalls – *1368*

Look at the whiskey and ale stalls – *155*

Or return to the street – *496*

1153

You place the key in the lock, and it turns easily, allowing the safe to open. Inside you find lots of correspondence on bits of parchment, many sealed on the rear. You scan them quickly hoping to find something of use and you see a note sealed on the rear to Admiral Jenkins in London. You open it and unwrap a folded piece of parchment which states it is from Eagle and that part one is solved. "Bearing 324 degrees true from the smiling face" are the only other words on the parchment. **Tick codeword Bearing B.**

You quickly tidy up and lock the safe again. What next?

Look at the desk – *1167*

Check the rug that's slightly lifted – *169*

Look at the other rug – *366*

Decide this is a bad idea and return to Timmers, saying you should get back to the ship pronto – *351*

1154

The day is dark and overcast as you see the shores of the abandoned island. There is no name for the place, and you can see rich vegetation on the shore, almost jungle like. There is a small mountain at the heart of the island, and you think you can see some sort of temple at the north end. Towards the south is a small off-shoot island, barely connected and which seems to be easily accessible with a large white sandy beach.

Your crew are unwilling to come ashore and when you suggest it, they tell you that no one has ever come back from setting foot on that island. In fact, says one, no ship has ever returned after stumbling across the island. You wonder how much of this is true and not just wild tales of sailors, but you take the warning seriously. Nonetheless the island may proffer some detail about Captain Estes and where he went or where his treasure is.

It's time to gird your loins and prepare to tackle the island alone. But will you go to the north or south or maybe to the volcano? Or has this been a bad idea?

Do you

Tell the crew to sail to the north of the island – *468*

Order the vessel to be taken to the south – *254*

Route for the centre of the island – *746*

Or decide this is really a bad idea and decide to set sail again. If so, **expend one day on preparations and then consult the voyage chart**

The Treasure of Captain Estes

<u>1155</u>

You cry for all the sails to be unfurled to grab every last breath of wind and you forget your course, instead taking you the vessel wherever the wind will take you quickest. You are running for your life, and you know it, but will you be quick enough.

Roll 1D100 (2xD10). Check the result against the chart below.

<u>Your vessels Speed</u>	<u>Result</u>	<u>Section to go to</u>
Very Fast	20-99	*1206*
Very Fast	00-19	*627*
Fast	70-99	*1206*
Fast	40-69	*627*
Fast	00-39	*1285*
Moderate	90-99	*1206*
Moderate	50-84	*627*
Moderate	00-49	*794*
Slow	80-99	*627*
Slow	20-79	*794*
Slow	00-19	*1035*
Very Slow	60-99	*794*
Very Slow	00-59	*1035*

1156

If you already have the codeword **Shoulder Wound,** then go to *856*

Otherwise read on

You've been hit in the shoulder and it's starting to ache. Everything is becoming a little hazy and you feel like you might not last too long. Start the timer box at *App 08* at 10. Every time you turn to a new entry, reduce the timer box by 1. If the timer box reaches zero go to **97. Make a note of this section now**. Now go to the street at *496*

1157

Do you have the code word **Shoulder Wound** – *1116*

If not the guard smiles at you but shakes his head. "Sorry, no slaves allowed. Run on now before someone sees you." He's firm but gentle and you take your warning with some grace. Return to the street at *1009*

1158

The jewellery stall has two large guards at either end who stare intently at everyone approaching. It must be nigh impossible in a place like this to run a stall safely. You can see diamonds, small but still worth a pretty penny amongst stones of much lesser value. There are a several ladies browsing as well as a few gentlemen and some men of the sea. You have no money so what will you do here?

If this is your third stall visited in the market, note the number of this section, and then go to *1336*

Otherwise, do you

Try to steal a jewel – *638*

Mingle with the other customers – *1026*

Try the provisions stall – *1368*

Look at the whiskey and ale stalls – *155*

Or return to the street – *496*

1159

"I don't have it," you say.

"That's disappointing. You'd better leave. If you stay they will fight to get you off the island. Best if you go find that Horn or else stay clear of here. Trust me."

You see the seriousness in the man's eyes and decide that you won't come back unless it is with the Horn. **Do not return to the small island unless you have the Kraken Horn.**

You take your small boat back to your vessel and plan your next course of action.

Do you

Tell the crew to sail to the north of the island – *468*

Route for the centre of the island – *746*

Decide to set sail - **consult the voyage chart**

1160

You see the crude map before you which seems to be just a series of lines and circles with the occasional word. You don't know what to make of it but maybe it was important. **The map is at App 17, and you may examine it any time you wish.**

You are still in the hut. **Tick the codeword Wayfinder.** What now?

Check out the other writings – *9*

Just get on with things and leave the hut and

Strike out for the path – *1039*

Look at the poles – *703*

1161

As you approach the shore, you see the man from the mountain, and he appears with what looks like a native carrying a musket. You come ashore and other natives appear. The man from the mountain runs forward and shakes you by the hand.

"Do you have it?" he asks. "The Kraken Horn?"

If you have the Kraken Horn and wish to give it to him – *1258*

If you don't want to give it to him, or simply don't have it – *1159*

1162

Reduce your time by 1. You step forward and feel clear water ahead but on your right you feel a large barrel blocking your path. On your left you can feel hatch handles but not the same feel as those you grabbed on the outside of the hatch to the forecastle.

Do you

About turn and step forward – *715*

Walk forward – *1344*

Open the hatch to your left and step through – *1209*

1163

You yell at the crew to retreat and watch as the vessel slips to the aft of the brigantine which allows you a run to freedom as the brigantine tries to turn its broadside to you and launch volleys as you retreat. Your vessel now has a chance but is it quick enough to avoid what will be brutal volley after brutal volley?

Is your speed

Very Fast – *546*

Fast – *283*

Slow, Very Slow or Moderate – *1207*

<u>1164</u>

You call out to the soldiers, dropping your gown off one shoulder, allowing them to come close to you. You can see they are captivated by you, and you run your fingers through your hair with one hand. But the other hand has the secreted knife in it and as they set their hands on your bare shoulders you quickly slit the throats of the pair, watching them drop gasping to the ground. You don't wait to see if they are dead but run out of the door to the fields beyond.

Go to **647**

<u>1165</u>

Everything happens so quickly, and a bull smashes you backwards knocking you to the ground and then you scramble as quick as you can back to the plain clear of any more bulls. You're back where you started but you have been winded and feel groggy. **Take 7 off your Island Time Chart while you recover.**

If you want to try and run the gap again – **59**

You could try and go through the jungle and around the rock formation – **923**

Alternatively you can leave the plains back down the jungle track – **1145**

<u>1166</u>

You are in the heart of New Southampton with Madame Le Vert's shop across from you with its collection of fine clothes for both men and women. There are guards outside the shop, however. Opposite is the courthouse which is open with gallows before it and people gathering around it. You think there may be a hanging in the offing.

You can see at the town entrance the market and a dark alley while in the opposite direction are the docks and the weaponsmith. Everywhere is hot and sticky but where will you go.

Do you

Make for the courthouse – *227*

Go to Madame Le Vert's store – *252*

Walk to the town entrance – *496*

Stroll further into town towards the docks – *1009*

1167

You walk around the desk and notice it has a drawer. You pull at it and the drawer comes out, dropping onto the floor. There's some parchment and a brass key that tumble to the floor.

Do you

Look at the parchment – *503*

Examine the key – *863*

Or replace everything and instead

Check the rug that's slightly lifted – *169*

Look at the other rug – *366*

Try to open the safe – *1289*

Decide this is a bad idea and return to Timmers, saying you should get back to the ship pronto – *351*

1168

You watch the water change colour and wonder when you should enter. Do you enter when the water is

Blue – *1208*

Green – *1122*

Silver – *882*

The Treasure of Captain Estes

1169

The bar maid shakes her head looking at you, but the pirates all start to fuss over you. They ask what you are looking for and seem a little disappointed when you say you need a vessel. One however turns to you and says he can offer you a vessel for some return of anything gained from the voyage. The other pirates seem annoyed he has something to offer, and he asks that you come with him to view his vessel.

Do you

Take him up on his offer – *848*

Or leave him for the rest of the tavern and

Talk to the gypsy woman – *711*

Walk over to the single pirate – *838*

Go over to watch the pirate playing the mouth organ – *1421*

Or leave – *1112*

1170

You take decisive action, much to the agreement of most of the crew. The infected areas are quarantined, and the cargo jettisoned.

Raise your crew morale by 1 level. Block off 1 section of your cargo hold for at least 30 days and remove the cargo within.

There is no spread of the plague, and you continue your voyage without further incident. Now continue your voyage at *654*

1171

You plonk yourself down on the sand beside the women and they shuffle slightly away from you. They seem afraid and after you hear some of the activity around you, you can forgive them.

Do you

Try to speak to them – *972*

Reveal your hair from under your hat so they know you are a woman – *979*

Offer them money – *1369*

1172

You wait until the patrol passes the hangman's pole and then race to climb up the structure. You know you'll have to be quick but which technique to climb will benefit you the most. You could lose your boots and shimmy up the pole. That would be quicker than climbing with your boots. You could also drop off your jacket before you climb but leaving behind all this stuff means you will need to hide them, or you could be quick enough to just leave them at the foot of the pole.

Do you

Climb the pole straight away – *292*

Kick off your boots and climb the pole – *668*

Kick off your boots and hide them before climbing – *190*

Drop your jacket, kick off the boots and climb straight away – *217*

Drop your jacket, kick off the boots, hide them and then climb – *1202*

1173

Reduce the Hot Strip by 1. If this places you on a Fire spot add 20 to this section's number and go there for the walls have moved. There are walls of fire to the south and east. You can route north or west from your current location.

Do you

Go West – *1403*

Go North – *75*

<u>1174</u>

Move Tabetha.

You are in a white walled room, bathed in the strange light, with two doors, one with a picture of a pirate flag above it, and the other with a schooner above it.

If Tabetha's number is 2 – *1459*

If Tabetha's number is 12 – **note this number and go to *1029***

If Tabetha's number is 8 – **note this number and go to *446***

Where do you go next?

Through the pirate flag door – *308*

Through the schooner door – *867*

Wait here - **return to the top of this section**

<u>1175</u>

You desperately run here and there, racing as hard as you can go. It's so dark and you react to the slightest noise until you finally realise that you have no idea where you are. Quickly you **hide** and then take a look around you. **Due to the amount of time you spent running, and then hiding, reduce your time by 6. But where are you?**

Roll 1xD100 (2xD10)

00-19 – *42*

20-39 – *103*

40-59 – *1393*

60-79 – *1435*

80-99 – *785*

The Kraken Awakes!

The Treasure of Captain Estes

<u>1176</u>

Reduce your time by 2. If your time is in the following gaps (46-41 or 16-11) then go to *1126*. If not continue below

You are in the north quarter with an array of livestock around you. You can hear them mooing and bleating but believe these are the normal night noises and it's not you who is causing them to murmur. The place stinks as well, and you can see small gutters running through the quarter, passing out under the wall, taking away the animals' ablutions. You wonder what else to do here.

To the west side of the fort, you can see buildings that seem to be locked up tight but there are barrels nearby and other crates. They may be stores and supplies. On the east side of the fort, you see rather well constructed buildings and flags flying, which may indicate important people. Ahead in the centre of the fort, is a wall which has sentries patrolling the top of it, but you cannot see inside the wall. There is a gate at the foot of the wall.

Do you

Wait in hiding – *1418*

Check out the cows – *387*

Look at the sheep – *780*

Go to the gate – *319*

Move to the West quarter – *493*

Move to the East quarter – *678*

<u>1177</u>

If you have the codeword **Cheesy – *279*** You start up the banks of the river working the opposite way to its descent. You feel the spray as it has numerous drops causing a refreshing spray to hit your face. As you climb you see a wooden chest at the side of the river. It has a lock on it but it appears to be rusted and almost crumbling away. You look around but there is no one about.

Do you

Break open the chest – *1406*

Return down the mountain to its foot – *61*

Ignore the chest and climb the mountain – *1205*

1178

You ask if you can join in, and the pirates laugh at first until you insist that you want to.

"Well, welcome stranger," says one of the pirates. "I'm wondering what you have to bet with. Let me tell you how to play. First you put forward what you want to bet for. We have Promissory notes, whisky bottles, or pistols on offer. You can offer knives, pistols, bottles, or even body parts. Then we roll the dice and see who wins. Roll mostly coins and you win, roll mostly scales and no one wins, but if you roll mostly skulls you lose. However, if you roll all skulls you lose everything. You happy to play?"

If you want to continue – *1060*

If not, politely decline and return to the street – *262*

1179

Move Tabetha.

You are in a white walled room, bathed in the strange light, with two doors, one with a picture of a spider above it, and the other with a schooner above it.

If Tabetha's number is 7 – *1459*

If Tabetha's number is 3 – **note this number and go to *1287***

If Tabetha's number is 5 – **note this number and go to *446***

Where do you go next?

Through the spider door – **608**

Through the shield door – **1052**

Wait here - **return to the top of this section**

1180

You have stepped back onto the cliff edge and now must decide if you will try again or make a retreat from the challenge. If you want to try again, check the map at **830** and pick your start point again. If you want to make a retreat, turn around and enter the jungle path going to **1003**

1181

"Well here comes a gambling pirate if ever I saw one," says the one-legged pirate as you approach. He gives a wry smile, and points to the three cups in front of him. "Do you want to play? I can take a stake up to 200 Doubloons. Place your money down and we will start."

The other pirates look at you expectantly. If you want to play make a note of how many doubloons you are placing as your stake. Now go to **62**.

If you decide it isn't worth the gamble, then return to **1424** and pick a different option.

1182

"I need a crew," you say.

"Doesn't everyone, and why do you need a crew?"

"I'm after Estes. Heard he has a lot of money on his boat."

"That he does, sailor, the pirate from where God only knows. And he has a big boat at that. I hear they are looking for captains down the docks, maybe try there. Or just save yourself a lot of hassle and enjoy yourself down the alley. Either way, there's no boat here."

The man slumps back against the wall and pulls his hat down further. It seems he has no further chat, or a boat, so best to move on.

Do you

Route to the end of the alley – *828*

Walk back to the street – *496*

1183

You scream at the crew, urging them on to get the vessel turned in time and ready to fire a broadside at the creature whose appendages are surfacing around you.

Roll 1xD100 (2xD10)

00-49 – *692*

50-99 – *256*

1184

You grab the bars of your cell in excitement hoping to see the guard approach and at first you almost squeal in delight seeing the guard's feet. However, he is followed by Captain Fareham. The Captain knows the value to him of your father's lands although they have been ransacked and he forces you to become part of his plan and you are married in private.

He now owns your father's lands and keeps you locked up for the next year. When you don't respond to his advances and wishes to be a passive wife, he has you taken away in the night and disposed of. Your last thoughts are that your family remains unavenged. Try again at *1* and remember enemies are everywhere, even those people who help.

1185

Reduce the Hot Strip by 2. If this places you on a Fire spot add 20 to this section's number and go there for the walls have moved. You shield the treasure chest for a few moments hoping it will cool down and then grab its handles at the side. Thankfully they are cool. **Tick the codeword Fire Chest**. There are walls of fire to the north, west, and south, so you route east from your current location. Go to **456**

1186

A familiar mist surrounds your ship after black clouds form and the sea begins to swirl as before when you last saw the Devil's Sloop. You know what this means, and you hear the words in your head "Tribute". You freeze on deck wondering what tribute will be asked for this time.

Do you have the Codeword **Crossed** – **807**

If not, read on,

As if you didn't know, and the dark feeling in your soul wells up as you and Martha bow down on deck to your master aboard the Devil's Sloop which has appeared alongside. You see the crew panic, eyes wide in terror as the pair of you throw many of them overboard to the mercy of your master.

Lower your crew morale by 2 levels. Lower your crew by 1 level.

With the tribute paid the day returns to normal but not the crew who eye you with a horror deep inside. Now continue your voyage at **654**

1187

You barely overcome the main current to get to the eddy, and you suffer for it. **Reduce your Waters Strength Chart by 2.** You swim through to the eddy. Go to **1083**

1188

You turn your vessel towards the Brigantine making a direct line for it. As soon as you make a move towards it, the vessel turns and races fast in the water away from you.

Do you

Pursue – **66**

Resume your course – **814**

1189

The pirate at the gate takes one look at your gift and throws it back in your face. He shouts at some of the pirates around him.

"How dare you insult the king in such a fashion. Leave now and do not come back until you can bring a better gift. And don't come back for at least a month."

You are escorted back to your vessel and are told to leave immediately let you want to face the full force of every pirate ship in Hell's Deep. You have no choice but to set sail. **You cannot return to hell's Deep until another 30 days are up on your voyage chart. Mark this on your voyage chart. Now consult the voyage chart and set sail.**

1190

You watch the guard pass by from your hiding place, keeping a track on them, but unable to move freely while they are about. It takes them a while to clear the area as they look here and there. **Remove 6 time.** Finally they are clear but you have had to abort your previous action. Return to **1418** and choose again but ignore the time adjustment at that entry this time round.

1191

You wander along the path, sweat dripping from your clothes, and reach a junction. Which way now?

Left – *76*

Right – *664*

Turn back – *1357*

1192

"Yes," she says holding it up to the light, "that will do very nicely. You have engaged Martha Downham, known as the Bloody Mistress of the Sea, and a scourge to all who cross me. I have a vessel and a crew at the docks ready to send you on your path to vengeance. Come with me and we shall gain back what was taken from you." Go to *1042*

1193

Reduce your Island Time Chart by 1

You leave the fires behind you and reach a fork in the path, wondering which way to go. You can take either fork, or you could always head out into the jungle off the path.

Do you go

Left – *1433*

Right – *245*

Strike out into the Jungle – *1283*

Turn around back the way you came – *910*

<u>1194</u>

The man frowns at you but turns and walks to the door where he appears to whisper something as it opens by just a crack. After a few moments, he turns back with a serious look on his face and grabs you quickly forcing you in through the door. Go to *16*

<u>1195</u>

Reduce your Waters Strength Chart by 1. The current is pushing you east. However, you think you can reach an eddy that seems to allow a way west but to get there will be incredibly hard work. Do you

Swim West – *1187*

Float East – *8*

<u>1196</u>

This hasn't gone well and getting out of a fight now will be tricky. Let's hope you still have some manoeuvrability and speed.

Is your manoeuvrability

Great or Good – *1251*

Poor, Lacking or Reasonable – *402*

<u>1197</u>

Reduce your time by 1.

If your time is in the following gaps (32-28 or 12-08) and you are not hidden, then go to *1037*. If you are hidden, you see a guard on his patrol and must remain hidden until he clears the area. Reduce your time by 6. Now continue at the plain text below

If your time is in the following gaps (47-38) and you are not hidden, then go to *1128*. If you are hidden, you see a guard on the enclosing

wall patrolling and must remain hidden until he clears the area. Reduce your time by 6.

If neither of these apply, continue at the plain text below

You can see before you the shadow of a large building with a single person wooden door. There appears to be no one on guard.

To the north and east, you can see a similar building to what is before you to the south-west is a gate in the perimeter wall, the door of which appears to be open.

Do you

Hide where you are – *1367*

Route through the open gate – *519*

Creep East – *1435*

Go North – *1393*

Approach the building before you to break in – *156*

<u>1198</u>

You sail past vicious rocks and then realise you have reached clear sea. Currently you are to the southwest of the formation. You can re-enter here or try one of the other entry points. Of course you may have had enough and decide to go elsewhere.

Do you

 Sail into the north entry point – *1260*

Try the southwest entry point – *246*

Take the southeast entry point – *1300*

Or sail to a different destination – **Consult the voyage chart**

1199

1 Skull 3 Scales 1 Coins

That's a stalemate so no change. **Your stake item remains on your codewords, but you don't gain anything.** Return to *1060*

1200

The only wall of fire is to the East. You can route south, west or north from your current location.

Do you

Go West – *443*

Go South – *1389*

Go North – *929*

1201

You enter the water and it's pulling you to the east. However, you think you may be able to swim up an eddy to the north. Do you

Float East – *43*

Swim North – *204*

Yell at your friends to pull you out – *1056*

1202

Tick the codewords **Nocturne** and **Pace. Go to *628***

The Treasure of Captain Estes

<u>1203</u>

Move Tabetha.

You are in a white walled room, bathed in the strange light, with two doors, one with a picture of a pirate flag above it, and the other with a horn above it.

If Tabetha's number is 21 – *1459*

If Tabetha's number is 16 – **note this number and go to *1029***

Where do you go next?

Through the horn door – *637*

Through the pirate flag door – *442*

Wait here - **return to the top of this section**

<u>1204</u>

How many provisions did you decide upon?

1-6 provisions – *482*

7-12 provisions – *521*

13-18 provisions – *792*

19 or more – *543*

<u>1205</u>

You continue up the mountain until you reach the top where a small shack sits with a man lying down outside being attacked by rats. They seem to be gnawing at him while he screams in pain. Around the scene, you can see a purple fruit growing on long stalks, yellow berries on a bush, a wheat grass by the hut and some long branches from some type of tree stacked against the hut. You notice the rats are now looking towards you!

Do you

Attack the rats with your weapons – *1148*

Attack the rats with the branches – *980*

Throw some of the purple fruit over towards the rats – *226*

Toss some yellow berries over to the rats – *1266*

Try to tempt the rats away with some of the wheat grass – *941*

Flee the scene back down the mountain – *1449*

1206

You watch your crew with pride as they give everything they have, and your vessel races away like the wind itself. Behind you, a black splurge under the sea gradually drifts away and you know you have been fortunate to spot the beast before it attacked. With a sigh of relief you steer well clear of where the Kraken was spotted but resume course later that night.

Your crew are delighted at surviving. Raise crew morale by 2 levels. Add 1 day to your voyage time for your diversion.

Now continue your voyage at *654*

1207

Your vessel sails so slowly, and you see the inevitable as the brigantine turns broadside to you. The first volley obliterates your mast. The second sends great shards of wood flying from the deck. The third lands on you and you are gone. Fortunately, you don't see or hear the suffering as Jameson sinks your vessel.

Make sure you pick a fight you can win! You can try again at *1*.

1208

You wait until the water is blue and then step forward. Suddenly the curtain of water is behind you, and you are standing on a wooden jetty above burning sand. Before you is a maiden in white who steps forward and hands you a long scroll. You open it up and see a picture of the peak of a mountain. At the top sits a wooden chest. You look up but the maiden is not there. And then there's no sand and suddenly no parchment. Then you are back in the room and the water curtain has turned to rock. **Tick the codeword Rock.**

There's nothing else left in this room, save the ropes, so you should move on. Do you

Climb up the rope – *756*

Climb down the other rope – *843*

1209

As the hatch opens you see daylight in the water outside and realise you are back at the forecastle deck. You swim upwards as fast as you can and break the water, gasping for breath. You look around for the mast, but it is gone, and the vessel seems to have tilted over further than it had before. You realise that it is now unsafe and your time searching it is done.

You clamber back onto your own vessel where the crew look at you expectantly. Did you find anything inside the Maria Saratoga?

Yes – *18*

No – *1384*

1210

You dress in the long-coat and breeches you wore in the mansion and tuck your long hair inside the coat at the back of your neck. Stepping out of your room, you grab a hat you see lying about with a broad rim and pull it down over your face. Quickly you walk through the garrison, not stopping for anyone and cross through the busy courtyard, full of traders and servants. But no one pays you a second glance and you stroll out of the gate and along the path to New Southampton. As you approach the town, you see another path branching off, one that leads to Strangar, the pirate haven.

Do you

Make for Strangar – *671*

Or head into New Southampton – *1114*

<u>1211</u>

You tug at the hatches and although difficult, you manage to pull them open. Carefully you swim inside making sure you keep a hand on one hatch. As you start to look around in the poor light, the Marie Saratoga suddenly shifts, throwing you to one side and you lose your grip on the hatch.

Everything goes dark and you try not to panic. Will someone come to rescue you? Is the hatch nearby? How much breath do you still have?

Don't panic, you tell yourself. *There'll be a way out.* Or will there.

You'll need air and you'll need it quick, so you need to get out. However, it's now pitch black inside the forecastle and you'll have to feel your way around. Use the time chart *App 09* at the rear of the book and when instructed, count down the units of time you have left beginning at 60. If your timer reaches 0 go to *1468*.

PS. If you want the real feel of this, don't map it, write nothing down unless instructed. Are you brave enough?

You are in total darkness, completely disorientated after the ship's movement, and reach out with your hands to feel around you. The low ceiling means you can walk through the water. Ahead is a wall and to your right is also a wall. There's clear way to your left and behind you.

Do you

Turn and step left - *899*

About turn and step forward – *90*

1212

The starboard side of the vessel is an absolute mess with the side of the vessel deeply gorged as if something was struggling. Along the gorging, some form of orange algae has formed and gently waves back and forward in the light current. You touch it and it feels spongy and slips out of your hand easily.

You may take some of the algae if you wish. Tick the code word Orange Algae.

You're out of breath and surface again. Once you have sucked in enough air, what do you do.

Do you swim to the

Stern of the vessel – *1422*

Bow of the vessel – *94*

Keel – *1413*

Or instead

Clamber on board -*603*

Return to your vessel – *894*

1213

Move Tabetha.

You are in a white walled room, bathed in the strange light, with two doors, one with a picture of a shield above it, and the other with a pirate flag above it.

If Tabetha's number is 19 – *1459*

If Tabetha's number is 1 – **note this number and go to *239***

If Tabetha's number is 11 – **note this number and go to *1029***

Where do you go next?

Through the shield door – *491*

Through the pirate flag door – *686*

Wait here - **return to the top of this section**

1214

Robert Grimshaw tells you to watch how he deals with this, and he steps to the middle of the deck so that the others surround him. He calls the second officer to him and asks him to repeat his complaint. Halfway through his response to Grimshaw, the first officer, grabs the man and delivers two crippling blows into the man's stomach.

"What did you say?" yells Grimshaw.

"Nothing, sir, nothing."

"Good, now all of you back to work or I'll take this further."

The crew take a step back and Grimshaw shakes his head as they disperse. You see how they look at you though and you wonder if you have made the right move here. You can tell over the coming days as although they obey your commands quickly, they seem to watch you closely. **Reduce your crew morale by 2 levels.** Now continue at *654*

The Treasure of Captain Estes

<u>1215</u>

Go to *875*

<u>1216</u>

Is your vessel's manoeuvrability

Poor or Lacking – *225*

Reasonable, Good or Great – *282*

<u>1217</u>

Reduce the Hot Strip by 2. If this places you on a Fire spot, makes you pass a Fire spot, add 20 to this section's number and go there for the walls have moved.

If you have codeword Fire Chest, there are walls of fire to the north, west, and south. You can route east from your current location. Go east at *456*. Otherwise read on.

There is a treasure chest at your feet, but it is between the three walls of fire and could be extremely hot. You could wait for it to cool down as you shield it or you could simply grab it. There are walls of fire to the north, west, and south. You can route east from your current location.

Do you

Go East – *456*

Shield the treasure and wait for a few moments to let it cool – *1185*

Grab it – *732*

1218

You wander along the path, and jog a little before you reach a junction. Which way now?

Left – *526*

Right – *612*

Turn back – *1453*

1219

The pirate looks up at you and sneers. "The docks, if you live that long. Now, go away before I put you out of your misery."

You thank him and draw back quickly. Do you

Approach the bar – *669*

Talk to the gypsy woman – *711*

Go over to watch the pirate playing the mouth organ – *1421*

Or leave – *1112*

1220

You ask the helm to take the vessel in close to the underwater cave and you get near enough to swim easily to it. As you go to strike out for the cave you think about what weapons you might need when suddenly a crewman yells for you. He is looking over the side and says to you that he saw something.

"Captain, I tell no lie but I saw a crab as big as a man down there. Scuttling it was, sideways as they do but this one was enormous."

"Was it just the water's effect?" asks the first officer.

"I swear, Captain," declares the crewman, "that was no illusion!"

The Treasure of Captain Estes

Maybe there are dangers down there and you wonder if you should take a party with you.

Do you

Want to take crew with you – *379*

Tell the crew to stay on board – *432*

<u>1221</u>

You grab Diggory's hand and tell him to jump. You both take a few steps and leap up onto the outer wall before pushing off completely, abandoning yourself to the fall. You look down and see the water below, thanking God that the tide is in. You hit the water and begin to swim, seeing a sloop ahead. Diggory encourages you to swim for it as the water is peppered with musket fire. You swim strongly and soon there is a rope dropping into the water beside you both and Diggory is pushing you up it.

As you clamber onboard the sloop you see a well drilled crew working hard and turning the sloop away from the garrison which is now firing canon towards it. There's a loud splash on the port side of the vessel but Diggory is now barking orders at the men around him.

"Cut and run! We cut and run, everything we have!"

It takes the rest of the day but the sloop races clear of the New Southampton bay and navigates round to the other side of the island before taking shelter in a small tree covered inlet.

"We are in the shallows and their vessels cannot follow even if they knew where we were," says Diggory, smiling at you. "We are clear. Time to find out what you want to do next, Mary Hastings, for you are now a fugitive."

Go to *1460* to discover what life has in store for you

1222

You have treasure, more than enough for the crew, and plenty for yourself. You are a wealthy woman and buying back your home and lands is easy. The wealthiest person on the island you have influence and you have seen your family avenged as best you could.

You are asked by the British to be the island's governor, but you refuse, your wealth allowing you to deal with all parties. You become one of the most dominant traders in the area. Everyone knows your name. People want to be you and you are held in awe wherever you go, by authorities, ordinary folk and pirates alike.

Congratulations, you have succeeded and brought honour and justice back to your family. You have won. But there are greater victories if you dare to try again. More treasure to be won and more power and influence to achieve. Try again at *1* if you dare, or will you simply bask in your current victory?

1223

Reduce your Island Time Chart by 1

You trek along the path, your brow full of sweat. There's a fork in the path, and you wonder which way to go. You can take either fork, or you could always head out into the jungle off the path.

Do you go

Left – *509*

Right – *690*

Strike out into the Jungle – *1347*

Turn around back the way you came – *125*

The Treasure of Captain Estes

1224

You see lots of parchment on the desk as well as a half-finished bottle of rum. There are manifests of ships, but a quick scan reveals nothing that can help you in your search for Estes' treasure.

Go to *1400*

1225

"I require a vessel and a crew," you say.

The man laughs at you. "This is a pirate den, and no woman is welcome here where business is done, no begone..., or I will make you leave."

You can tell he is not messing about. You decide to leave and return to the street at *1256*. Don't return to the building unless you are dressed differently.

1226

You run hard but your legs are taken out from under you as you are hit by something just below the knee. As you try to get up one of the soldiers grabs you and picks you up throwing you over his shoulder. You kick and scream, but his grip is solid.

You hear them converse in Spanish, realising that the New Southampton garrison is here. They decide to retreat, and you are tied to a horse before being taken to a rowing boat in the dark just off New Southampton. From there, you are taken on board their vessel and your life becomes a hell as their "cabin girl". It is two years later when during a drunken argument, you are thrown overboard that your turmoil ends. Your family is unavenged, your life ended.

Try again at *1*

1227

You return to your vessel and ponder what to do next. You certainly will not return to the dark isle for a long while. **You may not return to the dark isle on this visit to the Hell's Deep.** What will you do next?

Go to see Blind Tom – *681*

Visit the provisions isle – *334*

Enjoy yourself at the wild isle – *879*

Approach the pirate king – *1348*

Decide you have had enough of Hells Deep and set sail - **Consult the voyage chart and set sail.**

1228

There's no cover and you run as hard as you can almost blindly through the fort. You feel like you have been running forever when you stop in a hiding place. But where are you? **Note you are now in hiding.**

Roll 1xD100 (2xD10)

01-25 – *519*

26-50 – *493*

51-75 – *1176*

76-00 – *678*

1229

You walk forward into the darkness and realise it is a true darkness. As you walk you feel a wind at your back pushing you forward, and you start to stumble. You are pitching along and cannot stop yourself. But the floor remains, solid beneath your feet.

Up ahead you see daylight and you emerge out into sunlight and more branching paths and a post and a board. This time it reads

The Treasure of Captain Estes

'What's the name of my first vessel?'

You look up above the dark entrances back into the cliffs and see three answers: *Yellow, Grandeur, and Margarite.*

Your blood runs cold at your choices as you stand high up above the island. Well, you have the same issue as before and you need to give an answer or turn around. Do you walk the path that leads to

Yellow – *1333*

Grandeur – *522*

Margarite – *1391*

Or do you turn around and forget these crazy questions to head back down to the jungle path – *335*

1230

You walk along the path, and find it becomes covered by the jungle canopy, so you are walking in a tunnel of greenery. The path this time seems longer and eventually it breaks out into the foot of a mountain. There is a river running down its side which will give you purchase to climb along its banks but otherwise the mountain is also covered in dense foliage. There is a path running around the mountain which shows you another path leading west from the mountain.

Do you

Climb the mountain – *1177*

Take the path to the west – *477*

Retrace your steps – *435*

1231

How fast is your vessel?

Very Slow or Slow – *339*

Moderate, Fast, or Very fast – *949*

1232

You make to intervene for the girl but as soon as you speak you are rounded on by the other customers and actually beaten. A few guards appear and you are thrown out into the street where you are tossed into the dust and dirt of the walkway.

Do you have the codeword **Prominent** – *942*

Otherwise pick yourself up and **tick the codeword Prominent** in your list. Now return to the street at *496* and please stay away from the market.

1233

That night you wait at the last alehouse in town and Simon Kilmer arrives to take you to your vessel. In the dark, you see he has brought you clothes and you change into the provided long-coat and breeches, complete with boots and a small array of weapons. You're not sure if you can manage the cutlass but you like the pistol you are given.

You walk through the night until you reach the docks of New Southampton. As you approach you see several men join you and you try not to stare at them. Simon directs you to a small vessel which has a sparse number of crew on board.

"This is the Hawk, Mad Mary, and she's a fast one, very fast. We don't have much firepower, but we can hit and run. There's a reasonable amount of room for treasure due to the small crew but then we don't require many provisions. She can spin on a doubloon and hide in the shadows. Just beware of storms as she doesn't take to them. Now come and meet the crew."

You spend that night surveying the crew and they seem decent, mainly ex British sailors, which makes sense as Simon was one of those. In the morning you sail off to a small inlet up the coast where Simon discusses with you what to do next and awaits an update on the

The Treasure of Captain Estes

whereabouts of Captain Estes. It takes a week for any news to filter through.

While you wait, it's time to fill in your vessel chart with the details of your vessel and crew. Look for the chart at the rear of the book. You may photocopy this for ease of use. Fill it in now.

Vessel: The Hawk – Sloop

Speed: Very Fast

Firepower: Light

Cargo store: moderate

Shallows: Yes

Manoeuvrability: Great

Storm Handling: Poor

Crew: Small

Initial Provisions: 4 sections

Doubloons: 300

Simon asks to see you in your chart room, and you can see the concern on his face. "Mary, there's a problem with going after Estes. It seems that he has died. It is reported he and his vessel went down to a British attack two days ago. However, rumour has it that he left his treasure on an island in the vicinity of New Southampton. The island, known only as the Dark Land, is only accessible at certain times and appears in different places, or so the story goes. I've never known anyone who has seen it."

"So, I have nothing," you say, "unless I chase this treasure."

"It may not be an island as such but maybe a tall tale to discover and then find the real island. Rumour and superstition does travel fast around these parts."

"Well then, the truth of it we shall discover. Where do we go?"

"I have no definitive sightings of Estes before his last battle which was southeast of New Southampton. If you look at the chart, Mary, there are six places in the general locale where he could have been before he died and which may be able to shed light on his travels, and where the island is. Once you have examined them all, give your crew orders of where to sail to."

Check the *chart of New Southampton at App 02* to help you in your decisions. You may photocopy it for use with this book. Turn now to section *1276* to learn about the six locations and about sailing around New Southampton, and then to make your first decision as captain!

1234

You wander along the path and reach a junction. Which way now?

Left – *613*

Right – *555*

Turn back – *564*

1235

You consult your chart for the pilotage into Birds Paradise and sail past all the narrow passages and strange loops within the rocks around the main structure. It does not take long for you to arrive at the massive bird covered rock before you. Go to *275*

1236

Reduce the Hot Strip by 1. If this places you on a Fire spot add 20 to this section's number and go there for the walls have moved. There are walls of fire to the south and east. You can route north or west from your current location.

Do you

Go West – *738*

Go North – *539*

1237

You see the alley approach and suddenly leap from the carriage rolling on the ground and then back to your feet. You pull up your skirt and begin to run. You can see the looks of the everyday person in town, and you make for the dark alleyway as fast as you can. **Tick the codeword Prominent** on your list and go to *160* to continue your escape.

1238

Reduce your Waters Strength Chart by 1. The current is pushing you south. However, you think you may be able to swim up an eddy to the west. Do you

Float South – *866*

Swim West – *624*

1239

If this is at least the second item you have examined then roll 1xD100 (2xD10,) and consult the table below

2nd item	3rd item	4th item
00-39 – *959*	00-59 – *959*	00-89 – *959*
40-99 – read on	60-99 – read on	90-99 – read on

Each desk is made of stout wood and must have been brought over from European shores for the style and quality smacks of the continent. You race through papers and notes but can find very little of note.

Do you

Check out the cabinets – *1405*

Look at the chairs – *120*

Peruse the charts on the wall – *371*

Or leave the room and return to tunnel – *558*

<u>1240</u>

Reduce your time by 1.

If your time is in the following gaps (57-53 or 42-38), then go to *1037*.

You creep up to the building and to the single wooden door. You feel exposed as you stand there and wonder if you should just pull at the door and enter the building to get cover. It would be madness to stand here, but what's inside?

Do you

Hide where you are – *103*

Route South – *1435*

Creep East – *174*

Go North – *42*

Sneak West – *1393*

Listen at the door – *12*

Open the door and enter the building – *382*

<u>1241</u>

Who is your officer?

Simon Kilmer – **764**

Robert Grimshaw – **860**

Diggory Hurst – **1103**

Timmers – **426**

Martha Downham – **722**

Black Robert – **997**

If you have lost your named first officer, you cannot use this method. Return to **17** and choose again.

<u>1242</u>

Quickly you open the door of your room and then walk out into the hallway. As you reach the end of it and look for the steps down to the courtyard, a soldier asks what you are doing. You run but he is too quick and catches up with you.

"Now, my lady, where are you going to?"

Do you

Say you are off to the courtyard for your transport into new Southampton – **436**

Tell him it's none of his business - **1286**

Strike him hard while he's relaxed talking to you – **841**

<u>1243</u>

Go to **1394**

1244

You send for your offering, and it is brought before Tom who touches it carefully, examining it. He smiles and a child takes your offering away.

As you wait to see what he will say a trapdoor opens beneath you and you fall into a chute which makes you tumble out of the barge and into the waters around it. As you surface, a few children are laughing at you from the barge. Indignant, you swim to your vessel to dry off and decide your next course of action.

Go to see Blind Tom again – *681*

Visit the provisions isle – *334*

Enjoy yourself at the wild isle – *879*

Explore the dark isle – *397*

Approach the pirate king – *1348*

Decide you have had enough of Hells Deep and set sail - **Consult the voyage chart and set sail**

1245

The man steps across your path and grins. He looks you up and down before shouting over at some pirates in the street who seem to be leering at you.

"You look very out of place, young lady. I don't think you're the sort to work in this kind of place. Take a hint and leave town, try the main port at New Southampton. They know how to treat a lady over there."

You get the feeling he isn't going to budge, and you turn back to the street. Go to *262*

1246

Reduce your Island Time Chart by 1

You trek along the path, head hung low in the heat. This path seems to never end. Suddenly there's a fork in the path, and you wonder which way to go. You can take either fork, or you could always head out into the jungle off the path.

Do you go

Left – *1115*

Right – *982*

Strike out into the Jungle – *1077*

Turn around back the way you came – *1088*

1247

The man is disappointed and so is Simon. **You cannot accept this offer in the future.** Return to *580* and make your next decision.

1248

Reduce your time by 1. You step forward and paw around. On your right is a chair that seems fixed down. On your left you can touch some hatch handles and they feel just like the exterior handles of the original hatch you opened. Ahead there is just water.

Do you

Walk straight on – *1330*

Open the hatch to your right and step through – *391*

About turn and step forward – *345*

1249

The man is disappointed and so is Diggory. **You cannot accept this offer in the future.** Return to *580* and make your next decision.

1250

Reduce the Hot Strip by 1. If this places you on a Fire spot add 20 to this section's number and go there for the walls have moved. There are walls of fire to the north and east. You can route north or west from your current location.

Do you

Go West – *1141*

Go South – *803*

1251

You yell at the crew to retreat and watch as the vessel slips to the aft of the sloop which allows you a run to freedom as the sloop tries to turn its broadside to you and launch volleys as you retreat. Your vessel now has a chance but is it quick enough to avoid what will be brutal volley after brutal volley?

Is your speed

Very Fast – *274*

Fast – *376*

Slow, Very Slow or Moderate – *1427*

The Treasure of Captain Estes

<u>1252</u>

Reduce your time by 1. You step forward and run into a chair that appears fixed into the floor. There's clear water on your left and right.

Do you

About turn and step forward – *709*

Turn left and walk forward – *1344*

Turn right and walk forward – *107*

<u>1253</u>

Reduce your Waters Strength Chart by 1. The current is terribly strong, and you are swept north. There is nothing you can do except float to *955*

<u>1254</u>

You crawl this time towards the entrance, down low on your belly aware of the winds that come. Suddenly the path completely collapses, sending you down the cliff side and killing you instantly.

 'And walk, don't crawl! These are cursed cliffs, enter at your peril.' Remember that bit? Clearly not! Such a shame as you were doing so well. But if you don't pay attention.

You can reset to the start of this puzzle at *1366* if you want or start all over again at *1*. That was a long haul, and you did so well, just not well enough.

<u>1255</u>

Roll 1xD100 (2xD10). For every point of damage you have already done to the sloop add 3 to the result. Check the table below for the result of this round of the sea battle.

00-59 – You get caught with a severe broadside. **Lower your vessel manoeuvrability by 2 levels and your vessel speed by 1 level.**

60-89 – A volley lands on deck killing many of the crew. **Lower your crew by 1 level.**

90-99 – A volley blows out some of your canons, but you hit back – **Lower your firepower by 1 level.** But you cause the following damage dependent on your firepower: **Light – 1 point, Moderate – 2pts, Heavy – 3pts, Very Heavy – 4 pts**

100-110 – You land a splendid volley. Note you have done the following damage dependent on your firepower: **Light – 1 point, Moderate – 2pts, Heavy – 3pts, Very Heavy – 4 pts**

111 and up - You catch them cold with a blinding manoeuvre. Note you have done the following damage dependent on your firepower: **Light – 2 point, Moderate – 4pts, Heavy – 6pts, Very Heavy – 8 pts**

If you have caused 8 points of damage overall to the sloop – *1097*

If not

Do you want to continue the battle – *1267*

Do you wish to run – *1196*

<u>1256</u>

The docks area of Strangar has stone steps leading down to various vessels, all of which have some sort of guard at them. Although there are many pirates about, they seem to be intent on their duties and you see only a few bottles approaching lips. Before the docks, there is a stone building with two floors and each room seems to have a lit candle or two behind the shutters for you can see where the light is escaping through cracks. You get the feeling this is the serious part of the town and there is a sense of foreboding to it. If you get caught here without good reason you may end up dead.

Do you

Approach the docks – **45**

Make for the building – **1109**

Return to the centre of town – **1112**

1257

You grab hold of one of the treasure caskets as it strikes your foot. Desperately you haul it with you to the vessel and feel the arms of your crew haul you aboard. Soaking you gasp for breath and look around to see who else has been rescued. All the crew from the small boat are standing there but some of the treasure caskets are missing. You realise you have lost 30% of the treasure that was in the small boat. **Adjust this amount now on the Island Time Chart**. There is a silence among the crew but there is little else you can do. Go to **725**

1258

You hand over the Kraken Horn and he runs with it to the native who came out with him. The native grabs the item and turns to his village where you hear loud shouts. **Untick the Kraken Horn.** He waves to another native who runs forward to you and presents you with a scroll and a chart. The chart shows the sea around New Southampton. The scroll details part of Estes' final journey and mentions that the island where his treasure was placed had a bearing from the Abandoned Tower. You can see the Tower on the chart. **Tick the codewords Empty Chart** and **Bearing A.**

The man from the mountain says that the natives will be leaving soon, now they have the Kraken Horn and maybe you should depart too. You gather your crew and re-join your vessel. Once on board you wonder where to set sail for next. **You cannot come back to this small island.**

Do you

Tell the crew to sail to the north of the island – *468*

Route for the centre of the island – *746*

Decide to set sail - **consult the voyage chart**

1259

You seem to go through your doubloons quickly with a number of pirates stepping forward and when you get back to the vessel you see that your new crew is there. **Increase your crew size by 1 as long as the vessel has room. If not, you have wasted money on a new crew that cannot come with you.**

Among the new crew is a young cabin boy who says he was on Estes vessel before his vessel went down. He says that the Captain left his treasure on an island and that to get to it he needed three points of reference. He managed to grab a scrap of parchment one night with one of the points noted down. He gives you the scrap of paper which contains a bearing from Brid's Paradise. **Tick the codeword Bearing C.**

What now?

Go to see Blind Tom – *681*

Visit the provisions isle – *334*

Go back to the Wild Isle – *879*

Explore the dark isle – *397*

Approach the pirate king – *1348*

Decide you have had enough of Hells Deep and set sail - **Consult the voyage chart and set sail**

1260

You steer in past the rocks, watching your bow carefully. It's tight but you believe you can make it. Your first officer warns you that the rocks may narrow here and there and that turning may be an issue, but you are keen to reach find out what this birds paradise is all about. Soon you reach your first decision. Go to **144**

1261

When you are asked to roll the dice in the very next section add 20 to the result up to a maximum result of 99. Now go to **1017**

1262

You call out to retreat and to turn the vessel but there's seems to be a struggle to get clear. You see the brigantine now coming alongside at point blank range and volley after volley is fired into your vessel. The mast falls and then you feel the vessel begin to tilt. Soon it is sinking in the water. You try to flee over the side, but an errant pistol shot hits you between the shoulder blades and you fall to the deck. As the blackness invades your view, you know you are defeated.

Make sure you pick a fight you can win! You can try again at **1.**

1263

You sail on until the rocks form a small pool with three exits. They route northwest, northeast and south. The channels look equally wide and passable, so you have a choice.

Do you

Sail northeast – **191**

Take the south channel – **1338**

Go northwest from here – **186**

1264

The crew are not happy with this solution but they seem appeased but only when you promise there will be no more half rations. **You may maintain half rations for another 7 days only. After that for 30 days you must maintain full rations.**

Now continue your voyage at **654**

1265

Go to **508**

1266

You grab some of the berries off the bush and throw them down in front of the rats. They stop for a moment and sniff them before starting towards you again This buys you a second and you flee. There are simply too many and you are forced to run down the mountain. As you reach the base of the mountain, you skip over the river and the rats start to lose interest.

Now at the base of the mountain, you grab your breath and decide not to return this way again. **Note you cannot climb the mountain again.**

There are two paths away from the mountain, one a canopy covered path to the north, the other a more open topped path to the west, although it is still surrounded by the dense jungle.

Do you

Head north – **435**

Take the path west – **477**

The Treasure of Captain Estes

<u>1267</u>

Is your vessel manoeuvrability

Great – *218*

Good or Reasonable – *561*

Poor or Lacking -*1255*

<u>1268</u>

Not fast enough it seems. Captain Fareham's guards catch you and bring you back to him. You are escorted to your room and a guard is placed at your door, blocking all escape. Fareham has seen you are unwilling to go along with his plans and doesn't let down his guard as you are married in private.

He now owns your father's lands and keeps you locked up for the next year. When you don't respond to his advances and wishes to be a passive wife, he has you taken away in the night and disposed of. Your last thoughts are that your family remains unavenged. Try again at *1* and remember enemies are everywhere, even those people who help.

<u>1269</u>

You've been caught unawares out in the open and have to scramble for cover. Will you be able to find somewhere to hide.

Roll 1xD100 (2xD10)

01-25 – *533*

26-75 – *1228*

76-00 – *1379*

1270

You sail past vicious rocks and then realise you have reached clear sea. Currently you are to the north of the formation. You can re-enter here or try one of the other entry points. Of course, you may have had enough and decide to go elsewhere.

Do you

 Sail into the north entry point – *1260*

Try the southwest entry point – *246*

Take the southeast entry point – *1300*

Or sail to a different destination – **Consult the voyage chart**

1271

Reduce your time by 1.

If your time is in the following gaps (22-18), then go to *1037*.

If your time is in the following gaps (57-53 or 17-13), then go to *1128*.

If neither of these apply, continue at the plain text below

You creep up to the building and to the single wooden door. You feel exposed as you stand there and wonder if you should just pull at the door and enter the building to get cover. It would be madness to stand here, but what's inside?

Do you

Hide where you are – *785*

Route South – *1393*

Creep East – *42*

Listen at the door – *1442*

Open the door and enter the building – *680*

The Treasure of Captain Estes

1272

Your first officer shakes their head but carries out your orders as cannon balls rip your vessel apart. As the battle becomes more and more of a lost cause, you eventually give the order to sail away and pray the cargo vessel does not follow. It takes a while before you can see clear distance between you through the smoke and you are able to assess the damage.

Reduce your vessel speed by 2 levels. Reduce your crew by 2 levels. Reduce your Firepower by 2 levels. Reduce your Treasure store by 2 levels due damage. 50% of your cargo is destroyed. Reduce your crew morale by 2 levels.

You return to your voyage but must **add 1 day extra to it** for this diversion. **Also, your new voyage time is that of your new reduced speed.**

Continue the voyage at **654**

1273

You wander along the path, with weary feet, and reach a junction. Which way now?

Left – **554**

Right – **483**

Turn back – **891**

1274

You see a black bull running directly at you and a white bull in the middle channel. You are in the left channel. What will you do?

Stay left – **298**

Go to the middle – **392**

Go to the right channel – **783**

1275

The mud path is dense, and you dare not step off it into the thick green plants that lie beyond, fearing that they will close up behind you, trapping you in an endless humid jungle. You hear nothing, no bird life, no animals or insects and everything feels eerie. Sweat rolls down your face as the path now forks before you, left and right. Which way do you go?

Left – *575*

Right - *1359*

Turn back – *612*

1276

You are about to set sail into the waters around new Southampton in search of Estes' last days and where he placed his treasure. You may encounter vessels of an English, Spanish or even a Pirate flag. You may find tales of the local seas and many different occupants of the islands and wrecks. One thing is for sure, this will not be a quiet voyage.

You will record the days of your voyage using *the Voyage Time chart at App 04*. When travelling around New Southampton it will take days to reach your destinations and you will be on the open sea in between when several things could happen. Also, when you travel, it will take a certain number of days to sail from one place to another depending on your vessel and its condition. After choosing where you are going you need to consult the tables to calculate your voyage time. Don't worry, if you haven't sailed before there's a section to explain it all.

Now to learn about your possible destinations:

New Southampton: Yes, you start here but you can return, not to go ashore but for provisions and extra crew. It's a detour but one you may need to make.

Malin's Town: This small settlement is a thriving place of commerce which looks above board but also welcomes its fair share of pirates and privateers as long as they behave. Estes may have come here, or you may find plenty of rumours about him.

Fort August: A major British fort where their ships come to replenish and transfer crew. Not a particularly friendly place to a pirate but British intelligence know many things, and you might sneak in when they're not looking.

Bird's Paradise: Home to many varieties of birds and little is known about the rock except for that. It has been subject to many rumours about dark arts and there are always the tales of mermaids, but you don't believe them, do you?

The Wreck of the Marie Saratoga: Taken down by what, no one knows, but a place of dark arts with an island that is known to be best avoided. Definitely a possible place to hide any gold or plunder they say.

Abandoned Island: It's abandoned and never been visited again after many ships were seen floating around it without crew. Not a place for the faint hearted.

Hell's Deep: THE Pirate stronghold. You'll be very lucky to be welcome here, but it was a place Estes may have visited, especially if he was depositing his gold away from the Spanish authorities. The waters around it are Kraken infested and above water isn't any friendlier.

So, Captain, if this is not your first time afloat, choose your first journey from New Southampton, note it in the voyage log, calculate your days of the voyage and then roll on the Voyage chart. Once you have your next section go there directly, and good luck. You're going to need it!

If this is your first voyage or you need a recap as to how the process works, then go to **51**

1277

The barmaid smiles and takes your money as you splash the cash for information. The afternoon is spent carousing and you have plenty of friends asking about you and what you are doing but there is little information of note. You also get the feeling they don't trust you but are happy to drink your ale. By the time you leave you are none the wiser about the New Southampton seas.

Dejected you return to the crossroads – *802*

1278

You wait in your vessel as Simon goes into Malin's Town to find your contact and give him the good news. He returns alone and has in his hands a piece of parchment. It has details on how to complete the "Walk of Fire" whatever that is. **Tick the codeword Walk.** Now decide if you should stay in Malin's Town or depart.

Do you

See to the needs of your vessel and crew – *903*

Try to earn some money by signing up to a cargo run – *1335*

Visit the taverns for information – *802*

Visit the Mariners' Guild for information – *124*

If you have had enough of Malin's town, then **consult the voyage chart and set sail**.

1279

You walk around the building and see there's an alleyway at the rear. Entering the narrow passage, you see a small window which you can just about reach. Pulling at the shutters, you manage to open them and pull yourself up and into a dressing room. There are a small number of wine bottles on the floor in the corner along with some boxes.

You can hear Madame Le Vert in the shop and if you enter, she will probably see you as an intruder so if you want anything in the shop you will need to overcome her, and quietly. Plans form in your mind.

Do you take a wine bottle and attempt to overcome Madame Le Vert with it - *597*

If you have the codeword **Standard Knife,** take Madame Le Vert on with it – *141*

If you have the codeword **Pistol**, attack Madame Le Vert with a it – *513*

Use your hands to subdue Madame Le vert – *614*

<u>1280</u>

You reply in French and hold your breath.

"We are outside if you need any assistance," says the guard and you let go a sigh of relief, seeing Madame Le Vert is out cold. You acquire a full outfit of breeches, boots, shirt, long-coat and hat, before organising the boxes in the dressing room and climbing out of the small window. It's a squeeze but you make it out to the alley outside and then to the main street. You tip your hat to cover your face and get ready to plot your next path. **Tick the codeword Incognito.** Go to *1166*

<u>1281</u>

Reduce your time by 1.

If your time is in the following gaps (57-53 or 42-38), you see a guard on his patrol and must remain hidden until he clears the area. Reduce your time by 6. Now continue at the plain text below

You keep to the shadows, but no one comes. What will you do now?

Do you

Hide where you are – *103*

Route South – *1435*

Creep East – *174*

Go North – *42*

Sneak West – *1393*

Approach the building before you to break in – *1240*

1282

The women are very annoyed with you and turn their backs on you. **You may no longer make a deal with them.**

Is there anything else in the tavern that interests you? Do you

Approach the pirates with the monkey figure – *305*

Join the main bar – *594*

Or leave the tavern and

Make for the small houses – *1304*

Approach the gambling groups – *1424*

Go to see the fights – *84*

Decide this is not a place you want to explore and return to your vessel - *314*

1283

You push out into the jungle and force your way through past several pieces of vegetation. Soon there is no sight of the path but neither does the vegetation in front of you ease up. Eventually you come across a path again, but you have no idea where you are or how long it took you to get here. You're not even sure you are in the same part of the jungle you started in. This place is strange beyond belief, maybe even magical, or cursed!

You strike back out on the path again but where are you?

The Treasure of Captain Estes

Roll 1xD100 (2xD10) and go to the result below. Deduct the time indicated from your Island Time Chart and then go to your next indicated section to see where you end up.

00-19 –*280*

20-39 – Reduce time chart by 5, go to *677*

40-59 –*280*

60-79 – Reduce time chart by 4, go to *509*

80-99 – Reduce time chart by 15, go to *1111*

<u>1284</u>

Reduce the Hot Strip by 2. If this places you on a Fire spot add 20 to this section's number and go there for the walls have moved.

If you have codeword Fire Chest, there are walls of fire to the north, west, and east. You can route south from your current location. Go south at *321*. Otherwise read on.

There is a treasure chest at your feet, but it is between the three walls of fire and could be extremely hot. You could wait for it to cool down as you shield it, or you could simply grab it. There are walls of fire to the north, west, and east. You can route south from your current location.

Do you

Go South – *321*

Shield the treasure and wait for a few moments to let it cool – *864*

Grab the chest – *119*

<u>1285</u>

There's a thunderous explosion and the tailing vessel is engulfed in spray and noise. You tell your crew to fire another volley and the same vast barrage sends towers of displaced water into the air.

"Captain, I can see the tentacles. Over by the vessel. I can see something."

You respond to the Crow's nest hail, and spy with your eye glass towards it. You see a tentacle rip into the air from out of the sea and then lash towards the vessel, one striking it amidships and rendering the mast broken. But you see other tentacles reaching towards you. Just how large is the Kraken? The tentacles lash out and rips into your sails and across the deck, sending crew scattering.

"Flee," you cry, "away from the other vessel and best speed!"

You don't look back as your vessel glides away, but you hear the cries as crewmen go overboard. There's splintering of wood but the giant tentacles slip off your vessel and you are gone. As you hang on to the deck for grim life, you look back and see the Kraken now devouring the other vessel.

Your crew are relieved, but you have lost crew. Reduce your crew by 1 level. Your vessel is badly damaged and will need extensive repairs. Reduce your vessel speed, firepower, and manoeuvrability by 1 level. Untick either Spanish Tail or British Tail as appropriate.

Now continue your voyage at **654**

1286

"Frankly, that's none of your business."

The soldier seems rebuked and steps aside allowing you to continue your passage along to the stone steps down to the courtyard. Across the dusty yard, you see the large double gates. They are open and you see traders coming and going with a few guards watching them carefully. There is a relaxed air about the place, and you see baskets of fruit and vegetables, and some casks among the goods being exchanged.

You decide not to hang about and walk towards the gates. As you go through them, several guards look at you strangely but don't react.

There's then a cry and you can hear Captain Fareham telling the guards to hold you. There's no option, you need to run.

How fast can you run?

This fast – *1268*

Or this fast -*888*

1287

You can hear scratching noises through the spider door. Sounds like Tabetha is through that door. You decide to risk that door would be foolish. Return to your noted section and decide which door to go through or to stay put **but you cannot choose the spider door**.

1288

The safe looks standard with one keyhole to open it. But do you have a key?

If so, which one?

Brass Key – *1365*

Silver Key – *1467*

Gold Key – *486*

Or if you have no key or decide not to use one

Look at the desk – *206*

Check the rug that's slightly lifted – *565*

Look at the other rug – *1356*

Try to open the safe – *1288*

Decide this is a bad idea and return outside – *174*

1289

The safe looks standard with one keyhole to open it. But do you have a key?

If so, which one?

Brass Key – *378*

Silver Key – *1153*

Gold Key – *350*

Or if you have no key or decide not to use one

Look at the desk – *1167*

Check the rug that's slightly lifted – *169*

Look at the other rug – *366*

Decide this is a bad idea and return to Timmers, saying you should get back to the ship pronto – *351*

1290

You worry that you may not have enough to get clear, and you are right in that the first volley from the galleon hits you sending wood into the air. But the vessel holds fast, and you are just out of range of the next volley. However, that first volley did serious damage, and your crew are battered.

Reduce your crew morale by 1 level. Also reduce your vessel Storm Handling and Treasure Store by 1 level each as they were damaged in that last volley. Because you fled in a random direction it takes you time to recover your course. Add 2 days to the voyage time to allow for this.

Continue the voyage at *654*

The Treasure of Captain Estes

<u>1291</u>

You cannot stop yourself, but you manage to take the pole and swing it sideways, jamming it into the rock. The wind howls and you stay flat as you crawl your way back to the entrance. The wind does not abate until you are back at the junction. You breathe a sigh of relief, but you are faced with the same choice minus your pole.

Remove the circle around your chosen pole and untick the codeword. You may choose another pole to use if you have one. If so, circle that codeword and continue.

What will you do now?

Walk and enter

Victory – *702*

Senorita Marie – *199*

Elmsdale – *832*

Or crawl and enter

Victory – *342*

Senorita Marie – *815*

Elmsdale – *1254*

Or do you beat a hasty retreat – *34*

<u>1292</u>

You throw the culprits in the brig, where they rot for the voyage. But there's still an underlying fear amongst the crew of each other, one you've only partly stopped.

Reduce your crew by 1 level if you can, if not reduce your speed by 1 level due to lack of crew, until your crew goes up a level. If you can do neither you're in bad enough shape as it is.

Also reduce your crew morale by 1 level as they now live in fear of each other.

Now continue the voyage at *654*

1293

You watch the guard pass by from your hiding place, keeping a track on them, but unable to move freely while they are about. It takes them a while to clear the area as they look here and there. **Remove 6 time.** Finally they are clear but you have had to abort your previous action. Return to *433* and choose again but ignore the time adjustment at that entry this time round.

1294

You say that you cannot afford the time and ask the crew to get back to work. They are disappointed but still in a good mood after the wedding.

Increase your crew morale by 1 level.

Now continue the voyage at *654*

1295

You find the pull of the main current tough to overcome to get to the eddy, but you do it eventually. **Reduce your Waters Strength Chart by 1.** You swim through to the eddy. Go to *1087*

The Treasure of Captain Estes

<u>1296</u>

"She's powerful is this one," says your first officer, "but we are too. It's a poor vessel and we should be able to take it."

Do you

Sail away – *322*

Make a course for the square-rigged vessel – *538*

<u>1297</u>

"How much will it be to enter?" you ask pointing to some doubloons you have. The bald man rubs his chin and then tells you.

If you have the codeword Flunk, it is 4,000 doubloons.

If you have the codeword Rumour, it is 2,000 doubloons.

If you have the codeword Flop, it is 8,000 doubloons.

If you have the codeword Wanted, it is 1,00 doubloons.

The price is 3,000 doubloons if you have none of the codewords.

If you choose to pay, reduce your doubloons and go to *306*

Otherwise, do you

Leave it to your officer – *1241*

Decide you have an item you can offer to prove your worth – *229*

Decide the price is too high and leave Hells Deep – **Consult the voyage chart and set sail**

1298

You draw your knife and point it at the man but hear a musket click behind you. The barman has raced over and is now threatening to shoot you in the head. "Out," he says, "and slowly. Very slowly, or I will shoot."

You realise it is time to leave and you slow put your knife away and begin to walk away but feel the portly man pinch your bottom as you leave. It takes all your restraint not to turn and knife him. But there is still a musket at your head as you walk out the door back to the crossroads. **You cannot come back into the Admiral's Whiskers. Go to 802**

1299

You have a large crew compliment in the water with you and there is a tense standoff. You can see the cave in front but even with your numbers you will struggle to get in there and out, never mind search for something.

You can call this a stalemate and leave the island and the wreck – *632*

Or do you have the following codewords and wish to use the items

Spear – *271*

Orange Algae – *576*

Green Plant – *609*

Eye Charm – *1382*

Bodach Sword – *152*

The Treasure of Captain Estes

1300

You steer in past the rocks, watching your bow carefully. It's tight but you believe you can make it. Your first officer warns you that the rocks may narrow here and there and that turning may be an issue, but you are desperate to see if Estes left anything here. Soon you reach your first decision. Go to **525**

1301

You drop down to pick up the wine bottle and as you stand up you feel a sword being pressed into your back. The pirate was never asleep and he is now angry.

"Nothing doing here. Time to be about your business."

Do you

Walk back to the street with your hands in the air – **129**

Take a swing at him with the bottle – **1458**

1302

You see the darts fly out and fall to the floor scrabbling back the way you came. You stand up and see the darts now lying around but are unsure if the trap will fire again. Go to **843**

1303

The only wall of fire is to the west. You can route south, east or north from your current location.

Do you

Go East – **176**

Go South – **831**

Go North – **583**

Beware the Ghost Pirate!

1304

As you approach the small houses, made of wood and thatch, you understand that this is a place where ladies of the night entertain male pirates. There's clearly nothing for you here but you see several working girls talking around a fire with a pot on the boil over it.

Do you

Sit down beside them – *1171*

Offer them some money for information – *1369*

Or decide this is not a place you want to explore and return to your vessel - *314*

1305

You see lots of parchment on the desk as well as a half-finished bottle of rum. There are manifests of ships, but a quick scan reveals nothing that can help you in your search for Estes' treasure.

Go to *415*

1306

Who do you say your Captain is?

Simon Kilmer – *875*

Robert Grimshaw – *1215*

Diggory Hurst – *1394*

Timmers – *106*

Martha Downham – *1243*

Black Robert – *173*

1307

You step onto the pillar and feel a slight wobble as the wind blows past you. There are pillars to your left, right and behind. You can see a small item on the pillar directly behind you.

Do you step

To your left – *1363*

To your right – *1429*

Backwards – *448*

1308

Yes, it's in the middle cup. Double your stake money and get your stake back. Once you've noted that down, do you want to play again? Is so, with whom?

Look to join the one-legged pirate's game – *1181*

Engage in the stumpy pirate's game – *1316*

Play in the female pirate's game – *618*

If not go to *64*

1309

You send for your offering, and it is brought before Tom who touches it carefully, examining it. He smiles and a child takes your offering away.

"Beware the sea wind that blows from below only a needle shape can ever remain on the ground."

You wonder what Tom is on about, but you make sure to note what he says. **Tick the codeword Wind.**

What now?

Do you want to offer another gift - *1416*

Or do you take your leave of Tom and

Visit the provisions isle – *334*

Enjoy yourself at the wild isle – *879*

Explore the dark isle – *397*

Approach the pirate king – *1348*

Decide you have had enough of Hells Deep and set sail - **Consult the voyage chart and set sail**

1310

You take out some coins and show them to the door man and ask for access to the building. He grabs you by the collar and throws you into the street, shaking his head.

"Don't come back! I know your face."

You cannot return to the Mariner's Guild in daylight, during this visit to Malin's Town, as you are now identified as a loser.

Do you

Come back at night in an attempt to gain access when the building is closed – *742*

See to the needs of your vessel and crew – *903*

Try to earn some money by signing up to a cargo run – *1335*

Visit the taverns for information – *802*

If you have had enough of Malin's town, then **consult the voyage chart and set sail**.

<u>1311</u>

You listen at the window but cannot hear any activity outside. Do you

Climb back down the pole and leave the Guild – *212*

Or if you haven't already

Search the desk – *1224*

Look at the charts – *469*

Examine the sextant – *153*

Go to the portrait – *417*

Check out the drawers – *741*

<u>1312</u>

Reduce your Waters Strength Chart by 1. The current is pushing you north. However, you think you can reach an eddy that seems to allow a way south but to get there will be incredibly hard work. Do you

Swim South – *962*

Float North – *8*

<u>1313</u>

You remember the instructions you found with regard to the Drops of Daniel. They said you should ignore any items on the pillars but rather that you should make a Celtic cross pattern when you walk, reaching all four edges of the cross.

Now return to *830* and decide if you dare cross or turn away from the Drops.

1314

You think what you have on you and pull out your best item as a bribe. Handing it over the pirate stares at it and then glowers at you.

"You cannot bribe a man of Black Robert. He would kill me. Go now, before I strike you down."

You panic and run back to the street at *1256*. **Untick the codeword for the item you selected to bribe the pirate with. Don't return to the building unless you are dressed differently.**

1315

You walk up to Captain Fareham who looks delighted to see you. He takes his cloak and wraps you up in it, telling you it will be alright. Quickly he puts you on a horse and with a guard you are taken to the garrison where you will find out what plans he has for you.

Go to *1031*

1316

The small pirate looks up and scowls at you before pointing to the three cups in front of him. "Do you want to play? I can take a stake up to 400 Doubloons. Place your money down and we will start."

The other pirates look at you expectantly. If you want to play, make a note of how many doubloons you are placing as your stake. Now go to *1376*.

If you decide it isn't worth the gamble, then return to *1424* and pick a different option.

1317

You wait for the sentry and as soon as they are out through the gate you run inside to the interior of the fort. **Reduce your time by 2 for this effort.** Continue at *812*

<u>1318</u>

Roll 1xD100 (2xD10). For every point of damage you have already done to the galleon add 3 to the result. Check the table below for the result of this round of the sea battle.

00-29 – You get caught with a severe broadside. **Lower your vessel manoeuvrability by 2 levels and your vessel speed by 1 level.**

30-49 – A volley lands on deck killing many of the crew. **Lower your crew by 1 level.**

50-69 – A volley blows out some of your canons, but you hit back – **Lower your firepower by 1 level.** But you cause the following damage dependent on your firepower: **Light – 1 point, Moderate – 2pts, Heavy – 3pts, Very Heavy – 4 pts**

70-89 – You land a splendid volley. Note you have done the following damage dependent on your firepower: **Light – 1 point, Moderate – 2pts, Heavy – 3pts, Very Heavy – 4 pts**

90 and up - You catch them cold with a blinding manoeuvre. Note you have done the following damage dependent on your firepower: **Light – 2 point, Moderate – 4pts, Heavy – 6pts, Very Heavy – 8 pts**

If you have caused 24 points of damage overall to the galleon – *1001*

If not

Do you want to continue the battle – *761*

Do you wish to run – *87*

<u>1319</u>

"Hello there," says the figure as you approach, "you'd better get down the alley to the hostel. They don't like anyone touting their wares outside of the building. But maybe see you later."

The figure remains in shadow, and you decide it best to let things be and walk on down the alley. Go to *828*

1320

4 Skull 1 Scales 0 Coins

That was so close, you can feel the sweat dripping over your face. But it is a loss. (If you lost a body part go to *86*) **Untick the stake item from your codewords**, and return to *1060*

1321

As you wait to see what he will say a trapdoor opens beneath you and you fall into a chute which makes you tumble out of the barge and into the waters around it. As you surface, a few children are laughing at you from the barge. Indignant, you swim to your vessel to dry off and decide your next course of action.

Go to see Blind Tom again – *681*

Visit the provisions isle – *334*

Enjoy yourself at the wild isle – *879*

Explore the dark isle – *397*

Approach the pirate king – *1348*

Decide you have had enough of Hells Deep and set sail - **Consult the voyage chart and set sail**

1322

You suddenly hear movement. There's a guard afoot, patrolling the area and although you can hear them you are not sure where they are coming from.

Are you in hiding?

Yes – *1293*

No – *1269*

1323

You see a black bull running directly at you and it doesn't look like it will move to avoid you. You are in the middle channel. What will you do?

Go right – *1047*

Stay in the middle – *466*

Go left – *298*

1324

You hear a murmur from the guards but as you walk away, they seem to settle down. Maybe they thought you were simply someone else. Go to *1166*

1325

You walk slowly into the temple and before your eyes the jungle beyond becomes ablaze. Maybe it's the incense that did it or maybe this is for real but either way, you can feel the heat of the fires and see before a woman who is half sea creature and half human. Her black hair seems to have a life of its own reminding you of the snake pit.

You stand in terror as she wields a knife before you and approaches. You see that blood drips from the knife already and her mouth seems to salivate as she casts her eyes over you.

"Ah, one of my own, sacrificing your crew to the dark. Come my child and have this."

She produces a compass and hands it to you. As you open it you see it is pointing already, but not north.

"Find the map it needs, and you will have Estes' treasure. Do not return until you have my treasure. You are one of the dark now, I have your very soul."

Tick the codeword Devil's Compass.

The Treasure of Captain Estes

Suddenly you are alone on the beach of the isle beside your small boat. You take it back to your vessel and ponder what to do next. **You cannot return to the dark isle again on this adventure until you have found the treasure.** What next?

Go to see Blind Tom – *681*

Visit the provisions isle – *334*

Enjoy yourself at the wild isle – *879*

Approach the pirate king – *1348*

Decide you have had enough of Hells Deep and set sail - **Consult the voyage chart and set sail.**

1326

You take the frame you found on the wall and look at it. There's a portrait of a middle aged woman there. It looks nice but you don't know her and neither do any of the crew. Looks like a waste of your time.

Return to *18* if you have more items to check. If not, the island still looks unappealing and barren, and your first officer agrees it is not worth exploring. The wreck is now fully underwater and shifting, making it too dangerous to go back to. I guess you're out of luck here.

Set sail for a new destination by consulting the voyage chart. Tick the codeword Return

1327

You take the spear and attach the green plant to the end of it and then swing the spear at the crab creatures. You swim up and grab a breath before making for the cave entrance, still keeping the spear ahead of you. The crab creatures crowd you but stay back, fearful of the plant.

You enter the cave and see why they are so defensive of the place. There are crab younglings everywhere. And yet there is also a place in the middle of the cave that no crab seems to go near. You walk over to it and see a black cylindrical object. You grab it as you are short of air and quickly retreat from the cave.

Using the spear and plant combination, you return to your vessel and the cheers of your crew. Drying off you look at the item you found.

"It's the Devil's Compass, alright," says the first officer as you open it up. It's a compass, but the needle is simply spinning endlessly round. **Tick the codeword Devil's Compass.**

"Time to set sail," you say.

Set sail for a new destination by consulting the voyage chart.

1328

The volley from the canons rips through the air and you are again encompassed in smoke. This time you don't need to wait for the smoke to clear for a tentacle grabs the very deck you stand on ripping it to shreds. You fly into the air, unable to halt your progress and end up in the water. You find yourself being dragged down in a spiral of water and the air is driven from your lungs as you struggle. Soon you succumb to the water.

The waters around New Southampton are deadly, and the Kraken possibly one of its most dangerous inhabitants. You may try again at *1*

1329

You wander along the path, breathing heavily, and reach a junction. Which way now?

Left – *1230*

Right – *328*

Turn back – *707*

1330

Reduce your time by 1. Stepping forward you feel a wooden wall ahead. This wall extends to your left but to your right there is only water.

Do you

Turn right and walk forward – **90**

About turn and step forward – **899**

1331

As soon as you go for your weapon, Annie shoots and she shoots to kill. You fall to the ground, shot in the head, and soon everything is black. Maybe a bit more guile next time. Try again at **1**

1332

Reduce your time by 2. If your time is in the following gaps (52-47 or 22-17) then go to *1377*. If not continue below

You look at the scrolls on top of the barrel and most are to do with shipments of rum or fruit, or some other commodity. One takes your fancy though and seems to be a discourse on dealing with kraken. Unusual to find it here but you guess everyone has their favourite reading material – if they can read! **If you wish to take the kraken scroll, tick the codeword Human Bait.**

Do you

Wait in hiding – **926**

If you haven't already

Investigate the papers in the hut – **77**

Move to the north quarter – **1176**

Move to the south quarter – **519**

1333

You walk forward into the darkness and realise it is a true darkness. As you walk you feel a wind at your back pushing you forward, and you start to stumble. You are pitching along and cannot stop yourself.

Do you have pole in front of you – *464*. If not, read on.

You stumble with an unrelenting wind behind you. Suddenly the ground beneath you vanishes, realised by you as your feet find nothing and you fall. It is only a few moments before the ground comes up and hits you hard.

Where did you dig that vessel name from? New Southampton Harbour? Such a pity as you had got so far.

You can reset to the start of this puzzle at *1366* if you want or start all over again at 1. That was a long haul, and you did so well, just not well enough.

1334

You remember what you were told about having a ship that cannot be heard by the sea creatures or other vessels as it sails across the water. It may be an old seaman's tale but maybe it could work.

If you want to try to run silent – *265*

If not, return to *368* and choose again.

1335

Cargo runs are good earners, especially if you are short on your money. You take a walk along the harbour and find several buildings where cargo runs are being negotiated. The main routes are to New Southampton, Strangar via New Southampton, Fort August, and also a few small cargo transfers out towards the Bird's Paradise and the wreck of the Marie Saratoga.

When you visit there are three runs available for you to choose from, but which ones?

Roll 1xD100 (2xD10) and check the result below. Do this three times. These are your three options for transport.

The Treasure of Captain Estes

Die result	Route	Cargo	Payment
00-09	Malin's Town – New Southampton	Salted fish 10 cargo spaces (5,000 doubloons)	500 Doubloons
10-19	Malin's Town – Fort August	Cannonballs 5 cargo spaces (5,000 doubloons)	500 Doubloons
20-29	Malin's Town – New Southampton	Wheat 10 cargo spaces (4,000 doubloons)	600 Doubloons
30-39	New Southampton – Fort August	Barley 15 Cargo spaces	1,000 Doubloons
40-49	Bird's Paradise – Malin's Town	Asian Wood 2 cargo spaces (10,000 doubloons)	1,500 Doubloons
50-59	Fort August – Malin's Town	Empty Barrels 10 cargo spaces (100 Doubloons)	1,000 Doubloons
60-69	New Southampton – Malin's Town	Rum 15 cargo spaces (20,000 doubloons)	2,000 Doubloons
70-79	Marie Saratoga – New Southampton	Casket no cargo allowance (50,000 doubloons)	5,000 Doubloons
80-89	Fort August – Marie Saratoga	Wrapped package of a gold cross (15,000 doubloons)	3,000 doubloons
90-99	New Southampton – Bird's Paradise	Small casket no cargo allowance (20,000 doubloons)	4,000 doubloons

Having found what three cargo runs are on offer, select one (or none). Record the cargo run you want to attempt in the *Cargo Run Planner at App 12*. If your run starts in Malin's Town, place the required cargo in your hold. It takes a day to do this whatever the cargo is as you need to rendezvous for the smaller but more precious loads. If your run starts elsewhere, when you arrive at the initial loading point, then spend a day loading, and then a day offloading at the destination.

Note you are liable for the cargo you carry. Mark on your *Voyage Time Chart* when you load the cargo and then 30 days after. If you have not delivered within the 30 days you are considered to have stolen the cargo and will be arrested if you land at Malin's Town, New Southampton or Fort August. If you lose the cargo, you need to return to Malin's Town to pay its cost (the cargo's cost, not the job payment). The Cargo run guide will keep you straight, so consult it when you load cargo for transport.

You are given 200 doubloons on acceptance of the cargo run and then are paid the remainder on arrival at the destination.

Having completed your business and adjusted your vessel chart and the time chart, decide what to do next in Malin's Town.

Do you

See to the needs of your vessel and crew – **903**

Visit the taverns for information – **802**

Visit the Mariners' Guild for information – **124**

If your first officer is Simon Kilmer – **24**

If your First officer is Robert Grimshaw – **737**

If your First officer is Diggory Hurst – **786**

If you have had enough of Malin's town, then **consult the voyage chart and set sail.**

The Treasure of Captain Estes

<u>1336</u>

You have been walking round the market with many faces looking at you and you are bound to be noticed for who you really are. Have you a disguise?

If you are

In a long -coat and breeches then **return to the section you came from.**

Wearing a dress or a slave girl's outfit ripped from a nightgown then **continue below.**

You see the faces watching you and know people are whispering the name Hastings. You need to get out of the market and fast.

Do you have the codeword **Prominent - *868***

If not, you leave the market at a brisk pace. **Tick the codeword Prominent** and return to the street at ***496***. Don't return to the market!

<u>1337</u>

Reduce your Waters Strength Chart by 1. The current is terribly strong, and you are swept north. There is nothing you can do except float to ***1238***

<u>1338</u>

There is a break in the rocks, and you can see three paths out of this junction you have wandered into. You can route north, southeast or southwest, and all the channels look equally wide and capable of accommodating your vessel.

Do you

Sail north – ***1263***

Take the southeast channel – ***452***

Go southwest from here – ***1198***

1339

Reduce your time by 1. You walk forward and feel around. On your right is a chair that appears fixed. On your left and ahead is clear water.

Do you

Turn left and walk forward – **709**

About turn and step forward – **107**

Step forward – **1344**

1340

You made a dark pact when you sacrificed your crewmates, and you are tied to your master from that day. Despite being within sight of New Southampton, an eerie fog begins to surround your vessel and you feel an unearthly cold in your bones.

Beside your vessel another rises from the sea, one you have seen before for it is the Devil's sloop. Spectres begin to swirl around your rigging and the crew begin to panic. But as they start to take to arms, the spectres grab them all, including your first mate, and pin them to the deck.

One spectre, whose eyes contain an ethereal fire, approaches you. You kneel before it, but a wispy hand brings you back to your feet.

Do you have any of the following treasure in your cargo?

Treasure of Drops of Daniel

Treasure of Waters of Myra

Treasure of Wall of Fire

Treasure of Winds of the World

Treasure of Bulls of the Plain

Is so – **1353**

If not – **661**

1341

Your first officer glowers at you. "That is not how we command a vessel. I see I was wrong about you. Get off my ship," he yells, and he urges the crew to join him. You are picked up and unceremoniously thrown overboard where you fight to stay above water. You watch as the vessel sails off leaving you far from land. You try to swim but you tire quickly and then slowly sink into the vast water around you, never to be heard from again.

Try again at *1*

1342

"Your no Captain," says the man on crutches. "get out before we run you through!"

You see swords being pulled and a musket pointed at you. This is a fight you won't win and besides you wanted information which isn't going to happen. As you walk out the door, you hear the man sneer.

"Don't come back until you have something of note."

Dejected you return to the crossroads – *802*

1343

You see a guard atop the wall and take cover waiting until they have continued further along to the west. **Reduce your time by 6. Go to *42***

1344

You step forward but there's no floor and you sink down. You panic and, in a frenzy, reach out desperately, grabbing whatever you can. Your hand finds the rough edge of some floor and you pull yourself up and onto the safe wood. As you try to relax and think where you are in the dark, you realise you are totally disorientated and have no idea.

(Turn over the page)

Roll 1xD100 (2xD10)

00-33 – **600**

34-67 – **1426**

68-99 – **35**

1345

You send a volley at the creature and try to peer through the copious smoke from your canon. You wonder if your volley was enough.

Roll 1xD100 (2xD10)

00-49 – **936**

50-99 – **1016**

1346

You see a black bull running directly at you and it doesn't look like it will move to avoid you. You are in the right channel. What will you do?

Stay right – **547**

Go to the middle – **466**

Go to the left channel – **298**

1347

You push out into the jungle and force your way through past several pieces of vegetation. Soon there is no sight of the path but neither does the vegetation in front of you ease up. Eventually you come across a path again, but you have no idea where you are or how long it took you to get here. You're not even sure you are in the same part of the jungle you started in. This place is strange beyond belief, maybe even magical, or cursed!

The Treasure of Captain Estes

You strike back out on the path again but where are you?

Roll 1xD100 (2xD10) and go to the result below. Deduct the time indicated from your Island Time Chart and then go to your next indicated section to see where you end up.

00-19 – Reduce time chart by 2, go to *827*

20-39 – *280*

40-59 – Reduce time chart by 1, go to *758*

60-79 – Reduce time chart by 17, go to *854*

80-99 – *280*

<u>1348</u>

You decide to try and gain an audience with the pirate king. Your first officer tells you that not everyone is able to gain an audience and that to get one you will need to provide a gift but what you learn may be priceless. You'll need to decide on what to take to his isle with you before you enter his abode.

What have you got that you can afford to give away? Do you have any of the following codewords and can give the item or information associated with them as a gift for the audience with the pirate king.

Do you decide to give

Johnstone's Confuser, Bird Whistle, Bird chart, Instruction Book, Compass Map – *22*

Devil's Compass, Bearing A, Bearing B, Bearing C, Bearing D – *1041*

Bodach Sword, Sextant, Noiseless Horn, Eye Charm – *1360*

Gold Medallion, Gold Chain, Monkey, Argyle – *733*

Green plant, Orange Algae, Brass Key, Silver key, Spear, Empty Chart – *1189*

1349

You sail down the channel, but something seems wrong. All around your vessel a fog is gathering and consumes it in a matter of moments. Your crew cry out in fear, but you tell them to be quiet, listening intently as you can see nothing. As the fog begins to clear you find yourself sailing into another junction but are you in the same channel you started in?

Roll 1xD100 (2xD10) and consult the table below

01-20 go to *191*

21-40 go to *698*

41-60 go to *1448*

61-80 go to *1030*

81-00 go to *606*

1350

"You come in here and waste my time!" The doctor shouts for one of the pirates outside the room. "Get this bog rat out of here, and don't be too kind about it."

You are grabbed and taken to the street where you are thrown to the ground. Your attacker spits on you and then walks off leaving you with wounds that ache even more now. If you haven't used up your allotted turns, go to **1256**

1351

You take off your hat and let your hair hang down. You give a grin, hoping they will take you in as a sister.

"So, you are a girl? Well, the king will like that. Make sure you show your hair if you come before him. But are you a woman? What have you done to be a pirate?"

The Treasure of Captain Estes

Do you

Tell them a tale of your adventures – *636*

Offer some money – *213*

Or apologise, tuck your hair in and leave the deck, and then

Approach the pirates with the monkey figure – *305*

Join the main bar – *594*

Or leave the tavern and

Make for the small houses – *1304*

Approach the gambling groups – *1424*

Go to see the fights – *84*

Decide this is not a place you want to explore and return to your vessel
- *314*

1352

"The fugitive!" cries a man as soon as you mention Diggory's name.
You see others suddenly reach for swords and you can see a clear path
to the door, so you run for your life. As you reach the crossroads
panting you realise that was a rather dumb move. You need to
remember just where you are. **You cannot come back into the
Admiral's Whiskers. Go to *802***

1353

The spectre speaks.

"You have honoured our master and so he will reward you. Come,
Captain of the Devil's Sloop, he has need of you."

The spectre leads you on board the mystical vessel alongside your own.
You find yourself gliding over the deck rail and onto the strange vessel.
Behind you, you hear your previous vessel being dragged down to the

depths and the cries of men. There is cracking wood and screams. But you care not!

Your life is now in servitude to the darkest of masters and you are feared wherever you appear. In your twisted state, you find joy in every soul you dispatch, and your wickedness continues. It is over a hundred years before you finally face a holy man with a blessed spear who finally removes you from your corporate existence.

Was this a win? Was this the life you hoped for? If so, I do pity you. If not, at least you are released from your servitude to whatever hell the afterlife brings.

Go to *1* to try again

1354

2 Skull 2 Scales 1 Coins

You lose. (If you lost a body part go to *86*) **Untick the stake item from your codewords**, and return to *1060*

1355

Reduce the Hot Strip by 2. If this places you on a Fire spot add 20 to this section's number and go there for the walls have moved. There are walls of fire to the south, west, and east, so you route north from your current location. Go to *310*

1356

Reduce your time by 1.

If your time is in the following gaps (52-48) you see a guard on his patrol outside and must remain hidden until he clears the area. Reduce your time by 6. Now continue at the plain text below

This rug is slightly smaller and seems to be sitting trim to the floor. You pull it back revealing a trapdoor but with a finger hole punched to allow it to be lifted. Below is a dank passage, smelling of mildew and stale air. You wonder where this goes, is this one of the tunnels?

Do you

Enter the tunnel – *161*

Or replace the trapdoor and rug and then

Look at the desk – *206*

Look at the other rug – *565*

Try to open the safe – *1288*

Decide this is a bad idea and return outside – *174*

1357

You wander along the path, the quiet driving you mad, and reach a junction. Which way now?

Left – *1273*

Right – *172*

Turn back – *1191*

1358

You are hauled before the fort commander in the middle of the night, and he does not look best pleased, he tells you that you are obviously not working alone and there must be a vessel out there that you are part of. So, he throws you into the cells at the fort and you prepare for a lonely existence.

Who is your first officer?

Simon Kilmer or Robert Grimshaw –*355*

Diggory Hurst –*1445*

Timmers –*74*

Martha Downham or Black Robert or a replacement first officer – *729*

1359

You wander along the path and reach a junction. Which way now?

Left – *776*

Right – *347*

Turn back – *1004*

1360

Add a modifier of 20 when asked in the next section. Go to *207*

1361

You walk forward into the darkness and realise it is a true darkness. As you walk you feel a wind at your back pushing you forward, and you start to stumble. You are pitching along and cannot stop yourself.

Do you have pole in front of you – *928*. If not, read on.

You stumble with an unrelenting wind behind you. Suddenly the ground beneath you vanishes, realised by you as your feet find nothing and you fall. It is only a few moments before the ground comes up and hits you hard.

Guess you don't know your pirates. Such a pity as you had got so far.

You can reset to the start of this puzzle at *1366* if you want or start all over again at *1*. That was a long haul, and you did so well, just not well enough.

The Treasure of Captain Estes

<u>1362</u>

You've been caught unawares out in the open and have to scramble for cover. Will you be able to find somewhere to hide.

Roll 1xD100 (2xD10)

01-25 – *130*

26-75 – *1228*

76-00 – *1379*

<u>1363</u>

You step onto the pillar with a sigh of relief. There are pillars to your front and to your right. **Tick the codeword Aisle if you haven't already**. You can see a small item on the pillar diagonally to your rear right.

Do you step

To your right – *1307*

Forwards – *816*

<u>1364</u>

"Looks bleak but bring it in close and blast it!"

Return to *927* and make your decision.

<u>1365</u>

Reduce your time by 1.

If your time is in the following gaps (52-48) you see a guard on his patrol outside and must remain hidden until he clears the area. Reduce your time by 6. Now continue at the plain text below

You place the key in the lock, and it doesn't even begin to fit.

Return to *1288* and make another choice.

<u>1366</u>

You come out from the jungle path and find a winding path up a cliff which takes you high up.

Do you have the codeword **Still** – *79*. If not, continue below

At the top you see that there is a wooden post and attached board with words inscribed on it. Beyond, you see three paths disappearing off into the cliff face, darkness looming.

You turn to the board and read the inscription on it:

'My treasure is kept beyond the Winds of the World, a series of passages that may lead to doom or to safety. Understand a mistake will be fatal, and you will never lay your hands on my treasure. Before each branching of the path there is a question with an answer above each opening. Choose wisely for only one will take you safely on, the other two leading to your doom. And once you start do not turn back, for you cannot and live. And walk, don't crawl! These are cursed cliffs, enter at your peril.'

Chilling words and you ponder what questions may come up. Will they be riddles? Demonstrations of knowledge? Puzzles involving numbers or geometry? You have no idea.

You note that the paths are narrow and lead to darkness. You may take items with you including any poles if you have the codewords **Green Pole, Red Pole,** or **Blue Pole.** What use they may be who knows.

Do you

Walk forward to the first branch in the path – *801*

Forget about this piece of the treasure and turn around – *1019*

1367

Reduce your time by 1.

If your time is in the following gaps (32-28 or 12-08), you see a guard on his patrol and must remain hidden until he clears the area. Reduce your time by 6. Now continue at the plain text below

If your time is in the following gaps (47-38), you see a guard on the enclosing wall patrolling and must remain hidden until he clears the area. Reduce your time by 6.

If neither of these apply, continue at the plain text below

You keep to the shadows, but no one comes. What will you do now?

Do you

Hide where you are – *1197*

Route through the open gate – *519*

Creep East – *1435*

Go North – *1393*

Approach the building before you to break in – *156*

1368

The provisions stalls are many and staffed by people who know the value of their merchandise. It might not be jewels but it is what keeps people alive, and these traders guard it jealously. You can tell to try and steal something would be too risky and ultimately not of great use to you right now. After browsing for a few moments, you decide to move on.

If this is your third stall visited in the market, note the number of this section, and then go to *1336*

(Turn over the page)

Otherwise, do you

Approach the jewellery stall – *1158*

Look at the whiskey and ale stalls – *155*

Or return to the street – *496*

1369

You take out some doubloons and hear a cry from behind you.

"You stand in line like every other one of you insatiable dogs. Now get out of here while they eat."

You turn and find a brush shoved in your face knocking you back into the sand. Pirates laugh as a large woman keeps hitting you until you leave the area.

"Don't come back!" she says fixing you with an evil eye. **You cannot visit the small houses again during this visit to Hell's Deep.**

Do you

Explore the tavern – *363*

Approach the gambling groups – *1424*

Go to see the fights – *84*

Decide this is not a place you want to explore and return to your vessel - *314*

1370

You spend the next few days at Strangar beside Black Robert, and he kits you out in clothing suitable for a pirate. You have a smart long-coat, boots, and breeches, as well as a cutlass and knife on your person.

The Treasure of Captain Estes

He takes you to see his pride and joy, the Medusa, a large galleon he captured off the Spanish, and an impressive vessel. It has a formidable number of guns and a large hold for carrying stores and treasure. In the Medusa, Black Robert tells you that no storm will be a problem, even the Kraken could not take down a vessel like this. You can see the immense pride he has in it, and you feel inspired by his talk.

"You want Estes, the pirate from where God only knows," says Black Robert, "but first we need to find him. I shall send out word and see where he is, so we can hunt the dog down and take back what he owes you. But I'll do it quietly for all the authorities would love to capture the pirate king."

You spend a week in Strangar being taught how to use your cutlass while you wait for word of Estes.

While you wait, it's time to fill in your vessel chart with the details of your vessel and crew. Look for the chart at the rear of the book. You may photocopy this for ease of use. Fill it in now.

First Officer: Black Robert

Vessel: Medusa - Galleon

Speed: Slow

Firepower: Very Heavy

Treasure store: Large

Shallows: No

Manoeuvrability: Lacking

Storm Handling: Good

Crew: Large

Initial Provisions: 15 sections

Doubloons: 2000

One day, Black Robert calls you to his room and you can see the frustration on his face. "Mary, I'm sorry but Estes is dead. He ran into the British and was defeated somewhere near New Southampton. However, rumour has it that he left his treasure on an island in the vicinity of New Southampton. The island, known only as the Dark Land, is only accessible at certain times and appears in different places, or so the story goes. I've never known anyone who has seen it. Many say it is a legend but there are dark things in these waters, more than you know, and Estes knew all about the dark matters."

"So, I have nothing," you say, "unless I chase this treasure."

"Unless you seek the island you will find neither the remains of Estes or his treasure, I believe."

"Well then, when do we start? And where should we go?"

"I have no definitive sightings of Estes before his last battle which was southeast of New Southampton. If you look at this chart, Mary, there are six places in the general locale where he could have been before he died and which may be able to shed light on his travels, and where the island is. Once you have examined them all, give the crew orders of where to sail to."

Check the *chart of New Southampton at App 02* to help you in your decisions. You may photocopy it for use with this book. Turn now to section *1276* to learn about the six locations and about sailing around New Southampton, and then to make your first decision as captain!

1371

"We need to get to the gate and then to the shore," says Diggory. You remember seeing the courtyard of the garrison as being a busy place of traders and soldiers. The crowd could help making it easier to escape but you could also be running into a lot of soldiers. Alternatively, you could climb up the stone stairs beside the jail to the wall that surrounds the garrison and make your way round it to the gatehouse and descend there. There may be soldiers on the wall, but they cannot surround you on a wall like they could in a courtyard. Neither way seems easy but then again you are on the run. Whatever you decide, do it quick!

Do you

Go down through the courtyard to escape – *289*

Or run to wall surrounding the garrison – *352*

1372

The current is brutal and you are swept east. There is nothing you can do except float to *489*

1373

Your crew gets excited as you order your vessel to engage the schooner before you. But it appears that Jeboe doesn't want a fight and he turns away from you. He's as fast as they come and after a day's chasing, the vessel is long gone.

Add 1 day to your voyage time for the pursuit.

Continue the voyage at *654*

1374

Do you have the codeword **Anna** – *162*

If not go to *1311*

1375

The day is bright, the sails full and you are making good progress to your destination when the crow's nest shouts out.

"Captain, there's a disturbance in the water up ahead."

You race to the foredeck and stare at the ripples in the water, that build and build until you think there's a massive school of dolphins out there. You wonder just what is happening and cannot believe it as the disturbance seems to split in two to surround your vessel.

A woman's head pops out of the water, followed by another. There's blonde hair, black hair, brown, red, all colours and white skin, which all most shines in the water like a fish's scales. The women seem to rise until their top halves are above the water's surface, and you note they have nothing on.

A song begins amongst the women, and you don't recognise any words, but you see the male crew members begin to walk towards the edge of the vessel. There's a lilt in the song but it doesn't grab you and you struggle to find it pleasant. Not so the male crew members, who seem enticed, eyes wide and in complete wonder.

Do you have the codewords

Noiseless Horn – *146*

Female Crew – *752*

If not, read on

The male crew members begin to leap into the water, crying out their love for these women in the sea, mermaids as you now realise. You run to close down the hatches and doors to below deck. You need to move quickly for you have lost all of the crew above deck.

Roll 1xD100 (2 xD10). Check the result below. If Martha Downham is your first officer then take 30 off your result. If you then have a minus result treat it as 00.

00-15 - **You manage to close the hatches and doors so quickly that only the crew up on deck throw themselves overboard. Lower your crew by 1 level. Lower crew morale by 1 level.**

16-50 - **You manage to close the hatches and doors in quick fashion but some extra crew from below get up on deck and throw themselves overboard as well. Lower your crew by 2 levels. Lower crew morale by 2 levels.**

51-80 - **You manage to close the hatches and doors in quick fashion but some extra crew from are grabbed from where the canons are manned when the mermaids slam into the vessel causing a breach. Lower your crew by 2 levels. Lower crew morale by 2 levels. Lower your Firepower by 1 level.**

81-99 – **The escape of the men from below deck seems impossible to stop and you are overwhelmed. So many throw themselves to the water. Lower your crew by 2 levels. Lower crew morale by 2 levels.**

As soon as the men hit the water the mermaids dive on them, devouring them like wild sharks tearing at a fish. The sea runs red, and you fight to keep your vessel moving away from the blood fest in the water. It is the best part of a day before you can re-establish course from the direction you fled to at random when the mermaids attacked. **Add 2 days to your voyage time to return to your original course.**

Now continue your voyage at **654**

1376

The pirate places a coin into the central cup of three and turns them all upside down. His hands then become a blur as the cups are moved around at pace before being reset in a line.

"Now call," says the pirate, indicating you should choose the left cup, the middle cup or the right cup.

Do you choose

Left – **649**

Middle – **1025**

Right – **524**

1377

You suddenly hear movement. There's a guard afoot, patrolling the area and although you can hear them you are not sure where they are coming from.

Are you in hiding?

Yes – **148**

No – **403**

1378

You have run the gap and the rock formation widens allowing you to give further bulls a wide birth. You race up to the treasure casket, at the far end of the plain, and marvel at what is inside. Treasure beyond your dreams. Now you are on the other side of the rock formation, you are able to lift up the casket and run after the bulls, barely getting to the other side before thundering hooves race past you.

You have the Bulls of the Plain casket. Tick the codeword **Bullied**.

So, what now? How much time is left for more treasure?

Route back down the jungle path to **1145**

1379

Oh dear. Before you can find cover, you hear a shout and turn to see a rifle pointed at you. The guard calls out for reinforcements and soon you are surrounded. You have been caught. Go to **1358**

1380

You sail past vicious rocks and then realise you have reached clear sea. Currently you are to the southeast of the formation. You can re-enter here or try one of the other entry points. Of course, you may have had enough and decide to go elsewhere.

The Treasure of Captain Estes

Do you

 Sail into the north entry point – *1260*

Try the southwest entry point – *246*

Take the southeast entry point – *1300*

Or sail to a different destination – **Consult the voyage chart**

<u>1381</u>

Reduce your time by 1. Stepping forward you run into a wooden wall. On your right you can feel some crates but to your left is open water.

Do you

About turn and step forward – *541*

Turn left and walk forward – *588*

Examine the crates – *85*

<u>1382</u>

You hold the eye charm up in front of you in a dramatic pose. The nearest creature scuttles up and plucks it from your hand. **Untick the codeword Eye Charm.** Well, that didn't work.

Do you have the following codewords and wish to use the items

Spear – *271*

Orange Algae – *576*

Green Plant – *609*

Bodach Sword – *152*

If not, or you choose not to try them, you need to swim back to your vessel before the creatures get any closer.

If your vessel is in the shallows – *632*

If not, and it is anchored further out – *672*

1383

Do you have the codeword **Debbie** – *162*

If not go to *1311*

1384

You return to your ship, sodden and wondering what to do next. The island still looks unappealing and barren, and your first officer agrees it is not worth exploring. The wreck is now fully underwater and shifting making it too dangerous to go back to. I guess you're out of luck here.

Set sail for a new destination by consulting the voyage chart.

1385

You grab hold of one of the treasure caskets as it strikes your foot. Desperately you haul it with you to the vessel and feel the arms of your crew haul you aboard. Soaking you gasp for breath and look around to see who else has been rescued. All the crew from the small boat are standing there but some of the treasure caskets are missing. You realise you have lost 50% of the treasure that was in the small boat. **Adjust this amount now on the Island Time Chart**. There is a silence among the crew but there is little else you can do. Go to *725*

1386

You have returned to your vessel and now sit just off the island wondering what to do next.

Do you

Tell the crew to sail to the north of the island – *468*

Order the vessel to be taken to the south – *254*

Route for the centre of the island – *746*

Decide to set sail - **consult the voyage chart**

1387

Reduce the Hot Strip by 1. If this places you on a Fire spot add 20 to this section's number and go there for the walls have moved. There are walls of fire to the south and east. You can route north or west from your current location.

Do you

Go West – *929*

Go North – *394*

1388

You run quickly across the room, but you hear a swish as you do so. Small darts fire out from the walls, and you desperately try to avoid them. But are you quick?

Roll 1xD100 (2XD10) and check the result below

01-25 *241*

26-50 *819*

50-75 *1302*

76-00 *56*

1389

The only wall of fire is to the west. You can route south, east or north from your current location.

Do you

Go East – *321*

Go South – *552*

Go North – *1200*

1390

You order your first officer to keel haul them. The men are tied up to ropes which run underneath the vessel, and they are dragged across the bottom of it, their backs being ripped on the barnacles attached to the keel of the vessel. The men are in agony when they come back on deck, and you slap them both on the face to show your displeasure.

It may have seemed harsh but the punishment seems to have worked and the crew strangely seems to feel safer and less at risk from their crewmates.

Reduce your crew by 1 level if you can, if not reduce your speed by 1 level due to lack of crew, until your crew goes up a level. If you can do neither you're in bad enough shape as it is.

Now continue the voyage at **654**

1391

You walk forward into the darkness shaking as you do so. As you walk you feel that same wind at your back pushing you forward, and you start to stumble. You stumble along unable to stop yourself. But the floor remains, solid beneath your feet.

Up ahead you see daylight again and you emerge out into the cool sunlight with yet more branching paths and another post and a board. This time it reads

'What was my first captured vessel?'

You look up above the dark entrances back into the cliffs and see three answers: *Victory, Senorita Marie, Elmsdale.*

Here we go again! Do you walk the path that leads to

Victory – **702**

Senorita Marie – **199**

Elmsdale – **832**

Or do you turn around and forget these crazy questions to head back down to the jungle path – **335**

The Treasure of Captain Estes

<u>1392</u>

You can't resist it and start to grab a pair of breeches, a long-coat, and some boots. As you do so, the door bursts open and a guard casts his eye around the room, instantly sizing up the situation. He grabs you, telling the others to help Madame Le Vert. You have your hands bound and are taken back to the garrison to Captain Fareham.

The captain knows the value to him of your father's lands although they have been ransacked and he forces you to become part of his plan and you are married in private. Fareham now owns your father's lands and keeps you locked up for the next year. When you don't respond to his advances and wishes to be a passive wife, he has you taken away in the night and disposed of. Your last thoughts are that your family remains unavenged. Try again at *1* and remember enemies are everywhere, even those people who help.

<u>1393</u>

Reduce your time by 1.

If your time is in the following gaps (27-23 or 17-13) and you are not hidden, then go to *1037*. If you are hidden, you see a guard on his patrol and must remain hidden until he clears the area. Reduce your time by 6. Now continue at the plain text below

If your time is in the following gaps (52-48 or 12-08) and you are not hidden, then go to *1128*. If you are hidden, you see a guard on the enclosing wall patrolling and must remain hidden until he clears the area. Reduce your time by 6.

If neither of these apply, continue at the plain text below

You can see before you the shadow of a large building with a single person wooden door. There appears to be no one on guard.

To the south and north, you can see similar buildings to what is before you, while to the east there is another building and something further beyond, although the darkness makes it hard to see.

Do you

Hide where you are – *54*

Route South – *1197*

Creep East – *103*

Go North – *785*

Approach the building before you to break in – *989*

1394

You say your supposed Captain's name and Lord Buffington almost collapses.

"Robert! Robert! Bring your sword we have a pirate in our midst!"

Robert rushes into the room, but you manage to give him a shove and run past him racing to the front doors and out to the street beyond. Unfortunately, there is a cry to the air and you see yourself being pursued by the guild. They hunt you all the way back to your vessel which has to set sail immediately. You are a known face now and must lie low for a while.

For the next ten days on your time chart, you must avoid New Southampton and Fort August, and avoid Malin's Town for the next twenty. Now consult the voyage chart and set sail to a different destination

1395

The hut is made of straw but inside has a crude table with an empty bottle of rum on it. There is a wooden chair and some scraps of parchment. On one of the scraps of parchment is a crude map. There are copious writings here on other parchment as well, some scored out and then rewritten. Otherwise, there is nothing else in the hut but it is a great shade from the sun.

The Treasure of Captain Estes

Do you

Look at the crude map – *1160*

Check out the other writings – *9*

Just get on with things and leave the hut and

Strike out for the path – *1039*

Look at the poles – *703*

1396

"Yes, state your business," says one of the pirates stepping towards you. He looks full of menace, as if you don't belong here. You think about the items you have with you. Will they help?

Do you

Tell him you require a vessel and crew – *467*

Demand to see the man in charge – *219*

Tell him you are looking for Duncan Mackenzie (only if you have codeword **Letter Duncan Mackenzie**) – *720*

1397

Move Tabetha.

You are in a white walled room, bathed in the strange light, with two doors, one with a picture of a shield above it, and the other with a spider above it.

If Tabetha's number is 22 – *1459*

If Tabetha's number is 16 – **note this number and go to 239**

If Tabetha's number is 8 – **note this number and go to 1287**

Where do you go next?

Through the shield door – **442**

Through the spider door – **308**

Wait here - **return to the top of this section**

1398

You pull your pistol on the man. Do you

Threaten him – **977**

Shoot him and run – **619**

1399

You see that the battle is lost and order a retreat. The other captain clearly didn't want this battle either as they are happy to let you sail away. Once clear of all the smoke and confusion, you are able to assess the damage to your vessel.

Reduce your vessel speed by 1 level. Reduce your crew by 1 level. Reduce your Firepower by 1 level. Reduce your Treasure store by 1 level due damage. 25% of your cargo is destroyed. Reduce your crew morale by 1 level.

You return to your voyage but must **add 1 day extra to it** for this diversion. **Also, your new voyage time is that of your new reduced speed.**

Continue the voyage at **654**

The Treasure of Captain Estes

<u>1400</u>

How many items have you searched in the room?

1 item – *1374*

2 items – *1410*

3 items – *300*

4 items – *1383*

5 items – *475*

<u>1401</u>

You tell them that you mean them no harm, but they seem either unwilling or unable to comprehend you. Clearly, you are not welcome.

Do you

Attack them with your crew – *978*

Return to your vessel and fire your cannons at them – *1078*

Return to your vessel and leave the natives in peace – *1441*

<u>1402</u>

The guards look a little bemused at you but allow you to walk to the shop where you are greeted by Madame Le Vert. On entering the shop, you note the large collection of dresses and gowns on one side of the shop, but on the other, there are long-coats and breeches, boots and hats, everything a working man in this town could want.

Madame Le Vert begins to show you her latest collection and you try to feign interest in them as you ponder on your escape from the guards outside. Madame Le Vert asks if you wish to try any of the dresses on and you absentmindedly pick one and take it through to the small room at the rear of the shop.

Once the door is closed you scan the tiny dressing room and see a window up high. It is shuttered and certainly not wide in aperture, but you believe you could squeeze through. There are also a small number of wine bottles on the floor in the corner along with some boxes. Plans form in your mind.

Do you

Use the boxes to climb up to the window and try to squeeze through – *731*

Take a wine bottle and then sneak up on Madame Le Vert in an attempt to incapacitate her with it – *1013*

Lie on the floor with the wine bottles, empty them and pretend to be drunk, so you can then lure Madame Le Vert inside to incapacitate her – *796*

1403

The only wall of fire is to the north. You can route east, west or south from your current location.

Do you

Go West – *757*

Go East – *1173*

Go South – *456*

1404

You come up on deck to see a pile of rat carcasses being piled high. You look at them in wonder, but the first officer simply smiles.

"The cats we have on board have been busy. We think some cargo was heavily contaminated with rats, but the felines have sorted the issue."

You nod and stroke a few of the cats before returning to your cabin.

Now continue your voyage at *654*

The Treasure of Captain Estes

<u>1405</u>

If this is at least the second item you have examined then roll 1xD100 (2xD10,) and consult the table below

2nd item	3rd item	4th item
00-39 – *959*	00-59 – *959*	00-89 – *959*
40-99 – read on	60-99 – read on	90-99 – read on

You take a look at the cabinets, most of which are open. At the bottom of one you find a leather-bound set of papers. Opening them up, you see a title saying, "The Empty Chart - a Book of Instruction". May be interesting. **If you want to take these papers, tick the codeword Instruction Book.** Beyond this, you see nothing of potential use.

Do you

Examine the desks – *1239*

Look at the chairs – *120*

Peruse the charts on the wall – *371*

Or leave the room and return back to tunnel – *558*

<u>1406</u>

You grab the lock and tug hard. It comes away in your hand and you easily open the chest. Inside you find a rat eating a purple fruit which appears to be half rotting in the chest. There are also around 500 doubloons sitting in a string bag to the side of the chest. Tick the codeword **Cheesy.**

Decide if you want to take the doubloons, and if so add them to your inventory.

Do you

Return down the mountain to its foot – *61*

Climb the mountain – *1205*

<u>1407</u>

You come up on deck to find a party going on, with drinking and music. The crew stop dead as they see you arrive. You need to get to where you are going but maybe the crew need to blow off steam.

Do you

Join the party – *332*

Tell them to get back to work – *765*

<u>1408</u>

You casually ask the pirates if they know of anyone with a boat and almost to a man, they say if you need work or to hire you should go and see Cortez, opposite the docks. Well, you have your answer.

Do you now

Talk to the gypsy woman – *711*

Walk over to the single pirate in the dim corner– *838*

Go over to watch the pirate playing the mouth organ – *1421*

Or leave – *1112*

<u>1409</u>

You step onto the pillar and feel a slight wobble as the wind blows past you. There are pillars diagonally to your rear left and right, diagonally to your front right, and directly in front.

Do you step

Diagonally forward right – *166*

Diagonally backward left – *1429*

Diagonally backward right – *68*

Forwards – *142*

1410

Do you have the codeword **Barbara** – *162*

If not go to *1311*

1411

You see a brown bull running directly at you and a white bull in the right channel. You are in the left channel. What will you do?

Stay left – *547*

Go to the middle – *466*

Go to the right channel – *1165*

1412

Having made your stake, it's time to roll the dice. Pick one of the entries below and they will take you to your result and explain your winnings or losings. You can play as many times as you want but you could lose everything, including your life. If you are choosing for more than the first time, you may not choose an entry that you have chosen before. Good luck, you're going to need it.

Roll the dice and go to

50	*101*	*674*
1354	*1199*	*14*
312	*950*	*549*
1320		

1413

This time you dive down deep and come under the vessel where the water seems darker, hidden from the sunlight. You can barely see but you can feel and discover some plant life growing on the keel. As you touch it, it seems to prickle your skin. As best you can make out its green and you wonder if it's any use.

You can take some of the plant if you wish. Tick the code word Green Plant if you do.

As you return to surface you see a large circular shell in the seabed. It is half buried in the sandy surface, but it gives you shivers to think they have crabs that size around here. It would be enormous, almost man sized. You shake your head and happily swim for the surface as your breath is going. Once replenished, what do you do.

Do you swim to the

Stern of the vessel – *1422*

Bow of the vessel – *94*

Starboard side – *1212*

Or instead

Clamber on board -*603*

Return to your vessel – *894*

1414

You wander along the path and reach a junction with three paths off it. Which way now?

Left – *5*

Middle – *1050*

Right – *26*

Turn back – *73*

The Treasure of Captain Estes

<u>1415</u>

You tell him you'll enter anyway and a voice from behind the doors shouts, "Back off." The voice is female and shrill. The doors open and a woman standing only five feet tall dressed in a gown with her hair tied up glares at you. In her hand is a musket pointed at you.

"Go on. You heard him. I don't give two warnings."

Do you

Push on towards the doors – *839*

Reach for a weapon – *1331*

Take his advice and return to the main street – *496*

<u>1416</u>

Which of the following will you offer?

Ratcatcher: Monkey: Bodach Sword: Noiseless Horn: Johnstone's Confuser – *1430*

Eye Charm: Spear: Orange Algae: Green Plant: Gold Medallion – *1437*

Compass Map: Bird Chart: Gold Chain: Sextant: Argyle – *404*

<u>1417</u>

Robert Grimshaw seems to have a soft spot for you as he takes you to his house and helps you in your endeavour. He says he will put word out about Estes and find out where he has gone. In the meantime, he dresses you in a long-coat and breeches, complete with boots and a cutlass. On the third day he takes you to the New Southampton port where he shows you a vessel which is rather small but sleek.

"This is the Eagle, Mary, a fast and well-fortified ship. She only needs a small crew and will be useful for hunting down Estes. As long as we avoid any storms, we will be okay, but then we should be able to outrun them. We can't carry much either but then that is the price of pursuit. Look around, Mary while I check the reports on Estes."

While you wait, it's time to fill in your vessel chart with the details of your vessel and crew. Look for the chart at the rear of the book. You may photocopy this for ease of use. Fill it in now.

First Officer: Robert Grimshaw

Vessel: The Eagle - Schooner

Speed: Fast

Firepower: Heavy

Treasure store: Small

Shallows: Yes

Manoeuvrability: Good

Storm Handling: Poor

Crew: Small

Initial Provisions: 6 sections

Doubloons: 1500

Grimshaw brings you to his room a few days later with a frustrated look on his face "Mary, I'm sorry but Estes is dead. He ran into the British and was defeated somewhere near New Southampton. Rumour, for what it is, says that he left his treasure on an island in the vicinity of New Southampton. They call it the Dark Land, and the dull witted say it is only accessible at certain times and appears in different places. I've never known anyone who has seen it, but it will be a natural phenomenon that protects it, like a fog bank. It would be the sort of place Estes would hide treasure."

"So, I have nothing," you say, "unless I chase this treasure."

"That's the long and the short of it. Recovery of your assets and your life would seem to be the only course of action now."

"Well then, when do we start? And where should we go?"

"I have no definitive sightings of Estes before his last battle which was southeast of New Southampton. If you look at this chart, Mary, there are six places in the general locale where he could have been before he died and which may be able to shed light on his travels, and where the island is. Once you have examined them all, give the crew orders of where to sail to."

Check the *chart of New Southampton at App 02* to help you in your decisions. You may photocopy it for use with this book. Turn now to section *1276* to learn about the six locations and about sailing around New Southampton, and then to make your first decision as captain!

<u>1418</u>
Reduce your time by 2. If your time is in the following gaps (46-41 or 16-11) then go to *1126*. If not continue below

You wait in the shadows seeing no one move.

Do you

Wait in hiding – *1176*

Check out the cows – *387*

Look at the sheep – *780*

Go to the gate – *319*

Move to the West quarter – *493*

Move to the East quarter – *678*

1419

If you have the codeword **Spanish Tail** – *1099*

Otherwise, read on.

Out on the open water all seems well until you hear a cry from the crow's nest above. "Ship ahoy! Captain, I can see a vessel on the horizon."

"That's all good and well," you cry, "but what are we up against." There are numerous types of vessels out here and you might be facing a lightening quick schooner or a heavy gunned galleon. You grab your scope and peer out towards the vessel. You eye widens as you see your foe.

Roll 1xD100 (2xD10). Check the result below and go to that entry.

00 to 40 – *1423*

41 to 80 – *1032*

81 to 99 – *956*

1420

Reduce the Hot Strip by 1. If this places you on a Fire spot add 20 to this section's number and go there for the walls have moved. There are walls of fire to the west and east. You can route south or north from your current location.

Do you

Go North – *1455*

Go South – *548*

The Treasure of Captain Estes

<u>1421</u>

You wander over to where a pirate is playing a mouth organ and entertaining his fellow crewmates. Everyone seems to be enjoying themselves and a man taps you on the shoulder and tells you that you should watch this. You can see a monkey jumping around the pirates, and it makes you laugh. You try to ask a pirate about getting a crew but he shushes you and tells you to wait until the song is done.

Do you

Wait for the song to finish – **40**

Or decide to leave the music. If so, do you

Approach the bar – **669**

Talk to the gypsy woman – **711**

Walk over to the single pirate – **838**

Or leave – **1112**

<u>1422</u>

You swim to the stern of the vessel and see its broken rudder, half floating loose in the slow current around you. It has large scores on it as well. You can see something poking out of the vessel's side and on examining it you find a hard piece of shell. It is very flat, reddish in colour, at least that's how it looks underwater. You also have an eerie feeling you are being watched. You surface quickly before deciding your next move.

Do you swim to the

Bow of the vessel – **94**

Starboard side – **1212**

Keel – **1413**

(More options over the page)

Or instead

Clamber on board -*603*

Return to your vessel – *894*

1423

You see a Union Jack Flag on a Brigantine vessel, a fast vessel with about 100 men on board. "Blast," you cry out. You know that it has a lot of the options here, and now it seems to be following you.

Is your vessel *Fast or Very Fast* – *216*

If not, read on

As you watch the Brigantine it continues course with you, tailing you. It never gets too close, and you know that if you turn to it, it can outrun you before tailing again at a distance. You wonder what its intentions are but there's little you can do except continue course or change your destination. You now have the British navy watching you (Tick codeword **British Tail**).

If you decide to change course, use the voyage chart to determine your voyage length from your original departure point to your new destination. Then **add 2 days to your voyage** for starting off in a different direction.

If you maintain course use your original planned voyage days. Either way, continue the voyage at *654*

1424

You approach the gambling groups of pirates and see a number of games of chance in progress. They seem to involve picking a coin from a choice of 3 and if you guess right, you get twice your stake plus the stake back. However, there are three different sets of games, one run by a one-legged fat pirate, one by a small stumpy pirate and one by an older female pirate.

The Treasure of Captain Estes

"Careful," says a drunken pirate to you. "One of these games is rigged."

"Which one?" you ask.

"How should I know, I'm drunk!"

Do you

Look to join the one-legged pirate's game – *1181*

Engage in the stumpy pirate's game – *1316*

Play in the female pirate's game – *618*

Decide against playing and instead

Make for the small houses – *1304*

Explore the tavern – *363*

Approach the gambling groups – *1424*

Go to see the fights – *84*

Decide this is not a place you want to explore and return to your vessel - *314*

1425

You walk past the gallows and note there is dried blood on them. Maybe someone didn't die quick enough but with no crowd, they may not be in use today. As you approach the main building some of the guards get a good look at your face. They are discussing you quite feverishly.

Do you have the codeword **Prominent** – *96*

If not, you decide this is too risky and turn away. As you do so, one of the guards shouts and pursues you to the street, causing many people to look. You have to run to the far end of town to escape but you have been noticed. **Tick the codeword Prominent** to your list and continue at the far end of town at *1009*

1426

Reduce your time by 5. Anything you were holding in your shirt is gone. Untick that item. You feel around. On your left is a chair that appears fixed. On your right, behind and ahead is clear water.

Do you

Turn right and walk forward – *709*

About turn and step forward – *1344*

Step forward – *107*

1427

Your vessel sails so slowly, and you see the inevitable as the galleon turns broadside to you. The first volley obliterates your mast. The second sends great shards of wood flying from the deck. The third lands on you and you are gone. Fortunately, you don't see or hear the suffering as Rodriguez sinks your vessel.

 Make sure you pick a fight you can win! You can try again at *1.*

1428

Reduce the Hot Strip by 1. If this places you on a Fire spot add 20 to this section's number and go there for the walls have moved. There are walls of fire to the south and east. You can route north or west from your current location.

Do you

Go West – *1065*

Go North – *670*

The Treasure of Captain Estes

<u>1429</u>

You step onto the pillar and feel a slight wobble as the wind blows past you. There are pillars diagonally to your front right, rear left and right, as well as one to your left. You can see a small item on the pillar diagonally to your rear left.

Do you step

Diagonally forward right – *1409*

Diagonally backward left – *448*

Diagonally backward right – *531*

To your left – *1307*

<u>1430</u>

Which item do you offer?

Ratcatcher (the cats in your hold) – *1309*

Monkey (a monkey figurine) – *1244*

Bodach Sword (the ghost's sword) – *454*

Noiseless Horn (the horn without sound) – *716*

Johnstone's Confuser (the details of Kraken misdirection) – *1082*

<u>1431</u>

You order the guard to stay there and for the person to remain below deck.

Your crew are not happy, lower your crew morale 1 level. Tick the codeword Passenger Below.

Now continue your voyage at *654*

<u>1432</u>

You ignore the howling and laughter and place your hands on the chest, preparing to open it. Suddenly there are green ghostly hands on your hands as you try to open the chest. "I will curse you," hisses a voice.

Do you

Continue to open the chest – *128*

Leave the chest alone and leave the room by the rope – *470*

<u>1433</u>

Reduce your Island Time Chart by 2

You trek along the path, and it seems such a long stretch. Eventually there's a fork in the path, and you wonder which way to go. You can take either fork, or you could always head out into the jungle off the path.

Do you go

Left – *937*

Right – *245*

Strike out into the Jungle – *1077*

Turn around back the way you came – *758*

<u>1434</u>

"Martha Downham is my Captain."

There is a sudden hush over the assembled drinkers. The barmaid steps forward and invites you into the rear room asking what it is you need. When you tell her you are looking for information, she gathers some of the local drinkers who spend time answering your questions. You get several good titbits of information.

The Treasure of Captain Estes

"Beware Brid's Paradise, for Brid, a malevolent spirit resides inside. It is a spirit of tricks, tempting you before leaving you empty."

"The Mariner's Guild found something of Estes', but they keep it in the back offices. It has to do with his treasure."

"The Kraken stalks the waters around Hell's Deep more than anywhere else."

You thank them all for the information and take your leave back to the crossroads at *802*

1435

Reduce your time by 1.

If your time is in the following gaps (37-33 or 07-03) and you are not hidden, then go to *1037*. If you are hidden, you see a guard on his patrol and must remain hidden until he clears the area. Reduce your time by 6. Now continue at the plain text below

You can see before you the shadow of a large building with a single person wooden door. There appears to be no one on guard.

To the north you can see a building while to the west there is another similar to what's before you. A smaller fixture is to the north-east, although the dark makes it hard to see.

Do you

Hide where you are – *1010*

Route North – *103*

Creep West – *1197*

Go North-east – *174*

Approach the building before you to break in – *837*

1436

What now? Stay in Hell's deep and explore further or sail off somewhere else.

Do you

Go to see Blind Tom – *681*

Visit the provisions isle – *334*

Enjoy yourself at the wild isle – *879*

Explore the dark isle – *397*

Decide you have had enough of Hells Deep and set sail - **Consult the voyage chart and set sail**

1437

Eye Charm (necklace with gold eye) – *1082*

Spear (long spear) - *1309*

Orange Algae – (spongy underwater plant) - *716*

Green Plant – (prickly underwater plant) - *454*

Gold Medallion - (from the underwater vessel) -- *1244*

1438

You pick up a cask and begin to walk out of the gate. It's very heavy and you start to stumble, attracting a guard's attention. As he approaches you are forced to put the cask down momentarily.

"Have you got the right cask?" he asks.

Do you

Tell him yes – *902*

Apologise and say you're not sure – *1067*

The Treasure of Captain Estes

1439

You stand at the bottom of the main rock structure at the Bird's Paradise. Above you the birds squawk loudly, and you see a mass of bird droppings all over the rocks around you. There is a wooden door in the rock structure which is closed and has a brass engraved plaque on it with the already translated warning of:

A fool and his gold are easily parted, and you sir, are a fool for entering!

You step back and wonder what you should do and see a rope dangling down the outside of the structure. You could climb the rocks with the aid of the rope but there are so many birds around, many with young, that you are not sure of the wisdom of this idea.

Do you

Enter via the wooden door – ***303***

Climb the rock formation with the aid of the rope – ***362***

Decide this is a bad idea and leave the Bird's Paradise – **consult your voyage chart**

1440

"Drop gunpowder down and ignite it. Blow it out from under us!"

Return to ***927*** and make your decision.

1441

The natives seem happy to see you go after a tense stand-off but at least there was no violence committed by either side. Maybe you'll return later but for now you have more to explore.

Do you

Tell the crew to sail to the north of the island – ***468***

Route for the centre of the island – ***746***

Decide to set sail - **consult the voyage chart**

1442

Reduce your time by 1.

If your time is in the following gaps (22-18), then go to *1037*.

If your time is in the following gaps (57-53 or 17-13), then go to *1128*.

If neither of these apply, continue at the plain text below

As you stand at the door, you can hear snoring, and not just a single person. There's the odd creak as well but generally snoring.

Do you

Hide where you are – *785*

Route South – *1393*

Creep East – *42*

Open the door and enter the building – *680*

1443

Reduce the Hot Strip by 1. If this places you on a Fire spot add 20 to this section's number and go there for the walls have moved. There are walls of fire to the west and east. You can route south or north from your current location.

Do you

Go North – *877*

Go South – *375*

The Treasure of Captain Estes

<u>1444</u>

Reduce the Hot Strip by 1. If this places you on a Fire spot add 20 to this section's number and go there for the walls have moved. There are walls of fire to the north and south. You can route east or west from your current location.

Do you

Go East– *394*

Go West – *515*

<u>1445</u>

You languish in the cell hoping for rescue, but none comes. Eventually a rich trader sees you and convinces the fort commander that you can be purchased. You are taken back to England where you are a kept woman, beholden to a rich toff for everything. This may have been the worst fate that could have befallen you. You had hoped Diggory would have come for you, but he's got too much to lose where the British navy is concerned.

Looks like life didn't work out. Try again at *1*

<u>1446</u>

The brass sextant is of excellent quality and has the legend Lord Buffington inscribed on the side. If you take it, tick the codeword **Sextant.**

Go to *415*

<u>1447</u>

As you approach the door, one of the guards steps across and blocks your path. "I'm sorry, madam, but this is no place for a lady. I suggest Madame Le Vert's just back along the street."

You give a chuckle and try to walk past but he doesn't move.

Do you

Make a scene, calling him a pig – *516*

Try to slip him a bribe of an item you have – *447*

Return to the street as suggested – *1009*

1448

You sail down the channel and into a small pool where you can turn, and where several channels route away from. The channels route north, southwest, and south. The southern channel looks like it reaches the main rock formation, but you cannot be sure. The southwestern channel is very narrow and will require a vessel with great manoeuvrability. The northern channel seems wide enough for passage.

Do you

Sail north – *144*

Route southwest (only if your vessel has Great manoeuvrability) – *1465*

Make for the main structure to the south – *947* **and note this section's number**

1449

You flee and hear the rats coming after you, but you have a good head start. As you reach the base of the mountain, you skip over the river and the rats start to lose interest.

Now at the base of the mountain, you grab your breath and decide not to return this way again. **Note you cannot climb the mountain again.**

There are two paths away from the mountain, one a canopy covered path to the north, the other a more open topped path to the west, although it is still surrounded by the dense jungle.

Do you

Head north – **435**

Take the path west – **477**

1450

Go to **743**

1451

How many provisions will you throw overboard to feed the creature? You can only throw over what you have, remember. Decide now and then go to **1204**

1452

You wait in the your room before being escorted to a small carriage which is surrounded by four guards (**if you have the codewords long-coat or any Bottle on your inventory, untick them as you have to leave them behind**). Before you depart Captain Fareham tells you that you can exchange a promissory note to Madame Le Vert at her shop in town and he encourages to buy something pretty. The driver encourages the horses to walk, and you are soon on your way into New Southampton.

You know this is your opportunity but inside you are nervous. Captain Fareham has his eyes on your father's estate and you have no intentions of being his little wife. But he has not posted four guards on your carriage for no reason. You feel they are there as much to stop you running away as for your protection.

As you approach New Southampton, you see the familiar streets which you used to walk with your father and stepmother, and you can remember happier times with the hot sun and your father in full flow about town. You face will be recognised wherever you go in this town, of that you are sure.

As you approach the shop of Madame Le Vert, you see on your left the dark alley that runs through to the tavern of Geordie Graham, the laughing Englishman with his thick north-east of England accent. On your right is the food market with the daily act of buying and selling in full throw. Ahead is Madame Le Vert's shop and you wonder if you could make and escape once inside.

You need to make a move soon but is this the time? The whole town is around you for cover, but you are in a dress that says you are a woman of stature, and your face will surely be recognised.

Do you

Leap from the carriage and run to the alley – *1237*

Jump towards the food market to find cover amongst the crowd – *228*

Wait in the carriage to enter Madame Le Vert's – *463*

1453

You wander along the path, wondering if the world has died beyond, and reach a junction. Which way now?

Left – *797*

Right – *399*

Turn back – *1218*

The Treasure of Captain Estes

<u>1454</u>

On arrival on deck, you notice that the crew has started to mass, and they don't look happy. You stare at them angrily, but your first officer says that the crew need a word with their captain.

"What's troubling you, you ask?"

"Well, captain," says the second officer, "we aren't happy with the food. You see there's not enough of it and we could do with more. We think you're holding back on it."

You turn and stare at the crew.

Are you on half rations – *944*

If not, read on:

"You get plenty," you say.

If the crew have spoken to you about rations before – *253*

If not, they look at you somewhat disappointed. "Is that your last word on the matter, Captain?"

Do you

Tell them it's your only word – *278*

Tell them you'll increase the rations by 50% - *825*

Grab the second officer and throw him overboard – *1020*

<u>1455</u>

The only wall of fire is to the north. You can route south, east or west from your current location.

Do you

Go East – *1046*

Go South – *1420*

Go West – *176*

1456

Diggory's plan sounded good and so you come to the edge of your cell and ty to coax the jailer towards you. He looks at you leerily and you know you have him where you want him. With Diggory lined up behind you, you try to push the man back across the hallway to Diggory's arms. He is so heavy that you are not sure you can do this. You push hard but is it enough?

Did you push

This hard – **425**

Or this hard – **223**

1457

You walk towards the building and the pirate on the left approaches you. He shakes his head, indicating you should get lost. When you keep walking forward, he reaches for you and turns you around, giving you a kick up the backside and sending you to the dust.

"No slaves! Now get!"

You have to return to the street bruised and muddied. Continue at **1256** and don't return unless you have a change of clothing.

1458

You make to walk away but then swing the bottle hard at him. You catch him unawares and there is a dull clunk as you hit him on the head. The pirate falls to the ground, out cold, but his landing causes a fair noise.

"Grundy, you okay?"

The voice comes from inside the barn sending you into a slight panic. You could see who comes out but it might be trouble. It might be better to get away while you can.

The Treasure of Captain Estes

Do you

Wait to see who comes out – *536*

Lurk up by the door and await whoever comes out – *818*

Or run away to the street heading for the docks (*1256*) or for the edge of town (*262*)

1459

Standing in the room about to make your next decision you spot a black shape coming through one of the doors. You turn to run but the giant arachnid Tabetha has already punctured you with her stinger and is wrapping you up ready for her next meal. Looks like the Kraken's horn wasn't worth it after all.

You knew this was a winner takes all game and you lost. Life is but a game of chance and you seem to have rolled the dice very badly. Your crew depart after a few days wondering whatever happened to their captain. I guess they will never know.

1460

Diggory Hurst is leader of a band of former naval sailors who have cut loose on the waters around New Southampton. On the day after meeting you, he takes you around the hideout they have on the west of the island where you see a sloop and a little further out a square-rigged ship at anchor.

"We don't keep that vessel around for long," he says, "but I understand that you want to go after a certain Captain Estes. The sloop is needed closer to home but we can spare the Freedom, especially if there will be plenty of loot to place into its hold. It'll take most of the crew to man it, so we need to be sure where we are going. With that in mind I have sent out scouts to find out where Estes has made for. In the meantime, we will lie low, for the British want me, but in the meantime, we shall turn you into a pirate captain."

You are given a long-coat and boots, a tri corner hat and cutlass and Diggory tells you about the basics of navigating and sailing. You have to wait the best part of a week for any information to come back about your foe, Captain Estes.

While you wait, it's time to fill in your vessel chart with the details of your vessel and crew. Look for the chart at the rear of the book. You may photocopy this for ease of use. Fill it in now.

First Officer: Diggory Hurst

Vessel: Freedom - Square rigged Ship

Speed: Slow

Firepower: Moderate

Treasure store: Very Large

Shallows: Yes

Manoeuvrability: Lacking

Storm Handling: Good

Crew: Medium

Initial Provisions: 8 sections

Doubloons: 500

Diggory brings you to his hut by the coast a few days later with a frustrated look on his face "Mary, I'm sorry but Estes is dead. He ran into the British and was defeated somewhere near New Southampton. My informant states that he left his treasure on an island in the vicinity of New Southampton. This island is called the Dark Land, and it's not a place where you should go lightly. I've been around these parts long enough to know that not everything works as it would back in England.

The Treasure of Captain Estes

The tales say that the island is only accessible at certain times and appears in different places. I've never known anyone who has seen it, but there may be a curse around that island. Tales of people who visit do not end well. It would be the sort of place Estes would hide treasure."

"So, I have nothing," you say, "unless I chase this treasure."

"I know it's not the same as killing Estes but at least you could have his fortune."

"Well then, when do we start? And where should we go?"

"I have no definitive sightings of Estes before his last battle which was southeast of New Southampton. If you look at this chart, Mary, there are six places in the general locale where he could have been before he died and which may be able to shed light on his travels, and where the island is. Once you have examined them all, give the crew orders of where to sail to."

Check the _chart of New Southampton at App 02_ to help you in your decisions. You may photocopy it for use with this book. Turn now to section _1276_ to learn about the six locations and about sailing around New Southampton, and then to make your first decision as captain!

<u>1461</u>

Reduce your Waters Strength Chart by 1. The current is too strong and sweeping you south. Your foot scrapes the bottom briefly and you think you may be able to drop a pole and take a rest. Do you

Float South – _706_

Drop a pole – **Make a note of this section and go to _694_**

1462

You grab hold of one of the treasure caskets as it strikes your foot. Desperately you haul it with you to the vessel, but a tentacle grabs your leg, and you feel it down you downwards. You panic, flapping desperately with your arms and kicking with your free leg but down you go. Soon, you cannot help but open your lungs for air and water floods in. Soon your struggles are over.

You were so close to achieving your dreams, but you cut your time too fine. Your crew enjoy what spoils they manage to scramble from the water but leave you in the watery grave, far from New Southampton and the home you hoped to regain. Sometimes a pirate's life does not end well but in glorious failure. You can try again at *1*. But maybe rest first, because that was a long-haul effort.

1463

You see the plumes of smoke from the canons, but they seem to have no effect on the creature as it grabs your vessel and drags it below the waves. You were skilful enough but you lacked the firepower. Now you are seeing the watery death of your crew as you are taken deep down into the sea.

The waters around New Southampton are deadly, and you have succumbed. You may try again at *1*

1464

The weather is stormy but mild and you sail through with no issues. Now resume your voyage at *654*

1465

You sail along until the rocks part and you have three options of where to go, including routing back the way you came. You can go northeast but it is incredibly tight and twisty, or southeast and southwest from here, both along good channels.

The Treasure of Captain Estes

Do you

Sail northeast (only if your vessel has Great manoeuvrability) – *1448*

Route southeast – *191*

Go southwest – *606*

1466

You can see New Southampton ahead, the busy town beyond the docks and the impressive barracks further still. You are sailing in under a flag of peace and looking to trade but you decide you should stay below and not go ashore. Getting supplies will be easy for the crew but you need to give orders as to what you require. (If you have the codeword **Spanish Tail,** untick it as the Schooner will not follow you into New Southampton.)

At New Southampton you can pick up provisions, extra crew, and maybe a little extra to pick up the crew's morale. You can trade in doubloons or treasure (use the doubloon equivalent score for your treasure). Peruse the deals below and advise your quartermaster what is required. Once you have decided adjust your Vessel chart as necessary.

Provisions

- 5 doubloons per provision pack – 1 day to load
- A day's rum for the crew – 2 days cost (1 to acquire, 1 to drink to excess) Lifts crew morale by one level
  - Large crew – 100 doubloons
  - Medium crew – 50 doubloons
  - Small crew – 20 doubloons

Crew

- Recruit new crew at the New Southampton docks
    - 100 doubloons to lift your crew level by one level
    - 3 days to recruit each additional level
- Recruit new crew at Strangar
    - 50 doubloons to lift your crew level by one level
    - 5 days to recruit each additional level

Having done your deals at New Southampton and once you have adjusted your vessel chart and your time chart, it's time to set sail once again. Where are you going? Consult the voyage chart and set sail.

1467

Reduce your time by 1.

If your time is in the following gaps (52-48) you see a guard on his patrol outside and must remain hidden until he clears the area. Reduce your time by 6. Now continue at the plain text below

You place the key in the lock, and it turns easily, allowing the safe to open.

If you have the Codeword Bearing B you see the safe containing the papers you left behind last time. Go to the choices at the bottom of the section.

Otherwise continue below

Inside you find lots of correspondence on bits of parchment, many sealed on the rear. You scan them quickly, hoping to find something of use, and you see a note sealed on the rear to Admiral Jenkins in London. You open it and unwrap a folded piece of parchment which states it is from Eagle and that part one is solved. "Bearing 324 degrees true from the smiling face" are the only other words on the parchment. **Tick codeword Bearing B.**

The Treasure of Captain Estes

You quickly tidy up and lock the safe again. What next?

Look at the desk – **206**

Check the rug that's slightly lifted – **565**

Look at the other rug – **1356**

Decide this is a bad idea and return outside – **174**

1468

You panic as water begins to fill your lungs. You can't hold your breath any longer and you can't find the way out. Terror takes a hold and you soon succumb to the sea water that has this vessel in its hold.

Tough luck, but that was a nasty trap to fall into. You can try it again having just entered the darkness of the hold **1211**, or you can go all the way back to the start **1**. Better luck next time!

1469

The day has grown dark, and you are still on the island. Darkness falls and you can no longer see in front of you. There is a wild roar in the dark, and a scraping of vegetation. Something cries aloud, and then one of your crew screams briefly before the sound of him being torn apart fills your ears. You never see what came for you. Thankfully the end is brief if brutal. You found the island and were so close to Este's treasure. Maybe next time. Start again at **1**.

Appendix

Appendix Contents Table

<u>App 01- Codeword list</u>

☐ **Aisle**

☐ **Anna**

☐ **Argyle**

☐ **Barbara**

☐ **Bearing A**

☐ **Bearing B**

☐ **Bearing C**

☐ **Bearing D**

☐ **Bird chart**

☐ **Bird Whistle**

☐ **Blue Pole**

☐ **Bodach Sword**

☐ **Bottle Whisky Mackenzie**

☐ **Brass Key**

☐ **British Hunted**

☐ **British Tail**

☐ **Bullied**

☐ **Calm**

☐ **Caught**

☐ **Charge**

☐ **Charlie**

☐ **Check 200**

☐ **Cheesy**

☐ **Closed**

☐ **Crate Scroll**

☐ **Crossed**

☐ **Dampened**

☐ **Darkness**

☐ **Debbie**

☐ **Decent Chap**

☐ **Decline**

☐ **Devil's Compass**

☐ **Drop**

☐ **Ellie**

☐ **Emerald**

☐ **Empty Chart**

- ☐ Eye Charm
- ☐ Female Crew
- ☐ Fire Chest
- ☐ Flop
- ☐ Flunk
- ☐ Girlfriends
- ☐ Gold A
- ☐ Gold Chain
- ☐ Gold Medallion
- ☐ Golden 2
- ☐ Green plant
- ☐ Green Pole
- ☐ Holy Man
- ☐ Human bait
- ☐ Incognito
- ☐ Instruction book
- ☐ Jalibert
- ☐ Jog
- ☐ Johnstone's Confuser
- ☐ Kraken Horn
- ☐ Large Crew
- ☐ Letter Duncan Mackenzie
- ☐ Long-coat
- ☐ Middle
- ☐ Monkey
- ☐ Myra
- ☐ Nocturne
- ☐ Noiseless Horn
- ☐ North Beach
- ☐ Notes
- ☐ Orange Algae
- ☐ Pace
- ☐ Parley
- ☐ Passenger Below
- ☐ Passenger Cabin
- ☐ Password
- ☐ Pew
- ☐ Pistol

The Treasure of Captain Estes

☐ Prominent

☐ Promissory Note

☐ Ratcatcher

☐ Red Pole

☐ Return

☐ Rock

☐ Rosary

☐ Rumour

☐ Secreted Knife

☐ Sextant

☐ Shoulder Wound

☐ Silent Running

☐ Silver Key

☐ Small Crew

☐ Spanish Hunted

☐ Spanish Priests

☐ Spanish Tail

☐ Spear

☐ Spear

☐ Standard Knife

☐ Still

☐ Stowed

☐ Transept

☐ Trap

☐ Walk

☐ Wanted

☐ Wayfinder

☐ Well

☐ Whee

☐ Wind

App 02 - Chart of New Southampton and Surrounding Islands

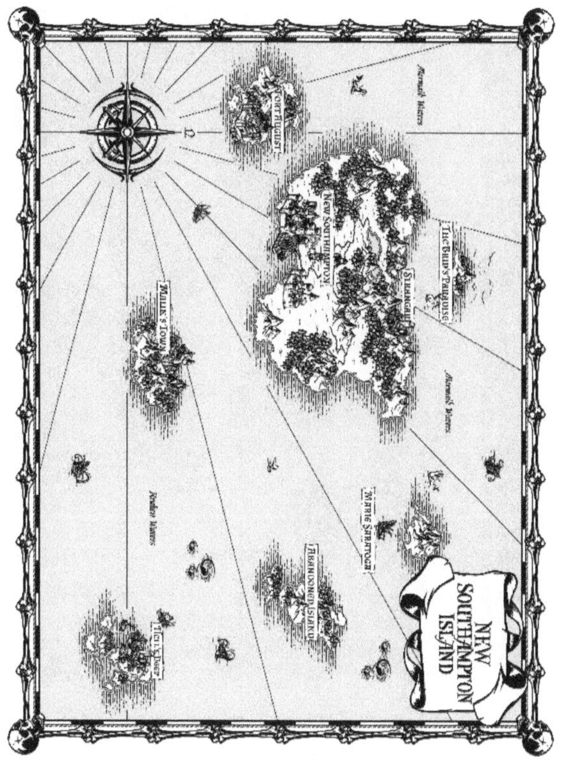

Further chart orientation over the page

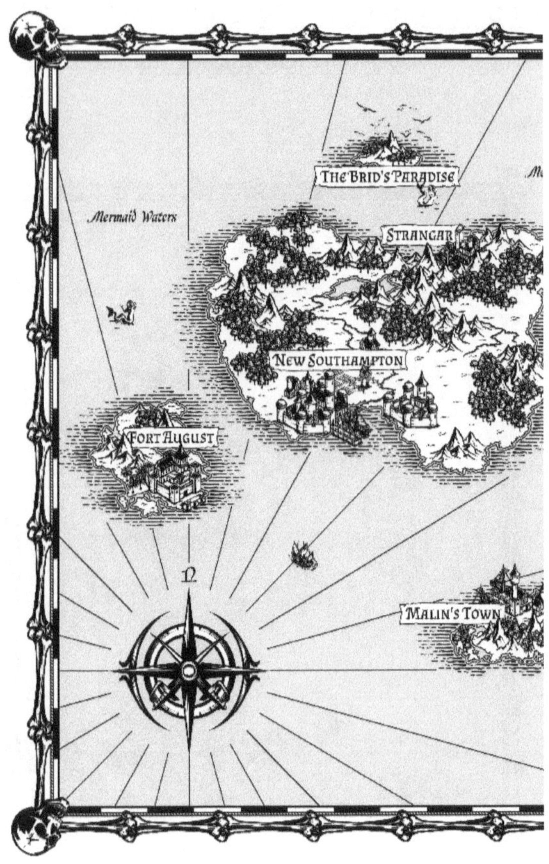

The Brid's Paradise
Strangar
Mermaid Waters
New Southampton
Fort August
Malin's Town

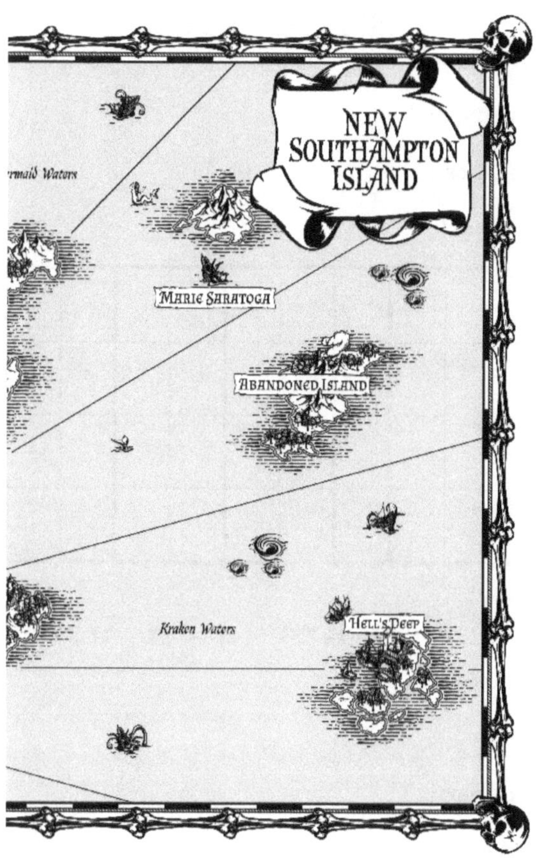
NEW SOUTHAMPTON ISLAND
Mermaid Waters
MARIE SARATOGA
ABANDONED ISLAND
Kraken Waters
HELL'S DEEP

App 03- Voyage Log

Vessel Name:

Vessel Type:

First Officer:

Cargo Hold:

I-   Very Small   -I-Small-I- Moderate -I-   Large   -I- Very Large -I

Doubloons:

Speed:

Firepower:

Treasure store:

Shallows:

Manoeuvrability:

Storm Handling:

Crew:

App 04 - Voyage Time

90	89	88	87	86	85	84	83	82	81
80	79	78	77	76	75	74	73	72	71
70	69	68	67	66	65	64	63	62	61
60	59	58	57	56	55	54	53	52	51
50	49	48	47	46	45	44	43	42	41
40	39	38	37	36	35	34	33	32	31
30	29	28	27	26	25	24	23	22	21
20	19	18	17	16	15	14	13	12	11
10	09	08	07	06	05	04	03	02	01

If your time is out, go to *150*

App 05- Passage Time Chart

Place From/ To	New Southa -mpton	Fort August	Malin's Town	Bird's Paradise	Marie Saratoga	Aband -oned Island	Hell's Deep
New Southam pton	XXXX	3/2/2/ 1/1	4/3/2/ 2/1	4/3/2/ 2/1	9/7/5/ 4/3	10/8/5 /5/4	13/10/ 8/7/6
Fort August	3/2/2/ 1/1	XXXX	4/3/2/ 2/1	5/4/3/ 2/2	9/7/5/ 4/3	10/8/5 /5/4	13/10/ 8/7/6
Malin's Town	4/3/2/ 2/1	4/3/2/ 2/1	XXXX	8/6/5/ 4/3	8/6/4/ 3/2	9/7/4/ 4/3	9/7/4/ 4/3
Bird's Paradise	4/3/2/ 2/1	5/4/3/ 2/2	8/6/5/ 4/3	XXXX	7/5/4/ 3/2	10/8/5 /5/4	13/10/ 8/7/6
Marie Saratoga	9/7/5/ 4/3	9/7/5/ 4/3	8/6/4/ 3/2	7/5/4/ 3/2	XXXX	3/2/2/ 1/1	8/6/5/ 4/3
Aband -oned Island	10/8/5 /5/4	10/8/5 /5/4	9/7/4/ 4/3	10/8/5 /5/4	3/2/2/ 1/1	XXXX	4/3/2/ 2/1
Hell's Deep	13/10/ 8/7/.6	13/10/ 8/7/6	9/7/4/ 4/3	13/10/ 8/7/6	8/6/5/ 4/3	4/3/2/ 2/1	XXXX

How to use:

1. On left hand side find your departure point
2. On top line find your destination
3. In the box where the row and column of these two points meet read the number that corresponds to your Vessel speed
4. Very slow / Slow / Moderate / Fast / Very Fast
5. This is your days planned of sailing.

App 06- Passage Start Point Chart

lace	New South-ampton	Fort August	Malin's Town	Bird's Paradise	Marie Saratoga	Abandoned Island	Hell's Deep
New South-ampton	xxxx	00-25 *1419* 26-50 *1099* 51-75 *373* 76-99 *1007*	00-25 *534* 26-50 *373* 51-75 *569* 76-99 *1099*	00-25 *1099* 26-50 *823* 51-75 *626* 76-99 *1375*	00-25 *1419* 26-50 *349* 51-75 *1099* 76-99 *203*	00-25 *1057* 26-50 *1099* 51-75 *569* 76-99 *203*	00-25 *1057* 26-50 *626* 51-75 *534* 76-99 *368*
Fort August	00-25 *569* 26-50 *1099* 51-75 *373* 76-99 *626*	xxxx	00-25 *1419* 26-50 *1007* 51-75 *1099* 76-99 *823*	00-25 *1375* 26-50 *1099* 51-75 *569* 76-99 *1419*	00-25 *1375* 26-50 *1057* 51-75 *203* 76-99 *1099*	00-25 *1099* 26-50 *349* 51-75 *1419* 76-99 *203*	00-25 *368* 26-50 *349* 51-75 *823* 76-99 *1099*
Malin's Town	00-25 *1057* 26-50 *626* 51-75 *1099* 76-99 *1007*	00-25 *1419* 26-50 *1007* 51-75 *1099* 76-99 *823*	xxxx	00-25 *1099* 26-50 *626* 51-75 *349* 76-99 *1375*	00-25 *1099* 26-50 *349* 51-75 *1419* 76-99 *203*	00-25 *569* 26-50 *1419* 51-75 *1099* 76-99 *1057*	00-25 *203* 26-50 *368* 51-75 *823* 76-99 *569*
Bird's Paradise	00-25 *1375* 26-50 *203* 51-75 *1007* 76-99 *1099*	00-25 *1375* 26-50 *1099* 51-75 *569* 76-99 *1375*	00-25 *823* 26-50 *534* 51-75 *569* 76-99 *1099*	xxxx	00-25 *1099* 26-50 *1375* 51-75 *569* 76-99 *349*	00-25 *1419* 26-50 *1099* 51-75 *1375* 76-99 *373*	00-25 *1099* 26-50 *1375* 51-75 *203* 76-99 *368*
Marie Saratoga	00-25 *1099* 26-50 *534* 51-75 *569* 76-99 *203*	00-25 *1099* 26-50 *1375* 51-75 *626* 76-99 *823*	00-25 *203* 26-50 *1099* 51-75 *569* 76-99 *1057*	00-25 *1375* 26-50 *1099* 51-75 *626* 76-99 *1057*	xxxx	00-25 *1099* 26-50 *1007* 51-75 *203* 76-99 *373*	00-25 *368* 26-50 *1099* 51-75 *569* 76-99 *1057*
Abandoned Island	00-25 *1099* 26-50 *349* 51-75 *1419* 76-99 *823*	00-25 *373* 26-50 *1419* 51-75 *1099* 76-99 *534*	00-25 *1057* 26-50 *1099* 51-75 *823* 76-99 *1007*	00-25 *1057* 26-50 *1007* 51-75 *1375* 76-99 *1099*	00-25 *1419* 26-50 *534* 51-75 *569* 76-99 *1099*	xxxx	00-25 *368* 26-50 *823* 51-75 *368* 76-99 *534*
Hell's Deep	00-25 *349* 26-50 *823* 51-75 *368* 76-99 *373*	00-25 *1419* 26-50 *1007* 51-75 *368* 76-99 *203*	00-25 *1057* 26-50 *626* 51-75 *569* 76-99 *368*	00-25 *1099* 26-50 *1375* 51-75 *203* 76-99 *368*	00-25 *823* 26-50 *1419* 51-75 *1099* 76-99 *1099*	00-25 *823* 26-50 *368* 51-75 *1007* 76-99 *368*	xxxx

How to use:

1. On left hand side find your departure point
2. On top line find your destination
3. Roll 1xD100 (2xD10)
4. In the box where the row and column of these two points meet, find your dice roll result and then go to the corresponding entry
5. If you may think you have enough information to find Estes treasure instead continue below:

The Treasure of Captain Estes

Finding Estes' Treasure:

You may believe you have enough information to find Captain Estes treasure, or at least where he took it. Let's see if you are right.

Do you have:

The Codeword **Devil's Compass** and one of the following codewords **Bearing A**, **Bearing B**, **Bearing C** or **Bearing D**

Or

Do you have three out of four of the following codewords:

Bearing A, **Bearing B**, **Bearing C** or **Bearing D**

If so, go to **499.**

If not, go back to the Passage Start Point chart, pick a destination, start your voyage and go find what information you are missing!

App 07 - Trip Planner

From:

To:

Days planned: Extra days:
          Total:

Provisions used: Half rations: Yes/No

From:

To:

Days planned: Extra days:
          Total:

Provisions used: Half rations: Yes/No

From:

To:

Days planned: Extra days:
          Total:

Provisions used: Half rations: Yes/No

From:

To:

Days planned: Extra days:
          Total:

Provisions used: Half rations: Yes/No

The Treasure of Captain Estes

From:

To:

Days planned: Extra days:
          Total:

Provisions used: Half rations: Yes/No

From:

To:

Days planned: Extra days:
          Total:

Provisions used: Half rations: Yes/No

From:

To:

Days planned: Extra days:
          Total:

Provisions used: Half rations: Yes/No

From:

To:

Days planned: Extra days:
          Total:

Provisions used: Half rations: Yes/No

<u>App 08 & 09 - Timers</u>

App 08 - Timer Box

15	14	13	12	11	10	9	8
7	6	5	4	3	2	1	Go to *97*

App 09 - Fort / MS Timer

60	59	58	57	56	55	54	53	52	51
50	49	48	47	46	45	44	43	42	41
40	39	38	37	36	35	34	33	32	31
30	29	28	27	26	25	24	23	22	21
20	19	18	17	16	15	14	13	12	11
10	9	8	7	6	5	4	3	2	1

Time is up! If in the Fort go to *799.*

If on the Marie Sartoga go to 1468

App 10- Walls of Fire

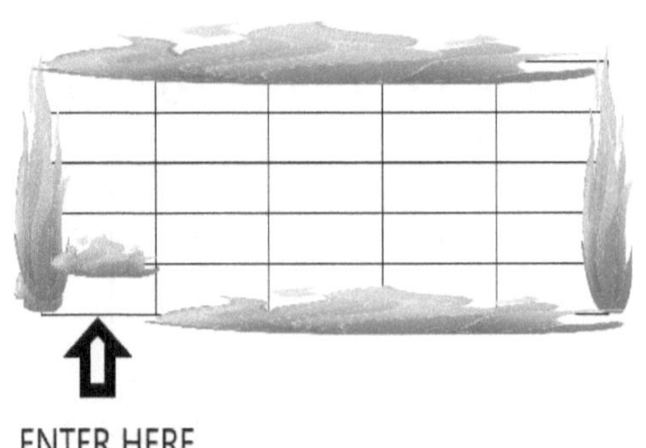

App 11- Hot Strip

25	24	23	22 - FS	21
20	19	18 - FS	17	16
15	14 - FS	13	12	11
10 - FS	9	8	7	6 - FS
5	4	3	2 - FS	1

Zero!!!!! You have been fried alive. Tough luck but it was too hot for you. You can start again at *1* for the whole adventure or go to *127* to start this challenge again.

App 12- Cargo Run Planner

(Mark your route)

Route:

Departure point:

(If you are at the departure point then mark the Voyage Time chart (*App 04*) 30 days from now to check the cargo planner. If not, do this on arrival at the departure point. Do not add your cargo or the loading days until you arrive)

Delivery point:

Payment on delivery:

Cargo:

30 day delivery limit passed:

Yes – You must avoid Malin's Town, Fort August and New Southampton until delivery is made, otherwise you are arrested and your game is over. You keep your initial payment but receive no extra money on delivery.

If the cargo is lost, you must go to Malin's Town and pay the cost of the cargo and an extra 200 Doubloons. If you land at Malin's Town and don't immediately pay you are arrested, and your game is over. Arriving at New Southampton or Fort August will result in immediate arrest and your game finishing.

<u>App 13- Dark Run Table</u>

First note the section you need to go to when back in Malin's Town.

Note the locations you need to visit in the table below and tick them off as you go. Note you must visit them in this order. Your cargo is very small as you travel and does not need to be noted in the cargo list. When you arrive at each location remove 1 day from your voyage log awaiting your contact. Once in Malin's Town go direct to the section you have been given.

Location 1		**Tick when here**	Cross out when 1 day removed from voyage log
Location 2		**Tick when here**	Cross out when 1 day removed from voyage log
Location 3		**Tick when here**	Cross out when 1 day removed from voyage log
Return to	**Malin's Town**	**Tick when here**	Section to return to

Location 1		**Tick when here**	Cross out when 1 day removed from voyage log
Location 2		**Tick when here**	Cross out when 1 day removed from voyage log
Location 3		**Tick when here**	Cross out when 1 day removed from voyage log
Return to	**Malin's Town**	**Tick when here**	Section to return to

App 14 - Island Time Chart

100	99	98	97	96	95	94	93	92	91
90	89	88	87	86	85	84	83	82	81
80	79	78	77	76	75	74	73	72	71
70	69	68	67	66	65	64	63	62	61
60	59	58	57	56	55	54	53	52	51
50	49	48	47	46	45	44	43	42	41
40	39	38	37	36	35	34	33	32	31
30	29	28	27	26	25	24	23	22	21
20	19	18	17	16	15	14	13	12	11
10	09	08	07	06	05	04	03	02	01

If you reach 05 on the chart go to *1469*

Treasure Found

App 15- Drops of Daniel Map

App 16- Waters of Myra

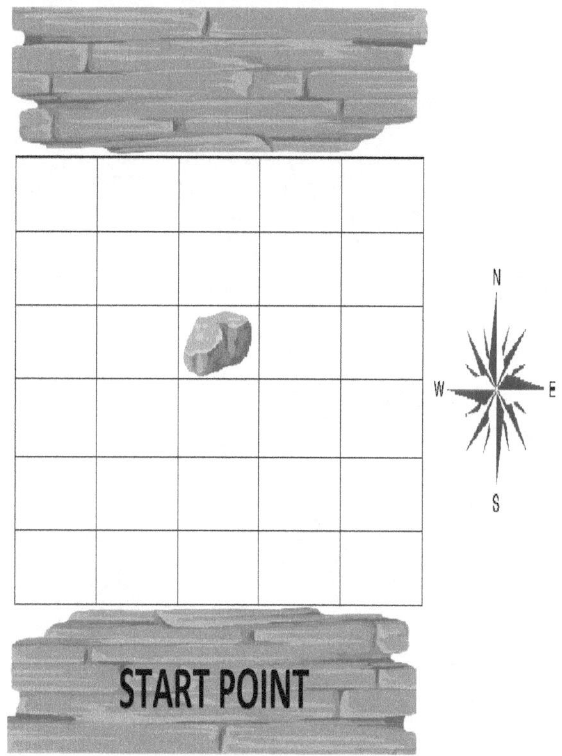

Waters Strength Chart

10	9	8	7	6
5	4	3	2	1

If this chart reaches zero go to *924*

App 17- Discovered Map

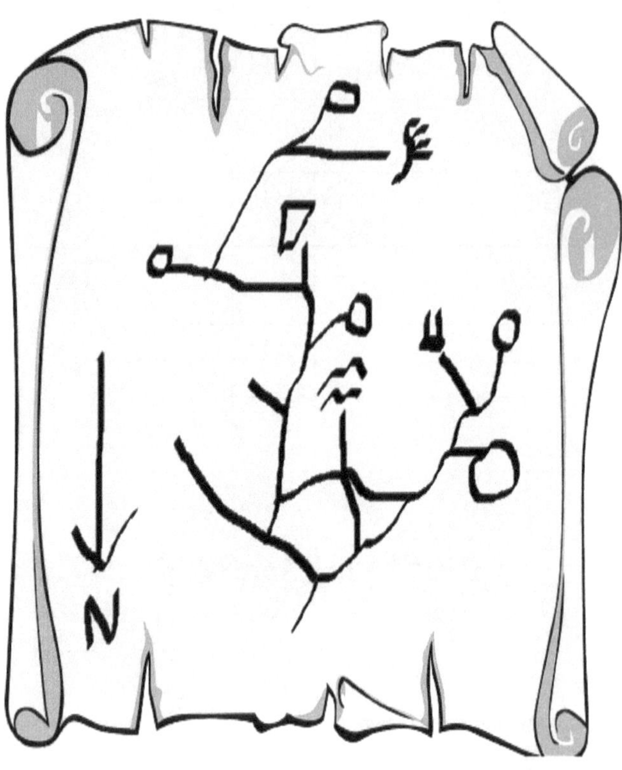

Notes

Notes

Notes

Notes

www.ingramcontent.com/pod-product-compliance
Lightning Source LLC
Chambersburg PA
CBHW061606210726
48287CB00001B/14